W9-BSH-864

"IMMENSELY EXCITING AND TERRIBLY
AUTHENTIC.
"WHITE-KNUCKLE TENSION AS THE
TWO MOST DANGEROUS SNIPERS IN EUROPE
HUNT EACH OTHER THROUGH THE
HELL OF STALINGRAD."
—Frederick Forsyth, author of *The Day of the Jackal*
and *The Fist of God*

"I DEVOURED IT. THE REPORTING AND
WRITING ARE AMAZING, AND THE
SNIPERS' DUEL WITH ITS LAYERS OF SUBTLE
TECHNIQUE AND IMAGINED MOTIVATION
IS SUSPENSEFUL AND POWERFUL. IT'S A VERY
GOOD PORTRAIT OF ONE OF THIS
CENTURY'S MOST IMPORTANT AND TERRIBLE
BATTLES, AND PROBABLY THE MOST
INTENSE URBAN CONFLICT IN HISTORY."
—Mark Bowden, author of *Black Hawk Down*

"A GOOD CANDIDATE FOR THE
THRILLER OF THE SUMMER AWARD...GIVES
A COMPELLING AND GRAPHIC SENSE OF
THE HEROISM-FILLED NIGHTMARE CALLED
STALINGRAD...A READABLE, GRITTY
ADVENTURE STORY."
—*The New York Times*

"BREAKNECK-FAST AND
LACED WITH REAL-LIFE VIGNETTES."
—*USA Today*

EXTRAORDINARY PRAISE FOR DAVID L. ROBBINS'S
WAR OF THE RATS

"Robbins creates an atmosphere so spectral and claustrophobic, and characters of such vivid authenticity as to elevate the material . . . to the highest levels of pure fiction. . . . *War of the Rats* is a must-read, harrowing yarn . . . a true tale of valor, gallantry, and sacrifice."
—Steven Pressfield, author of *Gates of Fire*

"Strikingly original—a novel so agonizingly true that a historian would be proud of it. The authenticity of Robbins' characters, the accuracy of his military detail, and the immediacy of his writing all bring the hellish combat of Stalingrad to vivid, gritty life. . . . Here is a book written with the art and understanding that few war novels can approach."
—Gary Solis, professor of law at West Point and author of *Son Thang: An American War Crime*

"Engrossing . . . Few suspense thrillers evoke the raw immediacy of *War of the Rats*. It takes reading only to page four to find it difficult to put down."
—Stanley Weintraub, author of *The Last Great Victory: The End of World War II*

"Based on one small historical drama . . . a terrifying and personal view from one of mankind's most horrific battles. A thoroughly engrossing story."
—*Rocky Mountain News*

"An engrossing thriller about a deadly, yet curiously romantic, war-within-a-war . . . Robbins can snatch a time and place out of history and make it come alive."
—*Kirkus Reviews*

Also by David L. Robbins

Souls to Keep

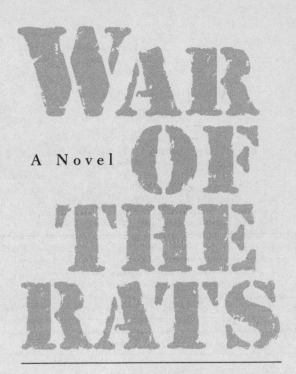

WAR OF THE RATS

A Novel

David L. Robbins

BANTAM BOOKS

New York   Toronto   London   Sydney   Auckland

This edition contains the complete text
of the original hardcover edition.
NOT ONE WORD HAS BEEN OMITTED.

WAR OF THE RATS

A Bantam Book

PUBLISHING HISTORY
Bantam hardcover edition published May 1999
Bantam mass market edition / June 2000

ISBN 0-553-58135-X

Published simultaneously in the United States and Canada

Bantam Books are published by Bantam Books, a division of Random House,
Inc. Its trademark, consisting of the words "Bantam Books" and the portrayal
of a rooster, is Registered in U.S. Patent and Trademark Office and in other
countries. Marca Registrada. Bantam Books, 1540 Broadway, New York, New
York 10036.

PRINTED IN THE UNITED STATES OF AMERICA

OPM   10 9 8 7 6 5 4 3 2 1

This book is dedicated to
my father, Sam, and my mother, Carol,
both veterans of World War II;
to my brother, Barry,
who served in Viet Nam;
and to those valiant men and women
of every stripe who have borne
honor into battle, who go unnamed
in history only because there
are so many of them.

I am the way into the doleful city,
I am the way into eternal grief,
I am the way to a forsaken race.

Justice it was that moved my great Creator;
Divine omnipotence created me,
and highest wisdom joined with primal love.

Before me nothing but eternal things
were made and I shall last eternally.
Abandon every hope, all you who enter.

—DANTE ALIGHIERI

The Divine Comedy: Inferno, Canto III

(the inscription above the gate to hell)

Next to a battle lost, the greatest
misery is a battle gained.

—THE DUKE OF WELLINGTON

(after the Battle of Waterloo)

INTRODUCTION

NOT EVEN NAPOLEON HAD STABBED AS DEEPLY into Russia as the German army had by August of 1942.

Adolf Hitler's forces plunged one thousand miles across the vast and hostile plains of Russia to the banks of the Volga River. It was by far the deepest penetration into this Asian land of any foreign legion in history.

The German plan was simple: place Moscow under siege to tie up precious Russian defenses, then race south into the Caucasus region and conquer the strategic oil fields there. Once in control of the Caucasus, Hitler could fashion a peace on his terms and divide Russia in half, enslaving the western portion of the huge nation for his dream of Aryan world expansion and "one thousand years of Nazi rule."

Late in July of 1942, Hitler called for a temporary shift in the *Schwerpunkt,* or main weight, of his Russian invasion, away from the southern oil fields to drive eastward, to neutralize a potential canker on his left flank. The city of Stalingrad, an industrial center responsible for almost half of Russia's steel and tractor production, a metropolis of over 500,000 residents, lay on the banks of a crescent in the Volga. Hitler sensed an important, and easy, victory.

The legacy of that decision was written thereafter in more blood and destruction than any other battle in history. The Red forces, under strict instructions from Stalin (for whom the city, formerly Tsaritsyn, was named in 1925 in gratitude for his role in defending it from the White forces during the Russian civil war) to take "not a step backward," put up an unexpected and vicious fight.

Stalingrad's five-month trial by fire began on August 23, 1942, when the first panzer grenadiers of the German Sixth Army reached the Volga on the city's northern outskirts. The German forces were under General Friedrich Paulus. He and his Russian counterpart, General Vasily Chuikov, commander of the Red Army's Sixty-second Army, presided over a terrible battlefield. The city, subjected to intense firebombings in late August, became a smoking charnel house. Soldiers fought and died in cellars, hallways, alleys, and the massive labyrinths of the wrecked factories smoldering beside the river. For months, the fighting was house to house and hand to hand, and the front lines swayed with each new clash, the rewards of which were measured in meters at a time. German foot soldiers called the fighting *Rattenkrieg*. War of the Rats.

The Sixth Army kept its strength inside the city at close to a hundred thousand troops, drawing on reserves of over a million men from German, Italian, Hungarian, and Rumanian divisions positioned on the great steppe outside Stalingrad. The Red force inside the city never exceeded sixty thousand soldiers and at times was as low as twenty thousand men desperately surviving until reinforcements could be ferried across the Volga. The two armies ground against each other with an incredible will, killing and maiming soldiers in unprecedented thousands.

By mid-October the Russians had their backs literally to the river. In some places they hunkered no more than a hundred yards from the Volga cliffs. Somehow they held out until finally, on November 19, 1942, the Red Army sprang its "November surprise." The Russians executed a sudden and immense flanking action that leaped out from both the north and south to close with terrifying speed behind the Germans and their allies, encircling them with a million and a half vengeful men. Hitler called his surrounded Sixth Army "Fortress Stalingrad" and told the world these men would stay in place and fight to the death. His encircled troops, freezing, starving, bedeviled by lice, and under constant threat of Russian attack, called their position *der Kessel*, "the Cauldron." Of the quarter of a million soldiers surrounded on the steppe in mid-November, less than a hundred thousand were alive to surrender two and a half months later.

The city's ordeal ended on January 31, 1943, when Paulus, a starved wraith of a man with a facial tic and a dead army, walked out of the battered Univermag department store in the decimated center of the city and surrendered.

The final toll on both armies was an estimated 1,109,000 deaths, the high-water mark of human destruction in the annals of combat. The Red Army reported 750,000 killed, wounded, or missing. German casualties were 400,000 men. The Italians suffered a loss of 130,000 out of their original force of 200,000. The Hungarians saw 120,000 killed, the Rumanians 200,000. Out of a prewar population in Stalingrad numbering more than 500,000, only 1,500 civilians were alive there after the battle.

For both armies, the outcome of Stalingrad was pivotal. Never before had an entire German army disappeared in battle. The Nazi myth of invincibility was broken. The Reds now had a major victory; Russia had withstood Hitler's best punch, and returned to him a death blow. Stalingrad was as far as the Nazis got; the Germans fought a rearguard action for the remainder of the war.

Two years later Red forces were celebrating in the streets of Berlin.

INTO THE MIDST OF THIS AWFUL CARNAGE, played out on this pivotal stage, strode two men: Russian Chief Master Sergeant Vasily Zaitsev and German SS Colonel Heinz Thorvald.

Each was reputed within his own army as its most skillful killer, a master sniper of extraordinary abilities. Both were assigned to find and destroy the other. Each knew his nemesis was looking for him in the colossal maze of ruin and death that was Stalingrad.

Three of the four principal characters in *War of the Rats*—Zaitsev, Thorvald, and the female sniper Tania Chernova—were actual combatants at Stalingrad. Their escapades and those of several of their comrades have been documented in a number of works of history, and this novel has been drawn from those works (see Bibliography). While Zaitsev's personal and family histories are recounted faithfully, I have presented the backgrounds of both Thorvald and Tania with some details imagined or altered for dramatic purposes. But the German sniper's and the female partisan's adventures and fates in Stalingrad have been left unchanged. The fourth character, Corporal Nikki Mond, is a composite German soldier who lives as authentic a life in Stalingrad as could be devised for him.

The dates, troop movements, and major battle details in *War of the Rats* are historical fact. In addition, most of the smaller vignettes, the personal struggles and interactions, are also fact, gleaned from interviews with survivors as well as written accounts. But like any novel, here—in the smaller, private moments—creep in the notions of accuracy and legitimacy. It is, of course, impossible to describe another's thoughts and unseen acts. It is possible, however, with study and understanding, to re-create what an individual might have done and how he or she might have gone about doing it in a manner that, while fictional, remains genuine.

DLR
Richmond, Virginia

WAR OF
THE RATS

1. Tractor Works factory
2. The Barricades factory
3. Red October factory
4. Lazur Chemical Plant
5. The Railyard
6. Ninth of January Square

----- Front as of September 12, 1942

.... Front as of September 30, 1942

The Khoper River

The Don River

R U S S I A

N

MOSCOW
900 km N/NW
of Stalingrad

BERLIN
3200 km W/NW
of Stalingrad

The Donets River

MOROZOVSK

THE MEDVEDITSA RIVER

THE ILOVLYA RIVER

THE VOLGA RIVER

① ② ③ ④ ⑤ ⑥

STALINGRAD

● KLETSKAYA

AIRFIELD

MAMAYEV
KURGAN ▲

The Tsaritsa
River

FERRY

KALACH

Krasnaya
Sloboda

Tsimlyansk
Reservoir

Miles
Kilometers

0   3   6

0   5   10

© 1999 James Sinclair

ONE

THE CORPORAL,
THE HARE,
THE PARTISAN,
AND
THE HEADMASTER

ONE

NIKKI MOND LOOKED OUT OF THE TRENCH INTO a smeared gray dawn.

The first light of the late October sky stayed clenched in a fist of smoke and dust. Fires from the night's bombing chattered in the rubble. Burned tanks and trucks smoldered on the front line four hundred meters away, pulsing greasy oil smoke. Brick and concrete dust put a dry, chalky taste on every breath.

Nikki laid down his rifle to stretch his back and legs. He opened his canteen; he did not swallow the first dram but rinsed the dust from his mouth. He hadn't touched the canteen in the night. Thirst helped keep him awake on watch.

"Let me have some of that." Private Pfizer walked up to start the new watch. "I feel like I've been breathing dry shit all night."

Nikki handed him the canteen.

Fifty meters away, Lieutenant Hofstetter came out of the officers' bunker shaking on his gray coat. He buttoned it casually while he walked to the two soldiers. Nikki and Pfizer stiffened at his approach. He waved them off with a yawn.

"Too early for that."

"Yes, sir," Nikki answered.

"Anything to report, Corporal?"

"No, sir."

"Well, the Reds never leave anything quiet for long. Let's see what we've got."

Hofstetter took Nikki's binoculars, then stepped onto a dirt riser. The officer raised his head slowly above the top of the breastwork and brought the binoculars to his eyes. Keeping his head level, he slowly surveyed the ruins of the Stalingrad Tractor Factory.

"Nothing," Hofstetter said. "Good. I think the Ivans took the night off."

Pfizer held the canteen up to the lieutenant. "Sir, have a drink on that."

Hofstetter lowered the binoculars. Turning broadside to the revetment, he raised the canteen and tilted his head back to take a long draught.

The lieutenant spasmed suddenly and threw the canteen into Pfizer's face. Water erupted from the officer's mouth, muffling a gurgled cry. His head whipped to the side; the canteen and binoculars fell from his rising hands. He tumbled.

The crack of a single, distant rifle flew past the trench. It circled over the morning like a buzzard, then was gone.

The lieutenant collapsed on Pfizer's legs. The private's face froze. He kicked the body off and scrambled to the opposite wall, ramming his back into the dirt.

Nikki snapped to his senses. He threw himself against the wall next to Pfizer, crouching low. He slid forward to lay his hand on the officer's back. There was no breath.

Nikki looked at the officer's helmet, still strapped under the chin. A red-rimmed hole gaped in front of the black eagle against a gold background, the emblem of the Third Reich. Blood leaked under the helmet to wet hair and ears, pooling on the Russian dirt. The lieutenant's left foot shivered once, quivering in the puddle spilling from the canteen.

"Fucking snipers," mumbled Pfizer. "We're half a kilometer from the front line. How can they hit us here?"

Nikki recovered his binoculars and canteen. He looked down on the lieutenant. Nikki had seen tides of death in the past two months. Death was part of the Stalingrad landscape; it was melted into the broken bricks and shattered skyline. He bore it on his back now like scars from a lashing.

Nikki put a hand under the private's arm. "Go get help moving the body."

Pfizer scrambled to his feet. Without looking back at the corpse, he bent low and hurried up the trench to bring back the punishment detail, soldiers who'd been caught drinking, fighting, or sleeping on watch and were given the duty of collecting bodies.

Nikki moved away from Hofstetter and sat. Dawn had taken hold. Green and red recognition flares lofted into and out of the sky to mark the German positions so that the Luftwaffe could avoid bombing their own men in the morning's opening sorties. Russian tracers flashed above, reaching for the screaming fighter planes. Flames danced in the decimated buildings while the constant flares exploded, flickered, and faded.

Waiting for Pfizer to return, Nikki composed letters in his head. He wrote a lie to his father on the family dairy farm in Westphalia. He told the old man not to worry; the war in the East was nearing an end, the Russian resistance was buckling. To his older sister, a nurse in Berlin, he wrote the truth, for he knew she was seeing the broken remains of this campaign firsthand in her beds and wards. Finally he drafted a letter to himself, a twenty-year-old corporal of the Wehrmacht dug in on the Eastern Front, crouched only meters from a fresh corpse. In his own letter he could neither lie convincingly nor tell the truth completely.

VASILY ZAITSEV PULLED THE BOLT BACK FAST. The smoking casing made no sound when it landed on the dirt beside him.

At his elbow, big Viktor Medvedev bore down through his telescopic sight. The first shot had been Zaitsev's; if a second target appeared above the German trench, Viktor would take it.

Zaitsev counted slowly under his breath to sixty. In one minute, whether or not Viktor pulled his trigger, they would move. That was the sniper's first rule of survival: pull the trigger, then pull out. Every shot can betray your position to eyes you cannot see but which are watching everywhere on the battlefield. Never stay in one shooting cell so long that it becomes your grave.

Zaitsev was sure his bullet had hit. The canteen was the first thing he'd seen, a round shape bobbing above the trench. He'd almost fired then: at a distance of 450 meters, it was hard to tell a canteen from a man's head. He'd increased his pressure on the trigger and waited. Five seconds later the head popped right into his crosshairs. Careless, stupid, dead German.

Viktor waited now for another target to move into his sights. On occasion a bullet blowing out the back of a man's skull would make the soldier next to him grab his rifle or his binoculars and search vengefully for the Russian sniper who had killed his officer or his friend, who had laid the silent crosshairs on him and snuffed his life with a single bullet fired from somewhere in the ruins. The shocked survivor sometimes vomited up one brave and loyal act for the still-shaking corpse beside him. Zaitsev and Viktor hunted courage as well as stupidity.

A minute passed. Zaitsev nudged Viktor.

"Time, Bear."

Medvedev lowered his scope. He and Zaitsev crept backward from the pile of bricks they'd hidden behind since before sunup, only fifty meters from the front line in no-man's-land. In a shallow depression, the two pulled dirty muslin sacks from their backpacks. They slid their rifles inside the sacks and attached ropes, then slipped away into the surrounding debris without them. This close to the front line, the rifles jiggling on their backs could bring the two snipers unwanted attention.

It took them five minutes to slither thirty meters across an open boulevard, then into the shell of a building. They reeled in the sacks slowly to betray no motion in the rising light.

They sat in the building for an hour, in case a Nazi sniper had seen them enter and was waiting for them to leave. The wait would try the enemy's patience—make him wonder if he'd missed them—as well as probe his physical ability to stay focused through his crosshairs for sixty empty minutes.

Zaitsev reached into his pack for his sniper journal. He scribbled in it, then handed the worn notebook to Medvedev.

"Sign this, Viktor."

Medvedev read the record of the day's kill: *17/10/42. NE quadrant, Tractor Factory sector. German bunker. Forward observer. 450 meters. Head shot.*

He signed. *Spotter—Medvedev, V. A. Sgt.* With a quick scrawl, Viktor sketched a pair of round ears, a snarling snout, and slitted, angry eyes. Under it he wrote "the Bear."

Master Sergeant Viktor Medvedev was a Siberian, a broad-shouldered, dark, and powerful man. His name came from *medved*, the word for "bear." His partner was another Siberian, Chief Master Sergeant Vasily Zaitsev. Zaitsev had the round, flat face of a Mongol. Smaller than

Viktor, he was wiry, yellow-haired, and quick, a scrambler. His name sprang from *zayats*, "hare."

Zaitsev and Medvedev were the only members of their division's sniper unit who worked directly along the front line. The other dozen shooters stayed burrowed in the rubble a few hundred meters back. Working so close to the Germans called on all their skills as hunters, testing their nerves and cunning, but it enabled the two Siberians to shoot several hundred meters deeper into the German rear. Their crosshairs found not just infantry, machine gunners, and artillery spotters, the fodder of war, but unsuspecting officers.

Viktor dug from his pack a half-full bottle of vodka. He inclined the lip toward Zaitsev. "Nice shooting, Hare." He took a swallow, then put the bottle in Zaitsev's outstretched hand. Zaitsev tipped it.

Viktor laughed. "You've got more patience than me."

Zaitsev wiped his lips. "How so?"

The Bear laughed harder. "I would have shot that fucking canteen."

SS COLONEL HEINZ VON KRUPP THORVALD FACED the applause.

His students clapped, fifteen of them who'd gathered on the distance range to see their teacher, the headmaster of the SS's elite sniper school, win a bet.

Lieutenant Brechner strode forward, ten marks in his hand. He laid the money in his colonel's outstretched palm, then bowed in a theatrical burst.

Thorvald accepted the money and returned the bow. He reached out to the puffing private who'd run back from one thousand meters across the field with the paper target.

Thorvald held the target up to Brechner and stuck his index finger through the perforation in the center of the bull's-eye. He waggled the finger. "This is a worm," he said, "sticking out of a Russian's head."

The men laughed. The remarkable ability of their colonel to make such spectacularly long shots was useless as a military tactic, for at such a distance it was impossible to tell if a target deserved shooting. Nonetheless it was an impressive feat, one that Brechner at least was willing to wager ten marks to witness.

"That's just how I got them in Poland," Thorvald said, handing his Mauser Kar 98K with a 6X Zeiss scope to the private, his attendant. "Two hundred of them. Back in thirty-nine."

Part of Thorvald's teaching philosophy was that his students should aspire to be like him: confident, calm on the trigger. They need not emulate his flabbiness and bookish nature, but he desired to see intellect in their marksmanship. He wanted them to reason out their shots, replacing the body—the enemy of the sharpshooter, with all its distractions and throbbing motion—with the still, sharp focus of the mind. He desired to see them behave and shoot like Germans.

Daily, Thorvald told stories of his own exploits on the battlefield as part of their training here in Gnössen, just outside Berlin. This morning, after the early practice session and the bet by Brechner, he gathered his charges under a large oak and had coffee served. While they sipped and settled on the grass, Thorvald told this class of young, eager snipers the tale of the Polish cavalry charge.

Within forty-eight hours of Germany's invasion of Poland, begun September 1, 1939, Thorvald had been transferred as a sniper to the Fourteenth Army under General Heinz Guderian. It was Guderian and his staff who'd conceived the lightning strikes, the overwhelming blitzkrieg tactic combining waves of air and land bombardment with highly mobile tanks and armored infantry. In the opening days of the Polish invasion, Thorvald, then a captain, found himself on his first live battlefield with little to do while the German forces easily split the Poles into fragments. Above the front lines, the Luftwaffe's Ju-87 Stuka bombers perforated the enemy's lines with their low-level, screaming accuracy. Then came a flood of armored cars, motorcycles, and tanks. Next came the rumble of infantry and artillery. When weaknesses were found, the German infantry knifed through to fan out into the rear, cutting communications and surprising supply stations.

By the third morning, the Polish army had fallen into disarray. Isolated units fought hard to beat off frontal attacks in Thorvald's sector outside Krakow. Finally his assignment came from Command: his eight-man sniper squad was to creep up during lulls in the fighting and shoot into the Polish trenches and strongholds. Command wanted its snipers to drain the enemy's fighting spirit.

For four days Thorvald and his men crawled at dawn to within five hundred meters of the enemy. Thorvald collected seventy-one confirmed kills, more than the rest of his unit combined.

While the other snipers bragged at the evening meals and compared journals, Thorvald read books. The commander of his division came around and handed out tin tokens, one for each kill. These were to be redeemable at the end of the war for one hundred deutsche marks apiece, the army's equivalent of a bounty. Thorvald gave his tokens away.

During the invasion's second week, Thorvald's company encircled a large Polish force. One morning at dawn, he looked out of his shooting cell at the sound of trumpets and pounding hooves. He watched in disbelief as a brigade of Polish cavalry leaped over the parapets and galloped across the open plain. Through his scope, he gazed at the colorful mounted soldiers, their gloved hands holding pennants and lances high, trying to rally their comrades.

He lined up his first target at six hundred meters and fired. The rider fell. Before he could acquire a second mark, the booming of tanks erupted behind him, raising columns of dirt and flame on the plain. He watched through the crosshairs; in minutes the magnificent Polish cavalry charge became a scattered collage of dismembered men and horses.

"And what," he asked the assembled class at the end of this day's tale, "do you think is the moral?"

Thorvald smiled at the young men. No hands went up. They knew better than to speak during his stories, even to answer a question.

They are so ready, Thorvald thought, looking at the faces, the ease of confidence in their movements, the juice of youth in their veins; they're tugging at the reins to go off to battle to earn their own reputations, to move their crosshairs over the hearts of real men. I know how a man can kill. But I wonder how he can be so anxious to risk his life to go and do it.

"The lesson, my young, ignorant boys," he said, holding his hands out to them as if to show the breadth of his sizable wisdom, "is this: don't be a hero, on horseback or otherwise. Stay behind cover."

TWO

MINUTES AFTER HOFSTETTER'S BODY HAD BEEN carried to the rear, orders came for Nikki's company to move from their position west of the Tractor Factory. The final assault on the next factory, the Barricades, was under way. This offensive would be the knockout punch; it should take just one or two more weeks to push the Reds out of the Barricades and into the Volga.

Captain Mercker split the eighty-man company into patrols of ten. Mercker was leery of snipers and migrating machine guns that might carve into his troops and bog them down in a firefight if they moved as one. He counted out the first ten men.

"Corporal." He pointed at Nikki. "You know our objective?"

Nikki nodded sharply. "Yes, sir."

"You're in charge of the first squad. Get to within fifteen hundred meters of the Barricades. Find a secure spot for the company to assemble."

"Yes, sir."

"Keep your head down. Move."

Nikki looked at the nine men assigned to scurry behind him through the gauntlet ahead. All young, pale, grimy faces like his own. All interchangeable, he thought, each one dispensable, like a throwaway rag. He said a quick and silent prayer that there would still be nine when he next counted.

"Go only where I go," he said. "Move only how I move."

Nikki bent at the waist and knees. His rifle hung in his hand almost to the ground. He stretched his neck like a tortoise and lifted his head. In this position, which was torturous but made a man as small a target as he could be when running, Nikki moved clear of cover and into the open street.

He ran in bursts, shadowing the contours of the buildings and rubble. His nine charges mimicked his every step. They ducked and waited one at a time behind the debris he chose. They lay panting for breath in the craters and ditches where he had lain. Nikki picked each position with care, knowing that every step he took had to be taken nine more times. He never allowed himself to be without cover for more than ten meters. In that space, a sniper would have to be extraordinarily good or lucky to line him up and hit. If he ran into the sights of a Red machine gun, he might still have time to dive for the ground and scramble behind something, anything. His biggest concern was his nerves; he knew that if he made a mistake, it might kill not him but perhaps the fifth or last soldier behind him.

Twice, rifle shots rang out. Nikki froze. The shots did not find his men and were not followed by more action. They were just the random convulsions of combat in Stalingrad, as if too much silence broke some unwritten rule. He caught his breath, then pressed on.

Nikki had the objective in sight for a long time. The three gargantuan factories stood in a line, their backs against the river—the Tractor Works, the Barricades, and the Red October. Around them for a kilometer in all directions lay open battleground plowed by bombs, the broken machinery of war scattered over it like coal shoveled across a floor. At fifteen hundred meters from the middle factory, the Barricades, Nikki sprinted across the remains of a wide boulevard and tumbled into an abandoned trench. He waved to his men to gather beside him and wait for the rest of the company.

After the grueling three-hour, six-kilometer traverse through the city, Nikki's reward was nine sweaty faces, their eyes rolling as if to say, Corporal, don't make us do that ever again.

The Barricades, like the other two factories, had been gutted and dismantled by battle to where it had fallen in on itself. A row of broken smokestacks rose above the giant heaps of steel. From this distance, the factory looked deserted. Nikki knew it was not.

To his left were the ghostly shambles of several stone buildings. The corner structure was the largest. Its top was missing, crumpled at its feet like a skirt that had been dropped. That building will make an excellent strong point, Nikki thought. We can occupy several floors and control the approaches from all sides.

The squad waited in the trench for the rest of the company to arrive. Nikki wondered about Lieutenant Hofstetter's body.

Where is it now, six hours after being alive for its last moments? Is it being readied to fly home, boxed in pine for a military funeral with flags and honors like we've all been promised? Or has it been dumped into an unmarked grave in the Russian sod with a hundred other corpses? Did his arms and legs fly akimbo when he landed atop the other dead, to stay that way into eternity, sliding down the pile, going to Judgment upside down?

I don't want to die like Hofstetter, a bullet in the brain fired from half a kilometer away blasting out the back of my head. He was just drinking from a canteen, he wasn't even fighting; he didn't get the chance to die thrashing or screaming to give his life some sort of send-off, a final moment of note. Drinking out of a canteen: he didn't know he was marked with the crosshairs of a sniper, a damned killer who crawled away with no blood on his hands.

I don't want to die like that, branded with an invisible black cross like one of war's ten million cattle. It isn't a proper death for a soldier; it's just an ending. It's even a bit stupid, a silly, facedown, ripped-open, awful ending.

I don't want to be buried in Russia, Nikki thought. I want to go home.

In ten minutes the first soldier from the second patrol appeared in the ruins to the rear. Nikki's men beckoned him into their trench. For two hours, the afternoon sun lowered its gaze and the rest of the company assembled. Captain Mercker arrived at dusk with the last group of ten. There had been no encounters with the enemy. The Russians must be withdrawing, Nikki guessed, to concentrate in the factories and ready themselves for the coming German hammer blow.

Mercker held a quick meeting with his lieutenant and five sergeants and corporals.

"We're going to take this big building on the corner, gentlemen. I want the men to move in their ten-man squads. Corporal," Mercker said, locking on Nikki, "you go in first again. You seem to be good at it."

Nikki nodded. A hell of a thing to be good at, he thought.

"Send word when the building is secure. If we hear action, we'll come running."

"Yes, sir." Nikki collected his squad.

Nikki led the way for his men, ducking and weaving. Bursting in the front door, his squad moved quickly down a long, dark corridor with machine guns poised and grenades ready. They scraped their backs against the walls before erupting into rooms. Every nerve was raw while they scoured the shadows for any sign of Russians. Nikki shouldered the last door. It opened into a large assembly hall, perhaps a ballroom. He sent a private to tell Mercker to come ahead. He suggested the large room at the end of the hall as the place where the unit should gather and spread out to fortify the building.

Once all eighty men were assembled, the captain ran down assignments. Spotters, large-caliber machine guns, and mortars would go to the top floor. Antitank gunners were sent to the middle floors to shoot down onto Russian tanks. For street-level defense, light machine guns and the rest of the men would be on the ground floor. Mess and communications were in the big hall.

Nikki stood beside the door to the hallway. At Mercker's signal, every man in the unit was to dash to his assigned position. Nikki prepared to fling the door open, plant his feet, and aim his machine gun down the hall to protect the men scurrying up the steps.

"Ready?" asked the captain. "Go."

Nikki flung open the door.

A grenade sailed past his face. On the other side of the hall a door slammed shut.

Nikki screamed, "Down!"

He flung himself to the floor. The grenade rolled into the crowd and exploded ten meters from where he lay. The blast was muffled. Nikki brought his head up from his arms to see the jerking body of a soldier who'd leaped onto the grenade.

Men recoiled from the door. Every weapon they could handle was pointed forward while they backpedaled. Chambers clattered as rounds were slammed into firing position. Eighty fingers poised on triggers as the boom of the detonation faded. Near the door, alone, the body of the dead heroic soldier lay smoking.

"Russians!" a voice shouted. "Goddammed Russians are across the hall!"

"How'd they get in there?" Mercker was furious. "Damn it, how? I thought we checked this floor!"

The captain stabbed his finger at six men; Nikki was the sixth. Mercker waved them beside the door, then made a fist, his battle signal for them to stand guard.

Nikki rushed forward with the other men. He sat quickly and hoisted his machine gun stock to his cheek. He aimed at the doorknob of the door across the hall. If it moves, he thought, I'm blowing it off its hinges. Another soldier slid along the wall and slammed their door shut.

The captain ordered two heavy machine guns set up and aimed at the doorway in case the Russians mounted a charge. Guards were placed at the three windows into the room. The Reds might try crawling around the side of the building to toss in satchel charges. Secure for the moment, the captain stepped to the center of the room.

"We're ordered to hold this building," he growled, "and that's what we're going to do. I don't know the strength across the hall, so we'll keep our position until we have more info. Or until we find a way to get the Reds out of here."

A soldier spoke up. "Why don't we just rush them, sir? There can't be more than a few."

"How do you know that, Private? There are eighty Germans in here. Would you like to hold us off with just a few? I don't think the Russians would, either. I doubt that's all they brought with them."

Nikki looked at the grimy faces leaning into the officer's words.

"No," Mercker said, "I'm not ready to turn this into a slaughterhouse. We'll wait them out. See who gets scared first. Probably they'll sneak out a window tonight and go report that the Reich has got this building now."

Nikki moved to the center of the room and sat. He watched two men lift the martyred soldier out of his smoldering blood and carry him to a window. It was Private

Kronnenberg. A boy his own age, nineteen or twenty. They'd spoken only a few times. Kronnenberg was new, just called up. He'd been hopeful, still certain that Germany needed Russian soil. A young patriot. He was no longer young, Nikki thought. Kronnenberg was dead. He couldn't get any older than that. He was lowered out the window gently.

Nikki's eyes fixed on the door. The Russians are just like us, he thought. There's a hundred of them. They're huddled in the middle of a big room. They're making plans to spend the night, too, figuring we'll creep out through the windows as soon as we're sure we don't want to die enough to keep this building.

Nikki was scared. He marveled that he could still be afraid for his life. When would the fear leave him completely? When would he have seen enough, run and crawled enough? He didn't shake after the battles in these buildings anymore. He no longer curled up in a corner under the clearing smoke, looking breathlessly at the dead of both armies. No longer. This was a bad sign. He didn't want to get used to this. But it was happening.

THREE

"COMRADE CHIEF MASTER SERGEANT. COME IN. Sit down."

Zaitsev stepped down onto the dirt floor of Colonel Nikolai Batyuk's bunker. Batyuk stood and motioned to a keg as a stool. The commander of the 284th Division was taller than Zaitsev but just as slim. His dark hair was combed back to show a high, pale forehead.

Batyuk's desk was a collection of planks laid over two barrels. Unlike the bunker Zaitsev shared with Viktor, this cave had been dug not by a German bomb but by sappers into the limestone cliff above the Volga, southeast of the Barricades plant. The walls and roof were fortified with timbers, recalling a Siberian sauna. Behind Batyuk, two women worked field radios, plugging and unplugging wires at a furious rate and speaking into microphones in low tones. Three staff officers leaned over another crude table to scribble lines on a map.

Zaitsev perched on the keg. He set his pack at his feet and rested his sniper rifle across his knees.

"You wished to see me, Comrade Colonel?"

"Yes, Vasily. You were stationed in Vladivostok before you were transferred here. You were in the navy. A clerk?"

"Yes, sir." I am not, Zaitsev thought, still a clerk.

Batyuk pointed to Zaitsev's neck. "I see you still wear your sailor's shirt under your tunic."

Zaitsev tugged at the blue-and-white striped jersey beneath his outer shirt.

"Yes, sir. In the navy we say the blue is the ocean's waters and the white is the foam."

Batyuk smiled. "I've never seen the Pacific. I hear it's beautiful. Perhaps one day."

The two sat silently. Both wore thin, faraway smiles across their faces. Batyuk blinked and cleared his throat.

"Let me see your sniper journal."

Zaitsev handed the black leather booklet across the desk.

The colonel flipped through the pages. Without looking up, he said, "As you know, in the last two weeks the Germans have kicked us out of the Tractor Factory in all but the northeast corner. They're also threatening our positions in the Barricades and Red October plants."

Batyuk laid the journal on the desk. "Our bridgehead is dwindling. I'm going to tell you a few things you may not know. Then again, since you're one of the men who makes those lines on that map come and go"—he motioned to his staffers drawing and erasing at their table—"you might know a great deal."

Zaitsev looked hard at his colonel. Batyuk reached under the desk and produced a bottle of vodka and two glasses. He poured.

The two raised their drinks in toast. They gulped, then inhaled deeply through their shirtsleeves, the Russian ritual to make the sting of the vodka last a moment longer.

Batyuk exhaled. "I'm sorry I can't offer you any cabbage."

Zaitsev smiled. "Another time, Comrade Colonel."

Batyuk leaned across his desk. "Something's up. I'm sure you've noticed that we've had our ammunition cut every day for a week. That means it's being diverted somewhere else." The colonel picked up a penknife and tapped it in his palm. "We have to hold out, Vasily. We've got to keep the Germans' feet to the fire. I can't tell you why, because I don't know why. But something very big is up."

Batyuk motioned Zaitsev to follow him to the map table. He indicated the row of three giant factories, red and black lines mingled in a tangle of battle activity. Zaitsev thought how little the lines told of the destruction and terror inside those buildings.

"We have forty thousand men in place," Batyuk began. "We can stay at that level so long as we continue to get reinforcements. Whenever the Germans reduce our bridgehead, we just pack the men in more densely. Even though our positions are getting smaller, they're not getting weaker. The Germans have been slow to catch on to this. In fact, Zhukov and the rest of the generals who know what's going on aren't concerned with space. If we can keep that number of men fighting somewhere in the city, the Nazis can't pull out. Hitler won't let them. He's already announced to the world he controls Stalingrad. I think Hitler's just mad because the city is named after Stalin." Batyuk chuckled. "Who knows. Anyway, as long as they can't leave, you and I are doing our jobs."

The colonel moved his hand to an open area between the city center and the factory district. His finger came to rest over a black circle. "This is Hill 102.8," he said, referring to the hill's height in meters above sea level. Its real name was Mamayev Kurgan, the burial mound of Mamay, an ancient Tatar king. "The Germans control this hill. From here they can see every damned thing going on . . . here." Batyuk drew a ring around the city center. "Here . . ." He motioned to a five-kilometer stretch of the ruins of three huge factories: on the eve of war, these plants had produced 40 percent of the Soviet Union's tractors and 30 percent of its high-grade steel; the bombings of August and September had reduced them to gar gantuan tangles of steel, twisted rails, and forlorn brick facades.

"And worst of all, here." Batyuk stabbed his finger three times along the Volga at the landing stages: the Skudri crossing, behind the Tractor Factory; Crossing No. 62, at the rear of the Barricades; and the moorings south of the Banny Gully, directly across from Krasnaya Sloboda, the Red Army's main embarkation point on the east bank.

"From 102.8, German spotters are directing artillery and air strikes against our supplies and reinforcements on the river." Batyuk moved back to his desk. "With supplies already being cut, we could be in serious trouble if we don't maximize use of what we do get from the east bank."

Zaitsev sat again on the keg. "Do you want me to hunt on Mamayev Kurgan? I know it pretty well."

Batyuk waved his hand. "Not yet." He opened Zaitsev's sniper journal to the first page. "Tell me about your introduction to being a sniper."

Zaitsev had seen his first snipers during the battle for the Tractor Factory only eighteen days before, two lithe men crawling in the direction of the bullets while others dug their way to cover. Zaitsev had admired their courage, how well they seemed to work on their own.

"Do you like working on your own?" Batyuk inquired.

"I am not unaccustomed to it. It's how I hunt."

"Who commissioned you a sniper? When did it happen?"

"On October eighth. We were in a shop of the Tractor Factory, pinned down under a machine gun. I don't know—I just crawled to a spot, aimed, and fired."

"Distance?"

"One hundred and seventy-five meters."

"You took out the machine gunner?"

"Yes."

"And you shot the next two Nazis who got behind the gun."

"I did." Zaitsev was surprised Batyuk knew this.

"Lieutenant Deriabyn approached you and told you to report to the sniper unit of my division, yes? You, along with your Siberian friend Viktor Medvedev—another crack shot, I hear—began as snipers with your telescopic sights the next day."

Zaitsev nodded. Batyuk was not inviting comment.

"What kind of training did you get?"

Zaitsev said nothing.

"Hmmm?" Batyuk took up the penknife. He tapped it on the table. It said, quietly, Answer me, Chief Master Sergeant.

Zaitsev's first days as a freshman sniper had been marked by a funereal silence. The nine other snipers in the squad did not speak often. No one seemed sure how long any of them would live. Camaraderie did not exist. The snipers were fresh-scrubbed boys and weasel-eyed men, long-limbed athletes and stocky pugs, all volunteers. They had been recommended for sniper duty by their platoon commanders, each for his ability to kill one target at a time from a distance. It seemed they were all resolute to survive the same way, one at a time, alone, at a distance.

The unit lived in a dirt cave, a bunker dug by a heavy artillery round and then covered with rafters and debris to disguise it from Nazi dive-bombers. At night, when Zaitsev and Viktor returned to the snipers' bunker, they alone talked by the glow of the lantern of strategies and their similar childhoods in the Urals. They spoke of hunting the enemy in Stalingrad as if the Nazis were animals in the wild, driven by instinct more than intellect. War, they agreed, scoured away man's humanness to reveal the beast inside. The beast was what Zaitsev and Viktor tracked and killed.

There was neither structure nor training in place for

the snipers; experience was their teacher, the battle gave
them their orders. Some of the men were sullen; others
shone brightly, ready to prove their worth. Many had
strength; others had patience; some had brains. Few combined all three, and Zaitsev and Viktor watched the faces
come and go, disappearing into the giant meat grinder of
war in the decimated streets, cellars, rusted metal, and
pockmarked walls.

"None, sir," Zaitsev answered. "No training."

Batyuk turned back to the opening page in the journal.
"Tell me about your first sniper kill." He found a place on
the page with his finger. "October eighth. You had two
kills near the railway behind the chemical factory."

On Zaitsev's initial dawn as a sniper, he'd spotted an
enemy unit digging a trench to connect two shattered rail
cars. That evening he'd asked the sniper squad's leader, a
corporal, for permission to return and hunt them. Since
he was a chief master sergeant, the rank he brought with
him from his years as a naval clerk, and the highest-
ranking soldier in the bunker, he was told to do what he
wanted. Before dawn, he and Viktor crawled out to take
up positions three hundred meters from the trench.

Zaitsev and Viktor watched the Nazis through binoculars under the rising sun. The two snipers let the Germans
show themselves above the trench a few times to give
them confidence that the area was secure. They would
wait for one of the digging soldiers to finish his labor and
thrust the shovel into the dirt or lean on it. That would be
the time for a chest shot.

"Why in the chest?" Batyuk interrupted.

A chest shot, Zaitsev explained, would more likely
cause the target to drop the shovel and leave it on top of
the breastwork when he fell. A shot in the back would
increase the odds of him taking the shovel back down into
the trench. Just as planned, the first soldier to die—with
Medvedev's bullet in his heart—let the shovel fly from his

grasp before he tumbled backward into the trench. Viktor and Zaitsev trained their sights on the tool left lying in full view. In minutes a head and an arm appeared above the dirt wall to retrieve it.

Viktor whispered, "You."

Zaitsev's bullet pierced the Nazi's cheek.

"Where did you learn this tactic?" Batyuk sat forward, his fingers playing under his chin.

"It's a simple ploy for a hunter from the Urals, sir. Wolves and other animals in the taiga mate for life. You bait one with the body of the other."

Batyuk opened his hands. "Ah, yes, of course. In Siberia. I fear we're out of wolves in my home, the Ukraine." He turned more pages in the journal. "And this one? Last week you were on the southern slope of Mamayev Kurgan, hunting enemy snipers." Batyuk held the book closer to his eyes. "What is the 'mortar shell trick'?"

Again Zaitsev explained to his colonel. He'd picked up this ploy from a German sniper who'd feasted on Russian wounded during their evacuation through a ravine near Mamayev Kurgan. Zaitsev had crawled to a position high above the ravine. He lay behind cover for hours, watching with his artillery periscope. The periscope was an excellent tool, allowing him to stay out of sight and observe a wide range at four power, the same as his sniper scope. It was precise to 250 meters. Looking near the crest of the hill, Zaitsev saw a heap of empty brass mortar shells. He counted twenty-three shells. He noted that one among the pile had no bottom.

"You counted the shells?" Batyuk tapped his pocketknife in his palm. "I marvel at your attention to detail. That's fantastic."

"Not really, sir. Noticing details is a more important skill than shooting for distance. Movements in the terrain, even the smallest shift in a rock or a new hole in a wall, are the only clues you may get to the location of a sniper.

These are the tracks we read, just like footprints in the snow or animal scat on the forest floor."

Batyuk nodded. Zaitsev knew he was telling his colonel things the man did not, could not, know. Oh, well, he thought, Batyuk asked me. What can I do but tell him? Zaitsev reminded himself to try not to boast. You're just a hunter, hunting. It's what you do well. Let it speak for itself.

"When I saw the bottomless mortar shell, I realized it would make a perfect shooting tube. It could be buried inside a trench mound or hidden among other shells, as this sniper had done. It would make him almost invisible."

Zaitsev had focused his periscope on the shell. With his free hand, he raised his helmet on his bayonet. A flash appeared inside the shell. The helmet sprang off the bayonet, dented in the front. Zaitsev gave the sniper credit for his patience and cunning. He'd had the first shot. The next belonged to the Hare.

The following dawn Zaitsev crawled to the same spot and located the shell pile. He counted again. This time he found only twenty-two shells. The shooting tube was gone. This sniper was no freshman; he knew to shoot and move. He'd taken the open shell with him. Where? Using the periscope, Zaitsev looked in every pit in the ground, along every mound. After three exhausting hours he found the brass shell buried near the top of a trench a hundred meters east of its original site. The camouflage was sloppy; part of the tube was left sticking out of the trench. A yellow reflection glistened in the rising sun, enough for Zaitsev to zero in on.

He crawled to a new position, one where the sun was directly over his shoulder and shining into the eyes of the German. He laid his rifle between two rocks and focused his scope on the mouth of the tube. Leaving the rifle, he slithered three meters to a pile of bricks. Again he raised his helmet on the bayonet. Again the Nazi stung the helmet with a bullet. Zaitsev scrambled back to his rifle. He stared down his scope into the open shell two hundred meters away. At the other end of the brass tube, the sniper leaned down just for a second to pick the spent casing from the trench floor. Still following the rules, Zaitsev thought, like all good snipers. Leave no trace behind.

Zaitsev waited for him to straighten. When he did, he split the German's brow with his crosshairs. The bullet, Zaitsev's lone offering in this one-on-one battle, struck between the eyes. He saw the rifle, lying ownerless now, in the gleaming shell.

"Between the eyes?" Batyuk repeated. He seemed doubtful.

"Yes, sir."

Zaitsev held the colonel's gaze. It had been his shot, his kill. One bullet, one Nazi. That was Zaitsev's creed, his special gift. He did not doubt. He raised his finger. He put it between his own eyebrows. "Right here," he said.

Batyuk returned his attention to Zaitsev's journal. He read through the final entries, then laid the booklet on the desk.

"This morning you shot an officer near the Tractor Factory."

Zaitsev stretched his back. He'd been sitting for almost an hour. "The Germans change shifts at dawn. The ones coming on watch often light a cigarette or do something stupid like stretch. The sleepy ones get careless."

"What did this one do?"

"He took a drink from a canteen. His head popped up like a cork."

Batyuk waited.

Zaitsev shrugged. "And I blew it off. Sir."

Batyuk patted the journal. "It says here you've killed forty-two Germans in twelve days' work. How many bullets have you used in those twelve days?"

"Forty-three, sir."

Batyuk smiled. "What went wrong?"

"I was hunting some officers on Mamayev Kurgan. I crawled above them on the slope. They were bathing in a pool of rainwater in a crater. I forgot to take into account that I was firing downhill."

"And?"

"And I was tired and did not subtract one eighth of the distance from the total. I overshot. The officers jumped out of the pool."

Batyuk continued to smile. "What did you do then, Vasily?"

"I saw my mistake and I left."

Batyuk leaned forward, his fingers steepled above his palms. "You didn't shoot more at the officers? I assume they were visible long enough for you to get off another shot."

"Yes, sir, I could have fired. But it's not the good way. A sniper should not shoot after he's revealed his position. One or two officers in return for a sniper is not a good trade."

Batyuk stood up. He nodded in small bobs, then clapped his hands once. "Vasily, I have a job for you."

VIKTOR MEDVEDEV FOLDED HIS *RED STAR* NEWS-paper in the middle.

"He wants you to do what?"

The two were alone in the snipers' bunker in late afternoon. Viktor's custom was to prowl from sunset until noon, then rest during the day.

Zaitsev replied, "He wants me to start a sniper school."

"You?" Viktor tossed the *Red Star* at Zaitsev's chest.

Zaitsev crumpled a page into a ball and bounced it off his fellow Siberian's forehead. "Batyuk says he needs heroes."

"I'm going to be sick." Viktor lifted his girth off the floor to pace and raise his arms in mock exasperation. "He wants heroes. What's he got now? Sheep? Children?"

He bent to pick up the wadded news page. "Don't do this to my paper. I read this. You may not think what's in here matters," he said holding up the ball, "but I do."

The big man's peevishness amused Zaitsev. He watched his friend uncrumple the paper and smooth it on the table. He looks like a giant woman doing her ironing, Zaitsev thought.

"You'll need my help, of course," Viktor said.

"Of course. There are so many things I don't know."

Viktor folded the wrinkled page carefully. "These damn freshmen they send us are too fast, too hot. They last about a week before they get their dicks shot off."

"City boys," Zaitsev agreed. "Farm boys."

He smiled at Viktor, as good a hunter as he, better in some respects. The Bear was fearless, an excellent night stalker. He was astonishingly silent on the move—even with his bulk—and patient and clever in the hunt. He could squeeze off two shots in five seconds, accurate to 350 meters. Zaitsev needed six seconds. But give me enough time to set up a shot, he thought, and I'll nail a head shot ten out of ten at five hundred meters in the wind. Let's see the Bear do that.

We'll put together a unit of snipers to do exactly what Batyuk wants. We'll train them to make every Nazi in Stalingrad afraid for his life twenty-four hours a day, on the front line or deep in their rear. The Germans will be scared to lift their heads for fear of having them blown off. We'll be the Red Army's assassins. We'll be everywhere.

He took his sniper journal from his pack. He felt the booklet's weight, sensing its contents.

I'll be everywhere.

• • •

"EXCUSE ME, COMRADE. MAY I COME IN?"

Zaitsev opened his eyes and checked his watch; 4:00 A.M. A hand pushed aside the blanket hanging in the bunker doorway. A lantern appeared, followed by a dark-eyed, jowly head. On top of the head sat a fur hat dotted with a red star medallion, the mark of a commissar.

Zaitsev arranged his senses. He stood.

"Did I wake you?" The commissar stepped into the bunker. He was short and thick. His greatcoat hung almost to the floor, to the tops of his shiny boots. The first shiny boots I've seen in a month, thought Zaitsev.

"Come in, comrade."

"You are Vasily Gregorievich Zaitsev?"

The commissar did not hesitate for a response. He reached his hand out to Zaitsev. "I am Captain Igor Semyonovich Danilov, a reporter with *Red Star*. Colonel Batyuk requested I speak with you."

Zaitsev shook the commissar's hand. He motioned to the bare dirt floor.

Danilov sat, his back against the wall. He took a pad and pencil from his coat pocket. Zaitsev settled on his bedroll.

"Colonel Batyuk has given us both assignments. You are to begin a new sniper movement in the 284th. I have been asked by the colonel to be your political liaison. He has told me a great deal about you, Vasily Gregorievich." The commissar made a note, then continued. "I know you are to be the leader of the new sniper school, comrade. I believe the recruiting for your school will be helped if it gets some coverage in *Red Star*."

Zaitsev shrugged. "I don't know. I don't read it."

Danilov reached out to touch Zaitsev on the back of the hand. Zaitsev recoiled slightly at the familiarity.

"You should. There is plenty of useful information in

Red Star. Tales of courage. Hints, tips, instructions, announcements. Party news. Even the theater schedule in Moscow."

Zaitsev said nothing.

"Vasily. You have killed more than forty Germans in ten days. You are a hero."

Something swelled and tightened in Zaitsev's chest. He did not know if it was a good or bad sensation. He imagined a balloon expanding. Too big and it breaks. Enough and it is light, floating.

Again Danilov did not wait. "You have established techniques in your own sniper activities that go beyond what the other snipers are doing. Your methods are very effective. They must be shared with the rest of the defenders. You have shown what can be done by one man and one bullet. Yours is a story that will be told. It must be told because it must be reenacted over and over throughout Stalingrad."

The commissar looked squarely at Zaitsev. "I speak frankly, comrade. I don't care if you want to be a hero or not. It's not my concern. I do care, however, that the rest of Russia knows we are holding out here. I care also that the soldiers in the ruins and trenches believe that heroes are kneeling next to them. You understand, every Red soldier is not a superman. The least we can do is let them know they are fighting at the side of supermen."

Zaitsev looked at Danilov's gray grin, set in the thicket of a heavy beard line. It would be a mistake, he thought, if I interpret this chat to be a request for my cooperation. I haven't been invited by this commissar to a banquet of choices. Yesterday I was a sniper doing my job. Today I'm what . . . a hero?

But I can do this. I can be this. This hero.

Danilov touched his pencil to his pad. He began. "You are from the Urals, I understand."

Zaitsev nodded. "Yes. I am a hunter."

FOUR

IN 1937, WHILE JAPAN AND GERMANY RATTLED swords at the world, twenty-two-year-old Vasily Zaitsev enlisted in the Red Navy. Born in Siberia, he'd never seen an ocean, and the idea seemed a romantic one. He was stationed in Vladivostok, on the Pacific coast. For five years he kept accounting records and waited for Japan, only seven hundred kilometers away, to attack.

Zaitsev read reports on the German siege of Leningrad, the occupation of the Ukraine, and the battle for Moscow. He listened to Party speeches and read articles about the inconceivable Nazi plan to capture the western third of the Soviet Union. The vast territory was to become a slave colony of farms and forced labor to feed the growing Aryan empire.

Off duty, Zaitsev hunted in the forests above the naval base. Lying in the leaves and rich humus, he trained his rifle on rabbits and deer, pretending they were Nazis. He was at home in the woods. He'd spent much of his boyhood hunting in the taiga, the white-barked birch forests near his home in Ellininski in the Ural foothills of western Siberia. His grandfather Andrei was one of a long line of woodsmen. The old man, lanky and bone white, like the birch forest itself, taught Vasha about the taiga while the boy was barely old enough to chew the meat of the animals they killed. When Vasha was eight, Andrei gave him a bow. Because he had to chase the arrows he shot or else fashion new ones, he studied ways to ration his ammunition, to shoot only when certain. Vasha learned to read tracks and lie in silent ambush, keeping his breathing shallow and his concentration deep.

In the summer of 1927, Andrei took twelve-year-old Vasha to hunt a wolf that was preying on their cows. Several kilometers from home, in a copse of trees, the wolf sprang at them. Andrei whirled and killed it with the sharpened end of his walking staff. This, said Andrei, ramming the spear again into the shuddering wolf's heart, was a lesson in courage for the boy. Never forget how easy it is to kill. Never be afraid to kill when you must. Andrei wiped a warm streak of blood across the boy's cheek. He watched Vasha skin the wolf. Then he presented his grandson with the old rifle he carried. On his way back to the village, Vasha shot two hares and a wild goat. He was a hunter now, with his own gun and three hides he could throw on the pile at the hunters' lodge.

Vasha often spent more time in the forest than with people. Sometimes he smeared bear fat over his body and gun to hide his scent; often his mother refused to let him in the house because of the smell. On these evenings he slept gladly with his dogs.

Grandmother Dunia taught him to read and write. Zaitsev believed it was his *babushka*'s breadth of spirit and broad-hipped will that held his family together. His sisters, parents, cousins, and even the dogs obeyed her smartly swung birch switch with only the occasional grumble.

Dunia was a spiritual old woman. She fought with Andrei over God, determined to keep religious holidays in her home. Though Andrei did not accept Dunia's saints, he would not insult them, perhaps in deference to Dunia's God or more likely the whip of her stick.

Once, Zaitsev asked his grandfather about his beliefs.

"Grandmother says the soul leaves the body and goes to heaven after we die, Grandpapa. Is that true for animals, too?"

Andrei cuffed him on the side of the head. "Neither man nor beast lives twice," he snorted. "Come here."

The old man walked Vasha to a side of venison hanging in the smokehouse. "This dawn, you killed that animal." He pointed with a hand sharp as his spear. "If I see you killing it again, I'll shoot *you*!"

The old man motioned outside to the deerskin tacked to the side of the shed. "The hide is drying. The flesh is on the table, and the guts we throw to the dogs. Remember, Vasha, soul is shit. God is about fear, a way to make you afraid and obey. The man of the forest is without fear."

The family's interest in Vasily's hunting exploits gradually waned. On his fourteenth birthday he returned in the morning with several wolf and lynx hides strapped to his back. He received no notice. That evening Andrei told him to always come back to the village from a good hunt before dawn or at night so that no one would see the number and quality of hides he brought home. Pride is good in a hunter, Andrei explained, but boastfulness is not. Vasily knew he was now considered an adult. He was expected to perform like a man of the taiga. Now his rewards were a glass of vodka, some peace and quiet from his sisters, perhaps even some respect, and a seat in the men's place, the hunters' lodge.

At sixteen Vasily was sent three hundred kilometers away to Magnitogorsk to attend technical school at Russia's largest ore processing plant. In the workers' settlement he finished primary school and began bookkeeping courses. Numbers came easily to him. In his free time he hunted in the hills around town.

After six years learning the trade of a clerk and another five years filing papers in the navy, the twenty-seven-year-old Sergeant Vasily Zaitsev wanted to fight Germans. The Nazis had invaded Russia. Japan would keep.

Hitler had taken the city of Rostov in a bloody July campaign to cauterize his right flank on his thrust to the Caucasus. Before the Germans could continue south, their left flank also had to be secured. In the middle of that flank stood the manufacturing center of Stalingrad on a bend of the Volga.

A fierce battle was shaping up on the steppe west of the city. Throughout the summer the Red Army lumbered out to meet the Germans to fight intense tank battles across immense fields and steep ravines. At first the Russians proved no match for the rolling blitzkrieg. They retreated east over the Don River to lick their wounds. On the land bridge between the Don and Volga Rivers, the Red Army regrouped.

In the first week of September 1942, Zaitsev and two hundred other Siberian sailors in Vladivostok were mustered as marines into the 284th Rifle Division of the Sixty-second Army. They were assigned to the western front and the battle that Winston Churchill called "the hinge of fate."

They were sent to Stalingrad.

THE TRAIN CLATTERED DAY AND NIGHT, REST-ing only in the afternoons to take on fuel and food. The villages where they stopped seemed asleep, moving at the heavy pace of age, of exhaustion. Children chased through the alleys playing army, ducks-on-the-pond, or October revolution, but even their laughter did not enliven the pall over the tile rooftops and dull, smokeless mills. There were no young men left in the towns. They were all gone to war.

The townspeople approached the halted troop train, tears welling in their eyes, hands lifted with bread, vegetables, vodka, clothes, and photos of Stalin and Lenin. The fleshy girls handed up letters to the uniformed arms reaching from the windows; the envelopes were often addressed to "Brave Young Man."

On the fifth day the train stopped in a treeless vista of quivering wheat. The sailors set up tents. They were addressed by Batyuk and ordered to spend three more days on the steppe preparing for battle while waiting for the trucks to carry them onward.

Dusk settled over the flat, featureless land; a trembling orb of orange appeared low in the western sky. Silence blew like a fog through the men. Standing beside the train and their tents, one by one, they held up hands to quiet each other and listen. In the gloaming, a barely audible boom and howl came from the flashing dome of light in the west, its source still well below the horizon. Zaitsev heard the sailors around him, and himself, breathe the word: *Stalingrad.*

For three days and nights the company practiced street-fighting skills. The men learned to crawl and run, to kill with bayonets and rifles, knives, shovels, and fists. Grenades with pins pulled to make them live were tossed and caught, then thrown into trenches to explode. Straw dummies were sliced or blown open, and many real noses were bloodied.

The morning of September 20, a dust plume rose out on the dirt road. A staff car came and stopped beside the train. Out stepped Division Commander Konstantinovich Zhukov. He'd ridden from Stalingrad to watch the sailors of the 284th pursue their drills.

The men threw themselves into their training, putting on their most ferocious show for the general. During a hand-to-hand exercise, one of the sailors tripped over his bell-bottom trouser legs. Zhukov slapped his thigh to stop the action.

"Why aren't you men in army uniforms?" he demanded.

Lieutenant Bolshoshapov stepped forward and came to attention.

"Commander, we are sailors and are proud to fight as sailors." Bolshoshapov shouted the words over Zhukov's head.

"Have you been issued your army uniforms, Lieutenant?"

"Yes, sir."

"Change into them immediately. These damned things," Zhukov said pointing at the billowing pants legs, "will get you killed. Where is your navy discipline?"

Zhukov whirled to return to his staff car. Bolshoshapov called out, "Commander, sir. With your permission, we would like to remain in our navy shirts under our uniforms."

Zhukov turned back and saluted Bolshoshapov.

"On behalf of the Red Army and the Party, I gladly consent. Of course, sailor. And fight bravely in your navy shirts."

The Siberians let out a cheer and stripped down to their skivvies and striped navy shirts. Orderlies ran to the train to fetch the drab green uniforms of the Soviet army.

That evening dozens of American Studebaker trucks arrived to ferry the division to the Volga. For two hours the men bumped down the road in the open backs of the lorries. Every soldier watched the spreading glow in the west. The distant thumps of explosions swelled in their ears while the horizon rolled to them.

The trucks stopped on the threshold of a forest, and the thousand-plus men of the 284th lined up on a path that disappeared into a thick stand of poplars. The soldiers marched two by two, burdened with rifles and packs. Zaitsev resisted the urge to look up through the leaves into the flaring sky. He focused instead on the back of the man in front of him. As he walked under the canopy of trees the sounds and lights grew muffled, as if the forest, ever his friend, were soothing him and his company, quieting the conflict for their restive ears.

Along the road, posters and slogans were nailed to the poplar trunks. *If you don't stop the enemy in Stalingrad, he will enter your home and destroy your village!* one read. *The enemy must be crushed and destroyed at Stalingrad!* and *Soldier, your country will not forget your courage!*

Three kilometers into the forest, the march was stopped. Batyuk ordered the men off the path to darken their faces and hands with grease and dirt. While they handed around the greasepaint pots, a hundred wounded soldiers shuffled past on the road away from the battle.

Every one of the bandaged and bloodied soldiers held on to another; the able-legged helped others limp along, the sighted led the blind. Those who had both hands carried stretchers. It seemed the searing heat of battle had melded these men together, so they moved and bled as one giant mangled creature.

The Siberians gaped at the marching soldiers' misery. They spotted a sailor among the wounded, still in his bell-bottoms. They beckoned him to the side of the road, where he saw the navy shirts showing at their necks beneath their Red Army tunics.

"Comrade sailor! Come, sit down!" they called.

The sailor, grimacing in pain, stepped off the path and was seated on a backpack. Several hands stretched out with cigarettes and matches. The weary man accepted a smoke. He asked to have it lit and held up his right arm. It was cut short, without a hand.

A flask of vodka shot from the crowd.

The sailor dragged heavily on the cigarette. He looked up into the camouflaged faces around him.

"Na zdorovye," he said, and threw back a large gulp. Then he held up his truncated arm. "Don't worry about

this. I sold it for a very high price." He looked at the heads around him. "Where are you from?"

"We're Siberians. We've come a long way to fight."

The man blinked. "So have the Germans."

His head sank to his chest. Hands shot out to catch him as if he might collapse.

The sailor pulled himself to his feet. He turned to rejoin the shambling line of wounded. The men parted to let him through. They offered him more cigarettes.

The sailor passed Zaitsev and stopped to look into the broad Siberian face. He tapped himself on the chest with the fingers that clutched the cigarette. Glowing ashes tumbled down his torn navy shirt. He put the cigarette in the corner of his mouth and pressed his thumb against Zaitsev's chest.

"Do some killing."

THE SIBERIANS EMERGED FROM THE TREES ON the east bank of the Volga. Two kilometers away, on the far side of the river, they saw a volcanic city. Stalingrad, once home to half a million people, appeared now as if not a single person could be alive there.

The city was lit by a thousand fires. Above the limestone river cliffs, charred roofless walls stood along avenues clotted with smoking rubble. Red pillars of dust and brick erupted into the air. Buildings swayed and crumbled as if the quaking city were nothing but a jagged shell and something huge and determined below the ground was kicking its way to the surface.

Lying on the sand, staring at the firestorm across the black, oily Volga, Zaitsev thought of his *babushka* Dunia's descriptions of the underworld. A gust blew warm against his cheek. It carried the heat and carbon smell of a furnace. How can men be fighting in that perdition? he wondered.

Captain Ion Lebedev, a political commissar, settled in the sand next to him.

"Are you ready, Comrade Chief Master Sergeant?" he asked.

Zaitsev looked at the *zampolit*. The man's black eyes flickered red. His face was split by a gap-toothed smile.

Zaitsev asked, "Has anyone actually said, 'No, I am not ready,' Comrade Lebedev?"

"We have two hundred men on this shore. A few need prodding to enter that." Lebedev jutted his nose at the blazing city.

Zaitsev held no love for the commissars. He'd been subjected to their speeches, their "prodding," for weeks. He'd listened with less than rapt attention for hours without end, it seemed—on the train, on the steppe, and now, here, in the sand on the cusp of battle. He did not need simple advice on courage, did not like feeling he wasn't trusted to fight well and die for the *Rodina*. Zaitsev had been a good Komsomol member and hoped to become a member of the Communist Party. But the Germans had not invaded the Party. Their strike was at Russia. It was for the Motherland he would fight.

Many of the men feared Lebedev and the other *politrooks,* and with good reason. Stalin had given these political officers—all loyal idealists—the fiat to maintain the order of the Party throughout the army, from the highest general to the newest private. Their power came from Stalin's Order No. 227, called the "Iron Hand Rule." Not only had Stalin charged the commissars with keeping the Red soldiers politically focused during battle, even during the worst of it, they were also to judge on the field of battle each man's performance. The commissars shared responsibility with the Soviet officers for the troops' dedication to fighting until the last vessel of blood was emptied. If a man showed himself reluctant to fight, the commissar was to support, encourage, exhort, even threaten. But if a soldier displayed cowardice or retreated without orders, the *politrook* was to act with an iron hand. Zaitsev, like the rest of the men, knew that, too often, the "iron hand" meant a loaded pistol held to your head.

Lebedev handed a scrap of newspaper to Zaitsev.

"This was printed in *Pravda* last week. I show it to you, *tovarich*, because the men look up to you. They will follow you."

"We're Siberians, comrade commissar. We'll all fight without articles from *Pravda*."

Lebedev put his palm on Zaitsev's shoulder. He shook it once gently and smiled with his gap.

"Read. We have some time before we cross."

The article was entitled "They Know at Home How You Are Fighting." Zaitsev squinted to read in the shifting light:

Whether your home is near or far, it doesn't matter. At home, they will always learn how you are fighting. If you don't write yourself, your comrades will write, or your political instructor. If the letter does not reach them, they will learn about you from the newspaper. Your mother will read the communiqué, will shake her head and say: "My dear boy, you should do better than this." *You are quite wrong if you imagine that the one thing they want at home is to see you come home alive.* What they want you to do is kill the Germans. They do not want any more shame and terror. If you die while stopping the Germans from advancing any farther, they will honor your memory forever. Your heroic death will brighten and warm the lives of your children and grandchildren. If you let the Germans pass, your own mother will curse you.

Zaitsev returned the sheet to Lebedev. "Thank you, comrade commissar. It takes courage to be so direct."

Lebedev patted Zaitsev again on the shoulder. "Yes, it does. I'll see you on the other side, Comrade Chief Master Sergeant."

Well past midnight, the Siberians lay on the beach, watching and listening to Stalingrad scream to them. A flotilla of battered fishing boats, barges, steamers, and tugs appeared. A barge dropped anchor in the shallows in front of them. Zaitsev saw the holes in the ship's timbers. Two men forward and four aft bailed buckets of water over the gunwales as fast as they could. Supplies were loaded quickly into the barge's hold. Wooden crates of ammo were shouldered up the plank and lowered belowdecks. Several dozen cardboard boxes were stored; from them came the friendly sound of clanging, ringing vodka bottles. Crates of canned ham from America were carried up the gangway. The Red Army soldiers jokingly called this ham the "second front." For a year Stalin had begged England and the United States to attack the Germans in the west to ease the pressure on Russia. The Allies always responded with their many reasons for being slow and considered in their actions. For the Russian foot soldier, these tins of sweet, wet, red ham from places such as Georgia and Virginia were to be the only help they would get from the States. The ham alone would have to suffice as the second front.

The boats chugged onto the Volga. Flares split the glittering night sky. The men stared overhead, trying to pierce the coils of smoke and search for the first hint of a diving Luftwaffe warplane. The dancing light from the city scorched like a fever across their brows, making them blink and sweat.

Halfway across the river a Stuka whistled past. The men braced, but no bombs or bullets fell. The fighter banked hard and climbed to avoid flying over the flames of the city. The men waited; was there another plane behind this one? When the Stuka was not followed, they let out a sigh as if from a single giant bellows.

The leaking flotilla pushed to the central landing stage. No more aircraft shot out of the night. Zaitsev read the Luftwaffe's neglect to attack the reinforcements to be a bad sign; it showed the Germans' confidence in their taking of the city.

Ashore, the company huddled against the cool limestone cliffs. Above them, the city teetered and crackled. The river lapped at the stones under their feet, murmuring of tranquility in the darkness, telling the soldiers a thin lie of calm and peace.

With the dawn came a renewed spirit; none of the men was willing to be seen with fear staining his face. Each set his jaw and shoulders for action. The bravado in their voices climbed with the sun and the sounds of battle filtering down from the cliffs.

A sooty runner delivered orders to Lieutenant Bolshoshapov. The Siberians were to move three kilometers north along the river to reinforce another company pinned down at the Lazur chemical plant. Their landmark would be a bank of crumpled fuel tanks.

After a half hour of jogging over the sand, Bolshochapov spotted the fuel tanks overhead. The pop of gunfire, punctuated by the thump of grenades, leaped over the cliff. The Siberians clambered up the slope and took positions in the rubble. Two hundred meters away a Russian company hunkered down under fire from mortars and machine guns.

Zaitsev's unit moved up on the German right flank. The Nazis, surprised by the reinforcements, deployed their machine guns to cover the new threat.

The Siberians drew fire, and for the first time Zaitsev heard the ripping hiss of bullets fired at him. This was the moment he'd waited for in a confusion of fear and eagerness. Here at last was the ultimate hunt. The rounds whizzing past whispered to him in the hushed voice of his grandfather kneeling beside him in the forest: Get moving, Vasha. Quick. Careful. Silent. Go.

Without waiting for orders, he slid through the rubble of the first fuel tank. He wanted to get an open shot before the enemy could scramble for cover from his angle.

At 150 meters Zaitsev opened up. He knocked down three machine gunners with his first three rounds. Once these guns were silenced, his company leaped from cover and charged the Germans, firing and shouting.

A whistling yowl dropped through the smoke. Before Zaitsev could move, an artillery shell exploded behind him in the middle of his mates, knocking men off their feet and dropping others onto their faces to burrow for cover. Zaitsev looked back and realized with alarm that one of the three fuel tanks, though badly dented, had somehow not been punctured during the previous bombings. His question whether it still contained fuel was answered by the next salvo.

The tank blew apart in a thunderous explosion, sending a fireball up and over the Siberians. Flaring fuel rained out of the mushroom cloud. Zaitsev's clothes dripped with small, hungry flames.

He tore off his tunic, navy undershirt, pants, and ammo belt. His skin was singed, but his head was clear. He pounded on his crown to make sure his hair had not caught fire.

Around him, his friends lay dead. Their corpses were wrapped in sheets of smoke; yellow hornets of fire swarmed about their death poses. Through it all the Germans continued shooting.

Zaitsev fought down his horror. He stared across the smoldering battleground. The Germans had moved and were rearming their machine guns, swiveling their lines of fire. With his eyes moist from the smoke, he dropped and raised his rifle, drawing aim on a Nazi holding binoculars, perhaps an officer directing the attack. Zaitsev's blackened hands shook; he could not wait for his pounding heart to let the gun sight settle in his hands. This might be his last clear shot before the Germans opened fire or called in more artillery.

He followed the swaying sight, squeezing for the shot he knew would serve only to give his position away. Suddenly he heard a cry of "Urrah! Urrah! *Rodina!*" Lieutenant Bolshoshapov leaped from behind a charred brick wall dressed only in his white underwear, ammo belt, and boots. He held his rifle over his head and charged, followed by waves of seminaked, smoking Siberians. Zaitsev stiffened, not believing his eyes. Without thinking, his legs lifted him from behind cover. He took a deep breath and screamed, "Urrah!" He pumped his rifle in the air and joined the charge.

He felt like a demon, running and firing into the maw of the Germans. The sight of themselves, fearless in their underwear and boots, guns blazing, drove him and his company into the Nazi line with a fierceness Zaitsev had never known. He felt exhilarated, bounding over debris, running and shooting. Closing in on the Nazi positions, his wrath grew so intense that, screaming, he crossed his eyes. He lost his balance and tripped over his running feet. Just as he hit the ground, the sailor before him was struck in the chest. The man's arms flew open, his legs buckled in front of Zaitsev, and he skidded to his knees like a duck landing on water.

Looking over the body, Zaitsev saw the lieutenant and the men chase the Germans. The Nazis fled down an alley, firing over their shoulders.

One of the Red soldiers who'd been pinned down helped Zaitsev to his feet.

"You guys are crazy!" he laughed. "I've never seen anything like that in my life. In your underwear."

Zaitsev touched his bloodied knee. "I tripped," he murmured.

The soldier looked about at the many bodies on the ground. He patted Zaitsev on the back. "Go join your unit."

The men walked to the spots where they had stripped off their burning uniforms. Each put back on whatever tatters he could retrieve of his scorched navy shirt.

The company settled in for the night. Fresh uniforms and food were delivered. Couriers brought with them the report of a comment made by Zhukov to Batyuk. The general had been amazed at how much the Siberian sailors seemed to dislike their new army uniforms. Apparently the commander had credited the company with burning the outfits off while still wearing them.

THE VIOLENCE OF THE LAST WEEK OF SEPTEMBER branded the lessons of house-to-house fighting into Zaitsev's eyes. Before each attack, he crouched in a trench or a bunker, listening to the advice of veterans who'd survived in the city for a fierce month.

Often the battles for the buildings became hand-to-hand, the bludgeon as deadly as the bullet, the enemy's breath and blood as close to Zaitsev as his own. For a large number of the Siberians, the three days' training on the steppe had been worthless. During their first few days in battle, many of his friends had been killed taking unnecessary risks. But none had run away, and none had died without his weapon in his hands. The days lurched past. The bodies grew in grisly heaps under the smoking skies.

Zaitsev moved in the rubble with the grace and confidence of an animal. His taut frame and lean, muscled arms pulled him through the debris without rest, keeping enough in reserve to hold his rifle deadly still or whip a grenade almost as far as his big friend Viktor Medvedev.

In hand-to-hand fighting, Zaitsev could be savage. His army knife, though bulkier than the skinning blades of his youth, slashed like a talon in his hand.

The Germans did not adjust well to the special tactics of street fighting. While the Reds captured strategic buildings with small platoons called "storm groups," the Nazis simply threw more men into battle as if by pouring enough blood on a street they could win it. Sometimes during an attack, bodies piled so high in an alley that the corpses alone blocked the Nazis' advance.

At the end of Zaitsev's first two weeks in Stalingrad, the Germans had fought their way to the Volga in the city center to control the downtown area and the main landing stage of the Russians, Krasnaya Sloboda. By mid-October the Sixty-second Army had been cut in half, north and south.

The strongest Russian bridgehead was in the rubble of the factory district, five kilometers north of downtown. The Siberians were assigned to reinforce the Thirty-seventh Guards in defending the Tractor Factory, the northernmost of the three huge plants.

After a thirty-six-hour artillery barrage, the Germans attacked the Tractor Factory in the early hours of October fifth. Zaitsev, tunneling into the debris under a swarm of bullets, saw his first sniper team. The soldiers were small and thin, not powerful warriors at first glance. One man's helmet was too big for him, covering his ears. He tipped it above his eyes to see where he was crawling. Both snipers carried rifles with scopes attached.

Even while Zaitsev's unit dug deeper into the wreckage for cover, the snipers crept into the debris, like hunters, toward their prey.

FIVE

TANIA CHERNOVA STOOD ON THE SHORE WITH her company, 150 soldiers from the 284th Division. In front of her a barge rolled gently at the dock in the black shallows.

Across the Volga, flames loomed and snapped. German fighter-bombers sprang from nighttime clouds, glowing red on their undersides from the fires raging below them. The planes dove to unleash their bombs at low altitudes. Their engines screamed, wings whistling to bank up and out, speeding the pilots away from the blasts and smoke.

Tania stared at the misery of the city. This was the heroic battleground of Stalingrad; its name was on the lips of every Russian. Stalin, the *vozhd*, the Supreme Leader, had made it clear: Stand and fight here at all costs in that apocalypse across the Volga.

Eleven women were in Tania's company, each dressed in jackboots and uniforms without insignia. They did not have rifles; as radio operators or field nurses, they would not need weapons.

On the road to the river, Tania had marched past a hundred artillery pieces operated by women. She could have requested to join them, working the big guns and Katyushas, the fiery racks of missiles suspended on the beds of American Ford trucks. But Tania had spent the last year fighting with the Russian resistance in the forests of Byelorussia and outside Moscow. She'd left the partisans one month ago to come to Stalingrad and continue her vendetta against the Nazi "sticks." She could not think of the Germans as human. They were pieces of wood, sticks. Men could not do what she had seen the Nazis do.

In the center of her group, a general with a shaved head was ending his speech. "The defenders of Stalingrad need help," he cried, "to stave off the charging enemy. The Tractor Factory in the northern quarter of the city has come under heavy assault. Soldiers fighting in the factory and throughout Stalingrad are not taking a single step back. But their lives, and the life of Mother Russia, depend on fresh troops entering the battle."

The general thrust his fist over his head. He shouted, "Urrah!" Tania and her group raised their fists and bellowed, "Urrah! Urrah!" The eyes around her darted from the cheering general to the blazing city. Fear, she thought; it shows first in the eyes.

The rickety barge at the dock had been loaded with supplies and awaited its human cargo. The general finished his speech. Guards herded the soldiers into line to board the boat.

Tania shouldered her backpack filled with cheeses, bread, and a bottle of vodka, all given to her by townspeople along the road. A short man with a thick, hard belly strode to the head of the line. He ran up the gangplank with surprising nimbleness, jumping over the gunwales onto the deck. Tania recognized him as a commissar, a Captain Danilov, who'd addressed the soldiers on the beach before the bald general's lecture. He called the soldiers to join him, to "step into history."

The first men boarded and sat on the deck. Two soldiers in the line in front of Tania, boys no more than

eighteen, took a few steps, then froze in place. The other
men ignored them, sliding past them in the line as if the
two did not exist.

Tania came up behind them quickly. "Keep moving,"
she said. "Don't do this. They're watching."

Tania walked in front of the boys to face them. She saw
their eyes fixed across the river at the inferno.

She shook one of them. "Move to the boat. Move!"

The young soldiers turned to Tania, then looked to
each other. One licked his lips. An older soldier grabbed
Tania's arm to pull her away.

"They have their fates, comrade. We have ours. Come."

Tania let herself be tugged several steps, still looking
back at the youths. She turned her head and marched in
line.

After a few steps she heard Danilov scream from the
deck of the barge.

"Stop! Stop immediately!"

All the soldiers halted and turned back toward the
crowded landing. The boys had bolted out of line to run
for the trees beyond the beach, dropping their rifles and
ammo belts and shedding their packs to leap over barrels
and cartons. Their quick footfalls, hard and hollow on the
planks of the landing, mingled with the muffled roar from
across the Volga. The dock grew silent while the two
young cowards ran out their lives.

Tania heard their cries to each other, frantic and
afraid. "Run! Oh, God! Keep running!"

Guards fired over the boys' heads and yelled for them
to halt and come back. The two ran.

Three more guards in greatcoats appeared from the
trees at the edge of the sand. They hustled toward the
boys, shooting.

One boy went down, wounded. The other stopped running. He turned, looked, and died where he stood. A

guard walked to the wounded one, put his pistol to the boy's forehead, and fired.

Tania and the soldiers resumed their march to the barge. The older soldier walked beside her.

"A waste," she said to him.

He looked down at her. "Boys," he said. "Boys the age of my children."

Tania heaved her pack higher onto her shoulders. She moved away from him.

"Forget your children," she said.

TANIA CHOSE A SPACE NEAR THE PORT RAIL. She sat with her knees pulled up to her chest. Several men asked her to move to the safety of the middle of the deck. Tania tossed her shoulder-length hair and held her place.

The barge moved onto the river.

Three Stukas found the boat quickly. The crooked-wing fighters banked, buzzed high in triangle formation, and screamed down. Plumes of water erupted in the white light of phosphorus flares. Tania blinked at the geysers licking at the barge.

Along the rails, NKVD guards, known as "Green Hats," stood with arms folded. A few had their hands inside their coats. Fingers on triggers, Tania thought, in case anyone gets a notion to jump overboard. Tania knew the Green Hats well, knew them to be the grimmest and most ruthless organ of the commissariat. She'd seen plenty of their work: they examined credentials and asked curt questions. Any soldier caught leaving the front without orders was dealt with swiftly. Hundreds of bodies had littered the road to Stalingrad, dreadful reminders to Red Army deserters to rethink their fears.

Another detonation sounded deep off the starboard rail. Shrapnel bit into the hull. Cold water soaked the soldiers on deck. No diving Stuka had shrieked before the explosion. That was a mortar shell, Tania thought. The big cannons are throwing in alongside the Luftwaffe. We've been spotted by the whole German army.

Water ran off the sides of the tilting decks. Commissar Danilov made a show of marching to the bow, swinging his boxlike torso and arms. He climbed onto the large stack of ammunition cartons where everyone could see him. He raised his arms over his head and pointed his hands straight up like antiaircraft guns into the noisy, deadly night.

"Fuck you!" he cried at the sky. "You fuckers of mothers. You whores!" Danilov scowled down at the soldiers. They were bunched together, wet on the trembling deck.

"Come on, you Russian heroes! Fuck those Germans up the ass! Come on! Let them hear you!"

A few voices rose. Then, like an engine catching and throttling to a roar, every one of the soldiers screamed out curses, exiling their fears into the night at the planes and flames and explosions of water and earth.

Tania thrust her fist in the air. "Bastards!" she screeched. "Murderers!"

While the troops spent their rage, Danilov called for the postman to come forward. "Mail call!" he shouted.

The postman handed up his canvas sack of letters. The commissar dug into the bag. Above the bedlam, he called out the names on the envelopes.

"Tagarin!"

"Here!"

"Antsiferov!"

"Over here!"

The postman took the letters from Danilov and scurried among the men. Twice he fell into their laps when the boat shifted on the roiling river.

Another tower of water reared off the port stern. A hand tapped Tania on the shoulder. Behind her sat the

older soldier who'd pulled her away from the two deserters on the landing.

"Would you like some bread?" he asked.

"No, thank you. I have my own."

"Please," he insisted, "have some of mine."

Tania looked at the cropped white beard and tanned
face. The man's blue eyes were set in the middle of deep,
strong wrinkles like indigo marbles laid on straw.

"Of course," she said, "but only if we share my cheese."

They dug into their packs. A third, younger soldier
reached out a half-full liter of vodka.

"Please," he said, "may we have a picnic?"

The three began to exchange their food and drink. A
shell exploded on the port side, closer than the last. Tania
sheltered the bread from the spray.

The young one extended his hand. "My name is Fyodor
Ivanovich Michailov. From Moscow." He appeared to be
eighteen or nineteen, a freshman. His face had a peculiar
quality even in the flashing night—Tania couldn't recall
ever before seeing an entire face take part in a smile the
way his did. His forehead, nose, chin, and eyes all crinkled at once. He shines, Tania thought quickly.

"I'm a writer," he said, taking the cheese.

"What do you write about, Fedya?" the older soldier
asked.

"Love stories. Poems." He shrugged. "What can I write
about? I'm Russian. My choices are love, government, or
murder."

"Write about Stalin and you'll have all three." The
older man laughed alone. "Yuri Georgiovich Pankov." He
took Fyodor's hand. "From Frunze in Kirghizia. I'm origi-
nally from Tashkent."

"An Uzbek," Fyodor recognized.

"A simple man." Yuri tapped his chest. "No dreamer
like you. I've spent my whole life wide awake."

Tania looked at Yuri's hand shake Fedya's. His fingers

were thick and powerful, with blunt nails. The knuckles were gnarled from labor. She guessed he had worked on one of the millions of Soviet collective farms. In Fedya's smooth white grasp, Yuri's calloused hand looked more like a tan bag of chestnuts than flesh.

"Well," said Fedya, looking across the river at Stalingrad, "I'm awake now, I can tell you that."

Yuri smiled at Tania. "And you, little tough one? Miss Sit-by-the-rail? You have a name?"

"Yes." She wiped her hands on her trousers to clean off the bits of cheese. "Tania Alexeyevna Chernova."

"And where are you from?"

Tania pursed her lips and hesitated. "New York."

Yuri's blue eyes popped wide. "New York, America?"

Fedya leaned over the cheese and bread. "New York City?"

"Yes," she said in English.

Another bomb blasted ten meters from the port rail. Cold water cascaded. The bread and cheese in front of Tania were washed overboard. Near the bow, a soldier slumped and moaned.

Yuri and Fedya were distracted from their amazement at Tania. All the men on the deck fell silent save for the groaning soldier. His comrades slid aside to lay him down and cover him.

Fedya clutched the vodka bottle. He stood. Tania saw how large he was, with great shoulders and a midriff to match.

A kneeling Green Hat shouted, "Sit down, you!"

Fedya handed the guard the bottle.

"Here, give him this. Come on, man! Take it!"

The guard grabbed the bottle and threaded his way to the wounded soldier. Then Tania's heart sank: she caught the whistle of an incoming artillery shell, the first one she'd heard in flight. She knew why.

"Down!" she screamed at Yuri and Fedya.

The three huddled together on the deck. The mortar shell struck directly amidships. The deck cracked open into great splinters and blew apart in a ball of flame and debris. The explosion deafened Tania. She flew backward, up and out into the flashing waters of the Volga.

SIX

NIKKI TRAINED HIS HEAVY MACHINE GUN ON the doorway. He made sure the gun's ammo belt was taut. He slid his hand along the broad, round barrel. It was colder than the Russian autumn.

He stared down the machine gun sight. It's stupid to wait for the Russians to retreat, he thought. They won't retreat. The Reds die in their holes. They're not leaving this building. Neither are we.

He imagined himself pulling the trigger—saw Russians burst through the doorway, then twist and fall in front of his machine gun. They came, they leaped at him, he caught them with bullets, and they came, the bodies jamming the hall. The machine gun spit and spit, firing and roaring, mowing them down. And they kept pushing the bodies of their comrades out of the way to get to him. He let the trigger go and the gun kept firing on and on. He ran across the room, ran through the ruins. His unit ran after him, streaming out the windows, while here in this empty room the Reds kept running at the machine gun, falling in front of it, building the mound of dead, falling in front of it, falling . . .

"Mond. Corporal Mond."

The voice pulled Nikki abruptly from his vision. Captain Mercker knelt beside him. He put his hand on Nikki's right fist, clenching the grip. Nikki's knuckles showed the white of bone.

"Easy, Corporal," the captain said. "We're all a little tense. Back it off a little."

Nikki relaxed his hold and wiggled his fingers. The captain offered him a cigarette and a light.

"Mond, you were in the first group. Did you check that room on the other side of the hall?"

"Yes, sir. There was nobody in there."

"How big is the room?"

"A little smaller than this one. Three windows like these."

Mercker dragged on his cigarette. His cheeks hollowed. "They must've had the same plan we did to grab this building. We rushed in the front door while they were climbing in the windows."

Nikki looked in the young officer's eyes. He saw calm there.

"You're new, sir?"

Mercker smiled. "Depends on what you call new. I was at Leningrad last year. Moscow this spring."

Nikki ground out his cigarette to keep his hands on the machine gun grips.

"Stalingrad is new, sir. Never been anything like this. The front line can be a thousand meters or it can be a ceiling." He looked at the door in front of his barrel. "Or a hall."

Mercker said nothing. Nikki felt the invitation to go on.

"Russians are good at house-to-house fighting, better than we are. If they'd been here first, we'd never have gotten in. We'd have to blow the building up with them in it." Nikki shook his head. "They're not leaving, Captain."

Mercker lit another cigarette. "What did you say about blowing them up in it?"

Three weeks ago, Nikki's unit had occupied a house in

the workers' settlement west of the Tractor Factory.
They'd found five Reds holed up in the basement. The
men would not surrender. They did not retreat. After
three days of stalemate, with the Russians fighting like
crazy Ivans, they'd had to rip up floorboards and drop
satchel charges into the basement. For five Reds, his unit
had blown up an entire house.

Nikki told his captain this story. The moment he was
done, muffled voices issued from across the hall. A song.
The Russians were singing! Within seconds, a strong
chorus formed. The song was loud and lusty. A dirty bal-
lad, Nikki thought, from the laughter accompanying it.
The Reds are sending a message to the German company
across the hall. There are plenty of Ivans in here, they're
singing to us, and they're not going anywhere.

An idea gleamed in Mercker's eyes. "You blew up a
house for five Russians," he said over the racket from
across the hall. "We'll blow one up for fifty."

Mercker called for a messenger.

AFTER TWO HOURS OF NONSTOP SINGING, THE
Reds quieted.

Twenty minutes later, Mercker's courier returned
through the window. He brought with him three sappers
and their equipment: twenty kilos of dynamite, six shovels
and pickaxes.

In the center of the room, one of the sappers raised a
pickax. He struck a ringing blow on the concrete. Debris
scurried from the strike like mice across the floor.

Mercker raised his hand. "Just a second." He turned to
the men. "Those Reds have shitty voices, don't you think,
boys? We should show them how a German sings a song.
Loud. In fact, so loud that it's all they can hear."

The captain began the Nazi party song, *"Horst Wessel."*
The men joined in, even those with guns trained on the

door and out the windows. Mercker stood in the center, swinging his arms like a conductor, whipping up the spirit and volume. The soldiers' voices climbed to a roar. Mercker pointed with a flourish to the sapper to smack the concrete. The engineer swung down hard and the floor gave way in a jagged dent. The men smiled and applauded, and all they heard was their voices.

For three hours the soldiers sang. Folk songs, *Bräuhaus* ballads, popular tunes, even pieces of opera ricocheted off the walls to mask the digging. When the captain signaled the men to stop—again, like a conductor, with a wave of his hands—the tunnel had long since disappeared beneath the floor.

Nikki took his turn with a shovel for a thirty-minute shift, tossing broken earth out of the hole. The tunnel grew to five meters long, two meters wide at a depth of one and a half meters below the floor. Inside there was just enough room for two men to kneel side by side and swing pickaxes. The plan was to burrow to the opposite side of the hall. Once beneath the Russians' stronghold, two and a half meters below them, the fuse would be lit. "Twenty kilos of dynamite." One of the sappers grinned and spit on the tunnel floor. "That ought to lift those Bolshi bastards halfway to heaven . . . or wherever."

Weary and dirty, Nikki slumped against a wall. Three more men were in the hole now, shoveling out dirt. This made very little noise, so no singing was required to mask it. Mercker told the men to rest for a few hours, then another strong medley would be needed before dawn. "Think up some new songs," he said. "And no opera. I hate that shit. I want songs about women."

Mercker sat beside Nikki, drained and grimy. He offered a cigarette and closed his eyes. Nikki thought the young captain was funny, good for morale. He seemed a good leader with a ready ear and plenty of cigarettes. Nikki hoped the best for him, that he would not die here in Stalingrad and that he would live to hate opera as an old man.

On the other side of the hall the Russian voices struck up another song. "Goddammit." Mercker's eyes were still shut. "Can't there be five minutes without a blasted song?"

The captain's eyes sprang open. He sat off the wall, his face close to Nikki. "No," he hissed, "there can't."

Mercker jumped to his feet. He grabbed a pickax and handed it to a soldier who was not yet dirty. "Get in there! Dig!" He motioned one of the sappers into the hole. He pointed at another soldier and handed him a pick.

"Let's go. There's no resting now," he said urgently. "We can't wait."

Mercker carried the last shovel to the middle of the room. He pointed the tool across the hall at the singing Russians. "Those bastards are trying to blow us up, too!"

Nikki thumped his head against the wall. Of course. Damn. The Reds have a head start on us, maybe two hours.

All the men were awake now, all staring at the floor. Nikki pictured the race beneath the surface, wondering who was in the lead and by what distance, afraid that two meters below him a cask of dynamite sat sizzling.

"If the Reds stop singing," Mercker called, "have a tune ready. And loud. Understand?" Everyone nodded. Mercker disappeared into the hole.

The race was on. The men dug with a desperate strength. They worked under cover of the Russians' singing as long as it lasted, an hour or so at a time, then picked up their own chorus whenever the Reds stopped. When their voices flagged, the enemy burst into song.

Through the night, Nikki's company did most of the singing. They gauged the race in the tunnels by who flung the most verses across the corridor. We must be catching up, Nikki thought. We've even added a harmonica. The Reds don't have a harmonica.

Flickering lamplight glimmered from the tunnel. Silhouettes descended and the bent, blackened shapes of others staggered out. The round, glowing hole in the middle of the floor looked to Nikki like a threshold to the netherworld with its shadowy demons coming and going.

At dawn, Mercker emerged, his face streaked with muddy sweat. He sat and motioned for Nikki.

The man looked exhausted. He spoke in a rasping voice, his head hung.

"The sappers say we've got one more hour of digging. Tell the men to get into their groups of ten."

Nikki nodded. The captain tugged Nikki's tunic with a blackened hand. "You're in the first group. Secure that trench. Hold there until I get the rest of us out."

Gathering their rifles, Nikki's patrol moved to the windows. The guard nodded, and Nikki leaned out to search the debris-riddled street. He jumped down and waved for his men to follow. One by one they landed, and he pushed them toward the trench.

The Russians stopped singing. Nikki smiled at the guard in the window. "Give them some opera," he said. He turned and ran.

Ten meters from the trench, a roaring wave swept over him. The ground rose, then jerked down to trip him. The air reached for him. He was caught in the grip of a powerful, careless force that knocked him down, lifted him, and flung him in a somersault away from the exploding building.

He landed on his back and skidded on his shoulders. The part of the building held by his company leaped out from its foundation, walls bulging hideously. Deafened, his skin reddened by the blast, Nikki scrambled for the trench to tumble into the arms of his men while a massive fireball gathered behind him, orange and blue, and erupted. The side of the building burst with a shattering boom, then fell straight down as if a trap door had opened. It dissolved until the last grinding bits came to rest. Above the devastation, a mushroom of smoke and dust curled and shifted, forming a gray and ghostly marker where the walls had stood seconds before.

My company is dead, Nikki thought. Mercker, all of them. No chance.

On the morning breeze, a song seemed to come from everywhere at once. It merged with the sounds of the embattled city, bouncing off the empty, broken walls on all sides, ringing from the dead ruins.

The song was in Russian.

SEVEN

TANIA FLAILED TO THE SURFACE OF THE ICY
river.

She looked back at the burning wreckage of the barge.
The stern and bow had been cleaved into separate pieces.
They pointed up into the night to pirouette in slow, smoky
circles.

A touch at the back of her neck made her spin around.
The outstretched hand of a dead soldier bobbed into her
face. She swung wildly at the corpse and backpedaled.
Another hand fell on her shoulder. This grasp was firm
and alive—Fedya, the writer. Treading water beside him
was Yuri.

She could not make out what Fedya was saying. Her
ears felt stuffed by the explosion. She knew she was surrounded by sound—the cries of the wounded thrashing in
the water, the bombs seeking the rest of the fleet upriver,
even the shouts of Fedya and Yuri—but all were like
mumblings trapped in a bottle.

A timber floated past. Yuri grabbed it. Already they'd
drifted far south of the Tractor Factory landing stage. The
shore was four hundred meters off. Tania estimated the
current would beach them near the city center if they

kicked hard. She wondered who would control the land they stepped onto.

Gripping the beam, Tania stared at Stalingrad. She ignored the nervous, quiet chattering of the two men clinging to the timber with her; she could not hear them clearly, and soon they stopped talking. Inside this isolation she balled her fists and cast a vow into the ruins, driving it like a spike into the heart of every Nazi hiding in the rubble. She swore to renew her war against the Germans, a vendetta begun over a year earlier when the occupation army in Minsk had murdered her grandparents, a doctor and his ballet-teacher wife.

Tania had come to visit her grandparents only two months before their deaths, from the Manhattan apartment of her parents. She'd arrived to convince the two beloved elder folks with whom she'd spent several summers to come live in America and escape the gathering storm in Europe. There was not much time, she warned; Hitler's nonaggression pact with Stalin was a farce, and they shouldn't believe it. She brought money from her father, Alexander, the son of the Chernovs. She could take them away. But the doctor and his beautiful dancing wife, both of them gray—though not in the manner of ashes, not cold and old but shining—would not leave Minsk. There was work to be done there, they told her, bodies for them to heal and children to teach. There was family for them to protect, two daughters and grandchildren, and there was family history in Minsk, graves and relics and memories. Stalin was too strong for Hitler, they answered, Russia too strong; Hitler knew this.

Tania urgently wrote her parents in New York, begging them to come and beg themselves. But there was only one response, a telegram instructing Tania to return immediately to New York, and wishing the grandparents luck in the coming hard days. Tania's father had been upset when she left; it was dangerous, he'd said. She was only nine-

teen years old. Tania told him to give her money, enough
to rescue the old ones, or she would go without his money
and earn it there to bring them back. Alexander, a young
scientist who had brought his new bride to America in
1912 in the waning days of the czar, drawn by the promise
shouting out of America as if from a carnival hawker of a
new and comfortable life for the couple and for the child
they hoped to bear one day, cried when that child hefted
her baggage down the stairs to a waiting taxi. Tania cried,
too, tears of anger at her parents who had raised her to
speak and love everything Russian, to jeer at the memory
of the toppled Russian royals, to rejoice at the surging
Soviet Communist power as the salvation of the Russian
peoples, to be proud of her heritage. She took her parents'
rhetoric seriously. She joined the American Communist
Party as a teenager and visited their native land as often as
she could. She grew to love the faraway places and the
people and the myths that milled in her own blood. Minsk
and Soviet Russia became her spiritual sanctuaries, and
her grandparents there became avatars of Russian sim-
plicity and courage. Now her own mother and father were
revealed as two-faced, big thinkers and storytellers who
were Russian by birth only, not spirit. They hunkered in
their wealth and hearth, secure in New York, smug in
their mail-order intellectual loyalty to Russia. But when it
came time for them to stand up, to rise for the sake of
their *papushka* and *mamushka*, they would not. They cow-
ered in their brownstone, their Americanness, their freedom. Slamming the taxi door, Tania swore that her tears
would be the last she would shed until she returned with
her grandparents or saw them safe somehow. She did not
understand then how she would soon weep at their
deaths. On June 22, 1941, six weeks after her arrival in
Minsk, three million German troops swarmed across the
Russian border. Two weeks later, Minsk was encircled
and captured, with over 150,000 Soviet soldiers taken

prisoner. German tanks took up sentry positions on every street. Electricity and water ran uninterrupted in the city, market stalls remained open, but wings had folded over Minsk. Heads everywhere in the city were heavy; feet dragged, eyes darted. Where was the Red Army, where was deliverance?

Dark squads known as the Black Crows began to kick on doors in the city. Soon they came into the Chernovs' neighborhood, at first to the homes of the Jewish families, then to others, even the respected ones. Three weeks after the city's occupation, Dr. and Mrs. Chernov were taken from their small apartment as they sat at dinner with Tania. Tania herself was clubbed with the butt of a Nazi rifle when she resisted the kidnapping. Before she could rouse herself from the bludgeoning, her grandparents were marched to the city square only three blocks away and executed. The two stood accused of collaborating with the underground, a claim supported only by the fact that Dr. Chernov had treated many patients who bore the marks of the Nazis' brutal inquisitions. At the rifles' reports, Tania jerked off the floor. Bloodied and wobbling, she ran outside to the sound and arrived in the square, smelling the cordite smoke of the bullets. Neighbors she did not recognize held her back, screaming. That night, Tania went to the home of her aunt Vera and told her what had happened. Tania's tears flowed, squeezed from her in a spasm. When she was done, she was finally dry, without tears. Vera must have seen this in her young niece's swollen eyes, for she said, "Stay here with me. Don't go." Tania said only, "I'm leaving the city to find the resistance."

The older woman put her arms around the girl. Before closing the door, Vera whispered, "Then fight hard, my Russian niece."

She left the city and for a week followed the sounds of fighting in the forests and villages. In the hamlet of Vianka, sleeping in a barn, she was approached by a dark cast of men, hunting rifles crooked over their arms. She was interrogated and allowed to join them.

Among the resistance fighters, Tania soon lost the tastes of her former privileged life in Manhattan and Minsk. She came to know the skills of the partisan for the taking of lives. She laid mines and rigged dynamite along tracks and under transports; she learned to fire a rifle and pistol and the ways to use a stiletto or bare hands for close-in killing. She shared a kinship with the guerrillas: they were linked by pain. Each man and woman in the cadre had suffered some blow of Nazi cruelty. Tania put her loathing of the Nazis in place of her grief for her grandparents and her anger at her own mother and father; fighting the Germans became her mourning and her apology for what she felt was a stain of cowardice on her American clan. After a year of freezing and killing and running in the forests, of exulting over the smallest victories, Tania walked out of the woods to join a passing column of army regulars. She had long before thrown away her American papers. She claimed residency in Minsk, at her grandparents' address. She was given papers for the 284th Division, climbed on a truck, and rode five hundred kilometers south to Stalingrad.

Now, in the freezing waters of the Volga, Tania's feet finally dragged onto a sandbar. She let go of the timber and splashed toward the shore, followed by Fedya and Yuri. Her ears had cleared, and the noises of battle reached her from far upstream. Nothing else broke the dark quiet.

The three crouched, dripping and cold, on the cool shore. The beach was littered with abandoned machinery and crates. Tania decided the safest direction to travel would be not into silence but north, toward the fighting in the factory district. There they would find Russians.

They'd floated downstream several kilometers. We

could walk to the factories before dawn, she thought, if we're not caught. But if the Germans have taken the city center, there'll be patrols operating on the riverbank to stop infiltrators.

Tania whispered, "Follow me. We'll go north."

Fedya moved behind her. Yuri hesitated. "Tell me your name again," Yuri asked.

"Private Tania Chernova."

"Tania, then. Tania, I cannot follow a girl. Not even an American girl. I will lead the way."

She showed the old man an empty face. She had nothing to prove to Yuri. He'd seen her thrash away from the corpse in the water, but he knew nothing of the partisan who'd sliced a dozen throats or laid mines under a supply train, then walked among the wounded completing the job with her pistol. He'd not seen the doctor's granddaughter garrote a prisoner after he spilled his secrets to her guerrilla cadre, or hide all day until she could fire a rifle to kill at three hundred meters.

But the old farmer was with her now and he was here to kill Germans. For that alone she would try to keep him alive. Let him die being useful, not stupid, she thought.

"Yuri, I've spent the last year in the resistance. I've been fighting in the forests of Byeloruss, not pushing a plow in the fields. I know the Nazis and I know how to keep us alive. I'll lead or I'll go alone."

She turned to Fedya. "You, too."

Tania walked up the beach. From behind came quiet but firm words, then the crunching footsteps of the two men.

After an hour of starting and stopping at every noise, it was clear they would not reach the factories before dawn. Tania looked for a place where they could wait out the coming daylight, to continue their trek later under darkness.

They walked for another hour, searching the cliffs for

an abandoned cave or bunker. With first light playing at the fringe of the horizon, a foul odor wafted out of the night. Tania wrinkled her nose and stepped faster. A tall pipe emerged in the darkness; it ran the short distance from the base of the cliff to the river. The pipe was two meters high. Fetid air tumbled from its mouth, a stench Tania felt through her skin.

Fedya gasped, "It's a sewer drain."

Yuri and Tania locked eyes. Both nodded.

Fedya stepped back, repulsed by the idea. "Oh, my God, you're kidding. We can't go in there. That's shit! There's shit all over the place in there. We can't . . . there's no way!"

Tania moved closer to Fedya. She put her fingers to her lips. "We don't have any choice. It'll be light soon."

Yuri stepped forward. "It's just shit, Fedya. We throw it on the fields every day. It'll make you grow."

"It'll make me puke!"

Tania moved to the lip of the pipe. She turned to Fedya. "In here, no one will notice. Come on."

She took her first steps through the sewer pipe as if leaning into a gale. She brought the inside of her elbow up to her nose to filter the filth through her tunic. Even so, the smell crept in through her eyes and ears.

She looked back at Yuri and Fedya. Yuri laid his arms across his chest to walk with his head held high, as though he might lift his nose above the odor. Fedya took large, slow steps, flapping his arms and shaking his hands like a tightrope walker.

"Walk, Fedya," Tania whispered, "we've only just started."

"Oh, God," he mumbled.

Twenty meters from the mouth of the sewer, the dim light from the opening receded to leave them wrapped in total blackness. Tania ran her hand along the slimy wall to guide her steps. She felt a brush of cool air against her cheek. "There's an opening ahead," she said.

Her hand slid off the wall into open space. Another pipe had linked with the main line. "This seems to head north. We'll walk until it's past dawn. Then we'll look for a manhole and climb out. With luck we'll be behind our own lines."

Tania shook her boots. Excrement clung to them and her pants legs. She felt the muddy damp where it had splashed onto her thighs. Behind her, Fedya made very few splashes. He was probably on tiptoes, she thought, as if there were a way to avoid stepping on shit in a sewer.

"Tania," Yuri called, "tell us about America."

Tania licked her lips, sweat salting her tongue. She did not want to talk, but she recognized that Yuri was only trying to quell their fear.

"Do you read, old farmer?"

"Yes, of course."

"What do you read about America?"

"That it is a country of decadence. Bright lights, whores, businessmen squeezing money from the poor. Gangsters. Riches."

"Do you believe it?"

"Only the parts about the riches and the whores. The good stuff."

This made Tania laugh, and she closed her mouth to stop from telling Yuri he was wrong, that he had left out so much more, good and bad stuff. America was a giant land of peace and opportunity and, yes, decadence. That it was America the beautiful, especially for those who were white and male with English surnames. That America was a bully. That America was afraid of this war with the Germans, just like her parents. And that she was Russian; she would fight for Russia and she would hate the Nazis if America would not.

Tania wanted to divert the attention from herself.

"Fedya," she said, echoing over their sloshing footsteps, "tell us one of your poems."

"Yes, good." Yuri picked this up. "Tell us a favorite."

"Here? Now?" Fedya sounded shocked. "I mean . . . you want me to tell you a poem? I can barely breathe in here."

"Oh, come on. When will you have better acoustics?"

Good, Tania thought, Yuri is distracting the frightened boy from Moscow.

"My God," Fedya answered. "All right, but I never said I was good."

He stopped walking. Tania and Yuri halted also. The rippling echoes died.

"It's called 'The Washing River.' It's one I seem to recall quite clearly at the moment. I don't know why. I'm in a goddammed sewer and I'm scared out of my wits. But here it is."

He began in a whisper, in a voice oddly reverent for the surroundings.

"Her hands open rich and furrowed,
    hard as the rocks she crouches near.
    I have walked with her, smelled her
    breathing on our way to the river.
Mist clings to our faces.
    We unload thick, soiled clothes.
    The slap of soap and river runs through my
        bones.
    Dirt wrings through her red fingers,
    back to the quiet water.
Light flashes through her flushed tenderness.
I watch the trail of clustered suds melt
    downstream.
We pile up the heavy rags into our baskets and
    stare
    back at the blueness.

> *Her clean cool hand rests on my neck, and for a*
> *   moment*
> *   there is no work.*
> *Where are you, Mother, as I lift my palms to my*
> *   face?*
> *   As I read their lines and ache?*
> *   I hold my crouched body.*
> *   I hear the dark slapping.*
> *   You run through my bones in this place."*

Fedya cleared his throat. "Well, there you are."

Tania was stricken by the poem; she felt his voice woven directly into her. The poem, singular in the sewer's darkness, had become for its few moments the lone reality of her senses. She'd been isolated with the words. Now, with the poem finished, it echoed inside her, slapping against her memories, the rocks in her heart.

Yuri sloshed to Fedya and clapped him on the back. "Why do you poets always hate your own work? That was beautiful. It made me miss my own mother."

"I don't hate it. Why do you say I hate it?"

"I had to twist your arm to tell it to me."

"Yuri, for God's sake. We're in a sewer!"

"That's our poet," Yuri laughed. "Misses nothing."

Yuri moved closer to Tania. He found her with his hand. "General Tania. I can drag my hand along this nasty wall almost as well as you. With your leave, I'll take the lead for a while."

She smiled, though Yuri could not see it. "Yes, of course. Thank you."

She listened to the farmer's footsteps splashing away. Fedya's feet slogged behind her. Tania waited for him to approach. The big lad's hand touched her, nudging her forward. She held steady against his fingers and let the touch sink into her ribs. She closed her eyes and felt the hand with her woman's senses, almost forgotten. Something inside her, a twinge, a twist, pushed back against Fedya. She caught it, held it, and breathed once for it. Then she hid it.

They walked in unrelenting blackness for another hour. The watery echoes of their steps hurtled into the dark, scraping along the walls. Tania began to feel she was falling into an endless shaft. The stench seared her nostrils. She was light-headed; a gagging nausea choked her.

Once, her balance reeled. She reached into the dark to cross Fedya's path. Her fingers brushed his chest.

"Are you all right?" he asked.

"Yes. Just exhausted. Every breath, it's like sucking in a garbage heap."

"Why haven't we seen any manholes? I'm sure it's dawn by now." Perhaps he believed she knew the answer.

She exhaled, looking into a darkness so total it seemed eternal in expanse instead of half a meter above their heads.

"They're probably covered up with debris from the bombings," she said. "Come on. We'll find one ahead."

Tania took another wretched step. "Fedya," she called out, "you go in front. I feel like following for a while. All right?"

Fedya squeezed her arm. Tania pulled herself forward. Minutes passed. Suddenly, Fedya's voice shot out.

"Yuri!"

Tania slid a hand against the muck of the wall to keep her balance; she held the other hand outstretched to find Fedya and Yuri. She came upon Fedya struggling in the mire. She laid both hands on his wet back. He was trying to lift Yuri from the sewer floor.

"Yuri!" he cried, his voice frantic. "Yuri, get up! Tania, he's fainted! What do we do?"

"Quick, lift him up!" Tania helped Fedya haul Yuri out of the filth. The old man's shirt and hair were soaked in water and excreta. Holding him close to lift him, Tania wrestled down her revulsion while her own clothes became caked.

"He's passed out from the fumes," Tania panted. They propped Yuri against the wall. "Damn it, he seemed fine."

"He was," Fedya insisted. "He is fine. He'll be all right. He just needs a moment to wake up."

Tania put her hand against Yuri's wet chest. His breathing was shallow. "Hold him." She stepped away from Yuri, measured the distance with her outstretched hand in the dark, and slapped him across his slumped face. Nothing. She slapped him again. Dampness sprayed from his cheek, sprinkling her eyes. Yuri made no sound.

"You'll have to carry him," Tania said. "Can you do that?"

"Yes. Of course."

Tania thought of Fedya laboring in this sewer, with Yuri a yoke across his shoulders. It would be only a short time before he, too, would succumb to the treacherous air.

"No, wait. Let's drag him. Put his arm around your neck."

Fedya and Tania hoisted Yuri's arms over their shoulders. They staggered on with Yuri's legs limp. Tania listened for any sign of consciousness from the old farmer's mouth.

After ten minutes of exertion and rising fear, she'd heard nothing from Yuri. She jabbed him in the ribs with her elbow. His breath jumped in an unconscious wheeze.

Tania asked Fedya, "How do you feel?"

"I can go on."

Tania walked on and thought, I can't. I'm exhausted and I want to throw up. Another few minutes of this and I'll be on my knees, if not my face, in the shit. I'm sorry, Yuri.

She pivoted Yuri to the wall and took Fedya's hands off him to let him slide to a sitting position. She held Yuri's head up.

"Take off his shirt," she said.

"Why? So he can breathe better? That doesn't make sense."

"No. Under his tunic he's wearing a farmer's longjohn. Take off your army shirt and put it on."

Fedya snapped back. "We're leaving him here? To die in a sewer? No! No! I can carry him! You're not leaving him!"

Tania leaned against the opposite wall. Fedya, she thought, you'll die here, too. So will I.

She was spent, too tired even to vent her frustration at ending her life beneath the streets of Stalingrad, in the dark and filth instead of out in the light, in the sound and heat of battle. Or I might have died old and in bed, surrounded by my children. Dying is blackness. Dying smells rotten, too. Look at me, where I am. Maybe I'm dead already.

She walked past Fedya, listening to her own stumbling footsteps. Her senses careened. She caught herself against the wall. Her stomach convulsed and she vomited on the wall. The sound of the spasm flew off like bats into the emptiness.

Tania righted herself and a weakness ascended in her legs. She recognized it as her death knell. Without intending it, she turned from the wall and walked, at least to die moving. The weakness tried to trip her. From behind came the splashing of quick footsteps. A hand appeared and held her up. The grasp bore her with a strength she thought could no longer exist in this hole. She reached to take Fedya's arm and felt that he was carrying Yuri's undershirt.

Tania walked in silence, unaware of time. She forgot her notions of traveling for more hours to reach any particular location in the city above. Her steps were measured now against her remaining strength. Her only goal was unfettered air, sunlight, and unechoed sound. Her feet grew leaden, and her breath came slow and labored.

She walked stiffly with Fedya for her crutch; her concentration was focused in her calves and thighs to resist the coming end of her power. She dragged herself onward, as if in leg irons, and clung to the arm around her middle. The blackness of the pipe threatened to infect all of her, blotting her out of consciousness, completing the darkness. She stumbled on, ticking off the list of her departing senses: I can no longer smell the tunnel, she thought. I can no longer feel my hands or Fedya's arm. I can no longer hear my footsteps. I can . . .

Something gleamed in the blackness ahead. My death, she thought. There it is. At least there will be light.

She lunged away from Fedya. A white spear twinkled ten meters ahead, shooting down at an angle. Tania thrust her face into the shaft of light as if it were a gushing fountain. Puffs of dust danced inside the beam, wandering slowly through it, tiny ballerinas floating across a spotlighted stage.

Tania heaved her chest against the wall to feel feverishly with her hands. She leaped to the other side.

"Here it is!" she croaked. "A ladder! It's a manhole."

Fedya lurched forward toward the ladder. "Let's go." She felt him ready himself for the climb, and she reached out to stop him. The touch of the ladder, of salvation, had rekindled some of her strength.

"No. Put on Yuri's shirt," she whispered. "Calm down. We're going to be all right. But I . . ." she smelled the foulness of her surroundings as if for the first time. She reeled and steadied. "I must go up first."

"I suppose I'm not to argue with you about these things, am I?" he said, pulling off his Red Army tunic.

"No. I'll signal you to come up. Walk away from the manhole. If I find Germans up there, they may climb down to see if anyone's with me. Stay silent. If you hear them coming down, lie flat. They'll fire soon as they drop.

They certainly won't chase you down here. Find another manhole and try again."

Tania laid her hands on the ladder's rungs. She climbed two steps. Fedya touched her leg.

"Tania."

"No. Walk away."

She waited for him to move beyond the ladder. She climbed to the manhole cover and shoved it aside as quietly as she could.

Daylight pushed in on her eyes. She ducked her head below the level of the street and blinked until she could see.

When her eyes adjusted, she raised her head slowly. They had been lucky. The manhole was shielded on all four sides by ripples of rubble. The facades of a row of large stone buildings had teetered into the street here and crumbled on all sides of the manhole, somehow failing to cover it. Tania clambered out of the hole and lay on her belly in the debris. She gulped the morning air. She heard nothing but the faraway pops of rifle fire. She hung her head into the manhole and said softly into the dark, "Come up."

Fedya climbed onto the street. He inhaled in great grateful swallows. She saw how filthy Fedya was, how scabrous was the front of Yuri's longjohn shirt. He wore the boots and olive khakis of the Red Army, but she hoped the longjohn and the overall condition of his dress would hide him from scrutiny. She looked at herself lying in the dust, coated like Fedya with a brown, rusty crust. She was just a young girl covered in shit.

The two climbed to the top of the rock pile. To the north was a line of Germans holding tins in front of a mess tent. Fedya stiffened at the sight of the Nazis as if he wanted to duck back into the debris. Tania hissed at him to stay straight up.

"No sudden moves. We're behind enemy lines. We can't run or crawl out. We'll have to walk out."

Fedya met her eyes. She smacked her dry lips once.

He grabbed her hand. "No, Tania. You're kidding." She shook loose his grip. "Tania," he pleaded, "nobody is that crazy."

She scrabbled down the mound, raising a dust cloud. At the bottom she called up to Fedya, frozen with his hands out from his sides, "Come on!" She waved him down with big gestures. "We've got to eat. I'm exhausted. I'm starving. This could be our last chance for the next twenty-four hours."

Fedya held his ground on the rubble heap.

"They won't know we're in the Russian army," she called. "We're not carrying weapons. We're walking around in the open. They'll just think you're some poor local worker who got latrine duty today and is taking a break for lunch."

"What about you?" he asked down to her.

"Me?" Tania shrugged. "I guess they'll figure I'm some whore who's working with you for food. Who cares? They'll make up their own stories so long as we keep our mouths shut."

Fedya slapped his hands on his hips in resignation. He picked his way down with measured strides. Such a large man, she thought, covered in crap and taking such small steps.

Fedya landed at her side. He frowned.

"You're the devil. Do you know that?"

"I can be. Come on. Say nothing."

They walked across open ground and took places at the end of the mess line. Impatient soldiers tapped their knives and forks on their plates.

For these sticks to be standing about waiting for mess like this, she thought, we're far behind their lines. They're acting like they're very safe here.

The line moved a few paces. Tania looked into Fedya's face. He stared at his boots, still caked but now covered in dust. He looked like a peasant from the villages, not a poet from Moscow.

"Was im Himmel?"

A Nazi pinched his nose in disgust. He stomped to Fedya and pushed him out of line, pointing for Tania to move also.

The two stood several paces back. They waited for the last soldier to disappear into the tent. They crept forward, obedient looks on their faces. Once inside, the cook tossed them plates and hurriedly scooped up knockwurst and kraut.

Fedya whispered while they walked into the tent, "Let's eat outside."

"No, I don't want to draw attention."

"Attention?" he said in quiet amazement. "Tania, we smell like camels. What more attention could we get?"

She shushed him and moved ahead. Around them a hundred Nazis sat eating. At each table, heads spun about when they passed. Fingers hurried to noses on appalled faces.

They found an open table and sat quickly. They shoveled the food into their mouths, afraid they would be thrown out before they could slake their hungers.

Midway through their plates, an officer approached. He held a kerchief daintily over his nose and spoke to them through the cloth. His voice became shrill. Tania and Fedya got up slowly.

They did not seem to move fast enough for the officer. The man lowered the kerchief and pulled a leather crop from his belt. He swung the crop across Fedya's back. Soldiers at neighboring tables applauded and laughed.

The German, his face growing crimson, struck Fedya again, then leaned across the table and hit Tania on top of her head.

Fedya leaped to his feet and shoved him back. "Leave her alone, *prostituta*!"

The officer regained his balance and looked deep into Fedya's eyes. He slid the crop slowly into his belt. He unbuttoned the holster for his pistol.

"Ah." He smiled thinly.

The officer stepped back and drew his sidearm with a dramatic, sweeping motion. He glanced around the silent tent. He raised the pistol to Fedya's heart and looked around the room again. The hundred faces were still.

The grinning Nazi interpreted the silence of his fellows as their tacit permission. He was justified in the execution of these two incredibly odious Russians.

Tania stepped to stand beside Fedya.

"Da svidanya, Russ," the German said.

A commotion erupted in the kitchen. The din of pots and pans banging on the floor spilled into the mess tent. The officer turned from Fedya.

A short, chubby man in a greasy apron burst into the mess hall. *"Halt! Halten Sie, bitte!"* he shouted. The man rumbled through the seated soldiers to jump in front of Fedya and Tania, his arms outstretched. In one hand he held high a wooden serving spoon.

The cook pleaded with the officer in stammering German. He pointed to Fedya and Tania, then to himself, and hung his head. The Nazi lowered the pistol and shouted at the cook. The round little man cringed, wrinkling his dirty apron. Then he snapped upright and clubbed Fedya's chest with the spoon. With his other hand he twisted Tania's ear, turning her around. He kicked her in the rear and shoved Fedya in the chest again with the spoon to herd them toward the kitchen, hollering in Russian. Over his shoulder, the cook called in an appeasing tone, *"Danke. Danke schön, mein Herr. Danke."*

The cook shoved Fedya through the kitchen door and pushed Tania behind him. Still shouting and cursing, he marched them out of the kitchen to a small, garbage-filled courtyard.

Once outside, the cook quieted. He whispered urgently in Russian, "Who are you? What are you doing in my mess hall?"

Tania shoved the cook in his meaty chest. "What are you doing serving food to Nazis? You're a fucking *hiwi*!"

Fedya stepped between them. "Tania! The man just saved your life. And mine, too. Be quiet, show some gratitude."

"Gratitude? This pig cooks for those bastards. He's worse than they are! He's a traitor, Fedya! A collaborator!"

"Tania." Fedya put his hands on her shoulders. "I'll take the lead now. You will follow me. Understand? I'll get us out of here. You'll get us killed. Now be quiet."

Tania inhaled to say more, to tell Fedya about the *hiwis* her partisans had caught and shot, about the placards they'd nailed to the traitors' heads to warn others not to cooperate with the invaders. Fedya shook her shoulders hard. Tania jammed her fists into her pockets, glowering at the fat traitor.

Fedya reached his hand to the cook. "Thank you. You saved our lives. What did you say to that German?"

"That you are two Russian peasants working for me. I told him I sent you to clean out the shithouse and you must have fallen in."

"Really? Just like that?" Fedya turned to Tania. "A good story. A quick thinker, isn't he?"

Tania spat. "Fucking *hiwi*."

Fedya turned back to the cook. "Right. Let's just keep this between you and me, shall we? Can you get us some clean clothes?"

"No," said the cook. "Who are you? How did you get here?"

"We're with the 284th Division. Our transport was

sunk. Once we got ashore, this girl led us through the sewer."

"You followed her?" The cook pointed with his spoon.

Tania leaned forward. Fedya kept her back with his girth.

"I wouldn't do that," he warned the man quietly.

The cook lowered the spoon.

Fedya continued, his manner still friendly. "Can you give us more food?"

"Of course." The cook went back to the kitchen. He stopped in the doorway. "I'll bring it out."

Fedya spun on Tania. "What's wrong with you? How can you treat a man that way who's saved your life?"

"He's helping the Germans!"

"He's a nothing little cook. How do you know his story? He might have a wife and children they're holding. He might be just a simple scared fat man who got caught up in all this and only wants to live through it."

Tania leaned against the top of a metal trash can. "If he's a coward," she said, "then he should be shot."

Fedya folded his arms. She looked into his blue eyes and took in his powerful figure. I want to live through it, too, she thought. She felt the sadness overtaking her, prodded by Fedya's scolding. So badly I want to live. But I'm already dead. The Germans took my life, they took my homeland and my good grandparents. All I have left is this soulless body. And I've sworn on blood to hurl myself against them until my body breaks, or my life and my tears return one day when the sticks are gone. But I, Fedya, Yuri, this cook, Russia—we are all of us dead right now. And to live again we can only fight. We must not, cannot, do anything else.

Fedya unfolded his arms. "We are not all so brave as you."

He reached for Tania and held her lightly. She laid her head on his chest, then pulled away.

"You stink."

The cook returned with steaming plates of kraut and a thick brown hash. He set them on top of a garbage can.

"The fighting comes mostly from that direction," he said, pointing to a horizon of devastation. "The front line is three kilometers away. The other way is the Volga. Don't go there. It's patrolled."

The cook looked at Fedya and nodded. Fedya returned the courtesy. The little man's eyes shifted quickly to Tania, unsure of what they would meet there.

The cook spread his palms to her. His flabby chest shook under the splattered apron. He seemed about to cry.

"You can't understand," he said.

Fedya answered for her. "Who can?"

The cook wiped his nose on his sleeve and turned to the kitchen. Fedya and Tania emptied their plates. They climbed out of the courtyard and entered the ruins to find the Russian lines. There was little movement in the streets. Nazi squads patrolled the shadows; sandbagged machine gun emplacements glared from the gaping wounds in the walls. Small packs of homeless, ragged citizens wandered trancelike through the charred, pocked, and eerily placid ruins. They dug into the debris to pocket bits of clothing and utensils to help them survive the holocaust of their city. The Germans left these mortal phantoms alone. Tania and Fedya hoped to be similarly ignored, counted among the forsaken.

If they did encounter a suspicious patrol, she'd told Fedya to act retarded, drool, and mumble. She would use hand signals to somehow tell the soldiers that the city asylum had been blown up and the large boy was just a harmless inmate. She'd found him in the streets and was leading him to the Russian rear for evacuation. They were covered in shit because they'd fallen into a ruptured sewer, latrine, whatever. If Fedya could act the fool, the

Germans ought to buy it—at least until she could concoct a better plan.

"But don't worry," she assured Fedya, "they won't stop us. We're unarmed. We're walking around in the open, no threat to them. And besides, we're covered in shit, remember?"

"Oh. I keep forgetting that," he said. "Wonderful. I think I'll wear shit for the rest of the war. It's the safest way to go, don't you think? Like armor."

They zigzagged through the ruins into the afternoon. A German squad passed them, the soldiers clopping and jingling in their heavy boots and packs. She cursed in a mad, high-pitched Byelorussian dialect while Fedya whooped like an idiot. Only one soldier in the patrol looked at them. He held his nose. The squad jogged into the shell of a building and disappeared up a stairwell.

Ahead, three hundred meters away across a desolate boulevard, was a railroad yard littered with the twisted steel curlicues of torn-up track and burned-out train cars. Just east of the tracks was a large building, five stories high and two blocks long. The windows had been blown out, and streaks of soot showed above each broken window frame, evidence of a gutting fire. Blackened German tanks cluttered the terrain. From where Tania and Fedya stood, the base of the ravaged building, across the open rail yard, was no less than eight hundred meters away.

Tania looked back at the building into which the Nazi patrol had run. Gun muzzles bristled from several windows, all facing west across the tracks.

This is the front line, she thought. No-man's-land.

She looked up at the afternoon sun. It would be too dangerous to cross the tracks in daylight. They could easily be caught in a crossfire or mistaken for deserters or spies by either side. Across the boulevard sat a brick railman's shed. Tania tugged on Fedya's sleeve.

"We'll wait in that shed. After dark we'll crawl across

the tracks." She pointed to the five-story building across from them. "That's where the Red Army is."

Fedya looked over the rail yard. "How do you know?"

Tania walked toward the shed. She jerked her thumb over her shoulder at the enemy in the building behind her. She heard the clacking and scrambling as they set up their mortars and tripods in the windows.

"They know."

Behind the shed's wooden door, empty shelves held only dust and broken glass. Screws and greasy clamps littered the floorboards. The window was broken, but the roof was intact.

Along the wall crouched a spring bed frame and a cotton mattress. The bedding was covered with glass and dirt. Tania flipped the mattress to a cleaner side. It showed powder blue and gray pinstripes with russet stains. The air was close, reeking of oil and emptiness. Tania struck the mattress with the flat of her hand. She backed away from a billow of dust.

"Some curtains, some flowers in the window." She turned to Fedya in the doorway. "I could plant us a garden for fresh vegetables."

"Comfy." He entered and sat on the bed. "A writer's cottage by the tracks. Trains have always been a romantic topic for me."

Tania stood in front of him. "Take off that miserable shirt. It stinks, and it makes me think of poor Yuri."

She tugged on the crusted tunic. Fedya raised his arms. She slid the shirt off him and flung it out the window.

"Boots." She pointed at his feet. "You can take those off yourself."

Fedya untied the laces. Tania undid her jacket and kicked it into a corner. Her blouse was of a rough spun flax, the color of straw. Sweat stains darkened the armpits and collar. She reached for the top button.

Fedya looked up from his boots. She followed his eyes to the points of her breasts.

"Tania," he said quietly. "I, um . . ." His eyes went to her hands poised at her neck. "Are you going to undo your shirt?"

"Yes, I am." She unfastened the first button, then another. "We can't go anywhere until after dark. I'm tired, and I'm sure you are, too. I thought we'd get some sleep."

She sat beside him and bounced. The springs squeaked.

Fedya gazed out to the rail yard. "Is anyone going to bother us in here? Should we both sleep at the same time?"

"The only one who's going to bother you in here," she said, leaning down to untie her own laces, "is me."

She sent the boots flying into the corner to land on her coat, then reached behind Fedya to run her palm over his broad back. He leaned forward, chin in hand, elbows on knees. She kneaded the muscles along his shoulder blades.

"Ah," he whispered, closing his eyes, "that is magnificent. Really. After the day we've had."

She dropped her hand from his back, and he opened his eyes. She saw the quizzical, bothered look on his face.

"Did I say something wrong?" he asked.

She shook her head slowly. "Today . . . today was nothing."

She pulled back her hair so he could see her face, all of it. She didn't know if he could see what was in her eyes. Did it come through? Could she ever show it to him, or even express it? The months of running, fighting, killing, and surviving. Surviving for what? To live more scarred years, to turn the pages on fifty more calendars, marking anniversaries of hatred without respite, stretching onward to her own death? Hatred without compassion, humanity, or morality; hatred stripped clean of all else, like bones in the sun? This was her dowry; this was what awaited her, even if she survived Stalingrad. She could never outrun or outlive it. It would follow her even if she carried it back to bright America someday. But could she show Fedya, anyone, ever? Or was it just hers, alone, to the grave?

She took his hand. "Today Yuri died. But he was already dead. He died last night when he came across that river. You died, too. I died a year ago in Minsk when the Nazis murdered my grandparents. I died of shame when my own parents would not come with me to save them. Do you understand?"

Fedya took her hand. The rims of his eyes reddened. He blinked. A tear welled in his eye.

"This is what the *politrooks* are telling us," she continued. "The NKVD, *Red Star*, the Party—everywhere we turn, the message is the same. You are dead. You have no life. The Germans have taken it. They have trampled it."

Tania reached to Fedya's face, smearing the tear with her finger. "Fedushka, there's nothing anymore for the individual. Not love. Not fear. Not family. We're not alive. Nothing we do matters. We're like ghosts who can't touch anything. The only time we appear, the only time we're real, is when we're killing the Germans. When we're not killing them, we do not exist."

She pulled free from him to rub her hands along the sides of his face. She moved his face closer and kissed him.

Eyes shut, she listened to her own breath coming hard. She murmured under the strength of the kiss. Her senses felt along the length of her body, waiting for his caress, looking for it on her breasts, between her legs. She tasted salt from tears; whether they were her own or his, she did not know.

She moved the kiss upward and pulled his lip between her teeth. He sighed. She felt heat.

"We're not alive, Fedya," she whispered. "We're not here in these bodies even though we feel them."

Tania searched again for his touch on her body. She reached into his lap and moved one of his hands up to her chest. She squeezed her fingers around his, against her breast.

"Make love to me, Fedya."

His hands were on her, one at her breast, the other on her stomach. She inhaled. A tightness in her loins came as if from outside, from above. She began to rise off the bed.

He pushed her away. "Tania. No."

She opened her eyes, disoriented and swaying. She put her hands on his shoulders to push herself erect. Fedya lowered his arms while she gained control over her balance, away from him.

"Tania, no," he said again, looking up. "It's not . . ."

Her arms flew from her sides. "It's not what? What's wrong?"

Fedya got off the bed and stepped to face a wall. She sat in his place on the squeaking bed.

"Fedya, what's the matter?"

He rubbed the wall with his boot and said nothing.

Tania sat on her hands. The bed squeaked again. She thought angrily about the noise they could have made on those springs.

"Fine," she said, "don't talk to me. Talk to that wall. If you want to stay up and guard me, go ahead. I'm going to sleep."

Fedya leaned his back against the wall.

"It's not right," he said. "We shouldn't do this." He motioned to the corner where her coat and boots lay.

"Shouldn't do what?" She pulled her hands from beneath her and slapped them down in her lap. "Shouldn't make love? Here? On a battlefield? Is there something sacred about a battlefield?" She looked out the window at the blasted world. "Where else do we have, Fedya? This is it."

Fedya moved in front of her. "I don't agree with you. I don't feel like you do, that I'm dead, like I don't exist. But you! You act like you don't care what happens to you, like there's nothing left of you for them to kill."

He pointed in the direction of the enemy lines. "Look at the chances you take! I remember you on the barge. You had to sit in the most dangerous spot. You wouldn't move. Then after three hours in the water and six more in a sewer, you walk me straight into a Nazi mess tent! You screamed at a patrol of Germans . . . in Ukrainian or something, I don't even know what that was! And your idea of a precaution is to tell me to babble like a moron in case we get stopped. Great plan! Is every American that insane?"

As Fedya stomped back and forth, waving his arms, she resisted the smile tugging at the corners of her mouth. He's right, of course, she thought. But dear Fedya, he never loses his charm. Even in the sewer, afraid of the dark and the shit. Even now, here, afraid of me.

His pacing covered the short distance between walls in a few strides. He flapped his arms at every turn. Tania looked into her lap to hide her smile. He looked like a giant mad goose.

"I don't think you put enough thought into these things," he said. "You act like you're invisible. That may be fine for you, but remember I'm right there behind you and I don't want to get killed in a Nazi mess tent! They don't give medals for that!"

He looked at the ceiling. "Oh, and I just can't wait for tonight to get here!" He spun on his heels, raised his arms high and held them there. "Tonight, I finally get to crawl behind you across a no-man's-land that is probably a minefield, worrying about who's more likely to shoot me, the Russians or the Germans! But first we get to make love as if it's something we ordered off a menu, like it doesn't matter at all. It's wrong, Tania. It's wrong to act as if things don't matter when they really do."

Fedya lowered his arms. He sat at her feet and shook his head, holding her eyes with his own. "I don't think I was ready for this. I joined the Red Army because Stalin said so, because, let's face it, it was the only thing possible. I trained for four weeks and then got on a transport. I ended up crossing the Volga in the water, holding on to a piece of a boat. I'm not like you. I didn't come to this war by choice. I didn't live with the partisans for a year. I'm scared of everything. Yuri dying in the sewer like that, that mess tent with Germans all over the place . . . You're wrong, Tania. This has been some day. And it mattered to me because it scared the shit out of me. Not that anyone would have noticed even if I had shit all over myself!"

He rubbed a finger behind his ear, looking away from her. "I'm not used to this. You might be, but I'm not."

She took Fedya's hand from behind his ear and pulled him onto the bed. She laid his hand high on her thigh. She put the top of her head against his cheek, nuzzling him with her hair.

"Are you used to this?" She rubbed his hand, feeling his veins, his fingernails. She pressed his hand higher on her thigh.

"I'm from Moscow, Tania. This is the one thing we're all used to there."

"Well," she whispered, "I'm in New York. It's so much smaller than Moscow, it's easy to get lost there. Why don't you lead me again for a while?"

She whispered into the ear hovering at her mouth. "Go on, Fedushka. Lead me. I'll take over when we get to the minefield."

Fedya whispered in return. She felt the warmth of his words on her throat.

"The minefield, Tanyushka?" he whispered. "Too late. I'm already in the middle of it."

FEDYA WAS WRONG. THE RAIL YARD HAD NOT been mined. Crawling in the darkness, Tania felt ahead with her fingers for detonator spikes, black barbs that would stick out of the earth only a centimeter. She found none.

She slid along the ground in as straight a line as the terrain allowed. She stopped at the hulk of a German tank. One of its treads had been blown off by an antitank rifle, further evidence for Tania to believe the Red Army was in the building in front of them. If not, the Germans surely would have towed this tank away and repaired the tread.

She and Fedya rested beneath the tank. They were halfway across the yard to the gray building rising out of the night, with another four hundred meters to go.

Tania was not worried about crossing the distance. The evening was quiet and dark. No flares scratched the sky. There was plenty of debris to slither behind. But she knew there were eyes behind and in front of her, sights fixed across the rail yard staring at each other in suspicion and hatred, watching for any activity. Her main concern was their first encounter with the Russians. They would be in the forward trenches, guarding their fortress from nighttime infiltrators. Like Fedya and her.

Tania lay still until her strength returned. Fedya's breathing eased long before her own did. He's powerful, she thought, recalling his strength in the sewer, his embrace on the dusty mattress.

Tania crawled from the cover of the tank. She led Fedya over more tracks and under rail cars to within seventy-five meters of the building. With the walls towering above them, Fedya pulled on her foot and dragged himself beside her.

"Now what?" he whispered.

"I don't know."

Fedya rolled his eyes into his brows. He laid his forehead on the backs of his hands in the dirt.

Tania stared up at the building. She scoured the ground, examining every bump and mound for the defense works and Red Army guards she knew were there. To surprise those guards in the dark would be fatal. To be caught in no-man's-land at sunup before they could make themselves known as Russians would also be certain death.

She touched the top of Fedya's head. "Stay here."

"What? Where are you going?" His head jerked up. "Tania?"

She pushed his head back down onto his hands. "Keep this down if you want to keep this."

Tania stood. She raised her hands over her head.

"Nicht schiessen!" she called out, walking forward, away from Fedya. *"Nicht schiessen, bitte!"* Don't shoot!

The night calm was splintered by rifle chambers slamming shut. She knew the barrels were aimed at her heart. She cried again, *"Nicht schiessen!"*

Russian voices called out from the debris twenty meters ahead. "Who's there? Identify yourself."

She inhaled to answer. Her lips formed the first sound in Russian. *Ya Russkaya.* I'm Russian. Then she stopped herself. She stepped carefully.

"Nicht schiessen, bitte," she called to the voices.

With a clatter, a dark shape leaped out of the ground and ran to her. The soldier seized her roughly, grabbing down one of her raised arms. Tania allowed herself to be pulled and then tossed over the lip of a trench. She tumbled onto the dirt floor.

A kicking boot rolled her onto her back. A rifle barrel

was thrust into her throat, pressed hard there, making her gasp.

"Who the fuck are you?" a shadow demanded.

He was joined by two others with rifles ready. "Talk!"

Another voice said angrily, *"Spreche!"*

Tania kept still, moving only her lips.

"I'm Russian. The 284th. My transport was blown up last night crossing the Volga. I floated downriver behind the lines."

The gun pressed deeper into her throat. Hands felt along her arms and legs, frisking her for weapons.

"How do you know German?"

Tania's voice gurgled. "I was a partisan in Byeloruss. We had to learn a little German."

The gun eased at her throat. She took a breath and cleared her throat. "Not like you Ivan dicks who only know how to sleep on guard and throw women around."

One of the voices laughed. The gun was taken away.

"The 284th?"

"Yes. Under Batyuk."

A soldier leaned down. She heard sniffing.

"Damn, what is that smell?"

Tania laughed. Fedya's armor, she thought.

"It's shit. I've got it all over me. It's a long story."

"Don't tell me." The soldier reached down to help Tania off the floor of the trench.

"Sorry," he said. "We didn't know who you were. All I saw was someone stand up right in front of me and shout in German. I thought you were an infiltrator."

Tania looked at the three soldiers. The hard treatment was no less than she'd expected.

"If I'd been an infiltrator, would I have called to you in Russian or German?"

Two of the three answered after a moment of considering in the dark trench. "Russian." The third nodded.

Tania smiled at her guess. Another chance I took. I'll hear about this one from Fedya, too.

She told the soldiers about leaving Fedya lying in the dirt twenty meters away. She called to him.

"Fedya, it's all right. Come in. We're back!"

He scrambled to the trench and was frisked as soon as he tumbled down.

Tania did not approach him. "Comrade Michailov," she said.

"Comrade Chernova." He nodded to her, then shook hands with the soldiers, smiling, thanking each of them for not shooting at them. "Good job," he said. "Nice work. Excellent."

Tania turned to the men. "Could you help us get some clean clothes? And a meal?"

One of the guards stepped forward. "Clean clothes will have to wait until morning. We can't leave our posts. As for the meal . . ."

The soldier reached into his coat to pull out a flask of vodka. He handed it first to Fedya.

"Welcome to Stalingrad."

EIGHT

"EVERYONE ON YOUR FEET. LET'S GO!"

Viktor Medvedev walked into the huge shop bay. Thirty soldiers jumped up from their seats on the scattered bins, barrels, and crates.

The high brick walls of the massive basement glowed with the salmon light of dawn. Once a machine shop for the Lazur chemical plant, the room's heavy machinery had been evacuated across the Volga in early summer, leaving a gray expanse of bare floor. Like all the large buildings in Stalingrad, the Lazur had been reduced by the Luftwaffe's bombings to scorched steel and cinder block until it could neither fall apart nor burn more. The Red Army had burrowed into the rubble of the Lazur and the wreckage in the rail yard surrounding the plant. The basement had survived intact beneath the mounds of collapsed brick and girders above. This morning the late October chill spilled through shattered windows high overhead. The room was quiet, its vast emptiness devouring sound.

The thirty soldiers standing before Viktor were the first sniper volunteers from the 284th. Commissar Igor Danilov had told the Hare and the Bear he wanted to limit

the school's first class to soldiers from their own division,
to encourage other divisions to start sniper initiatives.

Most of the volunteers had read about the formation of
the sniper unit and the exploits of Chief Master Sergeant
Zaitsev in the flimsy news sheet *In Our Country's Defense,*
put out twice a week by the Communists to the defenders
of Stalingrad.

Viktor stubbed out a cigarette and began.

"You are all here for one purpose only. You will learn to
be snipers to kill Germans."

The Bear held up a rifle with a telescopic sight. "No
matter what your battle experience has been before today,
fighting as a sniper will be different. You'll need skills beyond those of an infantry soldier. You'll need greater intelligence and discipline. You will no longer be part of a
thousand-man battalion doing only what you're told. You
will be snipers, acting on your own impulse. You must
think, then move, then act. If you don't, you'll be killed.
That I guarantee you."

Viktor stepped closer to the front row of recruits.

"This unit is the first of its kind. Until now the Russian
sniper has been a brave but largely disorganized and inef-
fective tool. We have served well, but we can serve better.
Over the next several days you will learn how to hunt
down your opponent. You will kill him in his own lair with
the silence and terror of distance. You will strike at him in
his most vulnerable moments: while he smokes his morning cigarette, when he takes a piss, scooping his evening
beans and horse meat into his mouth. You'll kill him when
he makes the smallest misstep. Fear will haunt him every
moment, the fear of wearing the silent brand of our
crosshairs. He won't know when the bullet is coming for
him or the man next to him. But he will know there is no
safe ground for him in Russia. That is your charge."

Viktor raised the weapon. "Your telescopic site will
bring your prey close. You will stalk and watch the enemy,

perhaps for hours or days at a time. You'll see his face, see his teeth, watch his head explode."

The Bear lowered the rifle. "This type of killing must be done with patience and without heat. This is cold death. You will know the man you're putting a bullet into."

Viktor sat on an empty crate. He laid the rifle across his knees as if resting an oar from rowing.

Through the shop door came Zaitsev, his footsteps clicking on the concrete. He cast his eyes over the recruits, continuing the scrutiny he'd begun outside the doorway, listening to Viktor's opening remarks. Six of the soldiers in the room he already knew: Baugderis, Shaikin, Morozor, the giant Griasev, Kostikev, and little Kulikov. In the past few days, he'd asked each personally to join the sniper unit after seeing them in action. He'd met Baugderis, Shaikin, and Kostikev while hunting on Mamayev Kurgan, watching the three, all farm boys from Tbilisi in Georgia, calmly drop Nazis at two hundred meters using only open sights. Viktor had found Griasev, a mammoth with arms and hands like jackhammers, at the Tractor Factory, throwing grenades over fifty meters with alarming accuracy, an unheard-of feat. Kostikev was a Siberian from Zaitsev's company in the 284th. He was as skilled with a stiletto as with a rifle and was the calmest man Zaitsev had seen in close combat. And Zaitsev had spent hours watching tiny Nikolay Kulikov at the Barricades Plant crawl a dozen times under enemy fire to bring supplies to a squad pinned down in a trench.

This first class of volunteers looked gritty and battle-hardened. Their sizes ranged from the hulking Griasev to a short and flabby Armenian woman, one of two women in the group.

"My name is Chief Master Sergeant Vasily Zaitsev. I am your instructor. I am assisted by Master Sergeant Viktor Medvedev." Viktor raised his cigarette in the air. "And of course by Commissar Danilov." Zaitsev smiled at the commissar, but the man scribbling against the wall did not look up.

"Your sniper training will last three days. Today we will discuss weapons, fieldcraft, and tactics. Tomorrow we'll teach you to aim and shoot with a rifle and scope. On the third day you will each be sent on a mission. Those of you who live to the fourth day will be reassigned to your companies as snipers." Zaitsev turned on his heels. "Viktor."

The Bear rose from the crate and snatched up two rifles. Screwed to the tops of both weapons were telescopic sights. Stopping in front of the trainees, he laid one of the guns down.

"When you came into this room this morning, each of you was told to leave your old rifle in the hall. Those rifles will be given to the infantry. You will be issued new weapons tonight."

Viktor surveyed the soldiers' faces. No one looked away. The Bear commanded attention. "I understand that two of you actually came in without any weapons at all." Viktor shook his head and smiled. "You two must be very dangerous fighters."

The group laughed with Viktor. He held up one rifle.

"This is the weapon of your enemy. The Mauser Kar 98K. It has been fitted with a four-power scope and fires an eight-millimeter load. This rifle is a piece of shit that can kill you."

Viktor snapped the stock against his shoulder. In a flash, he leveled the barrel at a private ten meters in front of him. The soldier recoiled, then gained his composure and sat up.

Viktor nestled in behind the scope, wrinkling his face to aim. "The optics are poor, with a limited field of vision. The scope has a cross reticle, which in my opinion worsens the sense of roaming. The balance of the weapon is pitiful. It jams frequently and can fail in cold weather."

He pulled the rifle's trigger. The hammer clicked. Instantly, without lowering the rifle from his cheek, he levered the bolt, pretending to chamber another round.

"The bolt is well located right above the trigger for fast reloading. The average Nazi sniper can get off two shots in four-point-five seconds with this rifle."

Viktor let the Mauser fall with a clatter. With his foot, he shoved it away to send it skidding against a wall.

The Bear picked up the second rifle. He held it over his head with both hands.

"This," he said, spinning the rifle like a baton, "is also the weapon of your enemy. It's the Russian Moisin-Nagant model 91/30 sniper rifle with a four-power scope. It fires a seven-point-six-two-caliber load, is reliable under all combat conditions, especially the cold, and is the weapon of choice for both Russian and German snipers."

The trainees smiled at Viktor. The Bear did not smile back. "Your job," he said, "is to not die and let these rifles fall into the enemy's hands. Let them keep using their German shit. These are Russian guns. Understand?"

Viktor again jerked the rifle up under his chin. He trained it at the head of the same recruit. The private, surprised for the second time, leaned away from the barrel, then righted himself again, embarrassed.

"Excellent optics, with a post and sidebar reticle, leaving the top of the field of vision open. The scope has internal windage and elevation adjustments. It's also mounted high enough above the barrel for you to see under it and use the open sight for shots under one hundred meters. The rifle is nicely balanced but a few grams heavier than the Mauser."

Viktor lowered the rifle, smiling now at the young soldier who'd been in his sights. "What the hell," he said, "we're Russians. We can carry it."

Viktor brought the weapon into firing position, again at the selected private, who this time sat stolidly. Viktor pulled the trigger, then slammed the bolt in and out without lowering the gun from his cheek. He squeezed the trigger again.

"It has one design flaw," he said, holding the rifle at his chest. "The bolt is too far forward for fast repeat firing. The average Russian sniper can fire two shots five to five and a half seconds apart. That means your first shot had better hit, because your enemy is going to be a second faster with the next bullet."

He tucked the Moisin-Nagant under his arm. "You will all be issued this rifle later today." Then Viktor turned his back to the trainees. "Vasha."

Zaitsev rose from the crate. He handed over his half-smoked cigarette in exchange for the Russian rifle. Zaitsev looked over at Danilov. The commissar remained bent over his notebook; he flipped to a new page, then shook out the fingers on his writing hand.

Zaitsev hefted the weapon. He walked up to the private who had jerked twice under Medvedev's aim. The soldier was seated with five others on a metal pipe.

"What's your name?" he asked.

The private began to stand for his answer. Zaitsev motioned him to stay seated.

"What's your name?"

"Chekov, Chief Master Sergeant. Anatoly Petrovich."

Zaitsev looked at the small rips in Chekov's uniform, the scruffiness of his boots. The man's eyes showed no fear. His lips were tight, his breathing was even.

"You've seen some action, Private?"

Chekov's eyes narrowed. His jaw muscles flexed.

"Yes."

"Did you hunt as a civilian, Chekov?"

"Yes. I was a poacher. In the Ukraine."

Zaitsev's eyebrows went up. A poacher? This is what I get for letting Danilov write the requirements for me. Well, this is no time to judge. He nodded and moved down the line, asking for names, sometimes homes, and if they'd been hunters. Or poachers.

"Vasilchenko. Um, yes, I did poach some."

"Druiker, from Estonia. I preferred fishing. But I can handle a rifle. You'll see."

"Volyivatek. Outside Kishinev in Moldavia. Hunted every day until I was drafted. Best turkey shot in my village."

"Slepkinian, from Armenia," answered a dark, thick-legged woman. "My husband was crippled in the factory years ago. I had to learn to hunt to feed my children."

Peasants, thought Zaitsev, like me. We're all peasants. All the better. Accustomed to hardship.

Zaitsev stepped before a tall, lithe blond girl. He noted her stare. This, he thought, is no peasant.

"Chernova," she said.

The large young man standing next to her called out his name even before Zaitsev could move away from the girl.

"Michailov, Fyodor Ivanovich. From Moscow."

Zaitsev looked at the two. Both appeared freshly scrubbed compared to the ruggedness of the rest of the group.

"Your uniforms are new. When did you arrive in Stalingrad?"

The youth spoke quickly; it seemed he was answering for both himself and the girl. "Two days ago. Our transport was sunk on the Volga. We . . . um . . . ." He paused, looking straight ahead, "Our uniforms were . . . um . . ."

Zaitsev said, "You're the ones who fell into the shit."

Viktor chuckled, rubbing his forehead into his hand.

Zaitsev looked at Fyodor Ivanovich Michailov. The boy was as big as Viktor. "It's all right, Private," he said. "It's just that stories like that one get around quickly. You're actually quite brave." Zaitsev looked at the girl. "Both of you," he added, smiling.

Zaitsev stepped to the middle of the floor, the Moisin-Nagant under his arm.

Well, he thought, now would seem to be a good time to start playing the hero. He spoke loudly, snipping the words off short the way Viktor did.

"Before we begin, I want to tell you something Comrade Danilov has not yet managed to put into print."

The commissar looked up from his pad like an animal hearing a curious sound. Hurriedly, he turned to a fresh page and bore down with his pen.

Zaitsev continued. "I want each of you to know why I have accepted the assignment to teach you. It's because I view you as my revenge. If I die in battle, yours will be the bullets I'll still fire at the Nazis. I'll fight them from my grave through you."

He paused to look over the intent faces of the recruits. "Each of you," he repeated, his voice solemn. He waved his open palm across the trainees as if in benediction.

"Each of you must know your own reason for being here, as I know mine. It will keep you alive."

Zaitsev extended the rifle to the poacher Chekov. The private took it, and Zaitsev held it with him for a moment.

"And it will make you die very, very dearly," he said. He released the rifle into the man's grasp.

The room was silent save for the echoes of Zaitsev's voice and the flipping of paper while Danilov whisked to a new sheet.

THE REMAINDER OF THAT MORNING WAS SPENT on what Zaitsev and Viktor called "fieldcraft."

Viktor presented the topic to the recruits in a simple fashion: fieldcraft was nothing more than hunting, right up to the point of pulling the trigger. The skills of silence and unseen movement were the most important abilities a sniper could develop. "Your shooting eye will improve with practice," he told them, "but missing a shot at three hundred fifty meters will never get you killed so long as your enemy doesn't know where you are.

"Stalingrad is not the forests or wheat fields of your homes. It's a giant pile of bricks, concrete, and metal. Hunting Germans in Stalingrad is not the same as hunting squirrels on the farm. Squirrels don't shoot back. To survive and kill in this city, you'll need new ways to move and hide. You must learn to use the ruins and craters, to run bent over with your head almost to your knees. We'll practice crawling and dragging your weapon in a sack behind you. Picking your routes through the debris requires a keen eye and patience. Most important—and this is something you may already know if you're really hunters—you must lie still for hours until the one shot presents itself. A move made too soon can be your last."

Viktor and Zaitsev led the recruits up the steps out of the basement to the first floor of the Lazur. Collapsed walls and ceiling joists formed a huge, jumbled wasteland. For four hours the two sergeants watched and shouted while the trainees crawled over and around the wreckage, dragging mock rifle sacks behind them. Whenever a head or shoulder popped above the debris, Viktor shouted "Bang! Dead Ivan! Now get *down!*"

The smaller recruits were better at escaping detection in the ruins. Many of the bigger ones, like Griasev and the freshman Michailov, bumped and jangled their way through the rubble.

To take advantage of these differences, as well as minimize the risks, Zaitsev divided the class into two teams. One squad, the "hares," would come under his tutelage. The hares would be the shorter, more slender soldiers, like Zaitsev himself, who could move undetected in the debris. Viktor's group would be the "bears," the larger men who needed extra instruction on how to keep their heads down and their feet from fouling each other's ropes but possessed greater physical strength.

In the late morning they ate a lunch of tea, soup, and bread. The hares and bears sat separate, as units, talking and laughing. Members of each group produced bottles of vodka.

Danilov approached Zaitsev, carrying sheafs of notes.

"Comrade Zaitsev," Danilov began, offering a cigarette, "tell me. What do you think of our new heroes?"

Zaitsev accepted the cigarette. "The women."

"You object to the presence of women in our sniper school?"

"They'll create problems among the men. They always do."

"Well, Vasily, let's see if you can't teach them to cause more problems for the Germans than for us." Danilov laid his notes aside. "You understand why it must be done this way. In the Red Army, there are tens of thousands of women serving alongside the men, on radios in the bunkers, stanching the men's blood as nurses, and working the artillery. This first sniper unit gives us the opportunity to tell the world that the Nazis are being defeated on the battlefield not just by Russian men but by the Russian people, all of them, men and women. We can say we have risen to fight as one. The Communist order is truly united, without distinction by class or sex. Think of the impact at home among the civilians to see pictures in *Red Star* of their sisters, armed and dangerous. Not even the Americans can claim that their women are shooting down their enemies with rifles."

Zaitsev ground his cigarette beneath his heel.

"I have less objection to your decision than the fact that I was not consulted," he said. "Please do Viktor and me the courtesy of asking our opinions in the future. For now, we'll make your women into killers." If they're not already, Zaitsev thought, walking away from the commis-

sar. The Armenian one, Slepkinian, though heavy, moved
well and claimed she was an experienced hunter. Viktor
had told him about the blonde, Chernova. The Bear had
shared a bottle with the guards who'd brought her and the
big boy, Michailov, in from the trenches on the edge of
no-man's-land. She said she'd been a partisan from Byelorussia. When she'd heard the Lazur plant was to be the
site of the new sniper school, she insisted on being among
the first trainees.

What has she seen? There's so little news from the
occupied areas. I've heard it's hard there, terrible. Is she a
solid fighter, the guerrilla's reputation, or just able to
mount a good stare on that pretty face? We'll find out.

Zaitsev looked at Chernova, sitting with the men. Her
spoon was tucked into her boot like a regular foot soldier.
She took a gulp of vodka and finished by inhaling through
her sleeve. The men enjoyed her. They ignored the other,
thicker woman.

He stopped his walk among the men and watched only
her. Even clapping his hands to break up lunch and move
on with the lessons, she tugged at his attention. Her voice
rose above the others. She was behind him, standing, her
hands on her hips. Ignore her, he thought.

Trouble.

ZAITSEV WALKED TO THE BASE OF THE CINDER-
block wall. He turned his back to the recruits, most of
whom sat cross-legged in a semicircle on the shop floor.
Late afternoon light flowed through the high, broken windows. Overhead, swirling dust glittered like mica.

"Out there"—Zaitsev pointed to the window above
him—"it's sometimes very quiet. That silence can be de-
ceiving. It can lull you into carelessness."

He walked to the middle of the group.

"Remember, you're not just infantry anymore. You're

snipers. You need new habits, new ways of thinking. A foot soldier's battles are fought with noise and explosions, screaming and shouting and rushing around. You will fight in silence. Just because it's quiet around your trench or your shooting cell, don't think you're alone. There are arms, legs, and eyes everywhere in the ruins. Every building, every destroyed house, every pile of rubble is under watch. Supply units are running through trenches carrying ammo, mines, and food. From the tops of buildings, artillery observers are training their binoculars in all directions. Sappers crawl through the debris to find enemy bunkers and tunnels. Runners from headquarters are carrying messages to units trapped without radios. Never forget: the battlefield is alive with activity, even when you can't hear it or see it. And you, the sniper, will lie in the middle of it all, unseen, unheard, watching everything, letting it pass you by until it's time to strike."

He paused. Every eye was on him. The soldiers craned for his next words.

Zaitsev looked at Danilov. The commissar's pencil wiggled madly, recording these first sessions of the new Red Army sniper school. *Vasily Zaitsev, head sniper,* Danilov must be writing. *Hero.*

"As a Russian sniper, you'll have the following duties when you return to your units. You will hunt the most important targets you can find in this order: officers, artillery observers, scouts, mortar crews and machine gunners, antitank riflemen, and motorcycle messengers. Never give up your position for a shot on a lesser target if you think an officer will come your way with a little more patience.

"Your company commanders will assign your platoon leader the day's objective. You will advance to the front line and spearhead the attack by taking out the targets I just named in that order. After the attack has begun, you'll move to the flanks to protect against machine guns and mortars."

Zaitsev paused to let what he'd said sink in, though he knew he would have to repeat it several times before the day was out.

He rubbed his hands together. "Like the wolf in the taiga, the Red sniper has only one natural enemy." He said this as if sharing a secret with fellow conspirators. "Your counterpart is the German sniper. He is your nemesis and you are his. Despite the list of targets I gave you, an enemy sniper is always a priority."

He smiled at the Bear, who stood behind the men, smoking and looking into the distance as if across a great open span.

"Nothing," Zaitsev said, reaching for the Moisin-Nagant to bring the sight up to his eye, "absolutely nothing will excite you and endanger you like a duel to the death with another sniper."

Zaitsev squeezed the trigger. It clicked in the quiet chamber. "He is your worthiest opponent."

Viktor spat on the concrete floor and rubbed it in with his foot. He stepped to the middle of the group and stood next to Zaitsev. The two linked arms.

"And we're going to show you how to kill him," Viktor said.

Zaitsev patted his large friend on the back. "One bullet," he said, "one kill."

THAT AFTERNOON, THE RECRUITS STUDIED WHAT Zaitsev and Viktor had learned about enemy sniper tactics and abilities. It had become clear that the Nazi sharpshooters were not trained for the urban devastation of Stalingrad but rather for operations as part of their blitzkrieg tactics. They were accustomed to moving fast and furiously across open fields and around deserted, bombed-out cities. Where do you learn patience, Viktor wondered aloud, when you're simply running behind tanks, conquering whole nations at once, like Poland in a month or the useless, gutless French in a week?

The Germans made good use of darkening agents such as grease or dirt to deflect light and blend with their surroundings. They wrapped their muzzles with light or dark cloth. On one occasion, both Viktor and Zaitsev were fooled by a Nazi sniper who'd set up a false position by linking a wire to a rifle, then pulled his trigger from twenty meters away. Zaitsev had fired at the position, certain he had a kill. His reward was a bullet skipped off his helmet and a hard fall onto the seat of his pants.

The German snipers' shooting skills were lethal to five hundred meters. Though deadly, the snipers could also be careless and overconfident, often neglecting to move after a shot. They didn't husband their ammunition, sometimes firing two or three rounds at a single target from the same position, presenting a patient Red sniper with the chance to repay a miss with a hit. The Nazis frequently repeated deceptions, bouncing a helmet on a stick high above the breastwork three or four times an hour as if the Russian sniper were nothing more than a fish that would bite on any worm. At times Viktor had felt insulted by the Germans. They would smoke cigarettes or pipes after dark or throw dirt into the open while digging a shooting cell. They sometimes made unnecessary movements or noises. "Never rely on your adversary to make a mistake," Zaitsev told the recruits. "But give him plenty of room to do so. Then punish him for it."

Viktor reminded them: "No mistake is small if it gets your head blown off."

The German sniper worked in relative safety, usually two to three hundred meters from the front line. His four-hundred-meter shot would therefore penetrate only a hundred or so meters into the Russian rear. This tactic posed little threat to Red Army officers, who stayed mostly far behind the lines. But the new Russian sharpshooter, with his greater fieldcraft skills, would prowl under the enemy's nose along the front lines to reach an inattentive German colonel or general half a kilometer behind the action. "Because of this bold fact, even our women snipers," Zaitsev said, "will make better men."

The Nazi sharpshooters never worked at night, allowing the Russians to operate twelve hours a day without fear of being spotted. "I don't like hunting after dark," Zaitsev commented, but added with a laugh, "though Master Sergeant Medvedev is quite the night owl." Viktor regularly took his toll on enemy machine gunners imprudent enough to fire tracers, or on artillery spotters who fancied the green and red flares they lofted above the Russian flotillas on the Volga.

Zaitsev believed the fiercer conditions under which the Russians worked kept them sharp. By contrast, the German snipers' concentration was eroded by working exclusively from the rear and only under the sun. As an added benefit, the Red troops on the front line got a morale boost from fighting alongside their marksmen. The German foot soldier never saw his army's snipers.

"The Nazi snipers think they're safe just because they're in trenches far behind the lines," Zaitsev said. "They are not safe, even there. Why? Because they're still in Russia."

That's enough for today, Zaitsev thought. I don't know what else to tell them. In fact, I didn't know I knew so much myself.

Zaitsev glanced across the room at Danilov. Incredibly, the commissar had scribbled all morning and afternoon. Danilov looked up to meet Zaitsev's eyes. He closed his notebook and gave the OK sign. With both hands, he held up the notebook with satisfaction as if it were a trophy he'd won. Danilov hurried from the shop with his long coattails kicking up like dogs running at his sides.

Zaitsev clapped his hands. "Everyone up. We'll start tomorrow with marksmanship. For now, the hares will come with me. The bears will go with Sergeant Medvedev. We'll show you to your quarters. Let's go."

Fifteen recruits followed each of the sergeants up to the ground floor of the Lazur to separate corners of the building. Once the decision had been made to divide them, Zaitsev and Viktor wanted distinct identities for the two squads, with military objectives that best fit their physical abilities and personalities, and Danilov had approved of the idea. The bears would work more closely with the frontline troops, softening up resistance before attacks and protecting the 284th's flanks during operations. Their weapons, in addition to the sniper rifle, would include the submachine gun and grenade. These large men would also be trained in night sniping operations, Viktor's specialty. On the other hand, the hares were to be the division's assassins, smaller, more mobile men—and women—with the nerve and fieldcraft, in Viktor's words, to "crawl into the enemy's mouth and shoot out his teeth." The hares would learn Zaitsev's abilities at dissolving into the front line with iron patience and unerring one-shot killing.

Zaitsev ushered his group into a large, windowless room with a blanket hanging in the doorway. A lantern glowed in a corner. Three buckets of water sat next to a tin washbasin. Beyond these, the room was empty.

"Dinner will be brought in a few hours. Get to know each other, because soon you'll be teaming up."

On the way out of the plant, Zaitsev met Viktor.

"What do you think?" the Bear asked when they had ducked into a trench behind the shelter of the huge building. The sun was almost down. The shadows were gone; an edgy chill crept from the ground. Zaitsev knew Viktor's routine: he'd return to their bunker, eat a hurried snack, read a few articles in today's *In Our Country's Defense* or *Red Star*, take a nap, and head into the night.

Zaitsev looked at his friend. "Well," he said, "before the first shot is fired, it's hard to tell. But I can tell you I'm glad I'm not a German."

"That's good." Viktor bent low to walk beneath the lip of the trench. Such a big man, Zaitsev thought. Not built well for this sniper business. How does he do it?

Zaitsev laughed. "I'm goddammed glad I'm not a bear, either."

Viktor grabbed a handful of dirt and threw it at Zaitsev's back. The Hare ran full tilt through the trench all the way back to their bunker, with the Bear growling at his heels.

NINE

MINUTES BEFORE MIDNIGHT, ZAITSEV ENTERED the hares' quarters.

"How are my rabbits?" His lantern threw amber shades against their blinking faces.

The recruits sat up on their bedrolls. Good, Zaitsev thought. They can sleep. An important skill for a sniper. Rest when and where you can.

He crouched. "I have a mission." Dark tendrils of shadow played on their faces when he lowered the lamp to the floor. "After school was out today, division head-quarters sent me orders. It seems some Nazi prisoners have pinpointed a German forward HQ. Command asked if I could take some snipers, set up positions on no-man's-land, and see if we couldn't get lucky with a few shots in the morning. I told them yes, we could do that, but I had a better idea. Why drill holes in just a few Nazi officers? Why not take care of them all at once?"

Little Chekov spoke up. "Dynamite 'em."

Zaitsev pointed at the private. "Trainee Chekov gets a star. Exactly. I'll take four of you with me. We leave imme-diately. I have the satchel charges assembled, and I've got a map of the location. Volunteers?"

All hands went up. Some recruits got to their knees to

raise their hands higher. Zaitsev tapped on the heads of the soldiers he wanted on the mission: Chekov, the poacher, a superb shot and intelligent; Kostikev, the silent Siberian killer; Kulikov, the most quiet and vigilant crawler in the class, who could literally blend with the rubble; and the resistance fighter, Chernova.

Each stood and walked to the doorway. Zaitsev turned to those remaining. "Get some sleep. You'll all have your chances. We'll be back before sunup."

The four followed Zaitsev out into the dark October hush. The nervous crackle of a far-off rifle or a machine gun's burst were the only noises to upset the chilly stillness. Zaitsev walked beside the high wall, holding his lantern low. The shadows of his squad lagged on the wall behind them.

Zaitsev put the lamp down. Waiting in a heap beside the wall were six backpacks and five regular-issue rifles. From his pocket, Zaitsev produced a greasepaint pot.

"Grease up," he told them. Chekov dug out a gob with two fingers and passed the pot around.

They darkened their hands and faces while Zaitsev spread his map beside the hissing light. He stabbed his finger onto the paper.

"This is the Lazur. Here are the outbuildings of the Red October plant. There," he said, and pointed again, "is the Stalingrad Flying School. And here between the two is a row of ice warehouses. In this one, on the top floor, is the German HQ."

He ran his finger along the map across the northern portion of the rail yard, which engulfed the Lazur on three sides. "We'll crawl north across no-man's-land. Our outposts are here and here. They've been alerted so that we don't get shot in the backsides. We'll enter the building from the south, climb to the third floor, plant our charges, light them, and get out."

He looked up from the map at the shiny black faces and white eyes of the recruits. All were looking down to study the layout—all except Chernova, who stared at him. He smiled at her.

"Clean as you please, partisan. Right?"

"Right."

"Let's do it." Zaitsev folded the map. "Each of you take a rifle and a satchel. You're carrying the dynamite. I'm carrying the fuses." He hoisted two of the packs over his shoulder. "If anything happens to me, make sure you take my packs."

He put out the lamp and left it beside the wall. He pulled Chekov beside him. "You know the way?"

The private nodded. "In the last two months I've spent a few years of my life in the Red October. I know all the ways there, Chief Master Sergeant. I know the icehouses, too."

Zaitsev patted Chekov on the back. The soldier was shorter than him by half a head, and he had delicate features and black hair. Chekov possessed the confident manner of an athlete; he'll make a good sniper, Zaitsev thought. He's quirky, cool. He'll be hard to predict.

"Good. You lead, Chekov." Zaitsev touched Kostikev on the arm. "You next. If we meet trouble, you take care of it."

The Siberian fingered the knives hanging from his belt, one near each hand. He said nothing but slung the rifle and satchel over his shoulder. He stepped close at Chekov's back.

"Nikolay," Zaitsev called to Kulikov. "If something happens to me, you're in charge. I want you in the middle. Go."

He turned to Chernova, her hair golden even in the night.

"You go in front of me, partisan. You'll check the work

to make sure the charges are set right. When we're ready, you'll light the fuse. Danilov will love that."

The girl's brows arched while she hefted her rifle. "Is that why I'm along? To be in one of Danilov's articles about you?"

Zaitsev tugged on her arm. "Do your job well and it could be an article about you."

The five soldiers walked in single file for a hundred meters to the north. At a signal from Zaitsev, they dropped into a trench leading to the edge of the rail yard. At the end of the trench, they were met by six guards posted behind heavy machine guns trained across no-man's-land. With a nod to Chekov, Zaitsev sent the lithe point man over the breastwork and onto the three-hundred-meter-wide plain of cratered earth and twisting rails.

At ten-second intervals, Zaitsev motioned for the next in line to crawl out of the trench. "Stay in Chekov's tracks."

Once all four hares were in the rail yard, Zaitsev slung his satchels over his back and greased up his own face and hands. He cradled his rifle and climbed out of the trench, lifting an oiled, dark thumb to the guards.

Once on his belly, he could barely make out Chernova's legs wriggling ten meters ahead. Neither she nor any of the other trainees made a sound.

For ten minutes, Zaitsev crawled in a crooked line, his eyes locked on Chernova's heels. He grew irked at the zigs and zags Chekov led them through. But as the route proceeded through craters, beneath rail cars, and behind debris, Zaitsev smiled admiringly at the craft of Anatoly Chekov's choices. Slow, patient, and silent.

A white flare shot up straight overhead. Zaitsev dug his chin into the dirt. Ahead of him, Chernova, Kulikov, and Kostikev were still as rocks. He was certain they were almost invisible against the dark, rippling dirt.

The flare twinkled and faded, riding a slow fall beneath a tiny parachute. Under the gleam of the drifting light, Zaitsev looked two hundred meters ahead to the huge outline of the Red October plant. Fifty meters to his right, almost astride their position, was the Stalingrad Flight School. Only forty meters more along this course until they would turn left; then the icehouse was just a short distance down that street.

The flare floated behind a row of ghostly ruins and extinguished itself. Zaitsev followed Chernova over the crest of a crater. The hares were there waiting for him.

Zaitsev pointed at a four-story building thirty meters away. The south wall of the building was missing. The stairwell to the upper floors was completely exposed to the outside.

Chekov nodded. The icehouse.

Zaitsev tapped Kostikev's leg. "You go first. Leave your rifle and satchel here. Light a cigarette from the second-floor landing."

Kostikev handed his pack to Chekov. Chernova took his rifle.

Kostikev pulled one of his knives from its sheath and gripped it in his mouth like a picture of a Turk pirate. He smiled at Zaitsev, his fellow Siberian, showing a flash of gold in his teeth. The stringy muscles in his neck stood out like buttresses under his jaw.

"See you in a minute," he uttered around the knife. These were the first words Zaitsev had heard him speak all day.

Zaitsev settled on the rim of the crater to watch the man disappear into the rubble of the fallen wall. Minutes passed. Then, out of the shadows on the second-floor landing, a dark form walked to the ledge. The shape turned and shuffled around a corner without lighting a cigarette.

A minute later a second form appeared on the landing and lit a cigarette. It inhaled deeply, giving off a glowing dot of orange, then flicked the cigarette down onto the debris below to bounce once in a shower of sparks.

Zaitsev whispered, "Stay low to the building. Then up the stairs fast. No noise. Nikolay—move."

Kulikov hefted his own rifle and Kostikev's and slid out of the crater. Chekov grabbed Kostikev's satchel and followed.

"Partisan," Zaitsev hissed, "go."

He waited until Chernova slid ahead of him with her rifle and backpack. He followed her over the rim of the crater.

He heard nothing, only the faintest scraping in the rocks from his scurrying hares. At the base of the steps, Kulikov squatted in the shadows, guarding. Zaitsev followed Chernova quickly up the steps, both on tiptoe. He looked out of the stairwell into the open air where a wall should have been. His heart pounded in his hands, which were clutching his rifle. He was unaccustomed to being so exposed in his hunting, as he was now in this stairwell. There was no camouflage, no trench, nothing to cloak him but silence and the gray-black night.

Two steps ahead, Chernova recoiled. She had just reached the top stair and stepped onto the second-floor landing. The girl stumbled back against Zaitsev. She fumbled to raise her gun.

He reached his arm up to the girl's waist and pulled her down onto his step. He flipped his rifle over, stock first, and lunged forward, the rifle poised to strike.

There in the dark, standing against the wall, was a Nazi guard. His rifle was slung over his shoulder. His helmeted head stared out past the demolished wall. Zaitsev knew what had happened. It was what he'd ordered, but with a flourish. He rubbed his foot against the toe of the German's boot and felt the slickness of blood on the landing.

Zaitsev reached under the chin and felt the haft of Kostikev's knife. The Nazi had been tacked to a wooden timber in the wall with his head resting upright on the knife, his chin on the white bone handle.

Chernova stepped up on the landing. Kulikov arrived on the steps below. He'd hurried up from his post on the first floor at the slight sounds of the commotion on the landing.

Zaitsev heard a "psst" from the steps to the next floor. Kostikev's gold teeth twinkled in the center of a loose grin.

"I had nowhere to put him, Vasha. I didn't want you to trip over him." The assassin shrugged, then climbed the steps.

"Guard the rear," Zaitsev said to Chernova. "Tell Kulikov to bring up his satchel. I'll come get you when the charges are laid." He followed Kostikev up the steps.

On the third floor, Chekov led the others into the middle of a large, open room. Thick wooden pillars stood on the outer reaches of an ancient oak floor. This is an old building, Zaitsev observed. It'll come down nicely.

They laid the four satchels in each corner. Kulikov hooked up the charges and fuses in the center of the room. Zaitsev's watch read 2:50.

"Ready?" he whispered to Nikolay.

"One minute."

Zaitsev crept down the steps to the second-floor landing. On his way, he heard not a whisper but a command.

"Hände hoch!"

His stomach tightened. Adrenaline needles welded his fists to his rifle stock. His lips curled in an unspoken curse. Chernova had been surprised by a Nazi on the stairwell, a guard Kostikev had missed. She was certainly at this moment staring down the barrel of a gun. The mission and all their lives were in jeopardy. The next five seconds would save them or lose them.

Zaitsev slipped down the steps quietly as he could. Reaching the turn, he peeked around the corner to the landing.

The soldier was frozen in place, his right arm extended to a pistol reaching at the girl's head. Zaitsev guessed the Nazi couldn't decide what to do next. What was he going to do with his prisoner? The man had to know there were more Russians in the building; the Reds wouldn't send one woman behind enemy lines like this. His dead mate hanging beside him, nailed to a timber, throat slit and blood dripping, was a fearsome sign. Should he run and save his own skin or take his prisoner down the steps? Or up? If he shouted for help, who might answer his call first?

The German shook the pistol in Chernova's face. *"Wo sind die Russen? Wo sind sie?"*

Again, Zaitsev turned over his rifle, readying it to smash the German if he got the chance. A shot would bring attention.

Hidden just behind the wall, he whispered, "Partisan."

Instantly, a dull thud was followed by a moan of pain. Zaitsev leaped, his rifle over his head, ready to lash out. There, doubled over but still standing, was the German soldier, with Chernova's foot clenched high between his legs. The guard's pistol clattered on the landing, then fell to the street below.

Before Zaitsev could surge forward to crush his rifle against the Nazi's head, Chernova leaped at the man's throat like a panther, pressing deep into his windpipe. The soldier gurgled and fought back violently. Zaitsev swung the stock of his rifle past Chernova's shoulder, hard into the Nazi's nose. The soldier collapsed backward and lay staring up through watering and panicky eyes. Zaitsev raised his rifle again and hammered it down into the soldier's face. The skull split against the concrete. He rolled the Nazi with his boot to the edge of the wall.

Chernova stood back, her hands clenched. Zaitsev brought his face close. "Come on," he whispered. "Fast."

The two sprang up the steps to the third floor. The charges were set in the dynamite. Chekov stood holding the central fuse.

Zaitsev and Chernova hurried to his side. The others moved to the doorway. "You do it," Zaitsev said. She took his matchbox and lit the fuse. It sparked to life. "Go!" Zaitsev called in a full voice to the men standing by the door. "Go!"

Forgetting all caution, the hares pounded down the stairwell, their boots clomping on the concrete. On the second-floor landing, Zaitsev passed Kostikev standing beside the nailed-up German. Kostikev yanked out his knife; the corpse crumpled.

They raced down the stairs into the cold open air. Behind them, voices shouted from overhead. Machine-gun fire crackled while they leaped over piles of bricks to speed through the rubble. Bullets ricocheted in the dark, though none came close enough to slow the hares down. They pumped their arms and feet and emerged into a narrow street.

"Go! Go!" Zaitsev called to the sprinters on all sides of him. Almost to the moment he'd expected, a roar shattered the night. The ruins suddenly shifted their shadows, flashing red on their wrecked, sad faces, winking at Zaitsev and the hares galloping straight for their own lines down an avenue leading to the rail yard. The rumblings of the explosion and the collapsing building rolled through the dead structures to veil their dash across no-man's-land and into the safety of the Red Army's forward trenches.

The five plunged onto the floor of a trench. They breathed hard, clutching their chests. Exhilarated, Zaitsev looked at the bobbing faces of the recruits. Through his heaving rib cage, he found his voice.

"Damn!" he said. "Damn! You think we used enough dynamite?"

Chekov and Kulikov patted each other on the back, laughing and breathless. Kostikev smiled his gilded grin. Tania coughed, struggling for air. She reached out to Kostikev's shoulder. She pulled her hand back, bloodied.

"Don't worry," Kostikev told her, beaming, as the others quieted. "I'm in love with a nurse. I get to see her now."

A guard in the trench handed down two bottles of vodka. Zaitsev gave the first swallow to Kostikev. The wounded man drank deeply, then reached the bottle back to Zaitsev. The clear glass was smirched with Kostikev's scarlet handprint.

Zaitsev looked at Kulikov. "Nikolay."

Kulikov helped Kostikev to his feet. Zaitsev gave them the vodka bottle. Arm in arm, the two men walked away down the darkness of the trench.

Zaitsev stood. He could not see the icehouse but could tell by a licking glow against the sky where the building had stood.

Chekov spoke. "I guess I'll get some rest, Chief Master Sergeant. Good night, Tania."

"Good night, Chekov."

The little soldier yawned. Leaving, he handed Zaitsev the other vodka bottle.

Zaitsev stood next to Chernova. The two of them were alone except for the silent guard at his machine gun. They watched the jumping light of the burning icehouse.

"A good night's work, don't you think, partisan?"

She spoke without turning her head. "My name is Tania, if you please, Chief Master Sergeant."

"All right, then," he said gently, "Tania."

He took a swallow, then laid the bottle on the breast-work.

"Good night, Tania," he said, and walked away up the trench.

TEN

TANIA WOKE IN A TORPOR ON HER BEDROLL. Zaitsev's boot nudged her gently in the dark. A steaming cup of tea was waved under her nose. She accepted it, and Zaitsev told her that Kostikev's wound was only a grazed shoulder. A few stitches, a roll with his nurse, and he'd be good as new.

At dawn, the hares and bears again assembled in the giant Lazur basement. A moist coolness seeped from the concrete floor and block walls. On the far wall a hundred meters away, a row of white circles had been painted one meter above the ground. The circles were in groups of three. The first circle was small and barely visible, perhaps the size of a fist. The ring to the left of it was slightly larger, and the third was twice the size of the first. Above each grouping was a number, one through thirty. A row of barrels and crates lay before the near wall.

Sergeants Zaitsev and Medvedev told the recruits to bring their Moisin-Nagant 91/30 sniper rifles and take a rifle and lie behind the crates and barrels. Each was given a number and told to aim at the largest circle. That circle, Zaitsev said, represented a chest shot at four hundred meters.

After the hares and bears had slid behind cover and

leveled their scopes, the two sergeants sat behind them. Tania smelled their cigarettes. She heard laughter from Medvedev. Maybe Zaitsev was telling him about the ice-house mission the night before.

The recruits were left behind the barrels and crates for an hour, eyes straining down their sights. If one turned to speak to the sergeants or even take an eye away from the scope, Medvedev delivered a loud lecture on patience and stamina.

Through her crosshairs, Tania watched the dawn light swell at the far end of the shop. After the first ten minutes, the white circle had begun to rise and fall; her heartbeat had entered her hands. She'd slowed her breathing and eased her grip. Finally, long after her legs and buttocks had begun to tingle from the chilly concrete floor, she heard Zaitsev walk down the line behind her.

"One at a time," he said quietly, "when I call your number."

He stood behind the recruits. Several minutes passed.

"Twenty-eight. Fire."

A shot rang to Tania's right. She held her breath to bring her target to the center of her crosshairs.

"Fifteen." Another shot.

"Ten." Chekov, at Tania's right elbow, fired. The bang made her jerk left. Immediately, Zaitsev called out, "Nine," Tania's number. She corrected a millimeter, squeezed the trigger, and took the jolt, then reacquired the target quickly. A puff drifted on the brick wall dead in the heart of the circle. She smiled on the rifle stock and held still while other numbers were called and more shots barked in the shop.

After the drill, Zaitsev and Medvedev inspected the circles. When they returned, they gave the volunteers permission to fire freely at the targets to practice aim and trigger pressure.

"Stuff something in your ears," Zaitsev told the recruits, who dug in their pockets for bits of paper and cigarette butts.

The morning wore on, and Tania fired over a hundred rounds. Her shoulder ached as if there were a bullet in it. Each pull of the trigger seemed to carry a different lesson shouted by the two instructors pacing behind the firing line. You're pulling too hard. You're drifting to the right. To the left. Get your cheek off the stock. Relax. You're too loose. Quicker. Take your time.

After an hour, the instructors again inspected the targets. When they returned with serious miens, those trainees who'd erred sufficiently were set back on the line for another session. Tania was not one of them, nor was Fedya.

She rose on legs like India rubber and wobbled from the crates to slouch against a wall. Fedya sat next to her, and she thought how good he looked. He hadn't shaved in the three days since they'd been flung into the Volga. His new uniform was dirty. His big face was a little less the all-seeing, all-worrying poet, the crazy goose, and showed some of the steel of the sniper volunteer. Something in his eyes was gone; the big stare, the look of wonder, white and broad like an opened book. Now he held his rifle across his lap, excitement on his body.

"Good shots, eh? We're both good shots," he said.

Tania touched his knee. "I didn't know you could handle a rifle that well."

Fedya sat straighter. "The Bear took me out last night."

"He what? What did you do?" Tania couldn't believe it. While she crawled with the hares, Fedya had roamed the darkness with Medvedev. She'd been eager to tell Fedya of her own adventure at the icehouse but now swallowed it. She motioned with her hands as if reeling in yarn, to draw out his story.

Fedya shifted his weight. "Sergeant Medvedev said since I was the only freshman in the group, he could teach me from the beginning and I wouldn't have anything to unlearn. At midnight we went through the trenches to the Dolgi Ravine. A machine gunner on the ridge was firing at the wounded being evacuated to the river. Sergeant Medvedev let me shoot him."

Tania leaned forward. "Just like that? You shot him?"

The poet from Moscow had killed his first German and on the morning after possessed so few words for it. Tania was amazed. She thought it would have torn his heart out.

Fedya ran his hand through his hair. "I don't know, Tania. It was . . . he was shooting at the wounded and the nurses. I got so angry. I didn't have any problem shooting him. I just . . ." Fedya looked at his feet.

After a moment, he arranged his rifle in his lap. "Yes," he said, bringing his eyes up to hers, "I shot him."

Fedya pulled from his pocket a fresh black notebook. He showed her the first page.

"There it is. October twenty-sixth, 1942. Two-fifteen A.M. Machine gunner. Three hundred meters. Chest shot. Dolgi Ravine. Witness, V. Medvedev."

Tania flipped through the clean white pages. Each page a life. A German life. A broken stick. I want my own notebook, she thought with envy. I'll fill up fifty of these.

Fedya tucked the booklet away. "I heard about your raid on the icehouse last night. The sergeant and I heard the blast. It was something."

Fedya waited for her to speak.

"I made a bet with myself you were in on that," he added.

She nodded. "It was something."

He reached his hand out to her. She folded her arms tightly over her chest and looked away at the others in the room, some walking about, some sitting in groups, others still with their attention fixed on their rifles. She shook her head, almost trembling.

"Are you all right?" He lowered his hand.

"Yes."

She rose, then leaned down and brought her face close.

"Don't ever touch me in front of the others. Ever."

"I'm sorry."

"I can't do it, Fedya." She turned away, then stopped and whispered to him angrily. "I must be as good as the others—better, even. And I will *not* be viewed by them as just a woman. I will not be a nurse or go work a radio in a bunker. That's where I'll end up if I'm seen holding your hand. There's time. There are places. But never until I say so. Do you understand?"

She looked into Fedya's face, wanting and expecting to find a ripple of pain there. She saw concern. She saw purpose instead of hesitation.

What have I done? she thought. The boy is in love with me.

"Tania, I only wanted to make sure you were all right." He rose also, shouldering his rifle, and turned to rejoin the bears. "And no, I don't understand or agree."

She stopped him. "Fedya?"

"Yes?"

She quietly asked, "Have you told anyone I'm an American?"

"No. And do you know why I haven't?"

He paced back to her the distance he had walked away. Close to her, his large chest near, she felt heat; the kill had not made him colder but had inflamed him. The poet, the scared boy, was impassioned with a gun in his hands.

Fedya spoke slowly. "Because if I did, they *would* treat you differently. They'd protect you and parade you like a show pony. I have enough sense to know that, Tania. Give me credit."

He spun and walked off, his rifle clutched in one mitt.

After thirty minutes, Zaitsev and Medvedev ordered everyone back behind the crates and barrels. The intermediate-sized circles represented a head shot at 300 meters. The smallest circle was also a head shot but at 450 meters, the maximum distance at which they could expect to work. These targets were to be fired upon at will.

"Begin," Medvedev called, and walked behind the trainees. Zaitsev stood near Tania for five minutes. Through binoculars, he watched the blooms of brick dust issue from her target. With each bullet, words of encouragement and invectives flowed into her ears while Zaitsev, and Medvedev elsewhere along the line, molded the volunteers as quickly as possible into snipers to bedevil the enemy.

TANIA LOWERED HER RIFLE. SHE WAS CERTAIN that she could not physically tolerate firing one more round. Her elbows, knees, eyes, and especially her right shoulder were pummeled and swollen. Her hips felt locked. She had to roll out of her sitting position onto her stomach and push up to get off the floor.

The trainees limped to the mess line. Each was given a bowl of warm gruel, a plate of sliced meat with bread, and a tin cup of tea. She sat on a crate and looked into the queue where Fedya stood. He nodded. She pointed at the crate next to her.

She wanted to dilute her angry comments of the morning. Perhaps there was a way to make Fedya understand her feelings without cramming them into his ears with such force. They had made love. It had been good, passionate, a release. But what baggage did the act carry? Did it mean they were joined, their spirits entwined the way their bodies had been? Had they been consecrated by Fedya as lovers, turned into pretty images in one of his poems? Or were they nothing more than what Tania felt them to be, two warriors on the edge of a battlefield sharing the last shreds of life left to them? Tania had not visited the depths of love while rocking on the bed with big Fedya. Yes, they had both cried out. But he had called her name.

Tania watched him collect his rations. She saw the agreeable confidence of his motions and thought, There's no room in me for Fedya's innocent love. I am full with sorrow and bitterness enough for a hundred hearts. I'll be his friend. Perhaps I'll sleep with him again. But I will not fall in love. He'll accept that. Or he'll step aside.

Before Fedya could join Tania, Danilov hopped in front of her. The commissar inclined his head in a mannered greeting and sat on the crate next to her. The crate groaned when the rotund little *politrook* unbuttoned his greatcoat. He took out a pencil and opened his notebook in his lap. A blur of scrawl covered every line and margin as he flipped to one of the few blank pages.

"My dear," he began, "I am Captain Danilov. I believe you know who I am and my own mission in this sniper unit. Of course, I do not have the honor of actually being a sniper. But I have taken a great interest in the activities of this first class of trainees. I will be describing your activities and lessons for the rest of the army through my articles in *In Our Country's Defense*. Perhaps you have read one or two of them?"

"No, comrade commissar."

"Well," he replied with a smile, his single eyebrow a cloud over his dark eyes, "maybe you'll read this next one. You will be in it for your part in last night's icehouse raid. What can you tell me?"

Tania looked to Zaitsev, who was speaking with some of the hares. She wished he'd save her from this unctuous, dangerous man perched beside her with his legs kicked out in front of him, croaking like a toad. She knew that with a word this commissar could send her out of the sniper school to a noncombatant role. And Fedya was right; if this commissar learned an American was fighting in their number, she would become a curio, a political and propaganda coup, too valuable for the *rodina* to risk her taking a bullet.

"Have you spoken with Comrade Zaitsev?" she asked. "He was the leader of the mission."

"We have spoken. It was he who insisted I talk to you. Apparently you killed a Nazi with your bare hands last night. And you lit the fuses that blew up the headquarters."

Tania looked at the commissar's little feet. His ebony boots were shiny. She wondered, How does he keep them that way?

Danilov continued. "What do you think of Comrade Zaitsev? And what do you think about being one of his hares?"

Tania searched for something to say. To her surprise, there was more than she expected in her storehouse of words. She realized they were not the words the commissar wanted to hear. He expects me to give him a heroic quote, she thought. How magnificent Zaitsev was in leading our most dangerous mission last night. What an honor it is to serve under such a man. I can't tell this commissar the truth, that I have no idea whether Zaitsev is a hero or a strutting coward; he seems to me to enjoy his growing status as a headline for *In Our Country's Defense*, one of the many new and improved icons of the Russian cause. No, I can't say true words to this little Chekist, that I also find Zaitsev disturbing, that I want to touch his veined hands and flat Siberian face; when his voice tells me to move or stop, to aim left or jump right, my body follows. How badly I want for him to be the hero that Danilov is constructing.

"Comrade Zaitsev is a bold man," she said, and the commissar set upon his notebook with his flying pencil. "He is indeed a hero, and all those who fight by his side will do heroic deeds. I am honored to be a sniper, one of the hares, under him."

"And after the building blew up last night, you ran, simply ran, through the streets to reach the Russian lines?"

"The explosion covered our sounds. I couldn't hear myself run. Chief Master Sergeant Zaitsev ran ahead of us. We followed. It wasn't my decision to make. But it was the right decision."

Danilov closed his notebook. "One last question, Private Chernova. In these dangerous times, it is important that Russia is defended by, let us say, committed fighters. As a woman, you would die for the *rodina*? You are prepared for that?"

The Communist bastard, she thought. His question carries the same stench as the Green Hats' queries on the Stalingrad road.

"Comrade commissar, I would not die for the *rodina* as a woman. I would die as a Russian." Tania cocked her head as if aiming her sniper rifle. "And I certainly will not die a coward. Comrade."

Danilov tucked his notebook under his arm and yanked in his legs. He stood from the crate. He was barely taller when standing than Tania was seated.

"Of course, my dear." He buttoned his coat with one hand. He stopped and reached the hand to Tania. When he spoke, the dramatic and false qualities of his voice were gone.

"Of course. Comrade."

Tania shook the flabby hand. She watched Danilov walk away. Zaitsev looked across the room. He nodded to Danilov when the little commissar bustled past him.

Tania replaced her spoon into her boot. She laid her plate down and walked back to the firing line. Three other soldiers were taking the time for extra practice. Their shots echoed in the great hall while she knelt behind her crate. She brushed aside empty casings, spilling them to clatter across the floor. She stuffed paper wads in her ears and threw back the bolt to send home another round. Fixing her eye through the scope on the smallest circle, she curled the second fold of her index finger over the trigger. She watched the target bob, riding her heartbeat. She waited, her breathing shallow, for her hand to steady. In seconds the target grew dead still under the crosshairs. It seemed huge, unmissable, summoning the bullet. She pulled the trigger slowly, evenly. The rifle cracked and recoiled into her tender shoulder. Through the scope, she found the sudden red breadth of the brick wall, struck in the center of the smallest circle. She pulled back the bolt to fire again.

THE AFTERNOON SESSION WAS BEGUN WITH Zaitsev's call: "Hares! Let's go! Bring your rifles!"

He led them up the basement steps with his rifle slung across his shoulders like a yoke. The recruits followed him to the Lazur plant's first floor. They wove through the maze of twisted metal and charred ceiling timbers to a row of sooty windows facing the no-man's-land rail yard. Zaitsev halted a few steps from one of the large openings; the window sash had long ago been blown in. His boots crunched on broken glass.

He pointed out the window at the German-held buildings beyond no-man's-land. The air drifting in was brisk, the Russian winter's first white blossom.

"You are looking west." Zaitsev spoke. "Right now, the sun is behind you. Whenever possible, set up your shots with the sun at your back. It makes it harder for your enemy to find you. Also, it prevents glare off your scope."

Tania looked out at the crater-filled rail yard, across which she and Fedya had crawled two nights ago, and the railman's shed and the trench they'd tumbled into. Now, in the afternoon light, she saw a dozen Russian machine guns, manned at fifty-meter intervals in the trench, aimed across the yard. Fedya and I could have collected a few bullets that night, she thought back. *Nicht schiessen.*

On all fours, Zaitsev crept to the lip of the window to set his rifle on the sill. He took from his pocket a pair of gloves, which he'd lashed together with string; he laid them on the sill. "Make yourself some sort of shooting bag," he said over his shoulder. "It'll keep your barrel from sliding."

He gazed down his scope. Without moving his head, he said, "See the second German tank, the one with the track blown off?"

Zaitsev fired. In the distance, Tania heard an impact, metal on metal, *ping,* ring through the report of the rifle.

The Hare turned from his shot. "The iron cross on the front fender of that tank is exactly four hundred meters from this wall. This row of windows is called the 'shooting gallery.' You will come here to calibrate your sights regularly or whenever you have any doubts about your rifle's accuracy. Approach the windows carefully, two at a time. Set your sights for the proper distance and wait for my order to fire."

Tania crawled to the window in front of her. Beside her was the Armenian woman, Slepkinian. She set her scope for four hundred meters and took careful aim at the Nazi tank's insignia.

Zaitsev slid back from his window and stood. He raised his binoculars and walked behind the two hares at the first window.

"Shaikin. Fire."

Tania braced at the report of the rifle to her right. From the field she heard nothing to indicate a hit.

"Nikolay."

Kulikov, next to Shaikin, fired. He, too, missed.

Zaitsev walked to the next window. Again, he instructed the trainees to fire, one at a time. Each, in his turn, missed.

Zaitsev said, "Partisan." She held the black cross on the tank's fender dead in her sights and squeezed smoothly. The rifle kicked. She listened for the *ping* of the hit. There was nothing.

After they had all fired, not one of the hares had struck the insignia. Zaitsev spoke calmly from behind. There was a satisfaction in his voice. Some ruse of his had worked.

"Firing at a wall in a basement is, as you can see, not the same as shooting at a target in the open air. Out here on the battlefield, you must take into account the wind, the humidity, the temperature, whether you are shooting uphill or downhill, even the time of day. Most of you have experience hunting. But none of you is accustomed to firing with a telescopic sight over these kinds of distances. You must develop the shooting instincts of the sniper. You must read the signs the terrain and nature give you. Now look through your sights at the target."

Tania fixed her crosshairs on the tank's insignia. Zaitsev's boots ground on the floor behind her.

"Look just above the fender. Today is cool but bright. The fender is dark. That means it's going to collect heat. You'll see heat waves rising off it. Which direction are the heat waves moving, left or right?"

Several voices answered. "Left."

"Yes. This tells you the wind is blowing from right to left. The waves are barely moving, so the wind is slight. But you're firing across a wide, open plain. You must reason that the wind is blowing unimpeded. Were it humid, or early in the morning after a cold night, you'd need to adapt your aim for those differences as well. Next, you're shooting slightly downhill. Take that into account. The trajectory of your bullet will decay more slowly and you will overshoot. The same is true when you're firing uphill;

your bullet will sail and you'll overshoot. Now turn around."

Tania lowered her rifle. Zaitsev held a bullet in his fingers straight out from his shoulder.

"When you're firing a round across a level plane, do you know how long the bullet is in the air?"

Zaitsev dropped the bullet. It clattered on the floor in a fraction of a second.

"That's how long. Your telescopic sights do more than magnify your target. They help you give the proper loft to your bullet for the distance you're shooting. This keeps the bullet in the air longer. You must learn to help your scope do its job by taking into account all the factors your bullet has to fight through to reach its target. Turn around and try again, on my signal. Think it through, set it up, then fire."

Fourteen rifle bolts rammed new cartridges into their chambers. This time, when the shots rang out at Zaitsev's command, Tania heard the *ping, ping* of many of her squad bouncing rounds off the Nazi tank below.

"Good!" Zaitsev called out. "Good shooting, hares! Let the Nazi bastards in those buildings out there hear you."

Tania set her scope to 425 meters, subtracting the one eighth required for shooting downhill. She allowed for windage by granting the right-left wind a millimeter. She waited in the midst of the rifle shots around her. Zaitsev gave her the word. She pulled the trigger evenly. The rifle punched into her sore shoulder.

Ping.

AFTER AN HOUR AT THE SHOOTING GALLERY, the bears walked through the rubble behind them. Zaitsev called the hares away from the windows, telling them to sit and watch quietly.

Like Zaitsev before him, Sergeant Medvedev lectured

his group on the advantages of keeping the sun at their backs when setting up a shot. The big Bear called their attention to the tank on no-man's-land. He explained its significance, then moved carefully to the window sill. In seconds, he lined up his sniper rifle and clanged a bullet off the iron cross.

The hares snickered amongst themselves without rebuke from Zaitsev while one by one the bears missed the target. Medvedev grimaced at them, but it served only to dampen their chuckles, not stop them.

After the dropped-bullet demonstration and the lesson on aiming, the bears began finding the target. The metal-on-metal sound of striking bullets rang in the rail yard below.

Once Medvedev was satisfied with the bears' marksmanship, he called them away from the windows.

"Come sit beside your comrades, the laughing bunnies."

Fedya lowered his large frame beside Tania. He crossed his legs and laid his rifle across his lap.

Zaitsev knelt at the front of the assembled trainees.

"This is the end of the second day of your sniper training. Now you know just about everything Master Sergeant Medvedev and I can teach you. You can only add to your knowledge by what you teach yourselves on the battlefield. Practice often, until the windage and distance rules become second nature. And don't forget: learn not only from yourself but from your enemy. I'll spare you any more wisdom. I know you're anxious to use your new rifles on the Nazis. Tomorrow each of you will take part in your first mission as a sniper."

Fedya whispered to Tania, "Not me. It'll be my second."

Medvedev joined Zaitsev at the front of the trainees. He looked to be the essence of the Russian fighter, big, dark, determined. Beside him, Zaitsev seemed small and light, yet like an engine, burning from the inside. They were day and night, these two. But Tania understood their reputations; they might well be the most lethal pair in all the Red Army.

Medvedev began. "Tonight, Sokolov's Forty-fifth Infantry is crossing the Volga. At least two battalions will be here by dawn. They've been given orders to keep the enemy away from the river between the Barricades and Red October plants. German machine gunners have moved to within five hundred meters of the Volga. That places our last ferry landing directly under fire. If we don't secure this area, the Nazi infantry will follow behind the machine guns and we'll lose another portion of the riverfront. Tonight you'll move to positions on the southern side of this corridor to shield the flanks of the Forty-fifth while they get into place in the morning. Chief Master Sergeant Zaitsev and I will come get you at midnight to take you to your positions. For now, you're dismissed. Go back to your quarters or go down to the shop and take some more practice shots. And get some rest."

Both groups rose and shouldered their rifles. Fedya stood tall next to Tania. Zaitsev and Medvedev left, wending their way into the rubble. The hares and the bears followed.

Tania said to Fedya, "Stay here."

He sat while Tania joined the group heading for the stairs. After walking in the rear of the line for a minute, she doubled back. She found him seated at the foot of a window, looking over the rail yard through his scope.

Tania sat next to him. She brought up her own rifle and surveyed the field with him.

"Do you see the railman's shed?" he asked. "It looks so close through the scope. I can almost see the curtains you were going to put up for me."

Tania moved her reticle across the shed's roof. It did not seem close to her. It looked and felt far away.

"Fedushka." She lowered her rifle. He continued to scan the battlefield. The rifle looks good in his big palms, she thought. He holds it well.

She laid her hand on his shoulder. He lowered the scope.

"Fedushka. Tomorrow morning we go into battle. It starts for us." She added softly, "Let's say our goodbyes now."

He set his rifle down. His gaze went into his hands.

"Please," she said. "Please, I can't carry anything more. Don't add to my weight." She took his hands in her own. "Another time, Fyodor Ivanovich. Maybe another world." She smiled. "Say goodbye to me."

Tania rose and stepped back from the open window to face no-man's-land; beyond it lay the horribly scarred city, the enemy running through its veins. She put her hands on the sides of his head and kissed him on the forehead. She rubbed his hair.

"Tania," he said quietly, "I can't."

"You will, Fedya. Whether you can or not doesn't matter. You will. Do it now."

She slid her fingers down his neck onto his shoulders and pushed away. She left him sitting at the window looking at the dusk dripping over the ruins.

Tania walked away several paces, then turned back to look at his strong, broad outline. His rifle lay at his side. Again, she thought of a stylized image of the Russian soldier, the Red Ivan, defender of the *rodina*. Fedya's sad vigil was a snapshot of it, a portrait in the dying light framed by the window.

It's good, she thought. It's proper that the poet from Moscow sits and stares. Keep your eyes and heart open, Fedushka. We will all need your poems when this war is over.

•   •   •

KOSTIKEV WOKE TANIA IN THE HARES' QUARTERS. His wound was dressed and he brandished a newer, wider smile to set off his golden teeth. After fifteen minutes and a cup of tea from the samovar, Zaitsev appeared in the doorway.

He brushed back the blanket. "Snipers, ready?"

Zaitsev led the soldiers out into the night wind. Tania hunkered into her parka while they hurried through the network of trenches. She wrapped her hair up under a black watch cap. At the edge of no-man's-land, Zaitsev did not take them across the rail yard. He turned east toward the Volga.

Walking along the cliffs overlooking the dark water, Tania spotted the outlines of a flotilla disgorging a thousand men onto the threatened landing stage behind the Red October plant. These were the first companies of Sokolov's division. The sky was quiet; no artillery or darting Luftwaffe planes broke the peace beneath the shrouded moon and the snapping, buzzing breeze.

The hares arrived at a wide avenue between the Red October and Barricades plants. On the south side of the street, Zaitsev deposited his snipers in twos and threes into the tallest buildings. His instructions were to go as high as they could to watch north across the avenue. Nazi activity was expected to build in the wreckage and alleys after word of the Forty-fifth's arrival spread to German headquarters. The trainees were only to monitor Nazi traffic. They were not to fire unless given the order directly from Zaitsev or Medvedev. The order would come in the form of two red flares from the western end of the street.

"No sense stirring up a hornet's nest if we can get Sokolov into place quietly," Zaitsev said. "We'll hunt later."

Before dawn Tania was dispatched into a five-story building with the lanky Georgian farmer, Shaikin, and the chubby woman, Slepkinian. They climbed to the top floor. Zaitsev assured them that this side of the street had been swept clean and was firmly in Russian hands. Wary little Shaikin told Tania he'd seen too many unlucky instances where the front line had changed unexpectedly.

"It moves like a snake," he said of the imaginary line between armies. Grenades in hand, they tiptoed up the stairwell. Tania was sorry Kostikev was not along. But Shaikin, built like a white whip, looked as though he could handle himself. She could not even guess what good the Armenian would be. For two days, Tania had been calling her "the Cow" behind her back.

The three slipped into a room on the western corner of the fifth floor, where they could see both up and across the avenue. Now, piercing the red shadows of dawn with her 4X scope, Tania looked over the broken facades to the German trenches beyond.

She sat as she had the afternoon before in the shooting gallery, at the base of a decimated window. She rested the barrel of her sniper rifle on the lip of a protruding brick, well back and hidden from view. Shaikin and the Cow sat crouched to her right, also eyeing down their scopes from behind cover.

She watched Germans scurry between trenches, following their movements three hundred meters away with her pointed-post reticle fixed on their hearts. A dozen times she imagined herself pulling the trigger. Her vision sharpened with the rising light, and she recalled Zaitsev's words on marksmanship: think it through three times; set it up twice; fire once.

She adjusted the distance in her scope by subtracting the required one eighth for downward shooting. She checked the wind; it was at her back, shielded by the building. The air was cold and would stay that way until April. She was ready now for the order, her first order as a sniper.

The three sat for two hours tracking the Nazis through their scopes. At intervals they took turns stretching, away from the windows. Tania's legs and hands ached with the tense inaction. Her vision frosted from keeping one eye closed and the other squinting. Her cheek and fingers grew stiff against the gun's metal.

The sun climbed, and Tania's patience chafed. How long do we have to wait? Sokolov must be in position by now. From where we sit, Shaikin, Slepkinian, and I can take out three Nazi machine gun positions in ten seconds. Wasn't that the idea, to help secure this corridor between the plants? Why are we waiting?

Shaikin rolled back from the window onto his back. The little man leaped with amazing agility to his feet. Tania looked away from her scope. Her ears picked up what he must have heard. Footsteps coming up the stairwell!

She reached into her coat for a grenade and rolled onto her belly. Slepkinian did the same. Shaikin laid his back against the wall beside the doorway. He held his open palm to them for silence. A knife appeared in one hand, a pistol in the other.

The footfalls were careless and loud, scuffing on the gritty steps. The sounds stopped in the hall just beyond the door.

Shaikin looked to Tania. She nodded back.

Shaikin flashed into the hallway, his pistol up.

Without a word or a glance back, he straightened and lowered the pistol to his side. He took two steps backward. Tania tightened her grip on the grenade. She glanced quickly over at the Cow. No surrender, she thought, clenching her teeth. I don't care what Shaikin is doing.

Shaikin backed into the room. Tania pulled the pin on her grenade and brought her arm back to let it fly. From the hall, she heard a whisper.

"Tania? Tania, are you in here?"

Fedya walked into the room, his hands still up, palms facing outward where he'd flung them when surprised by Shaikin's pistol. Behind him was the giant Griasev.

Shaikin smiled at Tania and Slepkinian.

"We should have known by the noise they were making," he said quietly. "Bears."

Tania slipped the pin back into the grenade. "What are you doing here?" she whispered to Fedya. She slid on her stomach back to the window.

"Medvedev sent us. He came up to the floor below you this morning and saw how good your vantage point was. We were in a building three blocks down where nothing was going on."

Griasev wagged his head. "Not a damn thing."

"So have you got plenty of Germans for us?" Fedya grinned.

"Take those windows there," Tania answered, pointing.

"And be quiet," added Slepkinian.

Tania was impressed with the Cow. She'd looked ready to fight it out, ready to die moments before.

Fedya and Griasev crawled to their places. Fedya set himself into shooting position, knees up. He wrapped the rifle strap around his wrist and elbow. He set a bundled pair of gloves on the sill and laid his barrel on them, careful to keep the muzzle back out of sight from below. He gazed through his scope to take in the German activity across the street. Tania watched him adjust his scope for distance. One-eighth, she thought, certain that he knew.

"What do you think, Tania?" Fedya asked. "Three twenty-five?"

The giant Griasev answered for her. "Three fifty."

"Three twenty-five," said Tania.

Fedya looked away from his sight for a moment. He caught Tania looking.

"Yes," he whispered, "lots of Germans."

Tania frowned. Fedya shrugged and tilted his head to look innocent, blameless for his sudden appearance here. He returned his attention to the Nazis.

Another hour passed in nippy stillness among the five snipers. Tania continued to curse Zaitsev under her breath for holding up the order to shoot. She followed the two dozen Nazis through her scope, noting how they grew more careless as their movements increased. They were digging new trenches, adding height to old ones and filling sandbags. Some even walked in the open, lugging ammunition boxes four hundred meters away.

They think they're unseen and clever, Tania thought. They think they're the ones with a surprise for us. But from this height, the five of us could easily wipe those sticks out. With a signal; that's all it would take. Where is it?

At that moment, a column of German infantry burst from an alley into the street, only two hundred meters away. Tania raised her head from her scope. There looked to be about twenty in the line jogging in formation directly below.

Tania's ears were clawed by the pounding of the Nazis' boots on the pavement. Her hands tightened on the rifle. The bitter taste of bile rose in her throat. She recalled the sight of her grandparents' bodies in the city square. The leaning shadow of Lenin. The footfalls of Nazis stepping in unison on the bricks. Arms restaining her, shrieks, her own voice and blood. But right now she was the one with a rifle in her hands, she was the one with *them* in *her* sights. She clenched her jaw, fleering back her lips, baring her teeth. The moments ticked; Tania felt as if she were swelling to a point where she could not contain herself and would burst.

She brought her eye down to the scope and took aim at the soldier running at the head of the squad. The black crosshairs bobbed from her pounding pulse, but the Nazis were so close below that it made little difference. She followed the one soldier running past in the street below, now less than one hundred meters away.

"Fire!" she screamed, surprised at the abruptness of her voice. Past thinking, as if she had kicked open a gate and now must go through it, she squeezed her trigger. She held tight through the jolt of the shot. The gray-green uniform jogging at the front of the line of soldiers crumpled in her scope.

The Nazis froze. Their heads jerked up at the report roaring above them.

Tania flung back the bolt. The Cow fired. A soldier in the rear of the line clutched his chest and fell.

In an instant, the room was engulfed in the sound of all five sniper rifles opening up. Those soldiers in the front and back of the line were dropped first, then the ones in the middle. The dark bodies piled up beneath the hail of bullets. Tania concentrated on the front of the line, knocking down men stumbling over corpses.

In less than fifteen seconds, it ended. Blue rifle smoke clouded the ceiling and slipped out the windows into the shattered morning. Shell casings littered the floor. Tania and her team sat hunched over their rifles. She surveyed the street through her scope, her heart pounding in her ears. She counted the victims in carnage below, stabbing each magnified body with her reticle. Most of the dead lay in a line, killed where they'd stood in the first few moments. Behind some of the bodies, smears of blood stained the street, marking the short trail of their last effort in life, crawling toward cover.

Tania's abdomen jittered. The scope danced in her hands. She called out, "Seventeen?"

Shaikin answered, breathless. "Seventeen."

Tania looked behind the buildings to the Nazi trenches they'd watched since dawn. These Germans had stopped their work to burrow behind their revetments and spin their machine guns back and forth to find the source of the gunfire. We're too far away, thought Tania, pulling back from the window. They didn't see us. Good. We'll attend to them later, and with a bonus of seventeen broken sticks. We got them all.

Tania turned. The other snipers had lowered their rifles. Shaikin and Griasev shook hands. Slepkinian looked left and right, beaming. Only Fedya seemed displeased. He slid bullets into his magazine and shook his head.

Griasev jiggled a meaty, happy fist at Tania.

"That was some ambush," he said, and exhaled. He clapped his great hands, rubbing them together as if eager to begin a meal.

Tania laid down her rifle and crawled from the window. Shaikin did the same. Slepkinian, Griasev, and Fedya continued to watch the German positions. The Armenian girl whistled at the mounds of dead in the street.

Well away from the windows, Shaikin walked up to Tania. "What do you think?" he asked.

"I think we put them in our books. Three each. And give the extra two to Fedya and the Cow."

"Then we wait for orders, I guess."

Tania walked to the doorway to sit on the stairs and collect the thoughts ricocheting in her head. She needed to grab them and cool the frenzy inside her. We've been taught to act with initiative, she told herself. To seize opportunities for targets, to make things happen. To wait, wait as long as we have to, then act. That's what we did here. We waited long enough. All morning. The sticks are the enemy. That's seventeen of them dead. That's revenge. What more can Zaitsev want?

Tania looked at her three comrades scanning through their scopes. The light was high in the northeast now, casting shadows behind them on the filthy floor.

Shadows. The light was in their faces.

Tania's ears pricked up. She heard a low hiss slither in through the windows. With her legs locked, her mind racing, the sound swelled into a whooshing whistle.

No, she thought. No!

The wall in front of her blew apart. Before her senses could leap, a ball of flame and a powerful black gust smashed her backwards. Bricks spewed on all sides, riding the shock wave of the explosion. Tania was hurled against the wall and collapsed to the floor. A sickening nausea spun inside her. She was deafened, numbed by the blow.

When she opened her eyes, the room was shrouded in thick whorls of smoke. Through the heart of the haze Tania saw the huge hole in the wall. The light streaming in gave the room a swirling glow.

Beside her lay Shaikin, his chin badly gashed and bleeding. He staggered to his feet and braced his hands against the wall as if climbing it. Blood was quickly covering the front of his coat.

"Up!" he screamed at Tania. "Up! Get out!"

Shaikin pulled her to her feet with a grunt. She stood and her knees buckled. Shaikin pushed her against the wall and held her there for a moment until her legs stiffened enough to support her.

Shaikin, his front stained in a crimson bib, gripped Tania's shoulders to push her to the doorway.

"No," she murmured, turning back to the room. "Wait."

Shaikin yelled in her ear, "They're dead! Dead, Tania! Go!"

He spun her around by the sleeves. She heard his shouts through the havoc. She saw the doorway and lurched toward it, dragging her feet through the rubble.

ZAITSEV PUSHED BACK THE BLANKET AND stepped gently into the hares' quarters.

She sat in a corner, where she had been alone for three hours. Shaikin, stumbling from blood loss, had been left with a nurse who'd spotted them retreating along the Volga.

Zaitsev crouched beside her. He leaned onto the toes of his boots, pulling his heels off the floor.

"What happened?" His voice was kinder than his face.

Tania fought back tears. She had not yet cried and did not want to do so in front of Zaitsev.

In an even voice, looking at his boots, she told him of the morning. She described the activity in the trenches behind the buildings, how easy the Germans would have been to pick off, how she and the others had watched patiently for hours. Then the patrol had surprised them, running in from nowhere. She'd reacted quickly, perhaps too quickly.

Zaitsev raised his head at this. Tania looked into his flat face. His eyes throbbed.

"What do you mean, you reacted too quickly?"

Tania felt a twinge of alarm flash across her shoulders.

"I—" She stopped.

Zaitsev's gaze narrowed. His jaw worked behind drawn lips.

"I fired first. I gave the order," she admitted.

Zaitsev's hand lashed across Tania's face, knocking her onto her side.

He stood from his crouch. "Get up!"

Tania rose. Her face stung, but she did not rub it. She backed against the wall and hung her arms at her sides.

"Comrade," she began.

"Be quiet."

Zaitsev stepped closer, his face only a few centimeters away. She felt heat move into the cheek he'd struck.

He shouted in her face. "What are you going to say to me, partisan? Tell me! Tell me you're sorry you disobeyed a direct order. All right, Comrade Chernova. You're forgiven. Tell me you're sorry you jeopardized a vital mission. Again, Comrade Chernova, you're forgiven. The mission continued anyway."

He caged his voice behind clenched teeth.

"Now tell me how sorry you are that your actions killed Slepkinian, Griasev, and Michailov. You alone are responsible for their deaths. No one else."

Tania swallowed hard. She felt immersed in dizzying, rocking waves of dread, as though she'd again been flung into the Volga.

"You didn't get them all, Private. One of them crawled away to a mortar crew with the coordinates to your position."

He balled his fist. "Your fucking position! You disobeyed my orders, you gave away your position and traded the lives of three of my snipers for seventeen infantrymen! Each of those snipers was worth a hundred Nazis. And you traded them for seventeen!"

Zaitsev pulled his face back, breathing hard through his nose. His wide-set eyes gouged into hers. She felt his pupils bearing down like the dark barrels of twin sniper rifles. Tania's mind was blank, producing no thoughts of her own. Everything she heard or felt, all her senses, were in Zaitsev's furious hands. Only a pulse of remorse cut to her surface to mingle with the mean flush in her cheek. All else waited.

Zaitsev shook his head. "We are not here to erase your memories, partisan. I don't know what you've seen or what you've lost, but whatever it is, your pain is not greater than Russia's."

He pulled himself erect. "Russia's, damn it! Not your pain, but Russia's! You are in the Red Army! You are no longer fighting a one-woman war! Don't ever forget this! Don't ever! It was your stupidity and selfishness that murdered three Russian soldiers!"

He leveled a shaking, angry finger at her. "From this

moment on, you will do what you are told to the letter or I'll have Danilov put a bullet in the back of your brain! Do you understand me?"

Zaitsev spun on his heels and stomped from the room. He yanked the blanket from its nails when he flung it aside.

Tania slid down the wall. Tears welled in her eyes. She felt them slipping over her cheeks. The tears tapped on the backs of her hands, limp in her lap.

Tania closed her eyes. She tried to listen to her own sobbing, but her ears were full of Zaitsev's anger. He'd screamed at her. He'd struck her.

She felt exiled from her body, floating beside it as if her spirit had become so full of grief and guilt she had to leave its bounds to contain it all. She looked down on herself, slumped there against the wall. She tried to feel pity for the weeping girl. All she felt was contempt.

I killed them, she realized. I, stupid and selfish, killed them. I am responsible. I am sitting here, crying, trembling, alive. And they are not.

She thudded her head against the wall. She searched for her voice to speak to the echoes of Zaitsev's boots disappearing down the hall, to answer the image in her mind of Fedya lying broken beneath a smoking pile of rubble, his young poet's eyes open, his stare no longer at this world.

She held her hands in front of her, making fists and releasing them, flexing the fingers until they hurt, as if she were clawing her way out of a dungeon. Pain delivered her back inside her body.

Her cheek glowed. She whispered, "I understand."

TWO

THE DUEL

ELEVEN

THE PANZER GROWLED AROUND THE CORNER, its iron hatches shut tight. Cautiously, the tank ground down the street, swinging its gray turret with a metallic whine. The crew inside looked for the Russians they knew were dug into the ruins ahead.

From behind, another panzer watched the progress of the lead tank, guarding it with a motionless cannon. Farther around the corner, out of view, an infantry unit waited to move in behind the tank cover.

A small explosion leaped from the second floor of a building at the far end of the street. A Russian 76 mm antitank gun had opened up at fifty meters and missed. The lead tank slammed into reverse and accelerated backward down the street, elevating its turret to the telltale flash of the antitank gunner's discharge. Farther back, the idling guard tank fired an antipersonnel shell into the ruins. A squad of Nazi infantrymen jumped from their hiding places to rake the now revealed Russian position with bullets and grenades.

At this moment in the battle, the way he'd learned over the past ten days on a dozen other streets like this, Corporal Nikki Mond raised his binoculars to the rooftops and teetering facades above the clatter. There, as if preordained, he spotted the bristles of Russian sniper rifles. They appeared only for a moment, like black thorns protruding from the buildings. With the sounds of distant, single pops, they picked off the German infantry one by one.

Nikki knew these sharpshooters had lain motionless for hours, since before dawn, in the eaves of those skeletal buildings. During this first week of November, what the soldiers had taken to calling "the quiet days," Nikki had grown aware of the increasingly deadly presence of enemy snipers. With the faltering of the Luftwaffe and the prevalence of smaller-scale battles, these silent assassins of the Red Army seemed to have crept into every crevice along the front line.

Nikki had witnessed several occasions where the action escalated from this point, each side calling in more and heavier weapons. If for some reason they did not, then the furor always settled down, with the dead left lying in full view. The wounded had to drag themselves to cover, then stay where they were until dark, unable even in their agony to cry out for help for fear that the snipers above or a creeping Ivan would finish them off. During the "quiet days," few prisoners were being taken.

This tedious taking and giving of alleys, streets, and buildings had become for the combatants of both armies the real battle of Stalingrad. Instead of the major confrontations of September and October spent pounding against the thin Russian beachhead, all the actions mounted now were disjointed local clashes at the company level, with each side trying to improve its position meter by meter. The bitter siege had become a grim bog, allowing only slow, torturous steps.

Both armies had gone underground. Cellars, culverts, tunnels, and a seemingly endless network of shallow trenches called "rat runs," like scratches over the city's frozen skin, now made up the contours of the battlefield under the gathering winter sky. The foot soldiers of the Wehrmacht called it *Rattenkrieg*. War of the rats.

Nikki lowered his binoculars to scribble hurried memos in his notebook. This was his new assignment: forward observer, assigned to German intelligence. His charge was to watch frontline infantry action and report on tactics and casualty counts.

After Captain Mercker and his unit were buried in the debris, Nikki had led his nine fellow survivors to a Command forward headquarters. There he'd encountered an intense young lieutenant, Karl Ostarhild. He told Ostarhild of the disaster while the officer poured him a cup of coffee. Ostarhild rolled out a map for him to locate the blown-up building where Mercker and his company had died. Hovering over the map, Nikki pointed out what he knew about the Red positions, strong points and weaknesses. Ostarhild had been impressed not only by the breadth of Nikki's observations and knowledge but by how hard he'd won them. The lieutenant asked Nikki to stay on under his command as an intelligence observer. Nikki accepted gladly.

Since then, he'd followed the sounds of rattling tanks and chattering automatic weapons across the city. He had not himself fired a weapon or thrown a grenade in twelve days. He did not even carry his rifle any longer.

Ostarhild was growing nervous about the information he was getting. He'd spent weeks compiling data from reconnaissance planes, visual observations, prisoner interrogations, and radio intercepts. He had no doubt that something very big was in the works on the Russian side. He didn't know what, but the signs told him it was of titanic scale.

The day before, on November seventh, Ostarhild had taken his data plus his preliminary conclusions to brief his superiors in Golubinka, several kilometers west on the safety of the steppe. He laid out his reports of a massive buildup of men and materiel in the northern, Kletskaya region. The lieutenant presented his theory that this might be a Russian attack army, armed and mobile, primed for a counteroffensive. He gave the assembled generals details about each Red unit, where they came from, even the names of their commanders.

Ostarhild related that the Russian Sixty-second Army, under General Chuikov, had been forced by STAVKA, the Russian high command, to suffer through a severe reduction in ammunition. Where was the ammo going? That morning, which happened to be the twenty-fifth anniversary of the Bolshevik Revolution, Stalin had made a surprisingly jubilant speech, monitored by shortwave from Moscow. Referring to the battle for Stalingrad, Stalin offered the cryptic reference that "soon there's going to be a holiday in our street, too."

Drawing partially on Nikki's observations and frontline savvy, Ostarhild presented a vivid picture of the current status of the battle. The attack on Stalingrad had become a series of violent, personal battles. The Germans, in small groups, might occasionally grab a block of ruins or even reach the Volga in or around the factory district. Once they'd consolidated their gains by digging in, the units often found themselves cut off by Russians who moved back across the narrow corridors the Germans had cut. The wounded were frequently unreachable; the dead were left to stiffen in gruesome postures on the ground. The men were losing all hope of personal survival. They continued to fight, but too often their strength was the result of alcohol or contraband amphetamines. Ostarhild depicted the Nazi soldier as unshaven, weary from lack of sleep or relief, ridden with lice, fearful of spending another Russian winter in battle, and having lost all sense of the Reich's greater purpose in bleeding for this city. Now, they fought—Ostarhild quoted the words of a battlefield reporter—"only for the ultimate obsession: to get at one another's throats."

The Russian position in the city was equally perilous. Along a three-mile stretch, the Reds clung desperately to their diminishing portion. In some places the riverbank was less than a hundred meters from their backs. Along with a throttled reserve of ammunition and a fantastic casualty rate, the Russians' looming problem was that the Volga—the Red Army's only link to its supply lines—was quickly growing unnavigable. The huge ice floes from the north that annually clogged the river had begun to tighten, but the Volga would not freeze solid enough to permit ground transport over it for another four or five weeks. Until then, the Reds' reinforcements and supplies would be drastically reduced, if not cut off altogether.

The young lieutenant was asked by his commanding officers if this, then, was not a good time to mount one more large offensive. Ostarhild had anticipated the question: he knew the instant he heard it that he couldn't answer honestly. A true response would not have been what the staff wanted to hear nor what they were prepared to pass on to General Paulus, the head of the Sixth Army. In his heart, Ostarhild felt the common soldiers had grown too disorganized, too cold in the shadow of their own doom to take part effectively in any more major assaults. As an intelligence officer, he'd censored hundreds of letters from the troops addressed to loved ones back home. Without exception, the letters displayed a deep brooding over their bleak prospects for returning to Germany alive. Command had responded by ordering all such letters intercepted and impounded. No sense depressing the home front with defeatist claptrap, they'd said.

Instead of laying before the officers the naked truth, Ostarhild spoke carefully, choosing terms he knew would be politic for their ears. The German soldier will fight bravely, he said, regardless of the assignment. But the generals had to act quickly before the window of opportunity closed. Ostarhild kept to himself his dread that the window had slammed shut weeks ago. Another offensive might be successful, he said, especially while the Russians' supply lines were threatened by the river. But Germany faced several new obstacles here in early November. The weather, the men's physical condition, and low morale certainly had to be addressed, but equally dangerous to the Reich's presence in Stalingrad was the growing number of enemy snipers.

The Red sharpshooters had adapted to the destroyed urban terrain far better than the Germans had, Ostarhild observed. They were rapidly becoming very effective. The enemy snipers were responsible for untold casualties, including many among the officer corps. A conservative estimate ranged between one and two hundred wounded or dead per day.

The casualties came in such a terrible way, too—from a distance, from an unseen rifleman who crawled off and escaped detection. The snipers delivered death always as an awful, bloody shock. The men in the trenches had come to believe there was no haven from them. Any movement, even while smoking or relieving themselves, could draw a sniper's attention. The thought of being hunted through a telescopic sight, of being marked unknowingly with invisible black crosshairs and then selected for a bullet in the brain and instant death, was a chilling, ugly prospect. The men were demoralized. Worse, they were becoming paralyzed.

Ostarhild showed the generals a file folder of clippings from the Russian military newspaper *Red Army* and the locally printed trench news sheet *In Our Country's Defense*. Attached were translations prepared by his staff. He brought their attention to the articles under the heading "From the Front" by a Russian commissar, I. S. Danilov.

These were stories of a newly formed Russian sniper school in the 284th Division under Colonel Batyuk. "Obviously," he concluded, "the Russian command has seen the value of just such a sniper movement. But I doubt even they could have foreseen just how troublesome their snipers would become."

General Schmidt, Paulus's aide-de-camp and the ranking officer in the meeting, nodded while he scanned the translations.

"These articles," he said, "make a very big show over this sniper Zaitsev, the one they call the Hare. He appears to be the brains behind this sniper school."

Ostarhild agreed. "Yes, sir. He's Siberian, a hunter from the Urals. Their press is building him up as their prototypical sniper, a great hero."

Schmidt tapped the papers with the back of his hand.

"Then I think it would be very good for the morale of our men to catch this hero Zaitsev and blow his goddammed head off."

Schmidt read a few moments longer. The general looked up and beamed around the room with a fat smile.

"And from the looks of things, this fellow Danilov has been quite a help to us." He held up the sheaves of *In Our Country's Defense,* shaking them at Ostarhild. "What we have here, gentlemen, is a catalog of all of Herr Zaitsev's tactics. It seems to be quite lengthy and complete, wouldn't you say, Lieutenant? How he thinks, what ruses he prefers, and so on. Tell me: in your opinion, will these help us catch this Russian son of a bitch? This little Red rabbit?"

The other generals in the room sniggered. Ostarhild nodded and said, "Yes, sir, they should."

"Then wire back to Berlin on my orders," Schmidt said, standing to conclude the interview. "Tell them we want to kill the best sniper in the whole Russian army. Send me the best German sniper. The very best. Immediately."

•   •   •

TWO DAYS AFTER OSTARHILD'S MEETING WITH
the general staff, on the afternoon of November ninth,
Nikki stood in a swirling snowfall at Gumrak airfield, fifteen kilometers west of the city center. Gumrak's single
landing strip and lone blockhouse formed the closest air
link between Germany and Stalingrad. In the last months,
the name Gumrak had taken on both joyful and dire con-
notations among the soldiers of the Wehrmacht embattled
in Stalingrad. Gumrak meant you were going home, perhaps bouncing in a seat, safely watching Russia grow
small and fade into the mist; perhaps, and all too likely, in
the darkness of a canvas bag. They've surely run out of
pine boxes by now.

Nikki squinted through the whipping whiteness of the
snow. He watched the Heinkel He-111 bomber roll to a
stop on the runway forty meters from his staff car. This
was the first snow of the winter. It came a full month
before the early dustings Nikki remembered from home in
Westphalia.

The roar of the bomber's engines peaked and cut back.
The blades flipped to a halt. The plane brooded in its own
silence for several minutes. No one came to meet it or
stepped out of it. Nikki bounced on his toes to stay warm,
his hands buried deep in his pockets, the flakes catching
on his eyelashes.

The door in the plane's midsection opened. A duffel
bag was tossed out. A man jumped down behind it and
landed heavily. He picked up the bag and walked through
the slashing snowfall.

The plane's motors spit and the propellers whirled to
life. The figure approached. He wore a long, black woolen
coat without insignia. His hat was ebony felt, broad-
brimmed and stiff, new. A brown muffler crossed his face
below his nose. The hat's brim guarded his eyes.

To the rising sound of the engines, the man handed his bag to Nikki, then strode past him to the waiting staff car.

Through the bulk of the stranger's coat, Nikki gauged him to be rather round, no taller than himself. This is the supersniper from Berlin, he thought. I expected to meet a titan, a rock-jawed veteran with eyes of blue granite. Oh, well, that was my own romance. This seems to be a soft man hurrying past me to get into the car and out of the cold. He must be very, very good.

Nikki started the car and steered off the runway. He did not slide the heater knob out, deciding to let the engine warm up before bringing in the air.

"Where's the heat?" the man asked through his scarf. "You could have let the car idle while you waited. It could have been warm when I got in."

"Yes, sir. I apologize." Nikki looked in the mirror. "Your plane was delayed, sir. I didn't want to waste fuel."

Nikki pulled out the knob to let cool air flow into the cab. The two rode in silence along the dirt road leading to Ostarhild's headquarters. Nikki stole glances in the mirror at the stranger. Only after the cabin had warmed did the man uncoil the scarf and push up the brim of his hat.

He smiled, catching Nikki's eyes on him in the mirror. "What's your name, Corporal?"

"Nikolas Mond, sir. From Westphalia."

"Ah, yes." The man nodded and looked out the fogged window at the gripping snow. "I've hunted there many times. Geese mainly, but wonderful ducks, too."

The man seemed to want conversation. The blue-gray eyes in the mirror waited for a reply.

"My family has a farm there," Nikki said. "Every harvest, we throw corn on the open fields. The ducks practically fly into the house and land on the supper table."

"Yes." The man laughed. "I love the taste of stupid ducks better than the smart ones."

He took off his hat and gloves and laid them across his

lap. His hair was cut short, light brown like the winter-dead steppe whisking by the car windows. His skin, cream pale, was stretched taut over pads of fat about the neck and ears that softened the angles of his face. Nikki noted the smallness of his ears, nose, and mouth, and how his eyes dominated his face as if they were two blue ponds and the rest simply gathered there to drink. When he blinked, it was slow and deliberate, but his head moved quickly, in staccato bursts. It made Nikki remember barn owls on the farm.

Nikki guided the staff car onto the paved road. A swastika fluttered on the front left fender to mark the passenger as important. Nikki drove slowly, guiding the car through droves of soldiers on foot. The men appeared to be ambling aimlessly, huddled against the snow. Some were wrapped in blankets. Many had stuffed newspaper under their helmets and inside their coats, evoking the image of scarecrows.

A horse-drawn cart stopped in front of Nikki. He brought the staff car to a halt. The soldiers on either side would not give way. Nikki did not want to blow the horn at the shuffling men, but he had to get through.

"It's all right, Corporal," the man in the backseat said. "Wait a moment."

Nikki looked at the load in the rear of the cart. Piled high against the rails were bodies, stiffened, clutching at nothing. Their heads were bent at violent angles. Bare feet protruded from the tangled mass of gray-green uniforms; boots and socks had been reclaimed by the cold hands of the living. A delicate shroud of snow nestled and built in the crevices of their crooked elbows and bent legs, unmelting white filling in eye sockets and open mouths.

An officer spotted the staff car waiting behind the cart. He ordered the men walking along the shoulder to make way. The officer waved Nikki around the cart. Nikki saluted the officer and turned onto the shoulder. The officer did not take notice.

In the mirror, the man's great eyes were closed, his eyelids like drawn curtains. He said, "You know who I am?"

"Yes, sir," Nikki replied. "You're SS Colonel Heinz Thorvald from Berlin."

The colonel opened his eyes. "From Gnössen, actually. I've been there for the past year teaching. Berlin is close, though. I go in for the theater every so often. Do you like the opera, Corporal? They have it in Westphalia, I know. I've been there."

"No, sir. There's never time on the farm."

The eyes closed again. "No, I don't suppose there is. The British bombed the State Opera House in Berlin. The Führer had it rebuilt. They're opening it at the end of this month. Wagner's *Die Meistersinger*. I want to be home for that."

Nikki concentrated on the road. Now that it had cleared, he stepped on the gas, speeding his passenger, the most dangerous long-distance killer in the entire German army, the supersniper Heinz Thorvald, to Lieutenant Ostarhild's offices.

OSTARHILD WALKED INTO THE SNOW TO GREET Thorvald. He came to attention and saluted. Nikki opened the rear door of the car. The colonel returned the salute and followed the young officer into the office. Nikki came with the colonel's bag.

Ostarhild poured the colonel a cup of coffee and offered a seat beside a coal brazier. Nikki hadn't seen the stove or the coal before. The lieutenant had scrounged them up for Thorvald's visit.

The two officers exchanged pleasantries about Berlin

and Stuttgart, Ostarhild's home. The pheasant hunting around Stuttgart, it seemed, was wonderful.

The lieutenant warmed Thorvald's coffee. He used the break in the conversation to shift to the colonel's assignment.

Ostarhild took from the top of his desk a collection of articles with translations attached by paper clips. The articles were from *In Our Country's Defense*. That morning, Ostarhild had let Nikki read them. The lieutenant handed them now to the Berlin master sniper.

"Colonel, these were written by a Red Army commissar. They directly concern your target, Chief Master Sergeant Vasily Zaitsev. It seems a simple hunter from Siberia has become quite a hero for the Russians."

Thorvald looked into his coffee.

"And quite a problem for you, yes?"

Ostarhild folded his hands. "More so than even these clippings tell. Zaitsev, nicknamed 'the Hare,' has become the head of a sort of impromptu Russian sniper school. In the past two weeks, more and more names have appeared in these articles, all students of his. You'll see them marked in the translations. Medvedev. Chekov. Shaikin. Chernova. The commissar believes some of the pupils rival their teacher in audacity, but none has surpassed him in skill. The Hare has taught three dozen snipers to work directly along the front lines. With their average range of three hundred to four hundred meters, they're doing no small amount of damage deep behind our lines. We're losing men to these snipers, yes, but worse, we're losing morale at a fearsome rate."

Thorvald looked up. "Three to four hundred meters. That's not so good for an expert sniper."

Ostarhild shook his head. "According to these articles, Zaitsev's is five hundred to five fifty."

"Mine," Thorvald said quietly, "is better."

Ostarhild waited for the colonel to finish his coffee and slide the cup to the corner of the desk.

"Colonel Thorvald, I have orders to assist you in any way I can. I've made provisions to quarter you here at my office. There is a room here that you may make your own until you complete your assignment. I've also arranged for one of our snipers to be your guide. Beyond this, what else can I do for you?"

Thorvald turned slowly, then moved his head in a quick jerk at Nikki. Nikki stood straighter under the gaze of the colonel.

"This man," Thorvald said to the lieutenant without taking his eyes from Nikki, "is he brave?"

Ostarhild shrugged, as if to admit he did not know what to make of the question.

"Yes, Colonel. He is. Very brave. And not foolish."

"Has he fought? Does he know the battlefield?"

Ostarhild raised his hand to Nikki. "Corporal, tell the colonel something of your experiences."

"You tell me, Lieutenant," Thorvald said, his voice even, dissecting. His look remained fixed on Nikki. "I don't want to hear what he thinks of his own courage. I want to hear what you think. If he is a brave man, a brave man will not say so."

Ostarhild spoke to the back of the colonel's head. "Corporal Mond has fought through the worst of Stalingrad. And I can tell you, Colonel Thorvald, the worst of Stalingrad is the worst of hell."

Thorvald's stare at Nikki broke, a smile riving his face like a sudden crack in white ice.

"Good." The colonel faced Ostarhild. "I would like him to be my guide and spotter."

The lieutenant sat forward. "Colonel, as I said, I've arranged for one of our snipers to be your spotter. He knows the battlefield as well as this corporal and he has experience with the Russian snipers."

"I don't want anyone with experience against Russian snipers. I don't want advice and tidbits. This Zaitsev has made a science of studying German snipers. I don't want someone who'll get me killed. I want someone who'll do what I say. This corporal of yours knows the battlefield. He's obviously a survivor. You say he's a fighter. And I know he understands fear. I can see it in his eyes. He knows what it can do."

Ostarhild shook his head. "Colonel, with all due respect, one of our snipers would be—"

Thorvald interrupted him. "Snipers are cowards. All of us are. We kill without fighting. Remember, Lieutenant, I taught your German snipers everything they know."

The colonel rose. "Corporal, have you killed men?"

Nikki nodded.

Thorvald spoke to Ostarhild. "I have never killed a man. I've shot hundreds but I've never killed a man. I merely take away their lives. They fall down when I pull a trigger half a kilometer away. That's all." The colonel pointed at Nikki. "I can't do what he can. I can't fight. I only shoot. That makes me a coward. I know it. This man is no coward. He comes with me."

Ostarhild stood also. "Yes, sir. Of course. Corporal, you will join the colonel at dawn. Go back to your quarters and get some rest. I'll meet you here in the morning. Dismissed."

Nikki saluted the two officers. He walked out the door into the dimming evening light. The snow had eased. He guessed it would stop within the hour.

Ostarhild's offices were on the first floor of the remains of a department store, across the street from a park. North of the park was the central rail station and a tourist hotel. East of the store was a set of concrete steps that once had led through statues and fountains down to a river walk, then along the river to the main ferry landing.

From the landing, pleasure boats had carried bathers out to the sandy beaches of the islands in the Volga. Shops, bakeries, kiosks, the local newspaper, a folklore museum, boat rentals, a political auditorium, an open-air market, a church—the shattered remains of all these lay around him like giant scattered skeletons while he walked to his quarters.

This city, he thought, has been stripped and smothered by a war so vast and powerful it can mow down a row of buildings like a scythe. Now this stomping, charging, consuming war is slowing down, shifting its focus to become personal. Now it's one man, flown in all the way from Berlin, assigned to kill one man.

Will this war overlook nothing, Nikki wondered? Is it beginning to hunt for us now by name, one at a time?

NIKKI LAY ON HIS BEDROLL. HE'D MADE HIS quarters in the basement of a bakery. Bread ovens and cooling racks stood against the walls. The strong flooring overhead had held through the bombings. Nikki knew he was lucky to have such a secure and private place to lay his head.

He spent several hours in front of a lantern with maps of the factory district and workers' settlements spread on the floor. He rummaged through his knowledge of the front, searching for clues to where the Hare might be operating. It's unlikely, he thought, that Zaitsev will stalk the northernmost of the plants, the Tractor Factory. We swept it of almost all resistance at the end of October. We own it, and it'll never be worth what we paid for it. The middle factory, the Barricades, is finally tilting our way after weeks of fighting. But every step there in that monstrous web of steel and concrete is incredibly dangerous. Besides, there's nothing but privates and corporals throwing their lives down like dice in the Barricades. Zaitsev likes bigger fish, the kind that make it into the Russian press: officers, artillery spotters, machine gunners. He likes drama. My guess is he's working the Red October or the corridor between the Red October and the Lazur. Or the eastern slope of Mamayev Kurgan. The Russians are strongest in these areas. Zaitsev wouldn't waste his skills or endanger himself in losing battles.

Nikki turned down the lamp. What did the colonel mean, that all snipers were cowards? Even the Russians? Was Zaitsev a coward? He thought back to some of his own battles, others he'd observed for Ostarhild. He recalled the Red soldier who'd been shot while holding a flaming bottle of antitank fluid. The soldier dropped the bottle and was engulfed in flames. Knowing he was as good as dead, the man picked up another bottle, ran through his agony at a panzer and smashed the liquid against the radiator to ignite the tank. Where were the Russian cowards? He hadn't seen one. The cowards had all died first. There couldn't be any left.

Lying in the dark, his eyes riveted open, Nikki stared into his memories. His mind soared like a hawk above the past two months. The houses. The factories. The green Volga. He listened to his heartbeat: it was the beat of mortar shells. His breathing rasped like the gasps of the dying. The dark cold and silence of the basement were the thumb of death pressing down on him. His senses swirled. He felt not only like he was falling but as if he'd been hurled downward.

He sat up. He had to skid it all to a halt; the parade of violent scenes and numbing explosions was overwhelming him. He tumbled in the heart of a fireworks display; the memories were so bright, popping and crackling on all sides.

Stop, he thought, stop it. Where is sleep?

•   •   •

NIKKI SAT UP IN THE DARKNESS TO THE SOUND of footsteps from above. Ostarhild called out to alert Nikki that he was in the building. It was a precaution not for Nikki but for the officer.

He lit his lantern and carried it to the foot of the steps. "Yes, sir, Lieutenant. Come in."

Ostarhild walked down the steps. "I'm sorry to wake you, Nikki. I need you to take care of something for me."

"Yes, sir."

"Early tonight, five battalions of the Three thirty-sixth Pioneers arrived. Paulus is going to make another big push at the Barricades. A telephone cable has been broken between my office and the rail yard south of the Lazur plant. I need this line open with the Three thirty-sixth while they get into place."

Nikki nodded.

"I've already sent one man out to fix it, but he disappeared. I've no idea what happened to him. He was a freshman private, so anything could've gone wrong. I thought I could let you rest, but now I've got to bother you."

Ostarhild handed Nikki a flashlight. "Let's go. This shouldn't take you too long."

Nikki set the lantern on the floor. He lit the flashlight to guide the officer up the steps. He left his rifle propped in the corner, where it had been for weeks.

Outside the office, Nikki threw the light's beam onto the ground. Ostarhild pointed out the black wire running into an alley. These thick, coated wires had been rolled out from giant spools off the backs of trucks to establish phone links between headquarters while the German army consolidated its gains. Whenever possible, the wires were laid along walls or on the inside of train tracks for protection and camouflage. Occasionally the lines were strung on poles to lift them over roads.

Nikki pocketed a set of wire strippers and a roll of black electrician's tape. Ostarhild patted him on the back.

"I've checked it to this point, Nikki. It's broken out there somewhere. Be careful. Just find it, fix it, and get back."

Nikki cast the beam on the wire and followed it into the alley. At the far end of the block, the wire rose up a flagpole and stretched across a street. He locked onto the wire with the flashlight and followed it, snaking through the city.

Walking, he kept alert. Even though this sector was well in the rear and the night was quiet, he was keenly aware that he was a German soldier strolling through the Russian dark behind a glaring flashlight.

Nikki kept his eyes on the wire, glancing only rarely at the shadowy ruins. He felt he had seen them all before, one just like another. Months ago, it had struck him how little character was left in this city that was Stalin's namesake, which once must have been beautiful. When Nikki first saw Stalingrad in early September, the bombings and combat had already stripped its flesh, reducing it to piles of debris and gaunt, defiant facades. It was a wasteland, all of it looking the same, its agony spread evenly. Only the wide, jade Volga and the steppe beyond Mamayev Kurgan were worth looking at anymore.

He tracked the wire behind the remains of a warehouse. A half-dozen empty coal cars sat on tracks there, all of them perforated by bullet holes. Nikki moved into an open yard; he heard footsteps in the rubble. He flashed the beam at the first of the coal cars. A private walked from behind it, raising his hand in greeting. The man shrugged and pointed down at Nikki's feet. Nikki aimed the beam down to the break in the wire. It had been cleanly severed, as if cut with a snipper.

What was this private doing? Nikki wondered. Had he wandered all the way out here and found he'd forgotten or lost his wire strippers or repair tape? Why hadn't he just gone back? Maybe he knew someone else would come fix the wire and so waited for the next soldier, figuring it would be safer to walk back together. Whatever his reason, Nikki, a corporal who'd been yanked out of his rest before an important morning mission, was going to give this freshman an upbraiding he would remember.

Nikki knelt and pulled out his wire strippers. The private stayed where he was. Nikki flashed the light at him.

"Come over here and help me. I'll show you how this is done, and then you're going to do it. Come on."

The little private shuffled over. The man's coat hung on him loosely, and his pantaloons, baggy at the knees, were bunched over the boots. The leather sheath of a bone-handled knife hung from a belt lapped around the soldier's waist.

That's not his uniform, Nikki thought.

The private walked up and stood over Nikki. The man brought his thin, pale head down to Nikki's eye level. Nikki raised the flashlight to look into his face.

The private grinned. His smile was golden.

PAIN WAITED FOR NIKKI. HE THRASHED TO THE surface of consciousness, to a stab of white pain at the back of his neck. His hands would not move. Water flooded his nostrils and mouth.

His cheek stung suddenly. His head snapped to the right, flinging open his eyelids. His jawbone sizzled with ache. Nikki coughed out the water in his nose and throat. He blinked his eyes to dry his vision. A bright light sprang into his face.

Quickly his senses took hold. He was lying on his back. His hands and legs were bound. He opened his eyes wide, and the light blurred into a starburst. It was all he could see.

A hand reached out of the light to grab him by the collar and jerk him into a sitting position. The pain in his neck sank and spread over his shoulders. His ribs throbbed. He'd been kicked while unconscious.

The light lowered to the floor. His vision adjusted, and he saw three men, one wearing the baggy German uniform. This one stepped forward. He leaned his face close and smiled with a mouth decked with gold-capped teeth. He drew a long knife and laid the blade under Nikki's chin. His face filled Nikki's vision.

"There's not a lot of time." A gravelly voice from behind the light was speaking accented German. "This one wants to kill you. I'm going to let him do it unless you give me a reason not to."

Nikki stared numbly into the face before him. The flashing yellow teeth disappeared behind thin lips. The man breathed loudly through his nose.

Nikki looked past the head in front of him into the shadows. From the spilling glow of the flashlight, he saw he was in one of the coal cars. These three were a commando team who'd sneaked over the line to capture and interrogate a prisoner. He could only guess how long they'd been waiting in the coal car. They'd snipped the telephone wire, then ambushed the freshman when he came out to fix it. They've killed him; now they have me, Nikki thought dully.

"You'll kill me anyway," he said.

The knife rolled under his chin. The blade scraped down his throat, over his Adam's apple, then again under his jaw.

Nikki swallowed. He gave his name, rank, and serial number. The face in front of him looked deep into his eyes, like an attentive dog that did not understand.

"Corporal, let me make this easy for you," the voice from behind the light said. "We know about the reinforcements moving into the Barricades. Several battalions.

We've been watching them. And even though the lad who wandered out here before you was quite a nervous talker, he didn't know anything of value. I suspect you do. Tell me something of value, Corporal. Now."

Nikki felt the blade curl under his ear. A glimpse of gold shone through the lips floating in front of him. This man spoke in a hiss; blood dripped along Nikki's neck from the slicing knife.

The interpreter said, "He wants you to know he will kill you in five more seconds. He says he wants to do it. I suggest you speak to me now, Corporal."

Now, Nikki thought. Now, he said! My God, this is a death I wasn't prepared for! My throat slit open, gasping for air, bound hand and foot like a slaughtered hog. Now! What can I tell them? Should I tell them? Tell them! Tell them what? What do I know? Value? What's of value to these madmen? What do I know? Start talking, Nikki. Anything. Something will come out, something of value. No, be quiet! Traitors and cowards talk. Die, just die. It's over. They'll kill you anyway. Oh, God. Father.

The knife left Nikki's throat. The face moved behind him. Nikki looked at the two standing men, specters in the downcast flashlight. They looked like all the other Russians he'd seen, in bulky padded coats, cartridge belts, and grenades slung about their bodies. Both wore the Russian fur hat, ear flaps tied up.

The light played again into his face, blinding him. The man with the knife laid his hand over Nikki's eyes and nose and yanked back hard. Nikki's neck stretched.

"Corporal," the voice said, "we must leave now. I give you this chance."

Nikki's brain flooded. He sucked in breath, baring his teeth. His hands and legs were strapped, useless. It's over. Over. There's nothing to tell them. It's nothing. All nothing.

A snarl escaped from his exposed throat when the blade was laid against it.

The light shut off.

Nikki relaxed.

Then, like a bullet, like an angel, a thought came to him.

"Thorvald."

"Wait," the voice said. "What was that?"

Nikki said again, "Thorvald. He's here."

The voice gave a command in Russian, and the light came back into Nikki's eyes. The hand released its pull on his face.

"Tell me, Corporal. Who is Thorvald?"

Nikki closed his eyes to think. Tell them. It doesn't matter. Thorvald's just one man; you're not giving away any big troop movements or secret plans. Tell them. It won't help them.

"Thorvald," he said, gasping, "is a colonel. An SS colonel. He was sent here from Berlin to kill one of your snipers."

The voice gave another order in Russian. The gold-toothed executioner behind Nikki moved in front, turning the knife over and over in his hand.

"Which one of our snipers?" asked the voice.

Nikki blinked into the beam. "Zaitsev. The Hare."

The Reds whispered in buzzing tones. The golden grin appeared close to Nikki's face again, blocking the light. His eyes were intent and his head skewed, again like the attentive dog.

The grin spoke. *"Otkuda ty znayesh pra Zaitseva?"*

Another voice translated. "How do you know about Zaitsev?"

"He's been written about in your newspapers. They tell us everything about him."

The three conferred in whispers. The man in the German uniform pointed at Nikki with his knife several times. One head wagged back and forth. The other, the interpreter, stood still, listening to the arguments of the other two. The decision clearly belonged to this man.

The gold-toothed one knelt beside Nikki to stare into his profile. He leaned on his knife and twisted it into the floorboards.

"When did this SS colonel arrive?"

"Yesterday."

"Is he good?"

Nikki nodded. The pain in his neck was rising again.

"He said he is. I don't know. I haven't seen him shoot. But he's the head of the Berlin sniper school, the special one in Gnössen. The generals asked for him specifically. They flew him in to get Zaitsev. They say he's the best. That's all I know."

"The head of the German sniper school?" The interpreter told this to his comrades. The gold-toothed man frowned and shook his head at Nikki's ear.

The leader rubbed his stubbly chin. "Hmmm. That is interesting, Corporal." His voice carried a musing tone. "A German supersniper, sent from Berlin to kill the Russian supersniper. Yes, that is interesting."

He paused to fold his arms across his chest. "But I do not believe it is all you know."

Nikki searched quickly for something more, any detail that might tip the scale. He'd just met Thorvald. He knew only what was discussed in Ostarhild's office.

"He says he's a coward. He wants me to be his guide."

The interpreter laughed at this. He told the other two.

He motioned for the man beside Nikki to come. The two in Russian garb shouldered submachine guns while the grinning one in the German uniform hefted a long rifle with a telescopic sight and walked toward Nikki, holding the knife.

He reached down and cut Nikki's hands free, leaving his feet bound. He leveled the barrel of the rifle at Nikki's forehead and pulled back the bolt. A bullet popped into the air. His hand flicked out and caught it.

He dropped the shell down to Nikki.

"Vot, dai etomu trusu. A sledushuyu on poluchit v lob."

He put the knife in its scabbard, then turned for the open sliding door of the coal car.

The interpreter stood before Nikki. He cut off the flashlight. In the darkness, the soldier spoke.

"He said, 'Here, give this to the coward. The next one he gets will be in his forehead.' Goodbye, Corporal."

The Russians jumped out of the door.

Nikki untied the rope from his feet. Once free, he crawled to the door to stare into the shades of night, straining his senses for any trace of his captors in the rail yard. Faced with no other choice, he slid out of the car and walked into the open.

They're gone, he thought. They left me alive.

Nikki blew out a breath. He stroked the warm metal of the Russian bullet in his hand. He pressed his index finger onto its point, feeling the ease with which it could pierce flesh. He dropped the bullet.

In the dark, on his hands and knees, he groped until he found his flashlight, wire strippers, and black tape in the dirt where he'd left them.

He repaired the break in the line through the throbbing in his head.

TWELVE

HEINZ THORVALD OGLED HIS IMAGE IN THE handheld mirror. This was his third morning in a row without shaving since he'd left Gnössen. Grow a beard while you're here, he thought. That Russian wind has needles in it.

He looked at his naked body. He always slept nude. It felt warmer pulling the blankets around his bare legs and under his chin. He had slept well the previous night on the cot in the storeroom Ostarhild had prepared for him, but more from fatigue than comfort.

Thorvald set down the mirror. He rubbed his stomach with both hands. His white skin held a reddish cast, the scarlet hue of childhood freckles still visible from head to toe. His shoulders and chest were soft. A layer of fat cushioned the lines of his muscles and bones like a jacket of snow. His waistline seemed to pout as if it were sticking out a lip.

He slapped his belly and jiggled it once to tell it he was going to give it some bread and jelly out of his bag in a few minutes. He gathered up the fatigues Ostarhild had sent at his request and pulled them on.

An opened wooden crate rested at the foot of the cot. Thorvald reached through the straw packing and lifted the canvas sack containing the new Mauser Kar 98K. He slid the rifle from the sack and undid the factory wrapping of oil paper. He felt the slickness of the packing grease and oil, the smell as sweet to him as morning coffee.

Thorvald broke the gun down, the stock, the bolt, the trigger assembly. He had an orderly bring him a basin of hot soapy water, then placed the parts in the suds. He shook out the canvas sack to rid it of straw and dust and laid it across the bed. After wiping the rifle parts down with clean rags, he set each on the sack and gave the metal bits a light coat of gun oil. He held the barrel up to the window and peered down it. Deep in the center was a single speck of dust, like a lone camel in a vast blue and perfect desert. Thorvald swabbed it out, looked again, and set the barrel on the sack.

He reassembled the rifle and washed his hands. He took off the oily fatigues and threw them in a corner. From his duffel bag he arrayed his clothes on the bed, dressing slowly, donning first his winter undergarments. He enjoyed the gathering warmth of each article: black cotton socks, gray-green woolen pantaloons, black wool turtleneck and large-cord sweater, then his insulated high boots. Last, he took out the reversible padded coat and hood, green on one side, white on the other. His white mittens were inside the pockets. He unrolled a pair of reversible drawstring pants and tossed them on the bed beside the coat.

After savoring three slices of pumpernickel slathered with Black Forest cherry jam from his duffel, he took up a small chamois sack holding his Zeiss 6X telescopic sight with crosshair reticle. He locked the scope into place.

Thorvald pulled on the pants and parka, white side out. Dressed and fed, he rubbed the blond stubble on his chin. They'll ask at the opera about the beard, he thought. I'll tell them I grew it on a mission to the Eastern Front.

He walked into the hall carrying the Mauser and a box

of shells. He passed Ostarhild's office, looking in for a moment to find the lieutenant away. He noted that the brazier and the coffeepot were also gone. The lieutenant's desk was a mess.

Outside, the first charcoal stains of dawn colored the sky. It's going to be a heavily overcast day, he thought. Good. They tend to be warmer. The clouds keep the heat in.

He counted only ten soldiers walking in the square across from the department store and in the streets around him. No cars or motorcycles broke the early silence. He wondered that there was not more activity, though he knew he was for the most part a stranger to the administration of war. In fact, he did not know how it worked on the large scale, outside the narrow range of his crosshairs.

Heinz Thorvald had never played more than a very specific role in the German military. He'd been a prized sniper, a gifted *Scharfschütze*, from the first day he donned the black and silver of the Wehrmacht as a twenty-seven-year-old captain in 1933.

Before his fifteenth birthday, Heinz had been a champion youth marksman in his native Berlin. His father, Baron Dieter von Zandt Thorvald, was a renowned sportsman in the southern forests. The old man had once hunted duck and quail with Field Marshal von Hindenburg himself. Heinz grew up a member of the wealthy industrialist Krupp family, his mother's clan, who held license to hunting grounds throughout Bavaria, and Heinz had been recognized early as a phenom with a shotgun.

But the boy's passion was not in the fields alongside his father. The baying of the hunting dogs, the wet dawns in the marshes, and the gritty, bloody meat of the wild kill were not to his liking. Instead, his heart beat for the time he could spend on the shooting range. He preferred the camaraderie and comfort of the clubhouse, the applause of admirers, and the competition with his peers. His favorite afternoons came with the matches against those elder marksmen who wished to teach the talented pup a lesson and rarely did. Heinz won most of the competitions he entered from the ages of sixteen through twenty. The matches he lost did more to improve his shooting than his victories. He analyzed every errant shot down to painful detail and did not repeat those mistakes next time out.

As a young man, he turned his talents to trap shooting. His gun of choice was the unpopular .410 small-bore rather than the more widely used 12 gauge. The shot pattern of the .410 was smaller. This shotgun required more meticulous aim than the larger-bore guns. Heinz accepted this voluntarily as his handicap. In his mind, it evened the contests. It helped him focus his will. The 12 gauge destroyed the clay targets, turning them into sprinkles of dust. Heinz enjoyed using the .410 to simply break the clays, then watch them fall. He sometimes practiced by shattering with a second shot a falling piece of an already stricken target. No one in Germany could best Heinz. His movement from high to low targets was as smooth as the flights of the spinning clays themselves. His balance was remarkable, and his reflexes were like a mousetrap. The clays were flung into the air at the call of "pull" for a high target and "mark" for a low one. Heinz moved the barrel of the gun in behind, then ahead, of the "pigeons" sailing twenty meters away from him in the first second, fifty meters away after three seconds. He knocked them down as surely as if the disks had been flung against a wall.

In 1928, when he was twenty-two, a wave of strikes shuddered through Germany. From his family's estate outside Berlin, Heinz sensed the unrest growing in the nation. His father, a veteran of the First World War, was a strong supporter of the military. Many times he told his son that the German army was the last lamp that could light the country's path back to its former glories.

The baron joined a militant group of veterans, the Stahlhelme, or "Steel Helmets," and marched with them in the Berlin streets against the encroachments of unemployment, the declining mark, the Weimar republican system, and the rising tide of Communism. He preached that the German people's most valuable traits were their industriousness and the skill of the labor force. Because of what he saw as the Weimar politicians' mishandling of the postwar peace, German workers were being laid off by the thousands. The nation was depressed. Its anchor of hard labor and daily production had been ripped from the shoal beneath, sending Germany adrift, the baron intoned often at dinner. Only a strong army could sink the anchor back into a firm purchase.

Heinz accompanied his father on a few of the Stahlhelme's raucous, confrontational demonstrations. The rancor of the crowd scared him, and he quickly retired to the sanctuary of his library and the rifle range.

Five years later, in 1933, the Austrian Adolf Hitler came to power. The year before, Hitler had been at the forefront in the Nazi party's election sweep. Hitler was now chancellor. His brown-shirted storm troopers, the Sturmabteilung, lock-stepped across the nation, which embraced the new nationalism. Hitler labeled both the Communists and the "Jewish terror" as the genesis of Germany's woes.

In the first year under Hitler, Germany's economy began to lurch forward like an engine that had sat idle for years and was suddenly oiled and cranked into action. The voices of dissent slowly disappeared when the Schutzstaffel, the SS, opened the first internment camps for political opponents. The nation began to shout as one, howling first at itself, then to the startled ears of the world. The

voices in the streets were young with the renewed power
of Germany rising again.

Heinz was enlisted by his father into the National Socialist Party, the Nazis. He was immediately scooped up
by friends into the storm troopers. Hitler called this
paramilitary organization, over half a million strong, his
"political soldiers in the fight to take back the streets from
the Marxists." Heinz was subjected, through meetings and
retreats, to an armylike discipline. He was ushered into
the labyrinths of Hitler's political aims and social suspicion of any thing or person termed "non-Aryan."

Heinz became upset by the fervor of his mates. The
storm troopers fought in the streets with fists and bottles
against Communist sympathizers. They marched in rigid
goose step in support of Hitler's mad dashes through the
halls of government. They were arrested for fighting, then
smashed benches and threw telephones through the windows at the police stations. Heinz could not join in the
violence. He was stalled by a fear he did not know he
owned until the first time his mates rushed into a crowd
of Reds. He'd stood on the edge of the melee, frozen on
the sidewalk, pressed against a building by his sudden
dread. He quit the brownshirts two months after joining
and was branded a coward.

The baron was not willing to accept this label for his
son and insisted that the error had been his. The storm
troopers, he said, were simply too proletarian. Heinz was
refined beyond the ken of those goons. The place for
Heinz was the Jungdeutsche Orden, the German Youth
Order, known as the Jungdo.

Here, young Heinz found an ideological home for the
sons of the bourgeoisie. The Jungdo marched in goose
step, but only because it was the fashion and they didn't
want to appear less committed to the National Socialist
cause than the other groups. But unlike the Hitler Youth
or the storm troopers, the Jungdo did not break ranks to

run down a group of men and women carrying Communist slogans or throw rocks and bottles at Bolshevik speakers. Their uniforms carried no insignia or rank to deemphasize age and status. Instead of the storm troopers' beer-sotted revelry, his group held brotherly and patriotic meetings. The members of the Jungdo carried themselves with the air of those bred to lead rather than skirmish. Heinz spent weekends on camping trips, engaged in sports and hikes. The Jungdo had a required reading list that closely tracked Hitler's preferred authors. Heinz was introduced to the great philosopher Nietzsche's belief that a self-willed, heroic superrace would emerge above conventional morality to sweep away worldly decadence. In Schopenhauer's *The World as Free Will*, one of Hitler's favorite bits of reading during World War I, Heinz encountered the idea of will as force. He marveled at the lessons of Darwinian selection and the unexpected parallels between math, physics, culture, and history set forth by Oswald Spengler in *The Decline of the West*.

Heinz's enthusiasm for Hitler's vision of Germany grew while he came to understand the influences behind the Führer's ideas. Under the guidance of Jungdo speakers and late-night discussions with comrades, he realized the danger of the Red peril. He saw the Jew merchant as the throttling purse strings of an Aryan nation striving for economic daylight.

During the summer of 1933, Heinz's life was filled with a sense of belonging he had not known before joining the Nazis. Though his family had always been a loving one and both his parents were children of wealth, Heinz had long walked only in the shadows of that love and privilege. He, like the other children of the estates, had become too accustomed to his position; he could no longer feel his life. If nothing else, he had this in common with the blue-collar workers and farm boys swelling the ranks of the storm troopers and Hitler Youth. The economy had slowed to such a crawl that the German youth felt isolated from itself. Their hopes and dreams had been mortgaged and their destinies shackled to the wreckage of the country's past. This was not the same past their parents remembered, the age of imperial Germany. Rather, the young men and women of 1933 Germany had grown up in the decades after World War I, after defeat and shame, in a Germany now mired in a worldwide depression.

There had been no intellectual or philosophical harbor for him before the Jungdo. He'd read books, listened dutifully to speeches, and wandered thoughtfully through the wildflowers and fields, like the rest of his breed. But most of his opinions were ones he'd usurped from his father. Now, through his nightly classes, he was versed in German folklore. He was conversant in the words of Thomas Mann as well as the soaring rhetoric of Hitler's *Mein Kampf*. He attended the riveting spectacles of Wagner's operas. He stood rapt in the middle of tens of thousands outside the capitol, the Reichstag, listening to Joseph Goebbels cry for "the struggle for Berlin." He marched with his father and a quarter million Stahlhelme through the Brandenburg Gate, flying the swastika and eagle standards beneath the stare of the Führer himself. Just as his body had found the sporting regimen of trap and target shooting, his mind found Hitler.

Before the Jungdo, there had been no spot on earth other than the shooting range Heinz Thorvald could claim to have truly made his own. He'd been a stranger to Germany all his life, invisible and disenfranchised.

Now he felt like an heir to the planet.

In November of 1933, his father approached him with news. The baron had secured for his son a captain's rank in the SS, the Nazi Party's own armed forces. His assignment would be as an ordnance officer, attached to the armory in Berlin. The Baron assured Heinz that his peacetime duties would include little more than participating on the SS's sharpshooting team and putting on displays of marksmanship for recruitment festivals. Heinz embraced his father and accepted.

For six years, SS Captain Heinz Thorvald developed his marksmanship skills. During the week, he refined the static shot, lengthening his distance eventually to one thousand meters with a 6X scope. On weekends, he honed his skills on the skeet field, swinging the heavier duck guns; he won dozens of contest and awards for the SS. Evenings were spent among books or attending the opera, especially those by Wagner.

There had been some women in Heinz's life. Their chief purpose had been to admire his manner. The prospect of loving a woman and sharing himself scared him; he used his loyalty to the Aryan cause to silence the whispers of worry and fright inside him. "The world," he told each woman when her string had run out, "is not right just yet for commitment to other than the Fatherland." Sipping a coffee and cognac after an evening at the opera, he told the girls the times were turbulent and tumbling.

"Not now," he'd sigh, looking away. "Maybe . . . I don't know."

Nineteen forty-one marked his eighth year in the army. Though Germany had been at war for two years, Heinz had spent only ten weeks on actual battlefields, in two campaigns: the invasion of Poland, where he'd sat at six hundred meters, knocking off frightened, defeated Poles across open battlefields, and Dunkirk, shooting a hundred retreating English and French soldiers waiting for rescue over the English Channel. In each case, Thorvald had fired with impunity from remarkable distances, confident that no marksman on the other side could counter him or even endanger him. In Poland and France, he'd collected over three hundred confirmed kills. He was ever thankful to be so safe in war, to be a sniper.

His impressive number of kills combined with his family's influence to secure for him a promotion to colonel. By the summer of 1941, the German war effort in Europe had shifted to the occupations of conquered nations and the relentless bombing of Britain. Very little ground action was taking place on the continent. Thorvald agreed to head a sniper school outside Berlin in the small town of Gnössen. He had SS engineers construct a state-of-the-art shooting range and skeet field, touting that skill in both disciplines was needed for accurate as well as fast aim. Thorvald hoped he would spend the duration of the war in Gnössen. He'd breakfast with his father on Sundays and spend his week creating lethal snipers to go into conflict and perform bravely on his behalf. He set himself the task of becoming too useful as a teacher to be sent into the field again.

Now the frosty Stalingrad wind slapped him out of his reverie, stirring again the sad sense in his breast that some promise had been broken. He stared down the steps of the river walk to the green Volga. The river was clotted with ghosts of ice floating under the surface. No boats are coming across that, he thought. Ostarhild told me about the Russians' supply crisis. I'm here during a lull in the fighting, but it's bound to increase the moment the Volga freezes and becomes first a giant footbridge and then a highway for the Reds' supplies. I want Zaitsev dead and a seat on a plane home well before that.

To the left of the steps were the ruins of shops; across the walkway were the remains of a row of statues and concrete fountains. All but one of the iron figures had been broken and knocked from their stands. At the end of the row, just before the cluttered boardwalk beside the Volga, stood a depiction of a Russian boy and girl. They held a sheaf of straw over their heads, the workers of the

Soviet future. They seemed to Thorvald to be four hundred meters away.

He took the rifle off his shoulder, looked down the scope, and subtracted one eighth for the shot downhill. Sensing the chilly clarity of the air, he subtracted twenty meters. The wind blew at him off the Volga, ruffling his hair under the white hood. Possibly eight knots. He gave the distance ten meters more.

Thorvald crouched and brought the crosshairs onto the dark forehead of the iron statue boy. He aimed for the left eye and squeezed. The report of the rifle roared at the quiet facades on his left, then bounced back and raced past into the open park. It was his first shot in Stalingrad.

He shortened his distance slightly when a trough in the wind appeared. He aimed and fired at the statue's right eye. Looking through the sight, he could not determine his accuracy. Iron boys, he thought, do not fall down from bullets.

Thorvald walked down the path to the statue. From this height above the river, he could see the huge islands splitting the Volga in half. Beyond the wide sand beach and evergreens on the islands were the flat plains of Russia, rolling away under the distant winter mist. He thought about how vast this land was. It could encompass Germany twenty times. He'd heard Hitler's plans for Russia, announced from a hundred podiums. He enjoyed watching Hitler shout his speeches, fists waving, beating his buttons, shaking while the words flew from his mouth as though he were a cannon and the words artillery shells. We will conquer Russia west of the Volga, then Moscow will sue for peace and the war will end. We will call the land from Poland stretching east to the Volga "Ostland." We will be its masters and populate it with our race. The Russians, the lowly *Untermenschen,* will serve us grapes and honey and chop wheat for our bread.

When I leave, Thorvald thought, I won't come back,

even when it is Ostland. I don't like this place, this gloom, this wind.

Standing before the statue, Thorvald stepped over the low marble wall onto the fountain floor. A gown of snow from the night before lay on the bottom, making the surface slippery. He slid up to the figure of the boy and ran his finger over the ebony left eye. A gray smudge came off on his finger. The copper jacket of the round had flattened upon impact with the harder iron. The muddy smear was a splash mark from the lead core. He checked the other eye and found the lead mark low on the cheek. The rifle is true enough, he thought.

Waiting at the top of the steps was the soldier he had requested that Ostarhild assign to him.

"Good morning, Corporal," he said. "How did you sleep?"

"Sir?" The young man seemed taken aback by the question.

"Just an inquiry. Manners. Like 'How's the weather?' "

The corporal reached for Thorvald's rifle.

"Yes, sir. I didn't sleep that well. The lieutenant sent me out in the middle of the night to repair a phone line."

"Was it close to the Russian lines?"

"Yes, sir."

"Did you repair it?"

"Yes, sir."

"Were you scared?"

The corporal shook his head and spit in the dirt. "I'm always scared, Colonel. You get that way here."

Thorvald walked alongside him into the street, north toward the Russian lines.

"Why aren't you carrying your rifle?"

"I figured today we were just going to look the front lines over, sir. If you want, I'll go get it."

Thorvald shook his head. "No. Don't worry. We won't get close enough to the Reds to get in any trouble. Let this Zaitsev work along the front lines with his balls in the mud. From the articles I read, he seems to be addicted to it. Besides," he added, clapping the boy on the shoulder, "I don't need to be so close to him as he needs to be to me."

The two walked in silence through the ruins. The corporal seemed quite certain of where he was going and knew the best routes to get there. Thorvald marveled at the destruction of the city. This was devastation, absolute and complete. There was nothing left whole. The buildings were mangled, ripped apart. Who could fight in this? Who could hold out through this?

The Russian wind seemed to say to him, I can. Thorvald huddled into his coat.

He waved his white-gloved hand at the ruins. "Where do you think he is, Corporal?"

Mond spread a map of the city on the ground. The colonel knelt beside him.

"Look here, sir. We've split the Russian force into three parts." Mond sketched with his finger three rings on the map.

"Here," he said as he pointed into the first, northernmost circle, "in Rynok above the Tractor Factory, they've got a full division. South of there, in the Red October factory, we've fought right through the middle of them all the way to the Volga, isolating this force." He jabbed the finger down into the Red October circle. "This small pocket deep in the shops is almost impossible to break."

Mond looked up from the map. "I've seen the Russians take artillery pieces apart in there, drag them through the rubble to the front line, then put them back together and blow us to bits."

The corporal laid his fingertip on the southeast corner of the Red October. He traced a line west from the building to the eastern slope of Mamayev Kurgan, the hill that commanded a view of the city. From there, he slid his hand south to encompass the Lazur chemical plant, the rail yards, and ten kilometers of riverfront to a point north of the main landing stage.

Thorvald looked up from the map into the top of Mond's head. The corporal did not take his eyes from the map.

"Where is he, Corporal?"

"My guess is he's in this southern pocket, the largest one."

"Why do you think he's there?"

"It's just a guess, but it gives him the most room to move, the most targets. He could get trapped in one of these smaller pockets. And I don't think they would want that. Besides, it's mostly a stalemate right now in these smaller areas. Zaitsev has over a hundred and forty kills. I think he'd want to work where he can find the most game."

"Game? Why do you say game?"

Mond shrugged as if to express how simple the logic was.

"He's a hunter from Siberia. That's how he thinks. He hunts. Sir, did you read the articles from *In Our Country's Defense*?"

Thorvald nodded. "Yes, Corporal, some. Not all of them. I perused them. Let's say I got the highlights."

The corporal lowered his eyes.

Thorvald responded quickly. "I'll read them all, I assure you. I was tired yesterday."

"It's all right. They're mostly brag."

"You say Zaitsev sees us as game. I take it you've read the articles. What kind of game are we to him?"

Mond studied the question, then answered. "Wolves. Siberian timber wolves. He thinks he's got us figured out. The Germans do this, the Germans do that. He reads tactics and routines like tracks, like we're animals."

"Then," Thorvald said, rising, "we will behave like Siberian timber wolves. We'll be dangerous but conventional. We'll let him think he has us figured out. And then we'll spring a surprise on him."

Thorvald smiled, liking what he was creating for the young corporal. After all, Zaitsev was right. The German sharpshooters were predictable. Thorvald knew it; he'd been the instructor for many of the snipers Zaitsev killed. He was certain they'd behaved like animals here in Stalingrad: dull and predictable. He'd seen it in their eyes while training them in Gnössen, the careless Aryan confidence of the Nazi youth, boys ruling the world before they'd fired the first shot. No respect for the enemy. No longer any respect for the power of fear. They'd fought in the streets with knuckles and beer bottles and considered those city squabbles to be their crucibles, their proof under fire. These young snipers entered the war already sure they were brave, convinced that the world waited to open before their courage like gates to a password. "Just show me how to do it" was all they seemed to want from him in training—"I'll take care of the rest, old man." They'd forgotten that fear, not the bullet or the bomb, is the most devastating weapon of war.

Hitler has taken fear away from the German people, Thorvald thought; that's the Führer's greatest power. He's almost done that for me, almost freed me from it.

"And this Zaitsev," he mused while Mond folded the map. "We'll treat him like a duck. We'll hide ourselves in a blind and then flush him into the open. We'll make him fly from fright and then shoot him down in a burst of feathers."

Thorvald looked at the corporal, who turned to walk north toward the Lazur plant and no-man's-land.

"I'm certain we can make Zaitsev come to us."

Mond nodded.

"The key,' he said, "is to let him know I'm here."

The corporal's face dropped. "How . . ." The boy hesitated. "How can we do that, Colonel?"

"Don't worry. I'm sure we'll think of something, you and I."

THIRTEEN

TANIA LOOKED UP FROM HER JOURNAL AT THE sound of metal clanging against the bunker. A tin mess plate clattered on the dirt floor. Sidorov, a young private with the sniper unit for only two weeks, had thrown the plate at Shaikin.

The two men's voices swelled. She stared across the room at them, both standing, ready for blows.

Zaitsev and Kulikov jumped to the two antagonists. Chekov did not move.

Kulikov took Shaikin's arm to pull him back. Zaitsev stepped between the two flushed faces.

"Shut up! Both of you!" Zaitsev shouted over them. He turned to Shaikin. "Ilya! What's going on?"

Shaikin yanked his arm out of Kulikov's grip. He rammed his finger at Sidorov. "I've had enough of this bastard! He's got seventy kills and he thinks it makes him a hotshot. He's over here running his mouth. But he's padding his kills."

Sidorov laughed. "You're a jealous son of a bitch." He said to Zaitsev, "He's only got thirty-six and he's mad at me. He ought to be mad at himself."

Shaikin snatched his sniper journal off the floor and shoved it at Zaitsev. "Here," he seethed, "look for yourself. Every one is a machine gunner, a spotter, a sniper, or an officer. Every one a priority target!" Shaikin glared at Sidorov. "Go ahead, hotshot! Show him your journal."

Shaikin wheeled on Zaitsev. "You know what he does? He shoots foot soldiers during an attack instead of machine gunners or officers. He's supposed to be protecting the troops, but he's just racking up kills for himself. He's a fucking menace."

Zaitsev faced Sidorov. He asked quietly, "And?"

The skinny private's eyes blinked with his own anger.

"That's crap!" He pointed out through the bunker wall to the battlefield. "The machine guns aren't operating in my sector. I shot one gunner a week ago and they haven't replaced him. This lying dick is just too slow to get seventy kills, and he's mad at me about it."

Zaitsev handed Shaikin's journal back to him without looking through it.

"Go sit down, Ilya."

Shaikin slumped on the floor next to Tania. He slapped his hands in his lap.

Zaitsev spoke now with Sidorov. "You have seventy kills. That's excellent. You know I have twice that many."

"Excellent for you as well, Chief Master Sergeant."

"And what do you think," Zaitsev asked, "of Shaikin's thirty-six kills? Truthfully."

Sidorov shrugged as if to say he would have chosen diplomacy but the Hare specified he wanted the truth.

"I cannot say the same, Chief Master Sergeant."

"Shaikin is not excellent?"

Shaikin tensed. He moved to push himself off the floor. Tania laid a hand on his arm.

Sidorov shook his head with dramatic reluctance.

"Comrade Sidorov," Zaitsev said, raising his chin, "you will transfer from this unit immediately."

Sidorov stepped back as if pushed. "Chief Master Sergeant, what? . . ."

"There's no room for your attitude in the hares, Sidorov. We are a small group and we are Communists. We do not bicker over personal achievements. Excellence is not measured in numbers or scores. Private Shaikin doesn't need seventy kills to be as good a sniper as you. Dismissed."

Zaitsev stared at the private. He and Sidorov were close in size, but Zaitsev seemed by far the bigger man.

"Dismissed, private."

Zaitsev waited for Sidorov to collect his journal, rifle, and pack and leave beneath the blanket hanging over the doorway. Shaikin got to his feet after Sidorov left. Tania stood also. She knew Shaikin to be a reliable and resourceful sniper. For the past three weeks, since they'd graduated from the sniper school, the two had worked the same sector. Almost half the kills in Shaikin's journal bore her signature as spotter and witness. In turn, Shaikin had witnessed twenty-three of her thirty-one kills.

With Sidorov's departure, there were now twenty-two hares and bears left of the original thirty. Zaitsev said that when the snipers got down to twenty, he would teach ten more to keep the strength of the unit always between twenty and thirty. He'll be teaching another class soon, Tania thought. Kostikev died last night, blown apart. He stepped on a mine during a commando raid deep behind German lines. Kostikev had been the mission's point man, their creeping assassin in the lead. The reputation of the hares was growing; their members were being requested throughout the division for special duties with squads outside the sniper cadre. Kostikev had been hurrying back; he was just south of the Lazur when he tripped the mine. Shaikin and Tania had tipped a bottle of vodka for Kostikev, the brave, gold-toothed killer whose mouth always flashed but rarely spoke.

Sidorov was the first in either the hares or the bears to be asked to leave. This was shameful. The others who'd departed their ranks had done so only by giving up their lives.

Zaitsev spoke to Shaikin. "Sidorov's sector bordered on yours, didn't it?"

Shaikin nodded. Sidorov had been one of four snipers assigned to an area on the eastern slope of Mamayev Kurgan, about twenty-five hundred square meters. Zaitsev and Medvedev had divided the entire front line into fifteen such sectors. Two two-man teams were assigned by the sergeants to work those areas with the most combat activity or to support Red troop movements whenever word came down from Command.

The sectors were reviewed nightly for shifts in combat activity. At all times, a minimum of ten sectors were manned with capable and experienced snipers. Zaitsev tried not to move the teams too frequently; he wanted them to get familiar with the terrain in their areas. Shaikin and Tania had been shuttled between sector five, their current sector, and sector six, swapping with Sidorov's unit. Both were on the eastern base of Mamayev Kurgan.

Each unit was assigned a leader; Shaikin, Kulikov, and Chekov were the heads of their sectors, as Sidorov had been in his. These leaders met nightly, whenever they could attend, here in the bunker Zaitsev shared with Medvedev. Tania had recently begun to attend these evening meetings with Shaikin, at her request. Shaikin, her friend and partner, agreed to let her come to the meetings, but only as an observer. Afterward, the two designed their next day's strategy together.

Now Zaitsev turned to Tania. He'd kept his distance since her costly error two weeks earlier. He had rarely addressed her in that time, communicating her assignments through Shaikin. For the first week, she was allowed only to spot for Shaikin. Finally, she was granted permission by Zaitsev to shoot. She set herself the goal of learning Shaikin's care and patience in the hunt, to gain better control over her passions when a Nazi was in her sights. She'd done so with deadly, gratifying results.

Tania thought constantly about the day Fedya had been killed. She knew she'd disgraced herself. After the incident, a chill had spread between her and Zaitsev like the ice growing in the Volga. Standing before him now, looking at his flat face, his hands, his body, all under such control, like a fox or a gliding bird, she wanted him to call her "partisan" again, to look in her journal and see how controlled she had been, what a good hare she'd become. She wanted to swallow vodka with him again in the trenches, to hunt with him, to be with him at dawn, to be in his eyes.

"Private Chernova," Zaitsev said to her, "you will take over Sidorov's place. He's been working with Redinov, Mcgolin, and Dyenski. You know the bounds?"

Tania nodded. "Yes, Chief Master Sergeant."

This was the moment she'd been piecing together in her heart, bit by bit like a puzzle. Now it was complete. She was renewed. Zaitsev had put her in charge of sector six. The probation, dating from the moment he'd struck her, was done.

Zaitsev looked at her sternly. "There are several German snipers working in that sector. Mamayev Kurgan is hot."

Shaikin, still standing beside her, spoke up.

"It's been hot for weeks, Chief Master Sergeant. Tania has dueled with a dozen German snipers. They're all in her journal with my signature."

Zaitsev smiled at her. The first smile from the Hare in too long a time.

Call me "partisan," Tania wished, but he did not.

Zaitsev asked Shaikin to make do for a few more days until he could assign him someone to replace Chernova in his sector.

Shaikin elbowed Tania in the side. "Better send two."

Tania felt the urge to go out right then, in the dark and blowing cold, to hunt. She touched Shaikin on the arm for his trust in her.

A bellow erupted from outside the doorway.

"Bullets and borscht!"

The blanket to the bunker swept aside. An icy wind followed the broad back of Atai Chebibulin, a burly old Bashkir from the village of Chishma in Turkmenia. Atai was the sniper unit's courier, the man who brought them ammo and rations.

Tania rarely heard Atai speak to the snipers other than to announce his arrival with his preamble "Bullets and borscht," and to say "T'ank you" in his halting Turkic dialect. But on one occasion the week before, Atai had come into the bunker earlier than usual, near dusk, when Tania was alone, waiting for more cartridges. She talked to him then. He told her he was a Moslem and that his son Sakaika had died here in Stalingrad.

Chebibulin knelt. He slid the harness for the large tin soup canister off his back. He laid the container in the center of the floor and took from a gunnysack a dozen boxes of cartridges. From his coat pocket a bottle of vodka appeared. This he handed to Chekov, who dove forward for it.

Since her first sight of Chebibulin weeks ago, while still a sniper trainee, Tania had been amazed at the Bashkir's ability to produce food every night for the snipers. He never arrived empty-handed; he was always burdened, grunting under the weight of ammo and rations. Chebibulin carried no rifle or grenades. All his strength was used to deliver whatever the snipers needed. If Atai were a sniper, thought Tania, he would certainly be a bear. He moves like an ox, with his banging tin canister and bowls and his shy mumble.

Chekov tipped the vodka bottle back like a circus

sword eater. After several gulps he called out, "Donkey! It's not borscht again, is it? I hate cold soup. It was cold last night."

Atai turned his back to Chekov, who busied himself again with the bottle.

Zaitsev walked to Chekov and reached for the vodka.

"Eat some soup, Anatoly, before it gets cold on you again."

Chekov handed Zaitsev the bottle and moved to the canister. He flipped open the flimsy top and kneeled to inhale the steam from the soup.

"Ah, the Donkey ran here fast tonight," he said, looking at Chebibulin's back. "Potato soup."

Shaikin said to Chekov. "That's enough, Anatoly."

Tania added her voice. "That's enough."

Chekov looked up from the cauldron. The vodka had already reddened his eyes.

"What's the matter? You two taking sides with the Donkey?"

Before Tania could answer, Chebibulin turned on Chekov.

"Donkey! Why Donkey! Why you call me that?"

The graying Bashkir's body was tensed, his big hands working at his sides. He blew out from under his large, drooping moustache. His chin, stippled with a dense salt-and-pepper stubble, worked as though he were chewing on his growing anger, trying to swallow it.

Chekov looked at Tania and Shaikin. Kulikov muttered and put his head back into his journal. Zaitsev, in his corner, ran his fingers up and down the vodka bottle.

"Come on, Tanyushka, Ilyushka, all this old man does is carry food back and forth," Chekov muttered. "He's no soldier. He doesn't fight. Don't give me a hard time sticking up for him. He plods back and forth. He's a donkey. So what? Let's eat."

Tania put her hand on Chebibulin's thick shoulder.

"Atai, tell me again about Sakaika. I want the others to hear it."

Chebibulin stared at the ground, chewing his mustache.

Tania watched Chekov spoon some of the white potato soup into a battered bowl.

"His name is not Donkey, Anatoly. It's Atai Chebibulin. And if you weren't such a mean drunk, you might have a little more respect. This man's son—"

Chebibulin raised his thick hands. "No, I," he said to her. "Is OK. I tell."

Tania sat next to Shaikin. Chekov stepped aside, reaching out his open hand in a gesture to the old man, ceding him the stage. He bowed with open sarcasm.

Chebibulin sat cross-legged in the center of the room with his back to Chekov. He grunted as he folded his legs.

"Three month ago, I take Sakaika, is my boy, to train in Chishma. He in army. I take him down in cart, long way. At train, I see army horses eating hay, drinking water. I think OK, I get free drink and hay for my horse, too. I tie him to post with army horses. Train crowded, many army. I lose Sakaika. I go in every car, calling boy's name. No answer. I lose."

The old Bashkir narrowed his eyes. His hand scratched his matted, graying hair.

"OK, I say myself, I say goodbye already. Sakaika know. I go back to horse, he gone. Army put him on train with rest of horses. I got no way home, no horse to pull cart. I need horse for farm. I go up and down, shouting, 'Army stole my horse!' I call horse name, Prinza, and I hear him stomp. Brrrrr."

Chebibulin blew through his moustache to make the flapping, rattling horse noise.

"I jump on train, find my horse with army horses. I go to soldier. 'Hey, this my horse.' Soldier shake his head, he say no can help. Another soldier, another, and no can help. Then train move and I try jump off. One soldier grab me. He say, 'Hey, where you going, old man?' I say I jumping off, you keep my horse, I walk home, OK. Man say we need you in army, all Russians fight. I say, 'Where Sakaika?' This soldier, he help find. I talk with Sakaika, we say OK, we go fight, we go father and son. Army give back my horse, one more horse and new cart. Me and Sakaika, we go in same regiment, Thirty-ninth Guards. Come to Stalingrad. Many fighting. Many dead. Day and night I going with dead boys to river, always coming back with bullets and borscht."

Chebibulin smiled beneath his moustache at his signature phrase. Then, knowing the end of the story, his smile fell. He looked down again into his lap and shook his head.

"Two week after we come Stalingrad, I find Sakaika. He got bullet in chest at fight for river landing. I put him in cart, drive like crazy man to hospital. Then big bomb kill my horses."

The old man looked up now, at Zaitsev. "I pull cart myself but too slow. Sakaika dead."

His eyes stayed fixed on Zaitsev. Tania sensed Chebibulin's determination that Zaitsev, head of the snipers, command respect for him from Chekov. It was not Atai's way to challenge a man to his face.

"I put Sakaika on boat myself. He got buried on other side. I go over there sometime, later, when war here over. First I go back to regiment, tell captain I fight for Sakaika, I got his gun. Captain tell me no, Atai, I get you new horse, you too important man for just bullets. You man for bullets and borscht."

Chebibulin rose. "Then," he said, "I meet Danilov. Fat little Danilov. Communist, OK? He ask me to take care of you, take care of snipers, important soldiers. You the best, he say to me, I the best. I take care of you," he said, looking now for the first time at Chekov, "and you call me

Donkey. I not Donkey. I Atai Chebibulin, father of hero Sakaika."

Chebibulin fell silent. After a moment, he moved to the canister and began to pour soup into the tin bowls. Chekov walked to Zaitsev and took the vodka bottle.

"Chebibulin?" Chekov spoke, holding the bottle out to the kneeling old man.

The Bashkir shook his head. "No. Is sin to drink spirits. Not Moslem way."

Chekov knelt beside Chebibulin to set the bottle on the ground. He held out his empty bowl. He let the old man pour another helping into it.

"Here," Chekov said, offering it.

"No, I not take your food. You soldiers."

Chekov pushed the soup at Chebibulin.

"And you are Atai Chebibulin," he said, "father of hero Sakaika. Here."

Chebibulin looked into Chekov's eyes. Tania watched closely. She saw the fearlessness of age in the old man's face. She understood the nature of his courage, knew it to be simple resignation. He had nothing left to lose now that he had lost his son, nothing left except the days that make up a life that has given up its gravity. Tania looked at Chekov. She saw him match the old man's stare, the daring of youth in his eyes, with not enough of life seen yet to understand what he stood to lose. She knew the hearts of both men, believed she had both of them beating inside her. She imagined that these two men kneeling in the center of the bunker, facing each other, were the two sides of a magic mirror. These are my two sides, she thought; I want to live, I want to die. She closed her eyes.

"No," she heard Chebibulin say, "I not take your food. Tell me I not Donkey."

Zaitsev answered. "You are not Donkey, Atai," he said. "I make you a hare. You are fast and brave, and a friend."

Tania opened her eyes. She smiled at Zaitsev, who was not looking at her.

"Yes?" Chebibulin looked at Chekov.

Chekov shrugged. "Yes."

"Then I give you this." Chebibulin reached into his coat for another bottle of vodka. He sat it on the floor.

Kulikov snapped his fingers. He popped his index finger against his throat, the Russian signal for vodka thirst. Chekov tossed the bottle to him. Kulikov pulled out the rag cork and tipped the bottle up.

Chebibulin lifted the empty soup canister, leaving the filled bowls on the floor. He hefted the container over his back and pushed the blanket aside, making to leave.

"Good night, hare," Zaitsev said. "Travel safely."

With his hand holding up the blanket, Chebibulin looked back at Zaitsev. "With all this drinking in your hares," he said, "it's OK. I stay Donkey. T'ank you."

CAPTAIN IGOR DANILOV WALKED UNDER THE blanket, letting it slide off him as he stepped sideways into the bunker. He kept his hands jammed in his pockets, shaking his shoulders from the night chill outside. Tania was surprised to see the speed with which the little commissar could shimmy his body. He was like a horse or a Tatar dancing girl. She smiled at the image of a round, dark, and hairy Danilov in a veil.

"Mail call," the commissar said. "The Hare has a letter." He held up two wrinkled envelopes and dropped one in Zaitsev's lap. According to Red Army custom, letters were to be read aloud so the gathered soldiers could share in the sentiments from home. The reader was allowed to edit bad news or sensitive words but was obliged to read out the bulk of the letter. Though mail was rare here on the front, Shaikin's wife had managed to get several letters through. She and his children had been transported from their home in Georgia to the far east, to Novosibirsk in Siberia, part of Stalin's industrial migration to save the Soviet Union's factories from the Germans. She had become Tania's favorite correspondent, telling her husband and, unwittingly, many in the sniper unit, about her garden, the poor quality of fabric available for the children's clothes, the ominous beauty of the Siberian autumn and other details of life far from the fighting. Now Tania leaned forward in interest to learn who was writing to Vasily Gregorievich Zaitsev.

He fingered the envelope, seeming to admire it for the ardors of its journey to him. He held the letter with both hands.

"It's from my unit in the Pacific navy. From Vladivostok."

All eyes were on him and his first letter. The Hare read:

> *"Dear Vasha:*
> *We have been reading about you in* In Our
> Country's Defense. *Who could have foretold our*
> *little friend, the clerk, would become such a hero?"*

Zaitsev's glare darted above the paper. The snipers looked at each other. Tania looked quickly from Shaikin to Kulikov. Both dammed back laughter.

"Yes," Zaitsev said calmly, "I was a clerk. That means I can add and subtract and I know the entire alphabet. Do you mind?"

Zaitsev cleared his throat for silence. ". . . such a hero," he repeated, looking up once more.

> *"We are here on the rim of the world, remembering*
> *you with affection and drinking toasts in your*
> *name. We keep up with your accomplishments*
> *through the newspaper and have a tally sheet posted*
> *on the kitchen wall. Every time you are mentioned*

*in the paper, we drink that night to the latest
number of your Nazi kills. You have gotten us all
very drunk, Vasha, but we can stand more. We read
where you still wear your navy shirt. Never forget,
Vasha, you are a sailor like us. Your strength comes
from the blue waves and the white foam, no matter
how far from us you are fighting. We know you and
your comrades will stop the Nazis in Stalingrad.
Victory will be won. Good luck. We embrace you
here.*"

Zaitsev folded the letter into the envelope. According to
custom, the snipers applauded. Tania thought, He's not
embarrassed by the attention. He's gotten used to the
spotlight.

Zaitsev sat, and Danilov stepped to the middle of the
room, holding high the second, unclaimed letter.

"I have a letter here from a girl in Chelyabinsk. She has
written on the envelope instructions that this must go to
the bravest soldier. Who would that be?"

Tania looked around the bunker. Her eyes settled on
Anatoly Chekov. He, like her, had not received a letter
since leaving his home. His family was in the Ukraine,
behind German lines. Anatoly often talked with Tania
about his worries, knowing that she, too, had family in an
occupied republic. Lately he'd shown signs of strain. The
ripples of tension circled his eyes and played on his brow
and lips. The ugly scene with Chebibulin; that was not
the brave, easygoing poacher. Chekov was cracking. Tania
and Shaikin had talked about it just the morning before,
how his drinking had increased and his moods swung un-
predictably. They spoke of the solitary regimen of the
sniper, how it was so different from the foot soldiers'. Not
enough sleep, constant assignments into danger along the
front line, the brooding presence of competition amongst
the snipers—despite Zaitsev's and Danilov's attempts to

keep the unit free of it and dedicated to socialist ideals—
and the killing. Even silently, from a great distance, you
saw the magnified blood, the flailing of the unsuspecting.
All this tired the spirit. Tania knew how barren was the
place inside where the sniper turned for relief. It was as
jagged and bleak as the bombed city waiting outside in the
cold night. There was no break in the pressure, no release
other than pulling the trigger. Over the past few weeks,
Chekov had quelled the visions by trapping them in a
bottle. Yet all the hares liked him despite his drinking. The
liquor never quenched his courage even when it clouded
his good humor.

"Anatoly!" Tania called out. "The letter is his, of
course." Heads nodded, Zaitsev's, too.

Danilov walked to Chekov's place on the floor. His legs
were splayed in front of him; the toes of his boots shook
nervously. Danilov handed down the letter and motioned
Chekov to rise.

Chekov fingered the envelope. After a halting glance at
the snipers, he tore the letter open.

" 'Dear brave soldier.' " He paused and looked behind
him at the vodka bottle resting next to his journal.

"Read, Anatolushka," Shaikin prompted him. "We want
to hear what your new girlfriend says."

Chekov licked his lips and continued:

*"My name is Hannah. I do not know who is reading
this letter, but I am sure you are the bravest one if
it was given to you.*

*I am seventeen years old. If that makes me your
daughter, then I will call you father. If not, I will
call you brother. The girls in my plant have
gathered presents for the defenders of Stalingrad.
We know it is hard for you in the trenches and our
hearts are with you. We work and live only for you.
Even though I am far behind the Urals, I have*

*hopes of returning to my native Smolensk. I can
hear my mother crying in the kitchen. Kill the
Nazis so we can go home. Let their families wear
mourning in their motherland, not ours. Let their
families wet themselves with tears. I am just a girl,
and I stand in a line assembling parts for trucks
and tanks. But I feel I am fighting, too, just by
staying alive, just by hating the Germans every
minute. I do not like to hate; it is not natural for a
Russian, don't you think? But we must, until they
are gone. Fight hard, my father, my brother, and I
will, too."*

Chekov rolled his head back, turning his gaze to the
beams supporting the bunker's ceiling. His chest worked;
the thin letter shook in his hand.

Kulikov applauded twice, then stopped, embarrassed.
No one else had clapped. Chekov was clearly troubled by
the letter. Tania wondered how Kulikov could not have
seen it.

Chekov handed Danilov the sheet.

"Keep this for me. I'll lose it."

He walked to a corner, picked up a bag of grenades,
and grabbed his submachine gun off a hook on the wall.
He left the bunker without looking around.

Danilov looked at Zaitsev. "Where is he going?"

Zaitsev motioned sharply to Kulikov.

Kulikov jumped up. Tania rose to go along. Zaitsev told
her to sit. Kulikov was a good friend to Chekov. He'd
bring him back.

Heavy silence lay on the snipers. Danilov refused to sit,
pacing in short strides. His stubby hands barely reached
each other behind his back. Then Chekov came through
the doorway. Behind him, Kulikov carried the sack of grenades and the gun.

Chekov slumped near the vodka bottle. He eyed it and

rubbed his chin, grimacing as if he were composing a response to a comment the bottle had made.

Kulikov stepped to the middle of the room. "Chekov has a plan," he announced. "It's a good plan, and I propose we carry it out. It's a raid on a German officers' bunker."

"Where is it?" Zaitsev asked from his corner.

"Sector six."

That had been Sidorov's sector. Now it was Tania's.

Kulikov looked at Tania. "Do we have your permission?"

Tania set down her journal and stood.

"I go." She met Zaitsev's eyes.

"Of course." The Hare stood. He was going, too.

Zaitsev asked Kulikov, "Do you know how to find the bunker?"

Kulikov pointed at Chekov, who was still staring at the vodka bottle. "I think Anatoly should lead us. It was his plan."

Zaitsev stood over Chekov.

"Anatoly, can you point out the location on a map?"

"I want to go." Tears welled in Chekov's eyes.

"No, friend, you stay here. Get some sleep, have a drink. Show me on the map."

Zaitsev spread out a map of sector six. The sad little sniper rubbed his nose on his sleeve while Zaitsev waited.

"Here." Chekov pointed at the southwestern corner of the sector at the end of a long run of trenches, one kilometer beyond the Russian forward positions.

One kilometer, Tania thought. Not so great a distance for a single pair of snipers to operate, especially under cover of night and snow. But to mount a guerrilla action that far into the German rear? Getting in is simply a matter of staying out of sight, a specialty of the hares. Getting out is different. Once the noise starts, the sticks know you're there.

Shaikin stepped forward. "I know every meter of sector six. I can get us there through sector five . . ." Shaikin ran his finger over the map. ". . . then down behind these shacks. There's a German trench here that Sokolov's Forty-fifth took last week. It's not on the map. But I know it. It goes right there."

"Nikolay," Shaikin said, looking up from the map to Kulikov, "is it still snowing?"

"Harder than ever."

Shaikin looked back to Zaitsev, excited. "Good. Vasha, we can move as silently as snowflakes."

Zaitsev handed Shaikin the map. Tania saw on his face that he was still considering the merits and dangers of the mission. It's spontaneous, she thought. This is not on orders; this is just for us, for the sorrow in Chekov's red eyes and in all us snipers. Will Zaitsev risk it?

She looked at Chekov curled on the floor. This man should be home in the Ukraine, chopping chicken necks and poaching quail on the state's property, not here in a dirt bunker, drunk and destroying himself even while the war destroys him. She looked at quiet, handsome Kulikov, so willing to fight, so eaten up inside by something she'd never heard him speak of, some blood in his past, that he could only cover it with more and more German blood. There stood skinny Shaikin, away from his children and wife. And behind them, in the air like corpses in catacombs, lay the dead. And all the dead to come.

"All right," Zaitsev said. "Everyone bring a submachine gun. Leave the rifles here." He walked to where Chekov sat sniffling.

"Anatoly," he told him, laying his hand on the man's head, "stay here. We can talk later. We'll do it right for you."

Chekov blinked, troubled and ashamed. Tania looked away before she could pity him more. She took Medvedev's submachine gun from the corner; she hadn't yet used a machine gun in Stalingrad. But it felt good in her hands; it was a weapon.

Zaitsev dug into his pack for the tin of grease. He tossed it to Shaikin. "Let's go."

Shaikin opened the tin and headed for the doorway.

"Wait."

Danilov, who until now had stood aside watching the dynamics of the hares, had both hands on his hips. The posture made him resemble a big gray sugar bowl.

"I'm going."

Zaitsev looked at the little commissar. He sighed, lowering his head in thought.

Danilov cut through the silence. "Don't waste your time finding a respectful way to tell me I cannot come. I'm not going to stay here and nursemaid your drunken sniper. I want to see this action for myself. I am coming."

Zaitsev raised his head. A thin smile was there, though his eyes told of his displeasure.

"Comrade," he said, "this is very dangerous. You are not trained for this type of maneuver."

Danilov, without moving, without even losing his smile, invoked his power. It was a dark force; it seemed to come from his jowls, which rose on his face while his neck lengthened out of his chest like a snapping turtle's. The commissar's single black brow gnarled over his eyes.

"Comrade Hare," he said in a voice murky with malevolence, "I do not want to remind you of the dangers I *am* trained in." Danilov glowered about the bunker. "The Communist Party will be present at this raid. That is . . . understood?"

With that pause and final word, Danilov released his hold on the room. His smile beamed genuine again.

"Comrade Zaitsev, I will put myself completely under your orders until we return. Is that sufficient?"

Zaitsev nodded.

"Besides," Danilov chuckled, his coat shaking up and

down on his sliding belly, his small hands on his buttons, "this won't be dangerous for me. I'm with the hares. You are the best.

"Now," he said to Shaikin, "toss me the greasepaint pot."

A WOMAN'S UMBRELLA KEPT THE FALLING SNOW off the soldier huddled behind the heavy machine gun. Tania could not tell the exact color of the umbrella. In the moonlight drifting down with the flakes, it looked pink. He doesn't use that during the day, she thought. Russian snipers would crawl through hell for shots at a German machine gunner under a pink umbrella.

The gun was mounted behind a high revetment of sandbags in the center of a twenty-meter-long trench. At one end of the trench, to the gunner's left, was a bunker entrance blocked by a blanket. The bunker was covered in debris to disguise it.

Shaikin had guided them here in under two hours, on a straight line through sector five, passing two Russian machine gun positions with sector five passwords. They'd entered this corner of sector six through a long, empty trench under the silence and limited visibility of the night and the snow, moving with near invisibility. Shaikin scurried in the lead, followed by Kulikov, Danilov, then Zaitsev. Tania brought up the rear, the place for the second in command. Zaitsev allowed her the proper prerogative. Sector six was hers.

In a crater twenty-five meters from the gunner, Danilov lay on his back catching his wind with deep breaths, his own hand over his mouth. His greatcoat was wet with snow, his shiny black boots were checked, and the knees of his pants were soaked through.

Zaitsev ducked at the lip of the crater, Shaikin at his shoulder. Zaitsev whispered something, then handed his submachine gun over. He slid out under the fine lace of hissing snowfall.

Tania moved beside Shaikin and watched. Kulikov crept up, too. Danilov rolled over and tried to crawl beside Tania, but there was no room and she shoved him back.

Lying on his back, the commissar tugged at her foot. Tania slid down and brought her greased face close.

"Comrade," she whispered, "while he is gone, I'm in command. You will stay low, understand?"

She did not wait for a reply but turned and resumed her spot next to Shaikin.

In the dark, Tania saw the outline of the Nazi soldier's head behind the gun, under the umbrella, but no more detail. She'd lost sight of Zaitsev slipping into the enemy trench. She could only imagine the Hare's movements along the wet floor of the trench, waiting, holding his breath, feeling ahead for debris that might creak or snap to give him away. In her mind she waited with him, held her own breath, flexed her fingers as his must have to dig through the cold dirt and mounting snow. She widened her eyes to increase her night vision with his. She came up behind the guard with Zaitsev, saw the soldier standing behind the machine gun, one leg up perhaps to ease his back; they waited for the man to yawn or stretch or rub his eyes. Then they sprang, slapped their left hand over the guard's mouth and slashed the blade held in the right fist down and across the neck, cutting the windpipe, deflating the lungs, keeping the left hand clamped over the gasping mouth, then thrusting the knife through the ribs into the heart or the aorta. They leaned the body against the trench, putting a piece of wood or a pipe under the chin to keep the head up. They righted the umbrella, settling it back into the snow, still wondering what color it was in the murky night.

A snowball landed in front of the crater with a quiet thump. Tania nodded to Shaikin. He rose out of the crater, not crawling but walking quickly, bent over. Tania followed. Behind her, Kulikov helped Danilov to his feet and over the crater rim.

Tania slid into the enemy trench behind Shaikin. Zaitsev met them. The Hare took back his submachine gun from Shaikin. Tania saw the blood darkness glistening on his hands, staining his sleeves. Kulikov and Danilov arrived and Zaitsev wagged his finger to send Kulikov and Shaikin to the far end of the trench to check for more sentries. Zaitsev squatted on his haunches on the trench floor, Tania next to him. Danilov sat in the snow.

Shaikin and Kulikov returned. Tania stood next to Zaitsev. She was glad for the cover granted by the dark and snow, but she knew that whatever kept the hares from sight could also hide the enemy.

At Zaitsev's signal, the group moved. They passed the standing dead sentry under the umbrella and moved to the end of the trench, to the blanket in the doorway.

Suddenly, Danilov elbowed his way past Zaitsev to stand in front before the hanging blanket. In his hand was a pistol. He pushed the blanket aside and stepped into the bunker.

Zaitsev ducked in quickly beside Danilov. His machine gun was leveled and ready. Shaikin, Tania, and Kulikov followed.

Inside the bunker, a lantern dangled from a rafter. The lamp's light was low, yellowing the still air and the earthen walls. On pegs beside the doorway were hung several submachine guns. Under the guns were helmets and flashlights.

Along the walls were three rows of berths, stacked four to a wall. Uniforms showing the stripes and bars of officers were folded and tucked on shelves. Snoring, easy breathing, and a sleepy mumble greeted the Russians while they formed a firing line.

Tania braced the stock of her submachine gun against

her waist. Her barrel was level with the guns of Zaitsev, Kulikov, and Shaikin. The Russian PPSh submachine gun had a rate of fire of nine hundred rounds per minute. She ground her teeth and planted her feet firmly in the dirt.

Danilov raised himself at the shoulders and spoke. "For the ruthless murders of children and mothers, you Nazi predators are sentenced to death."

Danilov lifted his pistol and fired into the berths. The report filled the bunker. Tania breathed the smoke of the powder. Heads and bodies in the berths sprang up, their voices buried in the hanging bang of the pistol. Before the others could react, Tania squeezed her trigger.

The submachine gun leaped in her hands. The barrel jerked above the berths to spit bullets up the bunks into the ceiling. Tania let go of the trigger to bring the barrel level again.

In that lapse, Zaitsev's gun roared, joined by Kulikov's and Shaikin's. Tania gripped hard and fired again. Danilov stepped back and the four gunners, side by side, blew a gale of lead into the berths.

Tania swept the gun across the bunks, shattering them, ripping everything in front of her, wood, mattresses, flesh, dirt. She could not tell where her bullets struck, mingling them with the pounding rounds spewed by the men at her sides. The bodies in the berths, still shrouded in the shredding blankets, rocked against the walls and spasmed on the beds. The jarring seconds passed and the room filled with noise like a bottle filling with water, the air shoved out and replaced with clattering explosions, smoke, and splinters.

Zaitsev reached out and pushed Tania's weapon down. She released the trigger. The others had stopped shooting. The room was thick with an acrid haze. Tania's hearing was blunted by the screams of the submachine guns in the small room. Her head throbbed; the only sound was a heartbeat coming strong in her temples.

The five stood still. Then Kulikov raised the blanket to let the oily cloud roil into the trench.

In the bunker, the lantern's dim glow strained to reach through the smoke. The berths were shot to pieces. The white innards of the splintered wood showed in a thousand holes. The dirt walls glimmered as if splashed with fresh wet tar. The lantern's small flame reflected off the walls in wet red dots. An uncountable number of shell casings littered the floor, mixed with shards of wood and tufts of bloodied mattress cotton.

In the raw aftermath, the blasts only now fading in her head, Tania's nerves jangled. A movement to her left made her jump. Kulikov stumbled out the doorway. Zaitsev was behind him, pushing. A hand grabbed her wrist. Shaikin turned her out past the blanket. Danilov was already in the trench.

Zaitsev spoke to her face; she could not hear him through the ringing in her ears. Shaikin, still holding her arm, began to run, pulling her along until she sped on her own. She followed Shaikin to the end of the trench. At the wall, he jumped up and flopped onto his belly to scramble to his knees. She handed up her submachine gun, feeling the heat of the barrel. She climbed out after Shaikin, then ran behind him through the white falling curtain against the backdrop of night. Her world was silent; the guns had stuffed her ears. She ran in the midst of the hares with the portly Danilov, knowing the Germans could be screaming at her, bullets flying by her, and she would not hear the rifles nor even see the bullets biting the ground around her. She ran, thrilled at escaping death by dashing through it.

They ran in their own footprints for two hundred meters away from the bunker. Safely distant, the snipers and the puffing commissar dropped behind cover. Zaitsev paused to catch his breath, then crawled ahead, telling them to follow in five minutes.

Tania leaned her head back to look into the falling snow. She felt dizzy, as though, instead of the flakes wafting down to her, she were flying upward into them. She let the flakes rest on her nose and eyelashes to melt on her hot, oiled skin. She cast her thoughts back over the past ten minutes. Images came to her out of order: the powerful quivering of the submachine gun, Danilov on his back, Zaitsev's bloody hands, the slivers of the berths on the bunker floor.

The umbrella. What actual color was it?

She opened her eyes. Damn, she thought. I forgot to look.

CHEKOV LAY SPREAD-EAGLED, SNORING. AN empty bottle stood watch beside him like a pet glass cat.

Zaitsev slipped under the blanket behind Tania, followed by Kulikov and Shaikin. Danilov had left their group the moment they'd scrambled back behind Russian lines, rushing to write the story of the latest sniper strike. This time the story was not about the distant and silent delivery of death by the hares. Tonight the snipers had crawled into an officers' bunker and massacred them in their beds. Tonight reeked of rabid brutality, of the abattoir, of revenge. And Danilov had been there, not just reporting events but for once making the news in person.

Zaitsev nudged the sleeping Chekov with his boot. The man snorted but did not wake up.

"Anatoly." Zaitsev slipped the toe of his boot under Chekov's side and lifted up, then let him roll back.

Zaitsev turned to Shaikin. "Take him back to the Lazur, Ilya." Then he smiled at Tania. "Viktor will kill him if he comes back and finds him in our bunker snoring like that."

Kulikov joined Shaikin. "We'll have to carry him, Ilya. I'll help you."

Together they lifted Chekov across Shaikin's shoulders. Kulikov picked up the three men's rifles and packs. Tania moved the blanket aside for them to stagger out the doorway.

She was alone now in the bunker with Zaitsev.

"Good night," she said.

"Wait. I'll walk partway with you."

Together they stepped out past the blanket. Ahead of them, Chekov continued to snore, swaying atop Shaikin's thin shoulders. Kulikov slapped Chekov on his upside-down head. "Shut up," Kulikov told him.

Tania reached into her pack for a cloth to wipe the grease from her eye sockets, cheeks, and neck. She rubbed fresh snow into her face, grinding the cold crystals like icy sand over her skin. Zaitsev watched Kulikov and Shaikin walk away with their drunken load into the tumbling snow and muffled night.

A breeze crossed her wet brow and chin, cooling her like a breath of mint. She looked at Zaitsev's face, still smudged with grease. He brought his eyes to hers. She looked down to his hands.

"You're covered in blood," she said. "Here." She scooped up another handful of snow. "Give me your hand."

She rubbed the snow over the back of his hand, digging it in with her palm. She scraped away the grease and blood. The flakes turned burgundy. His pale Siberian skin and high blue veins rose through the browning slush.

When she'd scoured both his hands clean, she daubed his face with the cloth. Zaitsev stood still, blinking under the cloth passing over his eyes.

Turmoil rose in Tania's breast. What am I doing, she thought? I'm cleaning him like a mother with a dirty child. She tried to rein in her hands, but stopping would only hasten the moment when they stood in the falling snow, face-to-face, with no nervous action between them to stall their words or give innocent purpose to the connection in their eyes. She knew this was the moment she'd waited for; standing with him now, so near to the coming touch. These few seconds alone had been rising with the heat of the evening's events. Before the raid, at the meeting, Zaitsev had forgiven her, reinstated her by giving her the leadership of sector six. Then had come the tumult of the killing of the German officers. She remembered tingling while the bullets flew from her submachine gun and then running in the snow and dark. Touching Zaitsev, even through the cloth, alone with him now, she tingled the same way.

Will he speak to me when I drop this ruse of cleaning his hands and face? Or will he choose silence, moving me to choose also? Will I act, or will I say good night and stumble off under my own burden? He'll speak to me when I drop my hands. He's waiting for me to stop. He will say . . . what?

Tania willed her hands to slow. With one final sweep, she wiped the cloth under his bottom lip.

"There," she said, smiling for an instant. She stuffed the cloth into her pack.

When she straightened and looked into his face, he was looking not at her but across the dim moonlit outlines of the ruins and the collecting snow down to the Volga. His reddened hands were tucked under his armpits.

"Tania, what did we do tonight?" He shook his head.

She did not understand what he was asking. She dug her own cold hands into her pockets. What's this mood? she wondered. Where is he all of a sudden?

"What do you mean, Vasily?"

She'd never called him by his first name. It fell from her mouth. But curled up into himself, gazing around like a man lost and unsure how it had happened, he seemed to have made himself smaller. His glow, the aura of the hero, the *vozhd* of the hares, had waned as if she'd rubbed it off with the grease and blood. This was not Chief Master Sergeant Zaitsev in front of her. This was Vasha. She could sense it. He was here, vulnerable, beside her in the snowy hush of the night.

She prodded him with her voice.

"What did we do?" She shrugged. "We killed a dozen enemy officers. We sent the Nazis a message."

Zaitsev's eyes leveled on her, though his sight still seemed far away. "What message did we send? Whom did we send it to? Who got it, us or them?"

What is he talking about? Those were invaders. What did it matter whether they were sleeping in their bunks, firebombing a peasant village, or executing civilians in a park? They were the same. They were vermin, sticks to be broken, marked for death. Any death, not just the clean and instant blackness from a sniper's bullet. Chopped up, pulped by a thousand rounds from five meters away—let them be found like that in the morning, let them tell that story on the German side of the line at dawn.

Zaitsev pulled his hands from his armpits. He motioned and started to speak, then halted, his hands left waiting for the words. His eyes were locked on Tania's.

"It's not . . ." he said, and narrowed his eyes; Tania saw how he cared about his next words. "It wasn't what I was taught. It's not our way. It shouldn't be. That wasn't killing. It wasn't even war."

Tania pulled his hands down. She stepped to him to hold his hands. They were cold; she held them tightly.

"Yes, Vasha, it was killing," she whispered, "it was war killing."

She took a last step to him, to press her chest against his. She pulled his hands behind her and felt them link around her waist to hold her. Tania laid her head on his shoulder. She looked at his neck, his ear, his short-cropped hair with no sideburns. She whispered again.

"You're right, Vasha. There was no honor in it."

She raised her head off his shoulder. His face still held distance and loss.

"But," she said, "there will be after Danilov writes it up."

Zaitsev's chest rustled in a short laugh. Tania pulled her arms tighter around his waist.

"Leave the killing to the rest of us," she breathed. "We'll kill for you. I'll kill for you. You hunt, Vasha. You hunt."

FOURTEEN

ZAITSEV TURNED THE LANTERN DOWN, ALMOST too far. Before the flame could gutter and go out, he raised the wick. Deep shadows gouged the dirt walls and floor of the snipers' bunker.

What am I risking? he asked himself. He looked at his watch: 2:30 in the morning. Viktor rarely returns before dawn.

He pulled Tania into the bunker. She held on to his hand as if hanging off a cliff: strong, tight, for her life. His mind was dispatched through his own hand into her long fingers. The strength in her grip made her real to him then, for the first time. Even when she'd held him outside moments before, he still hadn't been able to sense her. He'd looked above her, his mind on honor, death, war. What they'd done that night in the German bunker was acceptable to the soldier but terrible and foreign to the hunter. His grandfather would've beaten him for that. It was not done in the taiga, to kill wantonly.

He thought of Tania, submachine gun squalling, eyes blinking through the flying chips of wood and hammering noise. Tania gritting her teeth, running near me through the ruins and the night. Tania touching me through the snow cupped in her hands, the warm, dirty cloth on my face. Tania holding me. He looked at her now, in the center of the room, at the end of his arm. Her blond hair, thick as a wheat field, cast her shoulders and face in shadow. Only the tip of her nose was lit. He turned her so that the light played full on her face to bloom in her blue eyes.

From her first day as a recruit, Tania had been a distraction, even a worry, just as he'd predicted to Danilov. Indeed, she was Danilov's experiment, one that Zaitsev had thought would not last long. She was hot, eager, stupid with her emotions. She became a woman to him only when he joked with Viktor as men do, about her ass or her hair or whether Fedya, the big boy, dead now, had been getting any, or when he saw her with Shaikin, touching him in the meetings. But away from her, he did not think about Tania Chernova.

Now he sneaked into his own bunker like a thief. Why? Just because he had a woman by the hand? He was awash in sensation. What am I risking? he asked himself again.

If someone walks in, I'll laugh about it. I'll tell Viktor how I seduced the girl; she was good, and once was enough. He should try next, I'll say. But if we're left uninterrupted to hold each other, to be slow, to rock in each other's arms, to kiss and talk quietly, I don't know. I control all events now. What will I do with a situation I cannot shape? Do I want this?

Stop thinking, he told himself. This isn't up to you, anyway. You knew it from the moment she touched you outside.

Tania let go of his hand and turned her face away from the light. He watched her walk to his corner.

With her back to him, she unbuttoned her coat. She lowered her arms and the coat slid off to crumple on the floor, sleeves out, hood up, like a body melting into the dirt. Her hands moved to her neck. Elbows out, her wrists flicked, opening the buttons of her tunic. She leaned over to untie her boot laces. The lines of her pantaloons pulled tight against her bottom.

When she straightened, her hands worked at her waist. She turned to face him: all the barriers to her body had been unlocked. Her shirt hung aside from her breasts, the points firm beneath the gray-green undershirt. Her sleeves were unbuttoned at the wrists. Her belt was undone. The zipper to her pantaloons was down and her boots flapped open.

Tania kicked off the boots to stand in her socks. Her face was a white moon in the lantern light. Her eyes shone at him, reflecting the lamp in twin dots turned azure.

Zaitsev stepped toward her; he watched his shadow climb her legs, then shade her body and face. He reached to her shoulders to push the unbuttoned shirt back. She raised her head at his touch; her hair was heavy on the backs of his hands. Her collar opened and slid away. The tunic fell back and a scent rose from her undershirt, arms, and neck. The tang of sweat mingled with the smell of soil. He thought of the sweet loam on the floor of the birch forest. The shirt fell behind her. Tania stood between the coat and the shirt in a circlet of arms and buttons.

She raised her hands in the air. Her breasts pushed up against the undershirt, flattening and rounding. Zaitsev laid his open palms on her to feel her nipples. He pulled the thin cotton shirt over her head and dropped it at her feet.

Zaitsev reached for her waist, but Tania stopped him, pushing his hands down by his sides. She reached for his waist and unlatched the brass of the Red Army belt he wore outside his coat. She tossed the belt into the shadows where it rattled on the floor. The girl's hands moved to his chest. Her bare breasts and shoulders were ivory ovals in the hard linear shadows of the bunker. She undid the buttons of his coat and tugged the shoulders back to let the coat tumble.

She flipped open the buttons on his jersey. All the time, she avoided his eyes; she watched her own hands move on him.

The buttons freed. Zaitsev pulled his tunic and navy shirt over his head. He dropped them onto the growing heap.

Keeping her hands by her sides, she laid her breasts against his bare chest. She exhaled when her flesh pressed against him. Her breath was warm, full as fur against his cheek.

Tania locked onto his eyes. She sat on the floor before him, rolling her head back to hold his gaze. She pulled off her pants and socks and reached behind Zaitsev to gather in his coat and shirt, bunching them with her own clothes to form a mound at her back.

Zaitsev stepped out of his boots. He slid off his pants and dropped them to Tania, who made a show of adding them to the mix.

He sank to his knees on the stack of clothes. Tania pointed at his socks.

"Trust me," he murmured, breaking the silence, "they're better off where they are."

Tania giggled. Zaitsev was wrapped in her laugh, feeling it heat the cool bunker floor. Her laughter was like arms that moved his chest in front of hers and pulled him down over her.

Tania did not collapse back onto the cushion of clothes. She pressed hard against him with her chest. Her hands and arms stayed braced against the ground. This surprised Zaitsev and excited him. He covered her mouth with his to push her down in a kiss as though setting the spring of a trap. She allowed herself to sink back bit by bit, then relaxed and flung her arms about his neck. He laid his hands in the curves of her hips, then ran them up her sides, over her ribs, and behind her neck. She moved under him in a rolling wave.

He pulled his hand from the soft weight of her hair and looked into his palms and at his fingers. The hand was rough, callused from months of crawling through the ruins of Stalingrad. Dried blood from the night's murder clung beneath his nails. This is not a proper hand, he thought, to touch a woman.

Gently, Zaitsev pulled his other hand from beneath her neck. He rose up on an elbow.

"Give me your hand," he said.

Looking down at her closed eyes, Zaitsev put his hand on top of hers. Slowly he guided her fingers to her breast; he felt the question in her wrist. She relaxed the hand and entrusted it to him. He worked her forefinger in a small circle over the swollen nipple. Tania inhaled in a gasp, then let go in a murmured sigh. Zaitsev slipped her hand off her breast and led it into the cleft between the two mounds, then down onto the white plain of her belly. He moved her hand in languorous circles, pressing and releasing; her hips stirred under their hands. He led her touch down between her legs, sensing no resistance. She moved with him, taking his directions; her fingers began to swirl and glide under him on their own, on her skin, into herself.

He looked into her face and breathed with her sighs. He no longer led her hand but rode it, going where she pleased; he was saddled to her movements.

Zaitsev watched Tania bring herself to a climax. In a climbing quiver, she reached up with her free hand and pulled him down to kiss his face in the rhythms of her body. She pushed her stomach higher, pressing her thighs together over their hands. Within moments, her back flexed into an arch until she lay back with a heaving chest.

She opened her eyes. In her stillness, he felt the attention his own body clamored for now.

"Vasha," she whispered, "go with me tomorrow."

He looked down her length. Her knees were up. The smoothness of her legs ached inside him, pushing to come out.

"That's the way of the taiga," he whispered. He moved above her, sliding his knees between hers.

"The animals mate." He lowered himself. "Then they hunt."

MAMAYEV KURGAN'S SCARS SHOWED UNDER the morning light. The snow, which had fallen until dawn, did not hide the slashes of trenches or fill the craters that gave its eastern slope the look of a moonscape. The frost glistened diamond flashes in Zaitsev's scope while his crosshairs glided over sector six.

"Look at the top of the hill," Tania said. "There's no snow on it. I hear it's because the ground stays so warm up there from all the shelling."

Mamayev Kurgan commanded a view of the city and the Volga. Three months earlier, in August, Red soldiers standing atop the water towers on the hill's crest first saw the dust of the German army's advance tanks speeding over the steppe. This morning, Zaitsev knew, Nazi spotters were in command of the summit. The two armies had traded the hill several times, never keeping it for long, always attracting the worst the enemy had to dish out in order to regain the crest. The hill had been peppered with artillery shells so often and with such ferocity that the ground of Mamayev Kurgan carried within it an extra, pregnant heat.

Zaitsev and Tania hunkered down in a trench on the western edge of no-man's-land. Before them was an impossible maze of broken machinery, abandoned guns, and pitted earth. Bodies lay under the hummocks of small snowdrifts.

Zaitsev pulled the periscope from his backpack to scan deeper into the rising field in front of them. He thought, I've got to make something happen. He knew the hunting would be slow on Mamayev Kurgan. The fighting had been so intense, so nonstop that anyone left alive here probably knew how to stay that way. He didn't want to spend days with Tania helping her get her first kill as sector leader.

For a silent hour he peered through the periscope at the German breastworks. Tania crawled fifty meters away to look from a different angle and to avoid being conspicuous. The shadows shortened with the sun rising at their backs. The reflections from the glistening snow dulled. Twice, Zaitsev saw what might have been sniper movement. A wisp of cigarette smoke disappeared quickly; it might have been snow drifting on the wind. Moments after, near the same spot, he thought he glimpsed a helmet bobbing once, then twice, above the trench. This, too, vanished before he could focus on it.

Zaitsev was acquainted with waiting. But something about Chernova drove him at a faster clip. Her eager energy distracted him from his discipline, though she made no overt demands or even showed any hints of impatience with him. She has a heat, he thought, like a stove or the top of Mamayev Kurgan. Things boil up around her.

He set down the periscope and lit a cigarette, breaking a major rule of sniper engagement. He felt aggravated, restless.

Well, he thought, there's something I've been wanting to try for a while. Why not this morning?

He shouldered his rifle and crawled to where Tania squatted below her periscope. She did not look away from the eyepiece when he approached.

"You're smoking," she said.

"Stay here. I'm going to get Danilov."

Tania's head snapped around. "What? Why do that? He's no good up here. Leave him alone."

"I have a plan. Stay here." Zaitsev raised a finger at her. "And don't shoot a fucking thing. Understand?"

He wagged his finger at her hard to make his point and turned to steal back to the Lazur.

"SET IT UP RIGHT HERE."

Zaitsev stacked more bricks on the two piles he'd built above the trench. He stepped out of the way for Danilov to place the loudspeaker behind the brick mound on the left. The commissar let the bell of the speaker stick out a few centimeters to the right and pointed it up the hill toward the German lines.

Danilov unrolled the coiled cord between the microphone and the speaker. He sat on the trench floor with an effort and clicked the trigger on the microphone twice. The speaker blared to loud, tinny life.

"Wait." Zaitsev held up his hand. "Wait for my signal, as we discussed."

Zaitsev crawled on all fours to Tania. She stared at him, the rifle and periscope across her lap.

"So?" she asked.

Zaitsev made a quick study of her face. Her checks were flushed with the chill. A ring from the periscope showed around her right eye. Her lips held no smile but were left sour and pouting, the remnants of her one-word question to him: so?

He paused, appreciating her effect on him, her combination of beauty and will. He'd left her for ninety minutes on his trek back to the Lazur for Danilov. She'd had all that time to do nothing but stare up the slope. The stove, he thought, has warmed while I was gone.

He whispered. "Just do what I tell you, partisan." He glanced back at Danilov. "Our little commissar is really quite good at his job, you know. And his job is agitating. In a minute, he's going to get on his bullhorn and read some very nasty leaflets in German his brother *politrooks* have prepared. I suspect Danilov's German is not so good, but it's probably good enough to make every Nazi within earshot angry as hornets. Maybe just with his pronunciation, who can tell?"

Zaitsev grinned at his own jest. The corners of Tania's mouth lifted. A small blue wave broke in her eyes.

"My guess," he continued, "is that we're going to be in a shooting gallery soon after he turns it up. You go twenty meters to the left, and I'll stay near Danilov. If there's sniper fire, it'll probably be in my direction. I'll be set up for it; I've got a little trick I'm going to try. Anything else, machine guns probably, I think you'll see first. Any shots you get, take them. We move one minute after the first shot, either yours or mine."

"Vasha." Tania held out her hand, palm up as if to accept a coin. "You always say a sniper must guard the secrecy of his position." She pointed at Danilov to demand an explanation for the commissar and his loudspeaker.

"Exactly." Zaitsev grinned. "And that's why today we try the unexpected." He reached into her lap for her periscope. He laid it across her open hand, dropping his smile with the scope. "You wanted a hunt. Let's hunt."

He crawled away to set up his subterfuge, the stuffed cotton dummy he'd carried from the Lazur. He propped the dummy up behind the second, right-hand pile of bricks, moving it forward and to the left just far enough so that its helmet would be visible only in a roughly twenty-degree span to the southwest. Finally, he stuck a pipe behind the dummy's back to hold it in place.

Zaitsev had not been a frequent user of the dummies. No one in the hares was. The opposite was their specialty, as Tania had correctly cited: the hares strove to be invisible. A dummy was designed to draw attention to itself, a feint. The dummies were better for Viktor's line of work; the bears' style was a more confrontational one. He'd actually heard of Viktor's boys leaping out of their shooting cells during combat and charging. Not the way snipers should work, Zaitsev thought, but he would never tell Viktor Medvedev how to hunt or what to teach. But charging and shouting were not for Zaitsev's little, lithe assassins. Still, the dummies were always available. Their production had become an underground cottage industry for the thousand or so native Stalingrad women left in the city. Zaitsev held a mental picture of them sitting in a circle beneath a lantern in a covered shell hole or a basement, stitching dummies out of old blankets, stuffing them with mattress filling, giving the dummies names. This was how these old women fought, with needle and thread. Zaitsev was glad now to use one of their creations. He named it Pyotr and patted it on the shoulder.

Satisfied with the setup, Zaitsev took a position ten meters to the right of the dummy. With his pack shovel, he dug a slit in the lip of the trench. He placed a brick on either side of the channel for an embrasure. He laid his tied-up gloves in the trough and his rifle on top of them to face the twenty-degree arc he'd baited with the head of the dummy, Pyotr's head. He gave a thumbs-up to Danilov, who waited on the trench floor.

The commissar flicked the switch on the microphone and blew into it. The speaker pitched a noise into the air like a tree splitting. He had it turned up very loud.

The commissar arranged a few pages in his lap and brought the microphone close to his mouth to begin the propaganda. Zaitsev listened to the foreign tongue spit out through the loudspeaker. He'd never encountered German before he came to Stalingrad. When he'd finally heard it from prisoners and deserters, or on the lips of the dying, or screamed during close combat in the houses downtown, he'd judged it an ugly language, a battle tongue. German was spoken back in the throat, bitten and chewed with the teeth. By contrast, he considered Russian to be liquid; it was a language to be cradled on the lips, swirled in the mouth like cognac. Russian could be whispered through a keyhole to a lover on the other side to stroke her into unlocking the door. German was the language to knock the door down. It was how you spoke to your dog or cleared your throat.

Zaitsev looked past Danilov to Tania. She surveyed the field from behind cover through her periscope. He chose to scan through his rifle scope. The 4X rifle sight offered a smaller range than the periscope, but the optics were better for clearer definition. He swiveled slowly across his expected target range. Though the morning was aging, the sun was still behind him.

Danilov's amplified voice tore the air. The hard German consonants, sharpened by the loudspeaker, banged out an edgy echo flung against the hillside. That's obnoxious, thought Zaitsev, even if they can't understand a word he's saying.

The pamphlets in Danilov's lap were of the sort used by both sides, usually dropped from the air over the battlefield. The leaflets were a common sight, blowing across the ground between the two facing armies as if scurrying out of the way.

Zaitsev looked up from his scope. The rising landscape seemed void of life. Danilov's voice sailed over it like cawing electric buzzards. No movement at all. But Zaitsev knew that the depressions and gashes on all sides of him held soldiers and guns, German and Russian. He'd learned months ago never to be deceived by calm in Stalingrad.

He brought his eye back down to his scope. After a few moments of searching, he noted the barely visible barrel of a Nazi machine gun 350 meters away. It was not manned. That meant nothing. It could have been jammed and abandoned. It could just as easily be a fake position made of wood; it might also be a working machine gun with its crew hidden in the trench while a camouflaged spotter kept watch. Nothing is what it seems out here, thought Zaitsev. The softness of the snow is just a sheath over a jagged hillside. The stillness, seemingly blind, has a hundred eyes. Danilov's crackling voice even appears to come from a man's form that is actually a stuffed dummy.

Suddenly Zaitsev heard the thumping of bullets plow into the earth and bricks around the loudspeaker. The chattering of a machine gun flew past him. Danilov broke off his shouting; Zaitsev glanced from his scope quickly to the commissar, who was curled on the floor of the trench. He had dropped the microphone to shield his head with both hands from the brick shards and dirt falling on him while the machine gun raked the loudspeaker. In the heart of the action, Pyotr stood unscathed behind his bricks.

Zaitsev hunted to his left through the scope. The machine gun he'd seen moments before was still quiet. The gun firing at the loudspeaker must be operating to his right, outside his targeted killing zone. Before he could lift his rifle out of its slit, he heard Tania fire.

The machine gun fell silent.

Good. She got the bastard. One minute.

Zaitsev glanced at his watch.

Another machine gun came alive, aiming not at the loudspeaker but far to his left. Tania! They've spotted her.

Zaitsev rammed his eye against the scope and found the unmanned machine gun. It now had the head and hands of a soldier planted behind it, flailing away at Tania's position. Another German was beside the gunner, binoculars up.

Zaitsev exhaled to push his pulse out of his head. He watched the gunner work, to let the target take over his thoughts, away from the battle pitch. Let him draw the bullet. Let him open up for it. There's no hurry. Make it good. One shot. One squeeze.

Without anticipating it, the rifle jumped into his shoulder. He heard the loud report of the bullet on its way. This was how he accomplished his best shots: without telling himself "now" but simply thinking the bullet into the target, pulling the trigger on instinct, surprising himself a little.

In his scope, the gunner's helmet whipped backward when he fell from the gun. One of the soldier's hands caught in the grips. The gun swung upward under the hanging weight of the dead Nazi, still firing, bullets blasting into the air. The spotter pulled the snagged fingers free, then ducked behind the trench wall and, with the body of his comrade, dropped from sight.

Zaitsev gathered up his periscope and pack and scuttled to where Danilov sat dusting himself off. Bits of red brick and dirty snow lingered on his shoulders and fur hat.

Tania arrived, her rifle and gear in her hands, ready to go.

"Good work," Zaitsev said, kneeling beside the commissar. Danilov smiled, gathering his spilled pages. He dug between his legs and pulled the microphone out of the dirt.

"That worked well," Zaitsev continued. "But we need to get out of here now."

"Go? Why? I'm not finished."

Danilov's smile tightened and flattened like a pulled string. He pressed the microphone trigger and blew into it. The loudspeaker sizzled to life.

"I've got a bit more to say to you whores!" he shouted in Russian. His voice emerged from the battered bell with a buzz. Zaitsev was amazed the thing still worked.

"No. That's not a good idea." Zaitsev pushed the microphone down from the commissar's lips. "Our game worked well. Very well. Now it's time to go. Remember, we're on the front line."

"I know perfectly well where we are."

"Then you know we'd better move, and now."

As Zaitsev finished his sentence, his eyes locked onto Tania's face on the other side of Danilov. She heard it, too. The whining, falling whistle of a mortar shell.

Zaitsev grabbed Danilov by the lapels of his coat. He flung the commissar onto his face on the trench floor and dug down beside him.

The ground bucked with the explosion. The first shell landed above them, blowing shrapnel and shock waves past the top of the trench. More eruptions followed. Dirt rained onto their backs, pattering on the crowns of their helmets.

They waited with faces in the dirt through six explosions. The ground shuddered with each shell. When he sensed the bombardment was finished, Zaitsev tugged on Tania's leg. She raised her head.

Danilov reared up. Dirt and snow stuck to his mouth and eyebrows. He spit once to clear the debris from his lips.

"Comrade Zaitsev," he said, "I agree. We should go."

The three gathered their equipment. Danilov collected pages off the ground. Zaitsev grabbed at a few sheets to speed the commissar. He looked up at Pyotr. The dummy had stood through the barrage, the pipe firmly in his back.

With all his papers in hand, Danilov wound up the cord for the microphone and pocketed it. He reached his hand over the top of the trench to pull down the loudspeaker.

A bullet ricocheted off a brick lying just below the bell, splitting it into bits and dust. Danilov fell to the floor of the trench as if scalded. Tania and Zaitsev stooped quickly.

The commissar stared into Zaitsev's eyes. "What was that? Who the hell's shooting?"

"Stay low," Zaitsev replied.

He snagged his backpack and scrambled with it to the right. He pulled out his periscope and hoisted the mirror and lens above the top of the trench. Surveying the field quickly, he saw nothing of note against the rumpled white slope but the two dead machine gun positions.

He lowered the periscope. Just a German sniper who got caught napping, he thought. We woke him up with the broadcast and artillery and now he wants to get in on the show a little late. He figured he'd wait for someone to retrieve the loudspeaker. Clever move. I would've done the same. But I wouldn't have fired at a hand. I would've waited for a head.

Zaitsev decided to let the Nazi sniper have his fun. Maybe I'll come back tomorrow with Tania and take care of him. Maybe not. He's probably not worth it.

He looked up at Pyotr. Take him down, he thought, give the cotton boy a rest. Put him back up tomorrow and drill this snotty little sniper.

Zaitsev scooted over to Pyotr. He reached to pull the dummy down by the arm; suddenly, the cloth head snapped back. Pyotr's helmet rang out and jerked, flying off to fall backward. It hung there, caught by the chin strap wrapped around the neck.

Zaitsev leaped away. He looked at Tania and Danilov, and the faraway sound of a rifle report skittered down the hillside. Their eyes were fixed on Pyotr's head.

Zaitsev looked up at the dummy's face. In the center of the once featureless visage was a hole. Stuffing peeked out to give Pyotr a ragged nose.

Zaitsev hoisted his periscope again. This sniper must be in my killing zone, he thought. He must be. There's no other alley from which to see Pyotr's head.

Before he could focus the periscope, another bullet

ripped into the cloth face. The round clanged into the helmet strung behind the neck. Pyotr shivered but stood firm against the pipe.

Zaitsev was rocked. This bullet had struck within moments of the last, perhaps as fast as four seconds! The report of the rifle skipped by, faint and distant.

Another shot slammed into the helmet, fanning Zaitsev's amazement. It followed the bullet before at an incredible clip. Maybe three seconds, three and a half. Pyotr's head joggled back again as if in surprise himself.

Zaitsev flung his shoulder against the trench wall, lifting his periscope. He scanned the target zone furiously. The periscope had a range of 350 meters. This sniper must be inside 250 meters to have that kind of accuracy and speed, he thought. But the sounds of the reports were eroded, as if they'd rolled down from far up the hill.

Even if the enemy sniper was close, this quality of shooting was hard to explain. So fast to be so murderously accurate. Maybe it was a team of snipers taking turns with their shots.

Another bullet shook Pyotr. This one passed through the neck and cut the leather strap when it banged into the helmet. The helmet clattered to the floor of the trench, spilling the four spent slugs onto the trench floor. Zaitsev saw nothing. No muzzle blaze indicated a sniper's position; no bobbing head or cigarette smoke, no movement against the icy backdrop betrayed any of the hill's white secrets.

Shit, thought Zaitsev. Where is he? He's got to be close. I must've missed him, looked right past him. Them.

This is ridiculous, he thought. He lunged to the pipe buttressing the dummy and yanked it down. Pyotr fell and tumbled across his lap. The wisps of stuffing protruding from the holes made a skewed pair of eyes, a nose, and a small, marveling mouth.

Zaitsev picked up the fallen helmet. He took from its

bottom the four smashed bullets and hefted them in his hand.

Tania scooted over to him. She shook his outstretched leg.

"Let's go, Vasha," she said. "Somebody is crazy out there."

Zaitsev did not move or take his eyes off the shells. Deep inside him, he caught a glimpse, just a flash, of the two gray eyes of fear glowing in the shadows. The eyes crouched; the fear snarled once.

He closed his fist over the spent bullets. Tania jerked again on his leg.

"Vasha, let's go. We're in somebody's crosshairs. Somebody who's very damn good."

Zaitsev looked up at that. He licked his lips. His mouth had gone dry.

FIFTEEN

NIKKI ARRIVED IN THE ANTEROOM TO OSTAR-
hild's offices at dawn. The colonel walked out lazily just
after nine o'clock. "There's no hurry," he told Nikki. "The
sun doesn't shift to our backs until well after noon. Have
some Dutch coffee."

He led the colonel first to the spotter's hill, 102.8.
From there they could view the entire battlefield: the factories to the north, downtown to the south and the river
islands.

All morning Nikki carried the colonel's rifle and pack,
which was stuffed with food. He didn't mind; Thorvald
shared his stores liberally, proclaiming he wouldn't be in
Stalingrad long enough to eat half of what he'd brought.

After they'd roamed for an hour up and down a trench
network below the crest of Mamayev Kurgan, Thorvald
stopped and gazed down the slope. Nikki pulled up beside
him. A Russian loudspeaker on the hillside far below
them had cranked up, prattling in an irritating, tinny
treble. The narrator's German was so riddled with accent
that the words were almost unrecognizable.

"Can you make out what he's saying?" the colonel
asked.

"Barely." Nikki grimaced.

"Oooo." Thorvald shook his head. "That's bad German."

The speaker seemed unaware of his shortcoming. He shouted with conviction into his microphone. The awful metallic noise slicing up and down the hill would likely induce a headache long before the words could inflame any Germanic passion.

Nikki had begun to appreciate Colonel Thorvald. The man possessed a sense of humor, a lost thing in Stalingrad. He was clean, with no lice on him yet. He was generous with the cheeses and breads he'd brought from Berlin. Nikki liked his talkativeness, his confidence. He had not insisted that Nikki bring along his rifle. Though Nikki had yet to see him shoot, he suspected that Thorvald was what he said he was: the best.

Nikki hunched in the trench next to the colonel, admiring the man's white parka and pants. The outfit seemed to suck down into the snow on the trench floor. He must be nearly invisible from a distance, Nikki thought. He looked down at his own gray-green coat and filthy gray pantaloons.

Nikki had listened to the Russian agitators before, at least once a week during the heavy house-to-house fighting of September and October. He and his mates had laughed at the lectures then. In those days, the German army had been powerful, secure in its belief that the Reds stood no chance of holding the city. They're just squeaking like mice in a trap, the boys all had said.

Now everything was different. Now the message was not to be laughed at. The best he could do was ignore it even while the words drilled into his ears from the amplifier below.

The German soldier has been lied to, the loudspeaker blared. Russia is peaceful; come over to us and eat well. Consider the terrible harvest in your homeland this year, consider the hunger of your children and parents. Nikki tried to tune out the words, to hear only the scratchy warble and buzz of the shouting voice.

"He should turn it down," Thorvald snickered. "It's up way too loud."

Nikki closed his eyes. This is old news, this is miserable propaganda. The colonel wants to wait here and listen to this shit, fine, let him, so he can go back to Berlin and cackle about it there with his students and opera friends.

Thorvald spoke again. "He's right, you know."

Nikki gave no response.

"The harvest in Germany this year was awful. Bad year on the farms. Lots of people are starving."

"Pay no attention to it, sir."

"Of course. It's just . . . do they do this all the time?"

"All the time, sir."

"Does it work? Does it bother you?"

Nikki eyed Thorvald. He asks a lot of questions: Were you scared? How did it feel? Does it bother you? He's a colonel, he's a soldier. Hasn't he heard propaganda before?

"Yes, sir. It does work sometimes. And no, it doesn't bother me anymore. I don't listen to it."

Thorvald tilted his head. He looked into the sky filled with the rattling voice from below.

"It's good stuff," he said. "Current. They're good at this, the Russians. I guess they practice on their own people, hmmm?"

The sense of humor again. Nikki smiled at the colonel's eyes, still huge even when crinkled above a grin. Let's move on, he thought. Nothing doing here.

Below, a machine gun chattered. Nikki and Thorvald clambered to the lip of the trench. Both men trained their binoculars down the slope. One hundred fifty meters to their left was the machine gun position, sunk behind a row of sandbags. The gun crew had closed in on a spot near the base of the hill. Through the binoculars, Nikki barely made out two small piles of bricks being chewed at by the machine gunner.

Under the rasping of the gun, the loudspeaker fell silent.

Suddenly the weapon quit firing. Another machine gun far to the right of the bricks opened up.

After a few seconds, this gun, too, was silenced. Thorvald breathed under his binoculars. "Snipers."

Nikki bore down on the brick piles. With the bullet dust settled, he saw the small arc of a metal bell, the loudspeaker. Behind one of the brick piles was the outline of a form. A man in a helmet? Hard to tell. Must be four hundred meters away, maybe farther.

"Colonel . . ."

"My rifle," Thorvald said beneath his binoculars.

He wants his rifle. For a shot at this distance, downhill. Now I'll get to see him work and we'll know what we've got here in this soft white sharpshooter from the Berlin opera.

Nikki laid the sniper rifle in the snow beside the colonel. Mortar shells whisked high overhead. A second later, colonnades of dirt and smoke engulfed the loudspeaker. The explosions marched up the hill as the mortars on top of Mamaycv Kurgan slammed rounds onto the Russian trench.

When the shelling stopped, Thorvald took up his rifle. He spoke in a cool voice.

"This man with the microphone and the bad German. He'll try to retrieve his loudspeaker. It's very important to him."

The colonel worked only his jaw when he spoke. The rifle, the sight, did not move.

"His sniper friends are too far away to tell him to leave

it alone. He'll reach for it as soon as he shakes the dirt off."

Thorvald watched. Nikki waited, measuring the moments in breaths and heartbeats. Without warning, without comment, Thorvald fired. The report punched Nikki in the side of the head.

"Did you get him?"

Thorvald answered only with a flip of the bolt. A smoking casing landed on the trench bank beside Nikki's arm.

Nikki gathered his binoculars to track the colonel's work. Quickly, he acquired the brick pile. The bell of the loudspeaker was still there. The colonel must have got him, Nikki thought.

He looked past the bricks and saw the tiny shape of the helmeted head again. He's still standing. How?

Thorvald fired again. Nikki's shoulders twitched at the crack of the rifle. The helmet flew off behind the target's head. Before Nikki could ease the tension in his neck, Thorvald's bolt flew open and another smoking cartridge landed on the mound beside him. The colonel fired again. The head in Nikki's binoculars shook violently. Immediately, it righted itself. The head took two more rounds from Thorvald's flying hands as the German sharpshooter fired faster than Nikki could believe. Thorvald hesitated, another bullet already loaded in the chamber. Nikki saw the head disappear. Thorvald laid down his rifle.

How could he fire so fast? How could he strike something so small as a head so far below, four hundred meters away? Is he that good? And why didn't the head go down, explode, die?

Nikki gawked at the colonel. Thorvald returned the look for a moment with his twin lakes of eyes, then slid down the trench.

"Come down here, Corporal. They'll be the ones with the next shot."

Nikki squirmed backward and landed on the trench

floor. He opened his mouth to speak. Too many thoughts jammed in to seek expression all at once.

"It was a dummy, Nikki. A ruse. It was put there by those snipers to draw us out."

It worked. He fired at it. But how could a real sniper even raise his head when the man can shoot like that? Oh, my God.

Nikki took a deep breath. He arranged his juggling thoughts. He looked at the rifle at Thorvald's feet.

"But why shoot a dummy? What good did it do?"

Thorvald took a piece of bread from his pack. He pulled it in two and handed half to Nikki.

"I told you, Corporal, we're going to behave like wolves." He chewed. "We're going to announce ourselves to this Zaitsev with little stunts like this. We'll be very, very dangerous, even a little bit rabid. We're going to shoot everything that moves for a while and even, as you saw, a few things that don't. He'll hear about this little . . . exhibition of my abilities. He'll know something is different out here, someone new is operating for the Germans. Then we'll become his challenge, his monster. We'll be all he thinks about. Goodness, he'll say to himself, is there some sniper on the other side better than me? A better sniper? Impossible! He's going to worry about me, obsess about me. Then he's going to come looking for me. He'll ask for advice about me, try to figure me out, lose sleep over me. We'll draw him out, Nikki, like pus out of a wound. He's going to hunt me single-mindedly. And that will handcuff him to me."

Nikki watched the colonel talk and chew. He couldn't tell him that the Reds already knew about him, that even now Zaitsev may be hunting him. He had to keep Thorvald safe until he could maneuver him into position to kill the Hare. But he had to do it without revealing his own cowardice, his babbling betrayal to the gold-toothed face and the blade at his throat the night before.

Thorvald took the bread back from Nikki and put it away in the pack. He looked up, his eyebrows raised. He nodded.

"We'll make the Hare come to us, Nikki. Then we can kill him anytime we want."

SIXTEEN

NIKOLAY KULIKOV IS BECOMING A MASTER, ZAIT-sev thought.

He looked away from the eyepiece of the periscope to the side of Kulikov's head. He's really quite cunning. I'm going to make him a lecturer in my next class of hares.

Zaitsev whispered to him. "Ready?"

The little sniper stared down his scope. The strap of his Moisin-Nagant was wound tightly about his wrist to lock his hand in a sure grip behind the trigger. The battered wooden stock was pressed snugly against his shoulder. The rifle barrel rested on a piece of cloth in the rust of a huge steel girder.

Kulikov nodded his head in a tiny stab forward.

Zaitsev pointed at Zviad Baugderis, Kulikov's Georgian partner in sector two. Baugderis gave two sharp tugs on a string.

Zaitsev turned back to the periscope. It was his turn to spot while Kulikov shot. Two hundred fifty meters away, five bullet-riddled rail cars rested on tracks atop a meter-high embankment. He quelled his breath to still the magnified image.

Zaitsev bore down to pick movement out of the maze of

rails, bricks, and snowy earth. He caught a flicker of flesh. He hissed to Kulikov.

"There. The left car. Behind the back wheel. He's peeking."

Part of a German soldier's head came visible in the periscope behind one of the large steel wheels.

Kulikov's voice showed his concentration. He drew the words out as if singing a slow verse.

"Come on out, you fuck. Show me both eyes."

The German peered around the wheel. Zaitsev was amazed and even a little amused to see it. He knew this Nazi had been spooked; he'd heard something. What? A Red unit crawling through the rubble to stage a surprise raid? A messenger sneaking through the debris? It sounded like a tin can tumbling through the carnage, betraying the careless foot of a clumsy Ivan. Better take a quick look. Get ready, boys, the soldier whispers, something's going on. He pokes his head up and never feels the crosshairs split his brow, never sees the tin can rattle in the rubble attached to a string, the string in Zviad Baugderis's hand.

This was an ingenious ploy of Kulikov's. It also represented an impressive feat of silent slithering through the wreckage by two of Zaitsev's hares, worthy of mention to Danilov for inclusion as a new tactic in *In Our Country's Defense*. Zaitsev thought of how he would report this to the commissar. Like a recipe. Several hours before dawn, crawl under the noses of the enemy; lay out five tin cans attached to strings at fifty-meter intervals, all the strings running back to different camouflaged shooting cells prepared the day before; begin at dawn; pull one string, take your shot, then move at least one hundred meters away, two cans down, and pull another string. Be patient. Move after every shot so the Germans can't get a fix on you with their mortars. Work the cans like fishing poles, waiting for the waters to settle and the bait to appear tasty again.

Kulikov clucked his tongue. "Got him."

"Get him." Zaitsev clamped his teeth.

The rifle lashed out. Through the periscope, Zaitsev saw the German's head snap back, his hands flying wildly into the air. The body slumped down from its upward jerk. Two black dots leaped up beside it, the tops of more German helmets. When the soldier next to them burst, the frightened men under those helmets jumped. Then they dove below the level of the railroad mound that was their sanctuary like startled turtles dipping beneath the surface of a lake.

Zaitsev lowered the periscope to look at Baugderis. The dark-skinned farmer from Tbilisi dropped the string and shrugged. Kulikov chuckled.

"I can't believe it," Kulikov said when Baugderis crawled up behind him. "How stupid can they be? What's that, Zviad?" He turned to Baugderis. "The seventh one?"

Baugderis shrugged again. "Seventh. Eighth."

Kulikov was excited. "Let's move over to number five. We haven't hit them in a few hours. They've forgotten us by now."

He looked at Zaitsev. "Want another one, Vasha?"

Zaitsev shook his head. He'd arrived when the sun was high and the shadows hid nothing. The hunting had been good. He'd bagged two Germans quickly, then spotted for Kulikov and Baugderis.

"No, Nikolay Petrovich. I'm going to check on Shaikin."

He turned to crawl away. Kulikov grabbed his sleeve.

"Vasha, why are you making the rounds? Sector six this morning, here now, Shaikin next? This isn't how you hunt."

Zaitsev raised his eyebrows.

Kulikov let go of the sleeve. "I've seen you sit in one

place for three days with the same bullet in your chamber."

Zaitsev shouldered his rifle. He blinked at his friend.

Kulikov pressed. "What's wrong?"

"Nothing's wrong." Zaitsev scowled. "Do your job, Nikolay. I'll do mine."

Kulikov's voice came over Zaitsev's shoulder while he scurried behind the girder. "Go back to your bunker, Vasha. Take a rest. The Germans won't make a move without you, I promise."

ZAITSEV PUSHED THE BLANKET ASIDE FROM the doorway. Inside the dark bunker, the air was stale with lantern fumes. He pulled the blanket down from its nails to let cold, fresh air roll in. The last glow of dusk trickled in. He laid his pack and rifle in his corner and sat just inside the doorway, near the cleanest air and the best light, to look through his sniper journal.

Seven kills today, he thought. One machine gunner with Tania this morning in sector six, two more in sector two with Kulikov and Baugderis, and four with Shaikin and Morozov in an unplanned ambush in sector five on the slope of Mamayev Kurgan. All of a sudden, Morozov had perked up from his periscope. "Look! A whole unit! They're running, right over there. What do we do?"

Two of the Germans were dropped before Morozov could grab his rifle and join in.

That's one hundred and sixty-two kills total. That's good, Zaitsev thought. More than any other sniper, more than Viktor, almost more than any two of the hares combined.

I'm exhausted. Seven kills in three sectors. Kulikov was right. It's risky, stupid, selfish. Why did I do that? The four with Shaikin and Morozov in the late afternoon were just good luck, the right place at the right time. The sector-two kills with Kulikov took patience but involved very little risk. We moved often, we were smart, Kulikov and Baugderis were well prepared. They almost seemed to be enjoying themselves. The machine gunner with Tania this morning, that was tougher. I didn't even see the first one, Tania did. She got him. I hit the second. That could have been bad. My own fault. Too impatient, didn't look the area over closely enough before I went to fetch Danilov. Too damned impatient around Chernova. How does she stay alive? And the enemy sniper. Somebody damn good, Tania said. Unlikely. Must have been two of them trading shots at the dummy. Too fast for one man, three or four seconds between rounds, beyond three hundred fifty meters. Dead center on Pyotr's head, a face in the cloth. Two men, must have been.

Zaitsev breathed deeply. The fumes in the bunker had cleared out. Night settled into its nest over Stalingrad. He moved to his corner in the dark, on the cold dirt floor. The evening chill pecked about his legs.

The sound of boots hurried around the corner.

"Vasha!" Viktor stepped into the doorway, a huge silhouette. "Vasha, are you in here?"

"I'm here."

Viktor stepped into the bunker. "What are you doing here in the dark? Why is the lantern out?"

Zaitsev sat still, knowing that Viktor could not see him. "I suppose because you didn't refill the lantern this morning when you came back." Fatigue tarnished Zaitsev's voice.

The Bear peeled off his backpack and dropped it on the floor. "Fuck your mother. I've been looking for you all day."

"Why?"

Viktor reached into his pocket for matches.

Zaitsev sat up. "Viktor?"

The Bear moved to the lantern. He raised the windshield and struck the match. The wick did not drink the flame.

"Viktor, I just told you. It's out of fuel."

Medvedev struck another match and held it up, illuminating his big, frowning face.

"I've been following you since before noon," he said. "Why can't you stay in one place? Sector six, sector two, sector five . . ."

Zaitsev pulled his arms over his chest and crossed his legs. He looked up at the Bear, still irked with him.

Medvedev dropped the match. He spoke in the darkness. Zaitsev heard a huge smile on his friend's lips.

"You won the Order of Lenin, Vasha."

Zaitsev uncrossed his arms.

"This morning, right after I got back in, they came looking for you. A bunch of commissars. Vidikov was with them."

Vidikov. The vice chief of political intelligence. Viktor is serious. I won the Order of Lenin.

"I've been two steps behind you all day. Chuikov wants to see you."

"Now?"

Viktor lit another match. He reached down with his free hand and pulled the Hare to his feet with ease. Zaitsev felt Viktor's power and excitement.

The Bear laughed. "Excuse me, but I didn't question Vidikov for an appointment on your behalf."

He gathered up Zaitsev's rifle and pack, shoved them into Zaitsev's hands, then pushed him toward the uncovered door, propelling him into the night.

"Go, my hero. You son of a bitch."

Zaitsev quickened his steps to a rising thrill. Viktor's voice bellowed through the dark over his shoulder.

"Go and get it for all of us. You son of a bitch! Hurry!"

•   •   •

ZAITSEV'S PATH TO CHUIKOV'S BUNKER LED
him alongside the Volga. The river was a two-thousand-
meter-wide ribbon of unbroken darkness. No boats risked
the crossing, fearful of the jagged ice floes swarming under its surface. No planes rent the night sky, no red and
green flares burst and sailed down. It was all brooding,
waiting, punctuated only by the grinding of the ice giants
in the river.

Running, Zaitsev realized that he knew very little about
the man he was going to see, the defender of Stalingrad,
the commander of the Sixty-second Army, General Vasily
Ivanovich Chuikov.

He knew the city had become a pyre for the Germans
under this commander. But what else was a proven fact
about Chuikov? The man had never run beside Zaitsev
through the blistered nights and spitting bullets, hadn't
dived for cover under the metal heaps in the factories or
helped him stanch the spraying blood of a comrade's
wound. Chuikov was just a name. A man who made decisions from his bunker with his staff around him, with
women running his radios, with food and a cook and
plenty of good soldiers between him and the Nazis. Zaitsev pondered how he would soon feel in the presence of
General Chuikov.

He arrived at the command bunker and informed a
guard that he was expected by the general. The guard, a
burly private, escorted him into the bunker, then stood
behind Zaitsev while they waited in a doorway. A tall,
slender man in the next room looked up from a sheaf of
papers and approached, peeling off a glove. He thrust a
warm and dewy hand out to Zaitsev.

"Chief Master Sergeant Zaitsev. I am Colonel Vadim
Vidikov. Come in. Come in."

Vidikov led Zaitsev past a table covered with radio
equipment. Two men plugged and unplugged wires, never
saying a word. There were no maps in the bunker. Zaitsev

guessed it was because the Red Army controlled too little of Stalingrad to worry anymore about charting it.

"General Chuikov has been waiting for you all day, Comrade Zaitsev," Vidikov said. "He admires you greatly."

Vidikov pushed open another heavy wooden door. Inside, lit by three candles and a lantern, sat a short, thick-necked man. His nose and lips were heavy, almost swollen, under a shock of wavy black hair. Dark stubble took his chin into the fur collar of his officer's coat.

"Chief Master Sergeant Zaitsev," Vidikov said, closing the door behind him.

The stocky man stood at once, his hands left hanging at his sides. He appraised Zaitsev up and down.

"You are a very important man."

Zaitsev was surprised. The man who had just stood at the table had not said these words.

He turned quickly to the shadowed corner. The voice had come from there.

Out of the dimness walked a man shorter than Zaitsev, rounder almost than Danilov. The top of his head was bald; the hair on the sides was shaved close, white as the driest snow. His eyes were the blue of a clear, frostbitten sky. He held out a hand, puffy and soft. Zaitsev knew such a hand could belong only to a commissar.

"My name is Deputy Nikita Khrushchev. I am Comrade Stalin's political adviser in Stalingrad. I wanted to meet you personally, Comrade Zaitsev." Khrushchev pointed to the man standing beside the desk. "This is, of course, General Chuikov, your commander."

Zaitsev looked at the three men. The power in this room was not of his sort. He felt uncomfortable when Chuikov approached him.

"We are very proud of you," the general said, "all of us. You have done Russia a great service."

Zaitsev muttered, "Thank you, general."

Khrushchev floated forward. The size of his shoulders

and belly, the white of his skin and hair, made him seem as cold and large in the bunker as an iceberg.

The deputy spoke. "You are a member of the Komsomol, yes?"

"Yes, sir."

"Good. By tying up the arms and legs of the Germans here in Stalingrad, do you realize what we Communists have done?"

Zaitsev shook his head.

"The Party has taken upon its shoulders the weight of the world, not just that of the Soviet Union. The world is relying on our toughness and battle skill to keep the enemy here, to destroy them here. You see only the horrible details of the fighting. But believe me, the effects of what is transpiring in these streets and houses are worldwide. The Americans, the British, even the lowly French spill their coffee every morning when they read in their newspapers that we are still here."

Khrushchev's girth jiggled at his own humor. Behind him, Vidikov laughed at the back of the deputy's bald head, at the icy white crystals of his rim of hair.

"The world press is calling it 'Fortress Stalingrad.' And that is what it is. That is what we have made it. I can tell you, Comrade Stalin knows your name. Because of men like you, he avoids shifting troops south. He does not have to weaken the defenses of Leningrad and Moscow to reinforce Stalingrad."

Chuikov, motionless while Khrushchev spoke, sensed his turn in the ceremony. He picked a small medal from his desk, a round bronze medallion that hung from a red ribbon. On the emblem's face was the familiar goateed visage of V. I. Lenin, in profile, staring slightly upward against the backdrop of a five-pointed star.

The medal lay in Chuikov's palm.

"Comrade Zaitsev, there is so vast a land beyond the Volga. Can you tell me how we will look into the eyes of

our people there if we do not stop the Germans here? You
know the motto of the Sixty-second Army?"

"Yes, sir. 'Not a step back.' "

"Do you believe it?"

Zaitsev looked at his general, taken aback by the question. How can he ask me that? he thought. These fucking
Communists, always asking you if you're brave, if you can
cut it, if you'll die for the Party defending the *rodina*.

Why are they asking me this, to test my resolve? The
Nazis don't test it enough for them every day? Do I have
to come in here to this safe bunker dug into the side of a
cliff behind a shield of Red soldiers and have it tested
again? I'm a fighter, a hunter for the Red Army, for their
fucking Party. I've proven myself. What have they proven?
Just give them what they want and get out of this bunker.

Zaitsev turned to Khrushchev. In a full voice, he said,
"For us, there is no land beyond the Volga."

Khrushchev nodded. His gaze, though fixed on Zaitsev,
was inward. He spoke to himself.

"There is no land beyond the Volga," he repeated quietly, rolling the phrase on his tongue. "Yes. Yes." The stout
little deputy addressed Chuikov. "Give him the medal,
General. The Sixty-second Army has a new motto.
Vidikov, print that. Tell the men the noble hero Zaitsev
said it. That we are all bound by it. For us, there is no land
beyond the Volga."

Khrushchev clapped Zaitsev on the back, turning to
leave. "That's the way, young Komsomol member," he
said with a laugh. "That was very good." Then Khrushchev nodded at Chuikov, said, "General," and quickly
was gone, with Vidikov following in his wake.

Chuikov handed Zaitsev the medal. "Vasily
Gregorievich Zaitsev, I award you the Order of Lenin for
your efforts in founding the sniper movement in the Sixty-
second Army, and for your courage in battle."

The general patted Zaitsev on the arm. He smiled and

looked around the room. "Looks like it's just the two of us. Oh, well. We'll get ourselves a parade in Moscow sometime, eh?"

Zaitsev looked at the medal. The bronze was thick, with some weight to it. It's odd holding this, he thought. I have one of my country's highest honors in my hand, but I'd rather he hand me more ammunition for my hares. The copper in this medal might've made three bullet jackets.

Chuikov stepped back. Zaitsev looked up and met his gaze.

"I wouldn't pin that on, Vasha," the general said. "Not for a while. Keep it in your bag. It'll stay clean that way."

Zaitsev slid the medal into his coat pocket. He smiled at Chuikov. At least he lives on this side of the Volga like a soldier, Zaitsev thought. Not like that fat white rat Khrushchev. I've never seen that one over here, never even heard of him before. He's probably trapped by the freezing river on this side with the rest of us; he's handing out medals to pass the time.

"May I go, sir?" Zaitsev fingered the medal in his pocket. He'd show it to Viktor that night, and maybe Tania. But no one else. Of course, Danilov will insist on seeing it and writing about it. Damn, he thought. I'm a hero. Hero. Why did the word sound so repulsive in the mouth of Khrushchev? He made me feel like a show pony. Vasily Zaitsev, the hero trotter.

Chuikov pulled out both chairs to his table and motioned Zaitsev to sit. Zaitsev moved his hand toward the door, beseeching quietly, again, to be allowed to leave.

"Not just yet, Vasha. Someone else wants a word with you."

Zaitsev sat. Chuikov reached under his desk for three stubby glasses and a bottle of cognac.

Through the doorway stepped Colonel Nikolai Filipovich Batyuk, commander of the 284th Division. Zaitsev jumped to his feet. This, he thought, is my leader. Batyuk, the tall, skinny Ukrainian with the famous circulatory problem, the colonel who sometimes can't walk for the pain in his legs and has to ride on the back of one of his aides. Old Fireproof Batyuk. I've heard of him stepping out of a smoking bunker beating out sparks on his tunic, shouting orders like a mad fishwife.

Zaitsev saluted. "Colonel. Sir."

Batyuk returned the salute.

The two stepped forward and shook hands.

"Congratulations, Sergeant. General Chuikov approved your Order of Lenin with me. You deserve it."

Zaitsev had no answer. If they say so, he said to himself. It's in my pocket, anyway.

Chuikov poured three glasses of cognac.

"Na zdrovya." Chuikov hoisted his glass. He faced both men one at a time and threw back the liquor. Batyuk and Zaitsev wished Chuikov his health in return and drank. It had been months since Zaitsev had tasted any alcohol other than vodka.

This has been quite a day, Zaitsev thought, wiping his mouth on his sleeve. The medal in my pocket, the sticky cognac on my tongue, Tania in the warm pile of clothes, seven kills in three sectors, a toast from Chuikov and Old Firepoof. Quite a day.

"Comrade Zaitsev, I will not take long," the colonel said. He clinked his glass down on Chuikov's desk. "I know your medal was a surprise. It must be your lucky day, because I have another surprise for you. We have information that the Germans have brought in a specialist from Berlin. His name is SS Colonel Heinz Thorvald. He's the head of an elite German sniper school."

Zaitsev licked his lips, tasting the sweetness of the cognac lingering there. A sniper can become a colonel in the German army. That's excellent, he thought. That's respect.

Batyuk continued. "He's been sent here to kill you, Vasha."

Zaitsev looked down and shook his head, smiling to himself. He didn't want his officers to see him lack reaction; he took a moment to create one for them. By the looks on their faces, this was important. What's the big deal, he thought? They've all been sent here to kill me.

He rolled the empty cognac glass in his hand. He felt his own warmth in it. Well, now I've collected a specialist from Berlin. Yes, quite a day.

He looked up and widened his eyes once for their purposes. "What do we know about this Thorvald?" he asked.

"Not a thing." Batyuk shook his head. "He's an SS colonel. Draw your own conclusions from that. I can assume they think he's their best man for the job. It's rather ironic, really. Our best against their best."

Batyuk held out his glass for Chuikov to refill it. Zaitsev considered the word *ironic*. It fit. Irony was another thing his day had lacked. Now he had that, too.

"Oh, and there was something else, something about him being a coward," Batyuk added, "Don't believe it."

Chuikov approached him with the bottle. "Hold out your glass."

The general poured, and again the three men raised their glasses. Batyuk offered the toast. "Too bad they didn't send Hitler himself. That would've been a nice hunt for you, eh?"

Zaitsev lowered his glass from the toast to drink. With the fragrance of the cognac under his nose, he stopped and blinked; his vision fired out past the colonel and the general while their heads tilted back under their glasses. He flew back through the day, to the morning, to the battlefield, to sector two with Tania and Danilov in the trench, to Pyotr's quivering, perforated head. The sharp clang of bullets banged into the pit of the helmet again. It echoed behind his eyes, trickled down his spine, three seconds apart.

Not two men.

One.

The specialist from Berlin.

Zaitsev cleared his face. He wondered what he'd shown the two officers looking at him. He drank.

He swallowed the prickly liquor hard and fast, the Russian way. The cognac scraped nicely down the back of his throat. He exhaled, cooling the liquor that clung in his mouth.

He looked at Batyuk and smiled.

"I think the Berlin sniper and I have already met."

Chuikov cocked his head. "Really? Where?"

"On the eastern slope of Mamayev Kurgan this morning."

"How do you know it was him?"

Zaitsev rubbed his neck.

"He has a . . ." He paused to look for the right word. "Style."

"Good," Chuikov said. "You are off all assignments as of now, Vasha." He collected the glasses and laid them on his desk, then turned to Zaitsev. "Your one job is to find this German supersniper and kill him."

Zaitsev thought, Find him?

He lowered his face, to hide his eyes from the general and Batyuk. He collected all of Stalingrad he had seen in the past months, the decimation, the tangled wrecks of the factories, trenches ripping through the streets, blasted rubble and smoke, men running, men hiding, tens and tens of thousands of men living and dying and killing. A city full of this. The accumulation of Stalingrad was too much to consider in this way, to add it up and think on it as one thing in which to find one man, one supersniper who, in return, has been assigned to kill you.

Without thinking, for he would not have spoken, Zaitsev mumbled, "Find him."

"Yes." Chuikov held open the door for Zaitsev to leave.

Zaitsev moved through the doorway.

Batyuk patted him on the back and said, "Before he finds you, of course."

SEVENTEEN

NIKKI LED THORVALD DOWN FROM THE SPOT-
ter's hill. The colonel wanted to roam for a few days, to
"spread his scent around." Thorvald insisted on avoiding
any zones where he might be trapped by fighting. "Always
leave us a back door," he said.

Nikki thought it best to keep the master sniper clear of
the factories. Though the Germans controlled the Barricades and all but small corners of the Red October
and the Tractor Factory, those labyrinths were better left
off the tour. Nikki thought of the men in those metal
jungles as tortured, terrible creatures now. For six weeks
they'd spent their days and nights itching with blood lust,
clawing at themselves with hunger and thirst, scratch-
ing the welts left by lice. The war was forgotten in there;
all that was left was the killing. Thorvald needed distance
to conduct his wizardly marksmanship, and Nikki knew
that distance wasn't something you could ask for in the
factories. Most of the fighting there was still hand-to-
hand. Grenades and shovels shredded as much flesh
as bullets.

Nikki shook his head. No, the factories were no place
for the colonel.

We'll stalk the lines heading south. The Lazur chemical

plant is a strong Russian outpost, behind a giant no-man's-land of rail tracks. Also, the corridor to the Volga between the Red October and the Lazur has plenty of traffic. A third focus could be downtown in the five kilometers between Tsaritsa Gorge and Krutoy Gully. The gorge is like the spotter's hill, pregnant with crevices and bunkers, full of snipers and targets. Downtown, the Reds are crawling through the decrepit buildings, clinging desperately to the slopes of the riverbank, in some places within fifty meters of the Volga. The hunting will be good in any of these areas where the fighting has been reduced to waiting.

We'll draw Zaitsev out, just as the colonel said. We'll leave a trail for him to follow; then, when we're sure he's behind us, we'll stop hard, turn around, and catch him right between the eyes.

Nikki thought about what he'd seen Thorvald do on the spotter's hill, the way he'd fired his sniper rifle almost like an automatic weapon. Thorvald scared him, not because he was dangerous to Nikki but because he was too powerful to be left uncontrolled. He was like a machine that needed a strong hand on the wheel. Without a tight grip, the machine would fly into wildness. Thorvald will shoot a thousand men with those eyes and hands of his. In the process he'll get us both killed. It's hard to believe, but Thorvald seems inexperienced. He lacks patience and battle wisdom. How did he become a colonel in the SS? Connections? Obviously. No, I've got to contain him, manage him into this duel with Zaitsev.

Duel.

I can't even tell him this *is* a duel, that I made it one when I shouted out to the Russians his presence in Stalingrad.

Nikki stopped in the trench and turned to the colonel strolling behind him.

"Colonel, sir, could we talk for a minute?"

Thorvald held out his hands for his pack. Nikki slid it off his shoulder. The sniper laid it on the ground and sat on it.

"Yes, Nikki?"

Nikki squatted on his heels. "No disrespect, sir, but I've been noticing something."

Thorvald waited. Nikki felt his eyes on him, like hands. He imagined for an instant that Thorvald was staring down a scope at him. It set off prickles under his skin.

"Colonel, I don't know anything about being a sniper. But I've learned my share about staying alive on a battlefield. We can be a better team, sir, if you let me in on some decisions about when and where to shoot. I think if we don't work together, we're going to get killed out here. Sir."

Thorvald rubbed his hands together.

"You didn't like me shooting at the dummy."

"It wasn't that. Neither of us knows enough about what the other is going to do. I know I need to learn more about being a sniper, and you need to know—"

Nikki pulled up, afraid he'd chased his tongue over a cliff.

Thorvald cleared his throat. "It's all right, Nikki. I need to know more about being a soldier. Too right. Well, I suppose we are a team. Without you, we both know I'd get lost in a minute and wander right into Moscow. And without me, you'd . . . hmmm." Thorvald rubbed his chin. "Well, I suppose without me you'd be all right, wouldn't you?"

Nikki grinned. "No more so than anyone else in Stalingrad."

The colonel clapped once. "I'll tell you what. When we're done with this Zaitsev, I'll see what I can do about keeping the team together and taking you back to Berlin as my assistant. We'll get you out of Stalingrad. There. How's that for a deal?" Thorvald spread his palms like a magician who'd just made something unlikely appear. "Now you have to keep me alive."

Nikki breathed deeply. This was fantastic! It was better than he could have hoped for. He reached out to bind Thorvald to his word with a handshake.

Zaitsev was now Nikki's prey, too. He was Nikki's wings back to Westphalia. He thought of Thorvald's immense abilities in his own hands. We can do this. We can get him. And we can go home.

"Where do we start?" Thorvald asked.

Nikki cooled his excitement and thought about the translations of the several articles he'd read in *In Our Country's Defense*, the ones he was certain Thorvald hadn't read very carefully. Zaitsev isn't like Thorvald. The Hare will wait, he'll work, even suffer to let loose that one bullet for his one mark. He's a prideful man, living the legend as it happens to him, a day at a time. He'll never be unfaithful to the legend. He'll die according to it before he defiles it.

It's funny. Zaitsev is the man and we're the wolf, just like the colonel said. The man is limited by his humanity, his rules of engagement. Zaitsev's burden is to be a hero, an example for the Communists and his army, even his entire people. But the colonel and I don't carry that burden. We're the invaders; this isn't our land, so we can ravage it. These are not our people, so we can destroy them. We're not heroes, so we can act with purpose. We're free from the blinding glitter of humanity.

Nikki knew this about himself: Since his first moments in Stalingrad, he'd killed only to stay alive. Not once had he used a weapon in revenge or battle passion. He killed those who threatened him and his unit in their missions, none others. And though there has surely been enough killing in Stalingrad to fill ledgers and history books, he thought, there can be a few more deaths at my hand. And though it won't be my finger on the trigger, it will be me who kills Zaitsev.

So let's begin. Let's do some killing, Colonel. Just enough to be worthy of Zaitsev. It'll make him come at us hard and fast. He'll have every one of his hares out looking for you, Colonel. I know this, though I can't tell you. It doesn't matter. The Hare will run to wherever they report death that looks like the work of the master sniper from Berlin. We'll be there waiting.

Nikki considered the corridor between the Red October and the Lazur. He'd watched and made notes for Ostarhild while Russian sniper activity had trebled there in the past few weeks. "Let's go north," he said.

"All right. Why?" Thorvald picked up his pack. He tossed it to Nikki and handed him his rifle. Not everything changes just for asking, Nikki observed.

"Zaitsev won't notice if we shoot a dozen machine gunners or soldiers. Even a few officers won't make him sit up fast enough."

Nikki shouldered the rifle. He turned to lead Thorvald down the slope. "But if we take on some of his hares, he'll get the message. And I know where we can find them."

THREE HOURS LATER, NIKKI AND THORVALD sat in the basement of a gutted building, the headquarters bunker of Captain Manhardt of the Seventy-sixth Infantry. Manhardt slouched on a stool, speaking to Thorvald.

Nikki squirmed in his chair. The white camouflage parka and drawstring pants the colonel had secured for him that afternoon made him sweat. Thorvald had laughed when Nikki put on the outfit fresh out of a box, pointing at the crease marks: "You'll blend in well as long as the snow is neatly folded."

Captain Manhardt scratched under his arm absent-mindedly. He fidgeted while he spoke. Twice he interrupted his descriptions of how his men were being butchered in the Tractor Factory and in the corridor to murmur, "Fucking lice."

He answered Thorvald's questions. "Seven dead. Maybe more, I can't be sure." The man's misery was palpable, as if he were just trying to finish the interview and be done with these two white-clad meddlers so he could scream alone in his basement.

"Stupid bastards." The captain laid his tongue behind his lower lip, swelling it like he'd been punched there. After a sad moment, he continued: "They hear a noise in the rubble. A rattling sound, like someone kicking a can. Then some stupid bastard looks up over the trench and gets a bullet for it. It's been going on since dawn, up and down the railroad mound. I've been out there. I've told them, goddammit, this is obviously sniper shit! They're throwing those cans from somewhere or making that noise I don't know how. I've told them, I've ordered them! Don't look up when you hear that! But what can they do? They've got to look. They know the Reds. The Ivans'll do this for a day, two days, and they'll get the men to where they won't look over the trench for anything. The men will just sit there, blind, afraid to move, afraid not to move. Then at dawn, the Reds'll sneak through the heap and jump down my boys' throats because they wouldn't look up."

The captain scratched behind his neck. He wiped his hand across sleepless, shining eyes. "What can they do?" he asked Thorvald. "What can I tell them? Snipers. It's a goddammed sport to them."

Thorvald paused before speaking to pay his respects to the captain's woe.

"Let me see some of the bodies," he said. He made his

voice soothing, as though he meant it to be a poultice across Manhardt's brow. "The corporal and I will do something about it."

The captain stood. His body was laden with weapons; he bulged like a deadly fruit tree. Bands of bullets crossed his chest; a bayonet was strapped to his leg; grenades bunched at his waist. A Mauser pistol was jammed under his belt. He slung his submachine gun over his back.

He led Nikki and Thorvald up the steps and out of the basement into a gigantic grotto, a chamber left as a bubble in the heart of the building's ravaged interior. The high ceiling, like a crazy cathedral, was a jumble of bent steel beams and giant concrete shards. Scattered on the ground were wounded soldiers wrapped in red-soaked bandages, some reaching out their hands, some rocking, others lying still. Moans and whispers mingled with anguished calls for the two brown-clad nurses. These women scurried among the men, talking to them in low tones, nodding when they spoke, touching the men with wet cloths.

The captain faced Nikki. His eyes seemed to say, See all this blood. For what? He said, "The bodies are out here."

Thorvald and Nikki followed him through the bitter smells of wounds and gauze into a tunnel to the street.

Beside the charred and snowy remains of a German tank, seven bodies lay under gray-green blankets. The captain hung back while Thorvald approached the corpses. "You know your way around," Manhardt said. He turned and was gone around the corner. As he walked off, the captain's grenades and bullets rattled.

Thorvald knelt beside one of the bodies and peeled the blanket back from the head. Rivulets of blood had trickled from a hole in the dead boy's forehead. The blood had pooled in the eye sockets, then dripped alongside the nose and ears to form a dark spider sitting spread out on the gray face.

Thorvald looked up at Nikki. "At Gnössen I have a doctor who comes in to teach my snipers how to read wounds. It's a bit ghoulish, but often it's the only trail a sniper leaves behind." He touched the waxen face gingerly on the cheek. He said with a wan smile, "Now I wish I'd paid more attention."

The colonel blew out a sigh. He felt around the perimeter of the hole just above the corpse's left eye. Thorvald's breathing came in a heavy whisper through his nose.

He slipped his hand under the boy's head. Instantly he pulled his hand out. He grimaced.

"The back of the head's gone."

The colonel flipped the blanket up to cover the face and stood. His arms hung limp at his sides. He wiggled the fingers on both hands.

After a moment, the colonel knelt to uncover the second body. This head was clear and pale; he pulled the blanket down farther and found a rip in the coat, in the center of the chest. He unbuttoned the coat.

"Give me your knife."

Nikki pulled the knife from his boot. The colonel opened the coat and cut away the buttons on the sweater and the two shirts beneath.

The fatal wound was on the boy's hairless white breast, like a small crater on the ashen surface of the moon, below the left collarbone and near the heart. Thorvald took a pencil from his coat and inserted the tip a few millimeters into the wound. With his fingers, he worked the flesh around the hole, squeezing and kneading the muscles and skin.

Without a word or a glance to Nikki, he examined the next four bodies in the same manner. Two more had head wounds; in both cases, Thorvald reached under the head to find that the Russian bullet had blasted out the back of the skull. The other two bore chest wounds. Thorvald inserted his pencil into each of these and wriggled it while working the swollen flesh around the hole.

Nikki stood back, fascinated more by Thorvald's sleuthing than the wrenching tedium of death.

After ten minutes, Thorvald stood over the last of the seven shrouded corpses. He swept back its blanket. Nikki asked, "What have you found, Colonel?"

"Nothing yet."

Nikki looked at the body. He expected to see another perforated skull with a neat black hole stitched in the cheek or forehead with black blood dribbling down like seasoned lava. If not, then a simple rip in the uniform over the heart.

This body showed no marker of death. The head was unscathed. Thorvald stripped away the shirt. No wound spoiled the chest.

Thorvald yanked back the blanket to expose the full corpse. He sliced the uniform away; the stiff flesh was stained a dusky reddish purple in the shoulder blades, buttocks, calves and heels, where the blood had settled.

With his foot, Thorvald rolled the naked cadaver over. No holes appeared in the back. He raised his hands in frustration, then lifted the corpse again with his boot to turn it face up.

The dead soldier rocked and Nikki glimpsed a spot darker than the boy's hair just behind the right ear. It might have been a mole or a clump of dirt.

He pointed. "Look at the neck. Behind the ear."

Thorvald trailed his fingers through the short brown hair, down the nape, and under the ear. He leaned down to peer closer at the dot in the back of the skull.

"It's an exit wound. Look here around the cavity. There's no bruising, no abrasion ring."

The bullet had come out behind the boy's ear. Its

jacket had not flattened on impact to take the rear of the head with it when it left, the way it was supposed to do.

But where did the bullet enter?

Thorvald used the knife to pry open the mouth. The body's lips were clamped tight from rigor mortis. With some twisting of the blade between the teeth, the frozen jaw muscles gave way.

Nikki leaned over Thorvald's shoulder to look at the face. The mouth, wide open now, seemed out of balance with the repose of the shut eyes and the still, hard body. The mouth appeared defiant, screaming even as the rest of the body was resolved to its end.

Thorvald prodded with his pencil. He motioned to Nikki. "Look here."

He pointed at a chip in the left front tooth.

Laying the pencil under the broken place on the tooth, he slid the point into the throat, into a hole at the back of the wind pipe. He let go of the pencil. It stood straight up.

"He probably saw the sniper at the last second and tried to shout something. The bullet went in his mouth, clipped this tooth, and entered the back of the throat. It hit the top of the spine, probably cut it in two, then bounced out here under the ear."

Thorvald flicked the standing pencil with his fingertip. "This is the path of the bullet. It went in straight. He had his face turned at the sniper when the bullet struck. Let's see. . . ."

He fingered the hole beneath the ear, pulled the pencil from the mouth, and slid it into the neck. Again he kneaded the muscles and skin around the pencil.

Thorvald studied the wound, then withdrew the pencil and pulled the blanket over the body. He patted the head once when it was covered.

Still kneeling beside the body, Thorvald looked across the row of draped corpses. He spoke, addressing them: "The chest shots didn't tell me much. Once a bullet hits the torso's muscles and organs, it bounces around a lot. But . . ." He turned to Nikki. "Look here."

He turned back one of the blankets to reveal the pallid mound of a dead boy's bosom. He circled the wound with his finger.

"All the chest-wound entry holes are round," he said. "That indicates a ninety-degree angle of entry."

He touched a blue and red bruise ring around the hole. "See this circle of color? When a bullet penetrates, the skin stretches and becomes scraped. Then the skin snaps back and leaves this bruise around the hole. This abrasion, like all the abrasions on the other chest wounds, is symmetrical."

Thorvald covered the body and stood straight, easing his back. He pointed with the pencil down the row and shook his head.

"The head shots are useless. All except this last one. The mouth shot gave us a straight path in. I could only guess where he was looking when the bullet hit him. The exit wound was just under the ear, which tells me he was looking at ground level. If he'd been looking up, the exit would've been lower on the neck."

Judging by the angle of the exit wound in the last corpse, plus the even roundness of the entry wounds of the head shots and the abrasion rings on the chests, Thorvald concluded that the Red snipers were not in the buildings but on a level plain with the soldiers. If the snipers had been above, below, or to the side of the targets, the abrasion rings would have been wider on the side of the bullet's entry, like a slash or skid mark, and the holes would be oval, not round. From the accuracy of the shots, Thorvald put the distance at medium for an experienced sniper, about three hundred meters. There were at least two snipers working the area, a spotter and a shooter. These Reds were good; the targets, according to Captain Manhardt, had exposed themselves for only a moment.

The Reds were working close and unseen. This sort of killing was easy pickings.

Thorvald gazed at the seven shrouds a last time. The soldiers beneath them were boys, all of them; none had looked older than Nikki.

"These snipers are making sport."

Nikki led Thorvald through the wreckage to the aid station. He approached one of the nurses bending over an unconscious soldier. The man's chest was wrapped in seeping red gauze.

"Nurse, pardon me," Nikki whispered.

She kept her hands on the wounded soldier. The face she turned to Nikki was round and deeply lined. Her eyes and mouth were hung with the sort of soft flesh that holds exhaustion like a sponge.

"The colonel and I need to talk with some of the men," Nikki said. He looked at the bleeding soldier on the ground. "We want to know about the snipers who are working the railroad mound. Could you ask if any of the men were wounded there?"

"There are no wounded from the railroad mound, corporal." The nurse shook her head. "Every man shot there is dead."

Thorvald leaned down, quietly as a leaf falling.

"Madam, tell me, please, were you at the railroad mound?"

She turned her head to the soldier to wipe a froth of blood and spittle from his mouth. "Seven times. I carried them out."

Thorvald laid a gentle hand on the nurse's arm. She stopped wiping the cloth across the soldier's lips.

"We're here to fight the Russian snipers. We're specialists. Will you help us?"

The nurse laid the cloth on the soldier's chest and stood. Nikki saw the stains on the front of her uniform. Her broad shoulders and chest were blotched with a

rusted brown crust. She did carry them, he thought. She
had lifted the bodies in the trench and carried them out.
She laid them down and closed their eyes and covered
them with blankets one by one.

Thorvald spoke, deference in his voice. "If you could
show us where those boys fell, it would help us determine
where the snipers are. We won't take long. You can come
right back here."

She called to the other nurse. "Madeleine. This one
goes next." Pink bubbles boiled at the man's lips.

Outside, the woman ducked behind the frozen tank,
then scurried to a pile of rubble. With a nimbleness that
challenged Nikki to follow, she wended among debris
heaps and mortar holes to halt behind an abandoned Russian truck with its roof burned off. In a burst across an
open ten meters, she flew behind a line of ruined rail cars
sitting atop a dirt mound one meter high.

She slid into the trench behind the mound. Nikki followed and was relieved to have arrived without drawing
the attention of the Red snipers.

This nurse, Nikki thought, ran this route seven times
in, stopping, ducking, waiting; then straining under the
yokes of the dead men while she carried them out, dodging and weaving. We're three hundred meters behind the
lines, normally a safe distance. But the mere presence of
Russian snipers in the area changes everything. Each step
has to be careful and calculated or it's an invitation to a
bullet. When the Red snipers move in, you risk your life
just to walk upright, just to peek over a trench. Every
movement becomes strained and burdensome when enemy snipers are near; hot tension brands every second
with the crosshairs.

Once in the trench, gathered low behind the mound,
Nikki turned to look for the colonel. Thorvald was thirty
meters back, still hunched behind the chassis of the Red

truck. Thorvald pawed the air. This meant that Nikki was to go on without him. He'll be all right, Nikki thought. No sense risking my flight back to Germany across that open stretch. I can take care of this part without him.

The nurse led Nikki through the trench. It ran the length of the rail mound, over two hundred meters. Five cars were spread out on the rail, somehow refusing to crumble off their steel undercarriages. Behind the cover of each car, a unit of a dozen or so soldiers sat assembled around a machine gun boxed in by sandbags. None of the five guns was manned.

The nurse stopped at the first, second, and fifth of the units in the trench. At the first, she pointed down twice to the spots where she'd picked up bodies.

Each of the seven times the nurse pointed, she said only, "Here." Nikki asked if she could recall the order of her trips to the units. She could remember only the first two and the last two. He inquired what sort of wound had been suffered by each soldier she'd collected. She shook her weary head and looked away down the trench to the next unit. Nikki stopped asking.

He knelt among the men to question them about the sniper attacks. Had they seen anything? What had they heard, what was the sound that had made the soldiers look? Had it been the same sound each time before a sniper shot? Had they heard the sound again?

It had been several weeks since Nikki had been among regular foot soldiers. His work for Ostarhild had kept him isolated while he roamed the battlefield sketching out maps and scribbling notations. The sixty-odd men in this trench looked damned. Many of the vacant faces were cloaked behind beards. There was no warmth in the trench; the men sat huddled, mingling the clouds of their breaths and the closeness of their fear. Some offered him drinks from bottles that were cologne vials. Nikki was horrified. They're drinking captured perfume for the alcohol. My God, what's happening to these men?

Kneeling beside the soldiers, Nikki understood that these men were no longer fighting to win in Stalingrad. Here in the chill of November, their combat was not just with the Red Army but also with dread, the horror that howled when it snatched the fellow next to them without warning. Their enemies were men, yes. But every second they fought other, smaller battles: the wretched lice tormenting their skin, hunger and thirst that burned without warming, and the cold silence that threatened to close around them day and night.

Their downcast eyes and grinding jaws revealed to Nikki that these soldiers had at last glimpsed their fate: cannons, rifles, and grenades could no longer win their freedom from Stalingrad. Stalingrad was a filthy, decrepit tomb, without remorse, pity, or relief. The city was no longer a battlefield; it was an affliction. The last weapon against it was hope.

Slipping through the patches of lifting hands, Nikki heard the whispers. "Get him," they pleaded, "get that Red son of a bitch."

"Look at him, boys. He knows what he's doing."

"He was sent here by the generals."

"A sniper fighter. He'll get the bastards."

"They haven't forgotten us, lads."

That's why Thorvald was brought here, Nikki realized. The generals saw this, the erosion of hope among the men while the Russians built a stinking hero for themselves out of the Siberian Hare.

Nikki made an oath. We'll get Zaitsev.

He anointed his promise with the misery of these men. He pledged to remember forever the dried rivulets of blood hidden beneath the seven blankets in the street, and in the trench the sickening waft of cologne.

• • •

NIKKI FOUND THORVALD BESIDE THE CORPSES.
The silent nurse, no longer his guide, walked off without a
glance.

Nikki told the colonel what he had discovered. He described the layout of the positions in the trench: a dozen
men and one machine gun per unit, one unit each behind
the five rail cars, with fifty meters between units. The men
had heard rattling sounds in the rubble. When any of
them had looked up, he'd been struck down instantly by a
bullet.

Thorvald listened and nodded.

When Nikki finished, the colonel said, "The cans are
on strings. The snipers are pulling them."

He spoke as if he had devised the scheme himself.
Even though Nikki had figured it out, too, Thorvald possessed a peculiar, poised manner of pronouncing facts,
which Nikki found reassuring.

"The first bullet was fired at unit two," Nikki said, looking at the covered bodies to drive his memory. "The second was at unit five. The last three shots were at three,
one, and then four. The Reds are skipping around and
waiting."

"What do you suggest?"

"I think we should go down there in the trench and set
up between two and three. That's where I think they'll hit
next. When we hear the can rattle, we raise a fake helmet
or something, draw him out and shoot him."

Thorvald nodded. "Simple. Direct."

Nikki waited.

The colonel exhaled. "Suicide. Remember, there's
more than one Red sniper operating here. While I'm aiming at the one who shoots at the helmet, the other one has
spotted me. No, we stay out of the trench."

Nikki was dismayed. He wanted to kill the Red sniper

while surrounded by the haggard men, to show them how a German soldier can fight back. He envisioned himself and his colonel kindling a spark for them, giving the poor chaps something to cheer for.

Thorvald was going to propose some scheme in which they did their work anonymously; they would be deadly but unseen. The men in the trench wouldn't know. They would not clap Nikki and each other on the back, would not be watching firsthand when Nikki and Thorvald picked the lock of their cage.

Thorvald had promised Nikki his say. Now he'd had it.

"Follow me," the colonel said.

He walked away from his rifle, left leaning against the building. Nikki retrieved it, struggling to allay the aggravation in his gut at Thorvald's brusqueness.

"I found this position while you were in the trench," the colonel said over his shoulder. "If the Russians are at ground level, we need to be above them."

He led Nikki to the rear of the building's skeletal facade. They stepped over a window casing and skittered through trash and concrete. They climbed a metal staircase that had survived the bombings. At the top of the stairs, they made their way along the lip of what had been the third floor of the building. Ten meters in, the floor was gone, collapsed into the carnage below to leave a forty-meter-wide gaping hole. Nikki felt as if he were creeping along the rim of a volcano.

Moving carefully, Thorvald guided Nikki to a set of scorched window frames. Nikki approached one of the openings and looked down. Below was the rail yard, the five German positions behind the rail mound, and the ruined cars on top. Thorvald had brought him to a position twenty meters to the right of unit two.

Nikki estimated a distance of 350 meters beyond the unit and surveyed it with his binoculars. The Red snipers must be there, hidden in the wreckage, crawling in the trenches or snuggled into a crater. Or perhaps they're gone. The light was dusking now. What amount of killing satisfies the Reds in a day?

Thorvald sat below the window sill. He propped his rifle up and looked into the violet sky.

"The sun's behind us," he said. He raised his chin, pointing to the right of unit two. "You watch there. I'll stay to the left. The moment you see anything, I want to know."

He's going to sit up here and wait, Nikki thought. He's not even going to let me warn the men in the trench. I could tell them to stay down, don't look up, we'll get the snipers. I can tell them to put a helmet on a stick, stay down.

He's using the men in the trench for bait!

Nikki laid the binoculars on the floor. "Colonel?"

"Yes?"

"Let me go down to the trench. I can draw the snipers' fire. You can get them."

Thorvald shook his head. "No. I need you here."

"Then let me warn the men. They're scared to death."

Thorvald's face went taut. "You'll stay right here, Corporal. Pick up your binoculars. That's the best way to help."

"Colonel, those men—"

"Damn it, pick up those glasses." Thorvald pointed at the binoculars beside Nikki. "I don't care about those men! Will you understand that? We are not here to save them or accept their thanks. We have an assignment, Corporal! Find Zaitsev. Kill him. Then go home."

Thorvald's eyes narrowed. He paused and leaned forward. Nikki saw him weaving his head just perceptibly, like a snake tasting the air. "I will kill Zaitsev. You'll help me, or someone else will." Thorvald turned away.

Nikki looked down on the men in unit two. We're playing God up here, he thought. One of those soldiers is a dead man. I know it. I'm making it happen by watching. I can stop it. But I won't.

I'm not a hero for those soldiers. They can't have heroes anymore. Heroes are men, and men can't save them now. Hitler can't, Stalin can't, I can't—they can't even do it themselves. Zaitsev is a hero, and he's going to die. I'm not theirs. I am mine, and I want to go home.

Thorvald owns me. And Zaitsev owns me. They have a destiny, those two. And I'm sandwiched between them.

Thorvald stretched. "No, it's too dark now. They won't try it again. Go down and get us some food from the nurse."

Nikki rose without looking at Thorvald.

"Nikki." The colonel faced him. His eyes were softer. "You wanted each of us to do what he's best at. That was how we were going to get him. We agreed." The colonel drew his knees up against the cold. "That's what we're doing. This is what I'm best at. I'm the killer, and you're my guide and guardian. Don't break up the team. We'll get him and we'll go home together."

Nikki nodded. "Yes, sir."

Before he could turn, Thorvald added, "We'll spend the night up here. The snipers will try again at dawn, I'm sure of it."

Nikki knew he could thwart Thorvald's plan. He could give a word to the nurse or slip into the trench after dark to warn the men to stay down, no matter what sounds they heard in the rubble. But he knew he wouldn't.

"And Corporal," Thorvald called after him, "bring back those seven blankets."

DAWN RUMBLED AROUND THEM. NIKKI'S WAKing ears caught the grumble of tank treads grinding concrete into dust and the rattle of weapons carried in a thousand arms. Orders were screamed above the din. Radios crackled.

This is it, Nikki thought, Paulus's last-ditch thrust at the Russians burrowed in the factories. Far to his left, from the Banny Gully and the Barricades, came the pounding of artillery. Small-arms fire sizzled in the Red October corridor.

Thorvald was at his rifle, bearing down his scope.

"Start looking," he whispered. "We can't stay here long. Maybe our friends will take one last jingle on their cans before they're forced to retreat. Remember, they're at ground level."

Nikki scanned the rubble across from unit three. The sounds of tanks and men swarmed behind him, moving to his left, advancing on the Red October and the Volga.

"It's getting busy, Colonel," he said, pulling his eyes away from the binoculars.

"A bit." Thorvald looked agreeably at Nikki.

Suddenly Thorvald stiffened. His eyes grew wide, then slitted to focus over Nikki's shoulder. "Nikki," he said, not blinking or wavering the aim of his eyes, "find the third house in on the far side of the road. Do it."

Nikki whirled with his binoculars up. For a moment, before searching for the shacks, he looked down into the trench to unit three. The soldiers' normal huddle was broken. A few of them crawled away from the group on their knees, others were bent, looking to the floor of the trench. There, between the backs and shoulders of the soldiers, was a bloodied body, face up, shaking wildly.

Nikki swung the binoculars and found the houses quickly. They were simple brick shacks, part of the workers' settlement for the Red October, gutted months ago. He counted to the third one.

As Nikki scanned, Thorvald's voice came in his ears quietly, like a cinema narration to the magnified scene moving in front of him.

"Ten meters to the left. What's there?"

Nikki fingered the knob on his binoculars to sharpen the focus. "A sheet of corrugated metal. A roof, I think, from one of the shacks."

"Yes. Yes, good. All right, now move behind the roof. Find the small shack. It might be a pump house."

"Got it. Red shutters."

"Right. Now ten, twenty meters more, keep moving left. Is there a trench in front of that building with the . . . what is that?"

"It's a banner. It's . . . it's a poster of Stalin."

"Perfect. Is there a trench? I saw something in that area. Find a trench. Quickly, Nikki."

Piles of bricks and stone confused the terrain in front of the row of ruined shacks. Snow blotted out most of the detail. But in a jagged line, the snow and bricks seemed to disappear. There must be a depression there, Nikki thought. A trench.

"Yes. Yes, there is."

"Follow it. Find them. I saw a muzzle flash in that trench."

Nikki strained his eyes. The distance was at least four hundred meters, and the area was in shadow. He didn't know what he was looking for. Men, yes. But what would he see? A rifle barrel or a face at this distance? Impossible.

Cooling his frustration, Nikki stopped looking for objects and shapes and directed his eyes to recognize motion. In moments he glimpsed a gray lump bobbing just below the trench line. A helmet! It's coming this way!

The Red snipers are making one last round of their lines before they retreat. They're tugging, then watching for a shot. If a shot is there, they'll take it and keep moving down the line. Unit five, then four, just now three, next two. Right in front of us.

"Got him!" Nikki whispered. His eyes locked on the

helmet—There! Two of them! Two of them moving in the trench! Nikki talked Thorvald in, bringing him onto the targets.

He spoke quickly, concisely. He knew Thorvald was looking now through his sniper scope, his vision magnified, too, with a sharper but more limited field than Nikki's binoculars.

"The last shack, Colonel. See it? Now down five meters. A small crater, a wagon wheel sticking out of it."

"Yes."

"To the left again, a pile of timbers lying under another piece of metal."

"Yes."

"Ten meters down. A water cistern, or a barrel."

"Yes, yes."

"Now straight down from the tower. There's the poster. Five more meters left. They're right below a pile of bricks."

Thorvald paused. Nikki waited with him.

The colonel hissed, "Yessss."

"You've got them?"

Thorvald answered in a faraway tenor. "Don't speak."

Nikki was shackled to the moment, sharing through the binoculars the power and killing art of the Gnössen master sniper. He shuddered with a rush of excitement he knew the colonel did not feel.

The Russian snipers stopped opposite unit two, three hundred meters away. They split up; one moved ten meters to the right in the trench. They were only slightly more than specks through the field glasses, but Nikki felt that he could see them with the clarity of God's eye. One of the helmets dipped below the lip of the trench. The other stood firm. The standing one was the shooter; the other was the spotter. He must have ducked to lay down his rifle and take up the string and his periscope. Is this the way Thorvald is thinking? Is he following their movements like this, guessing what they're doing, predicting what they'll do next? Nikki could not ask, only watch.

He wanted to take his sight away from the snipers for a moment and gaze down at unit two. But he knew it would take him too long to reacquire the tiny shapes of the far-away enemy. He kept his focus on the gray dot, highlighted against the scrambled brown and white background. The other lump did not reappear to the right of it. There, Nikki thought, there's the shooter. But is it enough of a target for Thorvald to get a clear shot? Is he high enough above the trench? Thorvald won't waste all our effort just to bounce a bullet off the top of a helmet.

For two minutes they watched the Red snipers. The spotter stayed beneath the crest of the trench to gaze through a periscope. The shooter hunkered down, too low, waiting for the word from his spotter that a target was making itself available before he raised his eye to his gun.

Thorvald broke the silence. "They're not going for it."

Nikki was deflated. All this time shivering on the cold floor in this creaking building, sleeping under dead men's shrouds, and he and the colonel were going to go away empty.

"Nikki, how far can you throw?"

Nikki knew what Thorvald wanted from him. The men in the trench weren't rising to the Russians' bait. They'd heard enough of the tin can. They weren't biting, weren't going to look this last time. There's a German attack under way, there's no way the Reds are crawling toward them. They know this down in the trench. They're thinking, Fuck the Red snipers. We'll get them in a few minutes when the attack rolls over their position. We're not looking.

Thorvald couldn't shoot. Not yet.

He needed a soldier to raise his head. To freeze the

waiting Russian sniper in his scope, perhaps give Thorvald another muzzle flash to zero in on.

He needed a new mystery, a new rattle in the rubble. The master sniper needed a sacrifice. Now.

Only for a moment, Nikki considered refusing. But his reluctance flew away home, over his father's farm in Westphalia, into his sister's arms.

I'm defenseless, he thought. What does it matter? Shit, there's nothing left of me to defend.

Thorvald asked again. "How far can you throw?"

"Far enough."

Nikki laid his binoculars down and stood away from the window. He selected a rounded bit of brick that fit his hand well. It'll fly straight and far, he thought. Far enough.

Nikki readied his feet. "Now," he whispered.

He threw the shard with all his might. The brick sailed high over the heads of the German soldiers in the trench, like a hard little angel of death. Nikki didn't see it land, but he knew he'd thrown it far enough.

He stood back from the window, afraid a move forward might disturb Thorvald's concentration.

Only seconds after Nikki heaved the brick, Thorvald fired. His right hand moved in a blur, off the trigger, to the bolt, back to the trigger. He fired again the moment the smoking cartridge from the first bullet clattered on the floor.

Thorvald ejected the second cartridge and stared through his scope. Then he lowered the rifle and rolled over from the window to pick up the two spent casings.

Outside, tank and mortar rounds crashed to earth. The clamor, missing from Nikki's ears for the past several minutes, came flooding in on his senses. He wondered how close they were now.

Thorvald stood. A circle was pressed into the flesh around his right eye by the scope. It made him appear to be wearing a monocle. He jingled the two brass shells in his hand, trilling them like tiny bells.

Thorvald looked out across the rail yard.

"All right, Corporal," he said.

Nikki reached for Thorvald's rifle.

"I'll hang on to this for a while, Nikki," the colonel said. "I have one more chore for you."

EIGHTEEN

WHEN ZAITSEV RETURNED TO HIS BUNKER FROM Chuikov's headquarters, he walked into a celebration.

The party, fashioned by Medvedev, had gotten under way without the guest of honor. The Bear had told every sector head he could find about Zaitsev's award, told them that even though Vasha had the medal in his bag, they all had won it.

Zaitsev pushed back the blanket. Viktor, Tania, Shaikin, Morozov, Chekov, Voyashkin, and Danilov each held aloft a half-liter bottle of vodka, somehow secured by Atai Chebibulin, who'd brought them with the evening soup.

The snipers admired the medallion, raised bottles in a toast, and patted the Hare on the back. After half an hour of cheer, Zaitsev called the party to a discussion. He told them of the arrival of the Nazi sniper school headmaster and of the German's assignment: to kill the Hare, their chief. Danilov laughed a little drunkenly and guaranteed that this Nazi bastard would be made short work of. Zaitsev reminded the commissar that the German had the benefit of his notes in *In Our Country's Defense* on the Hare's tactics for the last month, even a photograph of Zaitsev.

Danilov was cowed for a moment, then smiled a black grin and held up his bottle and toasted, "So much the better!" The snipers waited for him to elaborate, but the commissar weaved out under the blanket with a wave, into his own night.

The council lasted until midnight. Each sniper expressed his thoughts on how to snare the Headmaster.

"He's just a schoolteacher. He's not a hunter. Go right at him! Challenge him!"

"No. Take your time. Trap him. Wear him down."

"Use your knowledge of the city. He's bound to be lost up to his ass most of the time."

"Get him into my sector. We'll take care of him there."

"Prick him, irritate him, distract him."

"Track him down and kill the fuck! What's the problem?"

"Don't wait. Take the initiative."

"Easy does it. Make him come to you."

Zaitsev listened. Each of the hares was right, each method they espoused had worked at one time or another. Use a dummy, set up false rifle positions, take prisoners, anger him, sneak up on him, follow him, bring him to you, draw him out, and more. This was the fascination of the sniper duel, little battles that would never be written up in strategy books. There were no classic and historic maneuvers to rely on, as there were in the grand tank battles on open ground or in giant infantry campaigns. There was no hedgehog defense prescribed against an encircling force, no flanking action required against an army's supply lines, no storm group sent in to nullify an enemy stronghold. Sniper against sniper was primitive and intuitive: it was hunter versus hunter, also quarry against prey. Each confrontation was molded from the characters of the duelists, each outcome the result of those characters. Each sniper carried one rifle. Each man worked in the same terrain, under the same sky. The chances and dangers were as evenly distributed as they got in war.

Zaitsev listened patiently, hearing nothing from his former pupils he did not know and had not considered himself. He would make no plans yet. Better first to learn the ways of this German, then decide. What will he try on me? Will he move or stay in one place? Will he hide or make himself known? Will he—

Enough, he thought, and took a final swallow of vodka. I know all these stratagems and feints. I taught them.

He sent the hares back to the Lazur, assuring them he would seek their counsel and keep them advised. He would also welcome any information they could gather about unusual Nazi sniper activity in their sectors.

Viktor set off on his nocturnal hunt. Minutes later, Tania slid back in.

She stood in the doorway, wordless, uninvited but possessing the room as if it were her own chamber. She moved toward him silently, her eyes fastened to his. She walked past, then behind him. He turned to keep his face to hers. He joined in her movements as if pulled by centrifugal force to circle behind her while she circled. Tania took off her coat and held it out with a straight arm into the center of their orbits. She dropped the coat and unbuttoned her jersey. Zaitsev followed her, prowling behind her, the two tossing their clothes into the center of their ring as if casting flowers onto a pond.

Two hours later, Tania stole away. They had both dressed in silence, pulling their clothes out of the mingled pile in the dark. One of these days, Zaitsev thought, she's going to leave the bunker with my pants on by mistake. He laughed: I'd better come up with a good tale for Viktor in advance of that one.

The next morning, Zaitsev woke late on his bedroll. Gray light dribbled in with the cold. He checked his watch. 6:45 A.M. He rubbed his eyes and scratched away the itching discomfort from sleeping on the drafty dirt.

He lit the lantern. His head roved from the lovemaking and the vodka. He dug into his pack to tug off a piece of bread and chewed absentmindedly. Where to start? he wondered. Where do I look for a master sniper who's looking for me?

He decided to return to sector two, to Mamayev Kurgan, where he and Tania had encountered Thorvald the morning before. Had he known of the Headmaster's arrival then, he'd have sent Danilov away and, with Tania, taken him on right there.

With Tania. The thought surprised him a little. Yes. She's good enough. I'd fight with her at my side now.

Well, he thought, up and out. Over to the Lazur, get Tania, and we'll go hunting in her sector first for this SS colonel.

Viktor burst through the doorway.

"Vasha! The Germans have attacked the Red October. It's big! Six, seven divisions!"

"Shit. Here it comes." This must be the Germans' last bid to capture the city. We all knew it would come before the Volga froze. This is it. November eleventh, dawn. And I overslept.

Zaitsev grabbed his rifle.

Viktor gathered Zaitsev's pack and extra ammunition, continuing to jabber. "They're on a five-kilometer front. Between the Banny Gully and Vokhovstroyevskaya Street."

"Who's defending?"

"Gorishny's Ninety-fifth in the factory and the corridor. Lyudnikov and the One thirty-eighth in the shops."

Zaitsev tossed the last of the bread to Viktor.

"They'll hold. Where—"

"I've already been to the Lazur. I sent every bear and

hare I could find over there. We need to hurry. It's closing up fast."

Zaitsev flew out of the bunker behind Viktor, his rifle in his fist. With his free hand, he shouldered the strap of his submachine gun. The heavy PPSh and its round, stubby magazine bounced against his spine while he ran. Viktor jangled under an assortment of grenades, cartridges, knives, field glasses, and guns.

Sectors two and three, Zaitsev thought. That's where the attack is. Kulikov is in two, Morozov in three.

Nikolay Kulikov. He wasn't at the celebration last night. He and Baugderis probably stayed in their trench overnight to work their tin can lines again at dawn. They're already in the thick of it. I've got to get to them.

Chuikov pulled me off all assignments to hunt down the sniper from Berlin. But it can't be helped at the moment. I'll get back to Thorvald later. He'll keep.

Besides, he might even be in sector two, waiting for me.

The Hare and the Bear ran through trenches and empty alleys to reach the Volga. There, behind the safety of its cliffs along the littered beach, lay the main route from the Lazur to the troops defending the factory district.

The Nazi general Paulus had made reaching the river a priority, to isolate the Russian positions into small beachheads, especially now during the supply crisis. But running, Zaitsev felt in his shaking bones that this last offensive spasm by the Germans was doomed. He knew Chuikov's Sixty-second Army was well dug in. To a man, the Ivans were fired up on vodka and stoked to a red glow by the bellows of the commissars' ceaseless bunker speeches, their foxhole whispers, their iron nudges.

Nearing the Red October, Zaitsev heard the boom of artillery and tank fire. Viktor slowed. Great puffs of steam heaved from his mouth. His wide shoulders slumped under the weights strapped to him.

Zaitsev patted Viktor's shoulder. "Bear, we need to hurry."

"Let's rest a moment," Viktor huffed. "No sense getting there and being too tired to kill any Germans." He trotted to a halt on the sand and bent over, hands on knees, breathing like a draft horse just in from the plow.

Zaitsev felt drops of sweat on his brow under his fur hat. He looked across the green river to the wooded islands two kilometers offshore. Behind those islands are food, ammunition, vodka, medicine, warmer boots, he thought. The Volga, the most beloved river of Russian lore, is even now shifting, deciding whether to help or destroy its countrymen.

The great ice floes drifted in the river; they bumped and grumbled below the surface. A milky skim of ice had formed in places along the bank, still too thin to walk on. But it was coming, the ice was gathering. How long until it was thick enough to drive a truck over? A month, perhaps? Will we still be here?

"I'll go ahead, Viktor." Zaitsev broke into a run up the beach. "Good hunting!" He left Viktor wheezing behind him. The sand hissed under his boots.

Vasha, the sand whispered, don't forget the Headmaster.

The Volga ice giants slid past each other and keened, Vasha, he's looking for you.

Once off the beach, moving through the streets, the barren buildings leaned over him to mutter in his ear.

Vasha, be careful, the city said.

He stopped in the street and looked around. A hundred Red soldiers ran past. Shouts and rifle reports surrounded him.

Thorvald, Vasha. Thorvald.

• • •

THE FIGHTING WAS BEHIND HIM NOW. HE DUCKED
into trenches and crawled through the windows of buildings in his path. His ears were as attuned as his eyes; he
was ready to freeze like a chameleon at any motion or
sound in the rubble. He advanced undetected, as he knew
he could.

He moved with a strength beyond what was in his
arms and legs. It was in his stomach, in his senses. He
knew that the war was not looking for him at that moment. It was absorbed elsewhere. He was at his zenith,
his most powerful and canny; he was alert to any
threat, ready to face danger and portion it out, creeping
along the seams of the battle, set on instinct to vanish
into the fabric of conflict. Though he'd tried over many
a bottle and cigarette, in dozens of trenches under
the flickering night-lights of tumbling flares with freshmen and seasoned veterans, he could never find the
words to express it: war, when you know it, when you
have it inside you, is an animal. You can scare it away,
hide from it, even anger it or feed it something other
than you. You can't control it, but you can think like it.
This was the skill Zaitsev could not teach to his hares.
It lived in him at the visceral level, beneath words and
intellect; it had breathed first in the taiga, been awakened in his blood by his grandfather. A soldier either possessed it, as Viktor and Chekov did, or won it, as
Tania had done, or didn't have it at all, no matter how
brave or clever. He remembered the dead boy, the young
bear Fedya.

He wondered about the Headmaster. Does he have it?
Is his killing skill in his intellect or his gut? Is he a
teacher, a soldier, or a hunter?

What will Thorvald show me? How patient is he?
Where is he? Is he waiting for me to move into his

crosshairs, or is he still stalking me? Will he try to flush me out, or will he set a trap and let me fall into it?

Zaitsev gazed at the hulls of the buildings opposite him. He looked to the burned shacks of the factory settlements, north to the remains of the Red October and, deep in the smoking distance, the Barricades. He thought about the city stretching behind him, tracing the arcing bank of the Volga in a crescent of desolation. It was all different now. Before, Stalingrad had been a battlefield, with maps, sectors, front lines, flanks, supply routes, the river—all building blocks defining the city. He'd grown to know it, learning the ruined terrain the best way a man could, by hiding in it. From his first days in the storm groups, the city had moved with a rhythm Zaitsev could feel, like the forest or the Pacific tides in Vladivostok. But now lurking within the shadows and cracks was a wild, unpredictable element: a single man with one mission, to find and kill him, the Hare. An SS colonel, a master sniper, skilled beyond what Zaitsev could guess, armed with his prey's photograph and sheets of Danilov's articles describing the sniper tactics Zaitsev had pioneered.

If Thorvald was the sniper who had shot up the dummy in sector two, then he was uncannily fast and deadly accurate. And, remembering Pyotr's ragged face, Zaitsev sensed that there was something else about him. Something skewed, perhaps bizarre.

Zaitsev moved far enough west to see the rail yard bordering the Red October workers' settlements. He was in the area of the icehouses, due north of the Lazur. Striakov counterattacked half a kilometer behind him. To his left, the echoes of tanks and boots clacked among the bricks and stark stone facades. The Germans were moving up to answer Striakov.

The shooting cells he'd shared with Kulikov and Baugderis were nearby. He scanned with his scope—the binoculars were better for the job at hand, but he preferred his finger on the trigger in uncertain situations like this—looking for the five ruined boxcars. They would mark the German trench, Kulikov's tin-can hunting preserve of the afternoon before.

He slid forward another twenty meters. The first boxcar became visible at the far end of the yard, atop a rail mound, below a bank of warehouses. He recognized the terrain. There, another fifty meters to his left, would be Kulikov's trench.

This last stretch was across an open yard. The ground was covered with debris. Resisting the urge to hurry this final distance, Zaitsev reached into his pack for a muslin sack. He slid his rifle and machine gun into the sack and pulled the drawstring. He moved slowly into the open, flat on his belly. He crept twenty meters in five minutes, stopping every five seconds to blend in with the cluttered earth. He crawled down into a shallow crater. He pulled on his rope and dragged the dirty tan sack just as slowly to him across the open yard. Gathering in the rope, he thought about the attributes of this sort of battlefield, how a man could turn them to his favor. If a man was careful and watchful, he could always find cover. If he knew how and when to move, he might travel at will throughout the city and remain invisible in the tangled shadows and rubble. The Germans surely had not thought of this when they bombed Stalingrad without relent in August and September, that they were simply building rats' nests, runs, craters, and shadows for the Red soldier.

After a half hour, he reached the lip of the trench, not knowing what he would find. He pulled his rifle sack to him quickly and put the weapons in his hands.

He stopped to cast his senses out into the yard and enveloping buildings. He was certain he'd arrived unseen. The German assault had moved behind him; he felt the emptiness of the rail yard. Here, less than a kilometer from the action, the buildings were quiet, spitting out only echoes of the fighting from the northeast Volga cliffs and the bowels of the factory.

He slipped into the trench, hoping he would not find the two hares. In the quiet of the yard, he admitted to himself he held little hope of finding Kulikov and Baugderis alive. If they're still in the trench, he thought, they're dead. Before dawn, this trench was on the very edge of the front line. The German advance would have swept right over them at full, sudden speed before anything could slow it down. They might've been able to retreat across the open yard, but only at a dead run, and that would have gotten them cut down by a hundred guns.

He realized that he'd followed an unspoken command to come to Kulikov and Baugderis. Even if he would only find corpses, he understood consciously now that he could not have left his friends to stiffen and blister under the winter sky. He knew also he could not expect to evacuate the bodies for a proper burial; that must wait until the Germans were run out of Stalingrad. But in order to write to their mothers to tell how their sons had died, he knew he had to come here. It was, in his secret way, what he wanted done for himself should he, too, be trapped and killed.

Honor for the dead; loyalty from the living. No man can desire these things and justly deserve them if he does not give them. This was fair. This was one of the rules of life and death.

Zaitsev moved fifty meters through the trench before he saw them. He hurried to the bodies slumped on the trench floor, and his heart began the quick descent into anger.

The first body was Baugderis. The Georgian lay against the trench wall, his arms spread, with his legs twisted under him. His posture seemed joyful, as if he'd leaped into the air to wave his arms and kick his heels. His face gave the lie to that. The right eye socket was a mass of dull color and flesh. Black blood cloaked his shoulder and right arm, spilled from the cavity Zaitsev knew was in the back of the man's head.

On Baugderis's right, a meter away, was Kulikov. Beside him was his helmet, a bullet hole punched in the side of it. Near his hand lay his artillery periscope.

Zaitsev stepped over Baugderis's body to kneel beside Kulikov. Blood had clotted over half of his friend's face and neck. A dark pool rested in his ear.

Zaitsev bent close to inspect the gash across the side of Kulikov's forehead. At the center of the wound, in the heart of the dried blood, a bright red cleft beat like a tiny tongue sticking out, pulling back. A trickle gathered into a drop, then ran a crimson ribbon down the crust. It stopped, but it had run far enough to tell Zaitsev that Kulikov was alive.

His hands flew to his friend's neck, his thumbs on his cheeks. He shook them hard. "Nikolay! Open your eyes!"

Kulikov exhaled and swayed his head. His eyelids fluttered, showing Zaitsev the whites.

Zaitsev patted Kulikov's cheek, harder each time until the eyes opened and focused. Zaitsev reached for his pack and canteen. He pulled open the man's mouth and poured water in. Most of it dribbled down Kulikov's neck until he began to swallow.

"Slowly. Slowly, Nikolay. It's all right."

Kulikov pushed away the canteen and coughed. He squinted and groaned. He brought his hand to his head but could not bring himself to touch the wound.

"Wha . . . what? . . ." Kulikov turned toward Baugderis. His eyes took in the pulp of his friend's face. "Oh. Oh, shit," he muttered, fear popping in his eyes.

"You're all right, Nikolay," Zaitsev said reassuringly. "You've just got a flesh wound on your head. You're not going to die. I'll get you back."

Kulikov closed his lids. He drew a deep breath. "The

attack. Where? . . ." he said in a voice searching for strength.

Zaitsev interrupted. "It's all right. They're behind us now. It moved past you."

Kulikov leaned his head back to look into the morning sky.

A grimace creased his lips. "I don't remember. More water."

Zaitsev handed him the canteen. What does he mean, he doesn't remember the attack? Yes, he's been unconscious for over two hours. But isn't that how Baugderis got killed, how Kulikov took his wound? The German attack ran over them, their retreat was cut off; they put up resistance and drew fire.

"Nikolay," he asked, "how did you get hit?"

Kulikov looked again at Baugderis. "Sniper."

Zaitsev's jaw tightened.

Kulikov struggled to sit up. "The attack came just after dawn. No way we could stay here. But . . ." He snorted, almost in a somber laugh. "I guess we did anyway."

Zaitsev waited for Kulikov to gather himself.

"We figured we'd head out from this end of the trench. Maybe we could make it to the icehouses if we ran. We moved this way, tugging on the strings one last time. We didn't wait long, just enough to see what we could flush out. We got one more."

Nikolay touched his cheek. His fingers trembled over the lumps of blood built up like gathered wax. He brushed his hair at the temple and found it packed hard.

He grunted when his fingertips neared the wound.

"Leave it," Zaitsev told him. "We'll get it fixed soon."

Kulikov dropped his hand and chuckled painfully, nervously, at his good luck.

He continued. "Once we got here, I pulled the string and spotted. We were in a hurry at this point. Nothing happened, and we were about to move to the last position.

Then, and I can't tell you why, I saw a German poke his head up. I called Zviad into the shot. He fired, and just like that he got hit."

On the top of the trench, lying in the dirt where it had been when the bullet struck, was Baugderis's Moisin-Nagant. Zaitsev pulled the rifle down and gasped.

The telescopic sight was shattered. A bullet had gone into it, smashing through the tube into Baugderis's right eye.

Baugderis had not had even the two seconds it took to fire and look away from the scope before the German killed him.

Zaitsev pulled back the rifle's bolt to pop out the spent casing. He hadn't had a chance to move a muscle, he thought. Baugderis fired, watched his bullet hit, and died on his feet.

"I didn't see where it came from," Kulikov said, shaking his head. "I . . . I was so . . . when he got hit, it came out of nowhere. It scared the shit out of me, Vasha. I guess I must have stood up."

Zaitsev nodded. "Just for a second," he mumbled, more to himself than to Kulikov.

Thorvald. He was here. And the bastard wants me to know it.

"Just for a second," Kulikov echoed. "There must have been two or three of them. We . . . we stayed too long."

Kulikov's eyes grew shiny. He looked again at Baugderis. A tear dripped a glossy trail over his bloody cheek.

"We were making a game out of it, Vasha," he whispered. "There was no reason. We should have left last night. But we stayed. Just for the fucking kills."

Zaitsev nodded. He understood. This was Nikolay Kulikov crying, one of the best and cleverest hares. This was a sniper, a trained and focused assassin, in tears, lamenting the killing. Zaitsev knew what Kulikov had witnessed:

he'd seen his own soul. He'd caught the stain of murder
on it and recoiled in horror. This was what the charnel
house had done to Kulikov and was doing to the men of
both armies. It turned them first into righteous killers for
their country, then into predators for sport and entertain-
ment, or for vengeance. How many times can you pull a
trigger and destroy a life before the realities switch on
you, until the thing you are doing is killing your own
spirit?

Kulikov had put bullets into close to a hundred men,
Zaitsev almost twice that many. Kulikov and Baugderis
had turned the art and need and ugliness of killing into a
game to ease the days. Zaitsev thought back to the slaughter in the Nazi officers' bunker. That night, troubled by
the senselessness of the act and its utter lack of military
necessity, he'd been lucky. He, too, had felt the malady of
his murders, as sharply as Kulikov felt his now. But Zaitsev had been near the flame of Tania to melt the ice in his
heart, to tame his pain until he could bridle it. Now Kulikov sat in this trench staring over his bloody shoulder at
the fruit of his own sport, the death mask of Baugderis,
and rued the rot of Stalingrad in his soul.

Whose fault is it? Zaitsev wondered to Kulikov's sobs.
Isn't this what we're told to do, every moment? Kill the
Nazis. Beat them into the ground, bite them, claw them,
blow them up, stab, shoot, kill them until they are no
longer on our soil. We're in a frenzy, all of us, we're rabid,
all of us. Every word we hear and read, in *In Our Country's Defense* and *Red Star*, kill the Germans. The *politrooks*, kill the Germans or die. The vodka which never
seems to dry up for us, stay drunk, stay dim-witted and
numb, kill the Germans. Wherever you find them, in battle, taking a piss, sleeping in their bunks, they're never
less than what they are: invading, miserable, stinking Nazis, the enemies of Communism, never forgiven, never
pitied, never saved. Kill the Nazis or die.

Zaitsev laid the rifle across the dead Georgian's lap. He unbuttoned the coat and ran his hand to the inside pocket to pull out Zviad Baugderis's Komsomol card.

"Let's go, Nikolay. Can you stand?"

Kulikov struggled to his feet. Zaitsev steadied him. He pressed on the wounded man's back to remind him to stay low.

Zaitsev picked up Kulikov's periscope. He looked around on the trench floor.

"Where's your rifle?"

Kulikov looked down also. "It's right . . . where is it?"

The rifle was gone.

Zaitsev felt as if he had fallen amidst the floes in the Volga. Cold needles nicked at his skin.

He's been here, he thought. He's been in this trench.

In his mind's eye, Zaitsev saw the high black boots of the Nazi colonel walking where he now stood.

Perhaps he left a clue? No, not him.

He looked one last time at Baugderis. This isn't enough? he thought. The bastard is making his own sport now, collecting trophies of his kills.

Or no, wait. Not trophies. He knew he'd shot two snipers today, didn't he? He had to come see if one of them was me. That's his assignment. When he kills me, he goes home.

He's got my picture from *In Our Country's Defense.*

The Headmaster waited for the German attack to move past, then he came out behind it. Now he knows he missed me. And he took the Moisin-Nagant as a bonus. It's better than his Mauser, and he knows that, too.

Zaitsev ducked lower in the trench and pushed Kulikov ahead of him. Is Thorvald still in those buildings? Is he dug in and waiting for me to come to the rescue of one of my hares? Is this a trap? Is Nikolay a bait? Or did he leave Kulikov alive to tell me how incredible his shooting was?

"Come on, Nikolay," he said. "Let's go. Quickly."

NINETEEN

THORVALD ROLLED HIS WHITE CAMOUFLAGE
sleeve down over his wristwatch. Nikki had been gone for
close to an hour.

He looked again out the window through the dust and
smoke wheeling under the swelling sun. He lay back. His
body recalled the night spent there, the tongue-and-
groove flooring unyielding to his back. The boy certainly
moves carefully, he thought. Four hundred meters out,
four hundred back, and it takes him an hour to do it.
Patience as a tool, a weapon. Nikki understands. Nikki
has the stuff of a sniper. I may train him myself when we
get back to Berlin.

Thorvald wrapped his arms again around his rifle to
rest them on his chest. He'd lain like this since Nikki left,
like a corpse clutching a rifle instead of a lily. He raised
his head to gaze down his white canvas tunic and pants to
his boots. He clicked his toes together once, enjoying the
slapstick of the move. Still alive, he thought. Still kicking.
He touched his nose to the rifle barrel. The gun had
grown metallic cold now, the warmth of the two spent
bullets long drifted out of its black skin. The smell of oil
and smoke, of flash and speed, trickled from the opening
onto his cheek. Thorvald hugged the gun. He rubbed the

bottom of his stubbled chin against the nub of the open sight at the end of the barrel. The rifle in his arms represented all that he was not. It was the missing part of him, the hardness and clarity not in his own flesh. The gun holds its spirit well, he thought. It smells of the kill, it feels of its nature: deadly, cold, hard. It is complete, resolved.

The sounds of the German attack flitted in the window. Before he left, Nikki had said that it probably wasn't Zaitsev lying out there in the trench. The Hare wouldn't have made those mistakes, wouldn't have stayed to the bitter end just for the kills. That's beneath him, not worthy of the legend. Bad form. No, Thorvald thought, this Zaitsev is not a sportsman, no mere marksman like me. He's a hunter. He likes his prey in the wild.

Thorvald looked into the charred rafters. He focused on a sliver of ceiling plaster, hanging by some thin force, swinging in the moving chill. He was learning more every day about Zaitsev even as he learned about Stalingrad. The two, he thought, the man and the city, are clearly inseparable. They are exact opposites and thus perfect complements. The city is a cruel, indiscriminate battleground. It is misery incarnate, with its lice, filth, and terrible faces, death and injury infecting every shadow. Stalingrad is a fallen thing, jagged and ugly. It screeches and shakes with each thrust of pain like an old dying mule. But Zaitsev, he stays silent under the city's screams. He is the solid, quiet ice and dicing cold of the Russian dawn. He has will. He's not stripped naked like the city. He's clothed in pride with his muttlike Siberian determination to endure. This sergeant with the forest in his veins, he doesn't even know where he is. He thinks he's still in the damned woods, somewhere in the mountains. He doesn't realize the colors are gone. The forest has burned down, and in that blaze the first victims were preordained: honor, order, and mercy, the very traits that elevate us above Zaitsev's precious wild beasts. As told in the great operas of Wagner, the ethics of Schopenhauer, the superman of Nietzsche, we are lifted above the animals, we are the more noble creatures. But in vicious battle, where men yearn only to kill each other, the raging heat of their hatred cremates their humanity. They become no more than savage, frightened brutes. Zaitsev hunts their animalness; he finds them by it and destroys them for it.

Zaitsev won't wake up, him and his one-man-one-bullet credo, his morality; he's sleepwalking. Ridiculous, the notion of killing with honor—it's an oxymoron. So there it is. The Hare is so different from Stalingrad that the city masks him, even protects him, because in some way, some intuitive hunter's way of being *in* but not actually *of* the forest, the city cannot even touch him.

No. That is not Vasily Zaitsev dead in the trench. Not yet.

NIKKI CALLED UP THE STAIRS. THORVALD HAD not heard him approach.

"Colonel, I'm back. Come down."

Thorvald rose stiffly to his feet. His joints ached from the ninety minutes of cold and inactivity. "Well?" he asked, descending the steps. "How did we do?"

Nikki hefted a long Russian rifle with a scope. "There were two snipers down, sir. No Zaitsev."

"Hmmm. Well, no surprise there. I suppose we'll have to be good instead of lucky, eh, Nikki?"

Thorvald pointed at the Moisin-Nagant. He'd seen plenty of them at Gnössen, had taught on them. They were good rifles, dependable in rough conditions if a little slow.

"If there were two dead," he asked, pointing at the Moisin-Nagant, "why only one rifle?"

Thorvald handed his Mauser to Nikki in exchange for the Moisin-Nagant. The Russian weapon was heavier. It felt awkward, crude, like a plow horse, he thought. But plow horses, the Russians understand, don't break down.

"Well, Corporal," he prodded, "where's the other rifle?"

"The other rifle," Nikki said, his face distant, perhaps back in the trench seeing something again, "was no good. I left it."

"That's fine. No need carrying damaged guns across that rail yard. You know, and I did mention it before you left, I thought something might be wrong with one of those Russian rifles."

Thorvald busied himself looking through the Moisin-Nagant's 4X sight. He turned his profile to Nikki and swung the rifle up and down—Mark! Pull! No, no good for traps, too head-heavy.

"What, in fact, was wrong with it, Nikki?"

Nikki paused. Thorvald concentrated into the Russian scope and waited for an answer in the confident way a man waits for a ball to drop when he has tossed it up.

Nikki shuffled his feet in the dirt.

"Nobody's that good, Colonel."

Without looking, Thorvald knew Nikki was staring at him. The young corporal was hooked to him now like a fish on a lure, to what he'd seen in the trench.

Thorvald swung the Russian rifle up, then down again. Clumsy. But reliable, deadly. I can hit with this, oh, yes.

"Indulge me, Corporal. Tell me about the other rifle."

"The other rifle had been shot through the scope."

Thorvald lowered the Moisin-Nagant. He grinned. "Really?"

Nikki slung the Mauser's strap over his shoulder. He reached out to take the Russian rifle from Thorvald.

"Quite a shot, Colonel."

Thorvald slid on his white mittens and walked behind

Nikki down the steps into the street. Soldiers scattered urgently in all directions.

"Not really a shot," Thorvald said into the air. "More of a calling card, actually."

Thorvald didn't care where he was going; he knew Nikki would guide him well. He'd been right to choose this boy over one of Ostarhild's snipers. The young corporal knew the battlefield. Even though Thorvald had done the actual shooting, Nikki had brought him to this morning's targets and thrown the rock that had sealed the Red snipers' fates. The young corporal had crawled out at his command to retrieve the Russian rifle, to ascertain if Zaitsev had been a victim, and to verify his "calling card."

Good, he thought. It's all working well. Nikki needed to see what I can do.

THEY TRAVELED FIVE KILOMETERS WEST TO-ward the rear, where the rush of men and machinery slowed. The battle sounds receded, and the thumps from mortars and tanks grew muffled in the maze of streets and alleys. A motorcycle messenger shot past them toward the tumult. Even the rasping spit of the speeding bike faded quickly into the blackened stones and brick piles around them. The decimated city seemed to swallow sound, light, life.

Thorvald stopped and sat on his pack. He called Nikki to sit also. He wanted to talk.

Thorvald glanced at the ruins. Over their tops, the sounds and smoke of the German offensive rose like newly released spirits into the sky. The city rumbled, the two armies clawed at each other.

"Look around, Nikki." He swept his arm over the smorgasbord of destruction. "Look at all this. Tens of thousands of men, all headed in one direction. And you and me, we're off on our own, just the two of us. We're fighting a different war."

The pounding of mortar shells amplified his point. "We're not using the same weapons as the rest of them. We're not knocking everything down, trying to root out every Russian we can find. We're working alone, on our own private seek-and-destroy mission. We're not looking for Red divisions with bombs and tanks and ten battalions. We're looking for just one man with these."

He jabbed his finger at the Russian and German sniper rifles Nikki had laid down.

"How do we do it? How do we find one quiet man in all this noise? It's got me confused and, I'll be honest, a bit worried."

Thorvald looked at the wreckage surrounding them. Concrete ghosts, he thought, carcasses of debris everywhere you look. Zaitsev could be anywhere, in any of those windows, cellars, trenches, gullies, gorges, ruins, tunnels. And the next day, the next hour, he could be someplace else. He could even be lying dead from another soldier's bullet or from a stray piece of shrapnel. And I'll be handcuffed here searching for a dead man, or at best a moving, hidden target who doesn't even know I'm looking for him.

What am I doing? I can't keep this up, I can't keep following this boy around Stalingrad, shooting at whatever he points out for me. I can't spend my every waking hour engaging Russian snipers in every quadrant of this infernal city, sending Nikki out two or three times a day to see if I've managed to put a hole in that bastard Zaitsev. No, this is an absurd and fatal plan. This is me, alone with a bold, bloody teenager trying to find one pinprick of a man in an endlessly hellish haystack. And Nikki wants me to engage every Red sniper we can find like a trick sharp-shooter in a traveling sideshow, just to catch Zaitsev's attention. At this rate, I'll probably draw a bullet long before I can deliver one to the Hare.

"Nikki," he said at last, pleased suddenly by the feeling of being conclusive, "we don't have time anymore to parade all over Stalingrad looking for Zaitsev. Even though we've just started, we have to change our plan. I wasn't sent out here to clean the city of snipers. Just one man. That's all we need to get us both a ride home."

Nikki's head hung. He fingered bits of gravel.

Thorvald continued. "Let's figure out a better way to let Zaitsev know I'm here. He won't be able to stand it. The legend, the hero, he'll come charging right at us like a mad bull. What do you think?"

Nikki made a fist around a stone and stared into the dirt.

Thorvald repeated, "What do you think?"

Nikki looked up.

"It's already done."

Thorvald laughed. What was the boy talking about? What's done? Zaitsev couldn't know I'm looking for him. He's not so powerful a hunter as to be clairvoyant.

Thorvald tossed a pebble over his right shoulder. It was a prayer for good luck learned beside the ponds of his childhood. Their waters shone behind the green estates of his kin, far away. "What? That fancy shot through the scope? I'd have to make that shot ten more times before Zaitsev would even notice. He'll think it was an accident."

"Not that shot, Colonel. Zaitsev knows you're here. He's known for a couple of days."

The words pulled Thorvald upright. He touched his fingertips together.

Nikki looked down again. He spoke into the ground.

"I told them."

Thorvald blinked. "You . . . you what? You told whom?"

"The Russians."

Zaitsev knows I'm here? Thorvald's senses rang with alarms. This boy told Zaitsev I'm here? How could he have done that? How could he have spoken with Zaitsev? What is this corporal, a Red agent? A spy, a traitor? Thorvald's thoughts raced, their brakes yanked off suddenly by Nikki's admission. Why is he telling me this? He looked at Nikki's feet, the two rifles lying there, both loaded. They were the only weapons within reach except for the knife on Nikki's hip.

Nikki continued. "I was captured. The night after you landed. The Russians were behind our lines; they caught me while I was fixing a telephone wire. They were going to kill me. I had to tell them something or they were going to cut my throat."

Nikki stood. One rifle hung in each fist.

"So I gave them you, Colonel. I didn't think it would matter. I told them you were here to kill Zaitsev. They liked that. A duel between their supersniper and our supersniper. They let me live so that I could tell you about it. But I didn't."

Thorvald glared up at the corporal. The boy's admission was plausible. Nikki was captured; he panicked and talked, just like I would have done, he thought. But the tale didn't allay his sudden suspicion of Nikki. This boy has known all along that Zaitsev is looking for me. He knew and didn't tell me. He's been manipulating me, risking my life, planning more confrontations that might have been with Zaitsev, the Red superman, without my knowing it. Well, well. Young Nikki. A killer, a liar, a traitor, and a coward.

No. This is definitely enough.

"Corporal," he said, his voice chilly, "I believe you. And I can see why you would hesitate to tell me about your adventure with the Russians. After all, giving information to the enemy is treason and punishable, I believe, by summary execution."

Nikki's knuckles went white on the two rifles. The boy's stance shifted. Thorvald wondered if the corporal was afraid that the SS colonel at his feet might rise, demand one of the rifles, and fire a round into his head for treason. Nikki tensed as if he might drop one of the rifles, lift the other gun, and just shoot Thorvald first.

"I also understand why you decided to tell me. After all, if Zaitsev blows my head off, you don't get to go home with me, do you? Is there anything else I should know about you, Corporal?"

Nikki stood still, looking ruined, like Stalingrad.

Thorvald gazed up to the low, scudding clouds to consider this new fact. Zaitsev knows I'm here. Well, that makes for a different game. I no longer need to let this child drag me all over the city, creating corpses just to get Zaitsev's attention. I've already got it. Now, if I were in the Hare's shoes, if I'd been told that a specialist had been sent from Berlin to kill just me, I'd hide and hope the bastard got killed by someone else first. But Zaitsev? No, the legend will come to find the German master sniper. The maniac is not living a life anymore; he's writing chapters for the Red newspapers. And it's going to be his anchor, his downfall. I can bring him to me now with ease. I'll give him a sniff of me and he'll head straight for it. I'll make this, what he hopes will be his greatest story—his chance to confront and destroy the master Nazi sniper in a one-on-one showdown on a stage watched by the world—into his obituary. I'll turn the Hare's pride into his tombstone.

Nikki was silent, waiting. Thorvald could tell, the boy had no idea what was to follow. I have him; I've stabbed into him so deeply that he's witless in front of me. I have the power of surprise in almost anything I do or say to him from this moment on.

We're going to stop chasing Zaitsev. Instead the Hare is going to be invited to a trap, into a duel he cannot win.

Thorvald tried to make his face stern; the moment seemed to call for it. But he knew from a thousand mirrors that his skin was too white, his cheeks too round. He made his voice firm instead.

"Well, Nikki, now that we are on what I hope is a level playing field, we're going to make a change. You and I are going to stop crawling around this city, looking for jousts like two knights-errant. Instead we're going to select for me a single position. It's going to be perfectly located. It will be undetectable. From that position I'm going to kill every Russian within sight. I'm going to turn a thousand-meter diameter into a killing ground. Zaitsev will come to me because, according to what you have just told me, he's waiting for me to appear. I'm going to oblige him. He'll come to me, just so. Then I will shoot him and I will go home."

Thorvald stood. He carried his pack two steps forward and dropped it at Nikki's feet.

"And I'll take you with me, Corporal. I can see now that you're no better than me. You need to get out of here as badly as I do."

TWENTY

ZAITSEV'S LEG QUIVERED. THE THUMP OF HIS boot against the dirt made Tania lower her scope and look at him.

His leg shook again.

"Can't," he mumbled. "Don't . . . find me . . . run."

Tania pulled her rifle from the lip of the trench facing the eastern slope of Mamayev Kurgan. She slid across the floor to him. She laid her hand on his knee and he stilled.

Zaitsev had curled around his rifle like a vine of ivy. He'd told her to wake him after fifteen minutes, but she'd let him sleep an hour. All day since dawn, she, Zaitsev, Shaikin, and Chekov had crept and climbed, looking for signs of Thorvald. She stroked Zaitsev's shin. He's been chasing the Headmaster pretty hard, she thought. He was up most of the night plotting strategies with Medvedev, poring over maps and reports.

For the three days since she, Zaitsev, and Danilov had accidentally met Thorvald here on the hillside of Mamayev Kurgan, little had been heard from the Headmaster. That's good, she thought; his signature on Baugderis was grisly. Maybe he got himself gunned down by someone else. Maybe he wasn't so good after all. That would be fine. It would help keep Vasha safe. The Hare has been exposing himself to the greatest dangers in each sector, talking with soldiers, interviewing wounded, artillery spotters, machine gunners along the front line, examining bodies, running under fire every step of the way, all just to find this schoolteacher.

I hope the stich from Berlin is already dead, she thought.

Zaitsev's body twitched; the rifle he clutched rattled. His eyelids fluttered and he raised his chin as if lifting it above a rising tide.

His breath quickened. "Where . . . ," he murmured, "where . . ."

Tania felt his leg muscles contract. She jiggled his thigh to rouse him.

Released from whatever gripped his rest, Zaitsev relaxed. He opened his eyes and tensed suddenly, startling Tania. She reared back on her haunches to give him room to sit up and focus.

"Where were you?" she asked.

Zaitsev sniffled and blinked. He drew in a sharp breath, the kind a man takes before hefting a heavy object.

"How long did I sleep?"

"An hour."

"An hour? I told you—"

"You needed it." She laid her rifle across her lap. The light had dropped to dusk. "You were exhausted."

Zaitsev rubbed his forehead. "Next time, do what I ask."

He sniffed again and looked down the trench to where the other team, Shaikin and Chekov, was positioned a hundred meters away, gazing up at Mamayev Kurgan's spoiled face.

"Anything?"

Tania shook her head.

"What was your dream?"

"Oh . . . um . . ." He paused, remembering it, or deciding not to tell her.

She prodded him. "You said 'run.' And 'find me.' What was the dream, Vasha?"

He ran his hand over his chin. The stubble hissed in his palm. "I was being hunted. In the taiga, I was running from a hunter. I had no weapon, just, . . . I just ran like an animal."

Tania waited for him to say it, then, unable to stop herself, said it for him.

"Thorvald?"

Zaitsev's eyes locked. His hand froze in the air.

That was stupid, she thought immediately. She reached to touch his leg. "It was probably your grandfather. You've said he was the best. Besides"—she pulled her hand back and shook her head—"you'd never run from Thorvald."

Zaitsev said nothing, but his eyes betrayed that she'd been right. It was Thorvald. The Headmaster's crosshairs had seared their mark on the dreams of the Hare. He was worried about the coming duel, even afraid of it, and she'd called him on it.

She'd been careless and forthright, had moved too close. Always rushing in, she thought, impatient and selfish. Not enough experience with men, not of this sort, anyway. Leave his ego intact, Tania. You can know his fears without making him say them out loud. Stupid.

"The light's dying," she said, to put words in the air and cover the mess she'd made. "What do you want to do?"

Zaitsev rose to his knees and shouldered his pack.

"Let's go." He didn't look at her.

"You go ahead." It was best to let him be alone for a while. Though innocently, she'd stung him. Let him walk away and curse her under his breath. She'd make it up to him that night.

"I'll get Shaikin and Chekov and see you later," she said.

Zaitsev gathered his sniper rifle.

She spoke while he turned from her. "I'll see you tonight?"

Zaitsev pivoted. His eyes softened above the roots of a smile, and he nodded to her. He turned again to make his way down the trench. She heard him laugh quietly at some private mystery.

"I WANT TO GO." TANIA FOLDED HER ARMS across her chest.

"Tanyushka, you can't!" Shaikin slapped his hand on his thigh. "It's not proper."

"Ha! Somehow it's proper for *you* to go? What would your wife write in her next letter if she knew? 'Dear Ilya Alexeyavich, I'm so glad you found a whorehouse in Stalingrad. I find it rather amazing, but I hope it helps ease the tension.' Yes?"

Behind Shaikin, Chekov chuckled.

"I'm going," she repeated.

"Ilyushka," Chekov said, resting a hand on Shaikin's shoulder, "let her come with us. Tania, do you promise to leave when we ask?"

"No. I'll leave when I'm ready."

"There!" shouted Shaikin, his arms flying up. "You see? She'll spoil it for us."

Tania kicked at the trench floor to shoot dirt over Shaikin's boots. "What could I possibly do to spoil it? Two women are running a bordello in a cellar in the middle of a battlefield! What could I do to interrupt them? You think they're shy? Or maybe I'll break down and cry?"

Shaikin's face hardened. Tania hadn't expected such resistance. She changed her tone.

"Don't worry, Ilya." She leaned over to poke her friend

in the ribs. "I'll be long gone before you drop your pants. I just want to meet these women. I'm curious. Let me come with you. I'll behave, I swear."

Tania walked away to let her friends decide. The sun squatted in the ruins to the west. Behind the buildings, the crest of Mamayev Kurgan bore a raw glaze like sunburned skin. The snowless peak, warmed from the constant shelling, remained in German hands.

She peered across the ruins, contemplating a brothel nestled in the midst of it all. How contrary, how opposite. How perfect; sex drained of love, dirty men and women grunting and digging a hole, searching for something soft and comforting only to find nothing awaiting but more emptiness, more hole, more Stalingrad. And yet, like me, when I lie with Vasha, how precious, complex, and confusing, how hopeful and doomed all at once.

Shaikin's suggestion that she might spoil their visit was ridiculous. She had no interest in watching or participating in sex with these women, and certainly not with her friends. She was merely fascinated by the notion, a little pleasure bunker in Stalingrad. But in her woman's heart she felt there might be something more heroic about these two women who "entertained" Russian soldiers, as Chekov put it. She sensed something fatalistic about them. Were these two women not simply cheap mistresses but in fact goodly and sad women driven to the edge—as she herself had been—by the deaths of their own loved ones, their lives sundered by the Nazis? Had they then been born anew into pain and degradation? Or were they just loose harlots hedging their bets? Certainly, should the Germans take the city, local whores would be among the more comfortable of the survivors.

She was insulted at the men's timid refusal to let her come along. Tania had dropped as many Germans as Shaikin. What would she see in a dirty cellar with two painted women lying about that would shock her? I won't stay long, she thought, just enough to meet these whores, see what they're like, maybe needle Shaikin and Chekov a bit. Then I'll come back tonight for my own diversion, my apology, with Vasha.

Shaikin and Chekov scurried over. Shaikin swept the backs of his hands in the air at Tania to shoo her before him as though she were a sheep in the road. "Fine, fine," he said in a high voice, "you want to come along, then fine. Go." He fanned his fingers at her. "Go, go, go."

Chekov moved past her in the trench. "It's not too far, Tania. Follow me."

He led them to the north end of the trench. On the count of one-two-three, the snipers jumped out and ran zigzag across twenty-five meters of open hillside to tumble into a crater.

Catching his breath, Chekov checked the sky.

"The sun's pretty low," he said. "We need to hurry."

Tania rolled over. "Hurry? Why?"

"They close after dark."

"You know these women well, Anatoly?"

Chekov's grin became a toothy smirk. "Well enough."

"Hmmm." Tania grunted, coiling for more exertion. "Let's go or you'll blame me for being late."

Chekov burst to his feet. He led them at a dead run for a kilometer, northeast from Mamayev Kurgan, across a wide boulevard and directly into the maze of workers' dwellings on the rim of the factory district. The front line was only two hundred meters away, but Chekov was light-hearted, as if he were leading his friends to his own home to introduce them to his family.

Tania weighed the danger they faced just to visit the whores. Though they were behind their own lines, there was enough light left in the day for enemy mortar crews or snipers to bear down from any of the taller buildings to the west. The setting sun and their fast gait lowered the risk, but what if SS Colonel Thorvald was one of those peering down a scope right now, looking for targets? Were they running fast enough?

Chekov stopped at the base of a pockmarked stone wall. He grinned at Tania and panted, "Almost there."

Another fifty meters among the burned and broken shacks of the workers' settlement and they halted. Chekov signaled Shaikin and Tania to duck behind cover and wait. He disappeared around the debris of a rubbled house; its charred clapboard showed pale yellow with white gingerbread trim between the scorches.

Long afternoon shadows cut the snowy avenue into jagged patches. Blackened, naked trees stood dead beside torn-up sidewalks. Houses here were nothing more than junkyard heaps, their histories squeezed out of them like dried rinds. In this extinct neighborhood, the only life, the only candle kept burning, was in the hands of two prostitutes.

As she caught her breath Tania smiled at the wreckage, thinking of the women waiting beneath it. The pair were like wild seeds sending out shoots into the ashes after a forest fire. Life, she thought, is a hard thing to snuff out.

Beside her, Shaikin rapped his fingers on his leg.

"Where is he?" he asked. "It's getting dark."

Tania clucked her tongue at Shaikin to play with him and shame him a little. He raised his eyebrows at her and drummed his fingers on the stock of his machine gun.

"Don't stare at me." He shrugged irritably. "You don't understand. You're not a man."

Tania winked at her friend's eyes, which could not stay on hers. "Silly as you men look right now," she said, "why would I want to be one?"

Chekov returned, beaming. "We're next."

Tania's mouth hung open. "Next?" She lowered her voice to a nasty hiss. "You mean there's a line?"

"Yes, of course," Chekov answered, unconcerned. "Every man in the Two eighty-fourth knows about these girls.

We're lucky today, though. It's so late in the afternoon that we're the last." He leered at Shaikin. "We can take our time a little."

Tania's surprise rose into indignation. Every man in the 284th? Risking their necks just to . . .

Quickly as her vexation had risen, it passed.

She took in the ruins of the city, with peril stamped on every brick and stone, and thought: Why not? Some tenderness for these men, even in the arms of whores, is a refuge. Perhaps it's the only respite left for them outside the glass of a vodka bottle.

Tania knew this power herself. To lie, even for moments, in warmth and gentleness was a haven in the long battle. She watched the last scarlet rim of the sun set behind the slope of Mamayev Kurgan—where she'd killed dozens of men, where fifty thousand more had fallen.

I'm not a man, Shaikin said. But he's wrong when he says I don't understand.

Tania heard footsteps. Voices too loud for the danger they posed floated on the air.

Three Red soldiers rounded the corner. One paused to give Chekov a friendly punch in the shoulder. The men hummed a lively tune in unison. The last one slowed to look at Tania. He made a shallow bow and moved on, rejoining his mates in their tune.

Chekov stepped forward. "Let's go."

"Wait." Shaikin spoke to Tania. "Please. You'll stay for five minutes, then come back here and wait. All right? Promise."

Tania looked at the backs of the men who had just sauntered away. She wanted the same cheerful mood for her two friends.

"Yes, Ilyushka. Of course."

Chekov led Shaikin and Tania around the corner. Ten meters ahead were the remains of a foundation in the ground. A square of broken cinder blocks stuck up from the snow like the jagged back of a rising beast. Other bricks marked where interior walls had once stood. The blackened remains of a pink wooden house lay behind the foundation.

A pair of hinged cellar doors showed in the ground just above the snow. The boards of the doors were pastel green with metal handles of sky blue. Shaikin yanked up one of the doors; the effect on Tania, looking into the darkness below, was of entering an underwater cave of shadowy aqua.

She followed Chekov down a short flight of steps. Shaikin lowered the door above their heads, and she became aware of the close, piquant smell of humanity in an oily mix with kerosene.

Tania stood at Chekov's back. Shaikin stepped in front of her. Hidden by her two friends, she folded her arms and waited to be either introduced or discovered.

"Anatoly Petrovich." A woman's throaty voice. Tania could not see its owner. The voice was energetic, not tired the way Tania expected a whore would be at the end of her day.

"Wait," the voice said. "I know the one you like."

Tania looked over the shoulders of Shaikin and Chekov. The room was square, no larger than five meters long and wide. The ceiling was made of the beams and floorboards of the house that had once stood above. The walls were concrete block, thinly whitewashed. In the amber light and deep, sharp shadows thrown by the lantern, she saw no cobwebs or dust in the corners. At least, she thought, these women are good housekeepers.

A gramophone scratched to life. Trumpets and woodwinds blared an introduction to a song promising to be lively. Tania looked down at Chekov's hips. The little sniper raised his elbows and snapped his fingers. He swayed to the tune, a tango.

The low voice spoke over the music. "Now who are your friends, Anatolushka?"

In time with the music, Chekov wobbled his right hip into Shaikin, knocking his friend sideways a step. Shaikin's hands stayed jammed in his coat pockets.

"This is Ilya Alexeyavich Shaikin."

Shaikin righted himself and Tania caught her first glimpse of the two women. They were arranged on a mattress on the concrete floor. One of the women, a brunette with a round, soft face, was larger than the other. She wore a white linen skirt and blouse. Her clothes appeared to be undergarments. Her bare arms and legs were heavy, not enough so to make them unpleasant, but large and soft. Like feathers, Tania thought, of a white dove.

Next to the brunette reclined a thin, pasty blonde. She wore an olive army undershirt above a skirt that had been stitched from a wool blanket. A frayed pink shawl wrapped her shoulders. The girl appeared sickly, brittle, with the hurting look of bruises under her eyes. The veins in her arms and neck were like blue streaks against frosted glass. Tania could feel the girl breaking even as she smiled up at her visitors.

Behind the two barefoot women were pastel pillows. Tania stepped forward between Shaikin and the swaying Chekov. The brunette on the mattress clapped her hands over her mouth.

"Oh. Oh, my," she said through her fingers. "Oh. Wait right there."

The woman dug down behind the mattress, through the pillows. She pulled up a small bronze tube. She rolled it in her hand, then put it to her mouth. Her lips began to glow bright red.

"Oh," she said, "wait. Let me get this on. There now."

She stood while the fragile blonde sat smiling absently.

"Hello." The big brunette spoke with the radiant lipstick, her mouth damask against the whiteness of her skin and the yellow cast of the lantern. She reached her hand to Tania and stepped with her knees high, still the large white bird, over the softness of the mattress through the scratchy tango.

She said, "I'm Olga Kopoleva. My friend is Irina Gobolinka. And you are . . . ?"

"Private Tania Chernova."

The woman shook Tania's hand. She looked back at blond Irina, who gathered herself deeper into her shawl. Olga grinned at Tania and shook her hand again, more firmly, as though greeting a dignitary. Tania thought quickly of Danilov. He should meet this woman.

Olga pulled Tania forward, ignoring Shaikin and Chekov. "Come. Please sit."

The woman's lips seemed to bite at Tania while she talked. "You are a soldier? This is your gun?" She pointed at Tania's submachine gun, strapped over her shoulder. Tania sensed herself holding back, keeping judgment bottled for now.

"Yes. Of course it's mine."

Olga turned again to the silent, wan Irina. "She has her own machine gun. She's a fighter. A woman." She returned her attention to her guest. "Tania, dear, do you like music? We have a few records."

"This is fine."

Irina spoke. "It's an Argentinean tango. We don't know the name." Her voice was unsure, fluttery, like a butterfly in wind. The pale girl giggled. "We can't read the label. It's in English, I think."

Olga continued talking, cutting Irina off. "Anatolushka likes this one best. It's odd, but most of the men that visit us like this one. I'll bet they don't even know where Argentina is."

Chekov sat next to Tania. "Tania's one of our snipers. She's one of the best. Silent as the night. As deadly as a woman."

Olga enjoyed this. "Anatoly, you bastard," she said, laughing and slapping at his leg, "we're not all killers."

"You are," said Chekov.

"Stop," laughed Olga.

Tania watched the large woman's lipstick smear at the corners of her mouth. Olga's breasts jiggled lavishly under her blouse when she shifted her attention from Chekov to Irina to her. Tania looked down at them. A woman's breasts are the only things in the world that can move like that, she thought. They can make any room in the world, even beneath the surface of a war, into a room rippling with sensation. I've done it before. Olga does it now.

"Tania." Irina opened her eyes wide. "You've killed Nazis?"

"Yes."

"How many?"

"More than a hundred. Between here and Moscow."

Olga asked, "You were in Moscow? In the battle?"

"No. I was outside Moscow. In the forests. I was with the partisans. We attacked German convoys."

The conversation, the eyes of the women and Shaikin and Chekov, had become focused on Tania. This had not been her intention, to take up space or energy on this visit. She'd simply wanted to observe, slake her curiosity, then leave. But with the unforeseen remembrance of her days with the resistance, her many sacrifices rose now to her surface. She realized that she was wearing them, without warning, in her face and voice. Her skin felt warm, prickled by the friction of the visions fleeing past her: her parents in their cozy home, whom she had not contacted in over a year—they must fear daily for her safety and for the grandparents, little knowing it was too late for their fears; Tania's friends back in Manhattan in their two-tone shoes flirting with soldiers and buying war bonds; young Fedya dead; old Yuri dead in a sewer; so many members of her partisan cell, dead in the fields; all

the mourning women, young and old, and children, in
Byeloruss, the Ukraine, Moscow, Leningrad, Stalingrad.
She looked down at Irina, the child whore, thin and white
as cobwebs. Tania thought of her own lost American girl-
hood: cars and parties, books and speeches, her heart
skipping at a handsome boy, her mind reaching for ideas.
She missed America with a pang in her breast; she missed
herself, deeply, in her marrow. And in that marrow, where
she could feel nothing keener, burned her hatred for the
Nazis for doing this to her.

Tania tried to fight down the visions, but the ghosts in
their scenery swarmed around her, as they did so often
when she was alone, or more recently after she'd made
love to Zaitsev. Sometimes when her woman's body came
alive in his arms, he brought the specters up out of her as
if they were rising out of a tomb. Now these whores were
doing it. The sexuality of their cellar, Olga's swaying bosom, Irina's pliant white skin, the Argentinean tango;
Tania felt them digging at her own body, unearthing her
sorrows.

Seated next to Tania, Chekov reached into his coat
pocket for a bottle of vodka. He handed it to Olga. The
woman cooed over the gift. She clutched the bottle to her
chest.

Chekov looked up at Shaikin, who had dug into his
own pockets. Shaikin walked around the mattress to Irina.
He handed the girl four packets of chocolate.

Olga's eyes returned to Tania. The business of the cellar had commenced. Tania found she had no questions,
no sisterhood to explore with Olga or Irina. She'd lost her
preoccupation with their nature. She knew enough now;
they were whores on their surface. Beneath that, she had
no interest. She would accept their purpose in Stalingrad,
even their contribution. Shaikin and Chekov smiled at the
women while they presented their tributes. This satisfied
Tania. These women serve, too, she admitted, because her

friends' smiles were indeed the same toothy smirks she'd seen on the soldiers who'd passed them ten minutes ago, young men skipping back from this cellar to their dooms with a song on their lips.

Tania had to leave. These women had kindled something in her body, some spark in her heart and loins that, when it glowed and caught, pulled her back into her flesh. The flesh carried memory and too much pain. When Chekov and Shaikin handed over their payments, the ugliness of the whores' trade gave her a reprieve from her visions. She flung down her warming heart in that moment to retreat without it back into the depths of what had become for her the empty husk of her emotions, her bare cell.

These two women are more of the wartime dead, Tania thought. I have that in common with them. They're like the corpses at the summer funerals my grandfather took me to when his patients would pass away. They were painted nicely, spoken of in whispers. They looked well and composed in their deaths.

Olga held her gaze on Tania. Irina busily unwrapped one of the chocolate bars. Tania, too, would present the women with a gift before she left the cellar.

"I have something for you," she said to Olga.

"Really?" The prostitute resettled herself into the mattress. She nestled the vodka bottle between her legs to hold it upright with her thighs and free her hands.

Tania reached to Chekov's waist. Quickly, she drew from Chekov's belt his captured German Luger pistol.

"Tania, give me that! What are you doing?"

She tossed the pistol onto Olga's lap. The gun struck the woman's thigh and bounced onto the mattress beside her. It lay there, ugly against the pastels.

Pale Irina pulled her knees away from the pistol on the bed as if it might strike at her. Olga looked at the gun

beside her. Her hands fingered the bottle between her
legs.

"Right now," Tania said, "this cellar is in our territory.
That's today. Tomorrow, this little nest of yours could be
behind German lines." She pointed to the stairs. "If a
German comes down those steps, you use that pistol. You
kill him. Do you understand me? You do it."

She stabbed her finger at Irina and Olga.

"I'll do your fighting for you, girls, but you die with the
rest of us. You die Russian."

Tania reached into her coat pocket. She pulled out two
chocolate bars and threw them backhanded at Irina. Then
she whirled and stomped onto the first step. She reached
up to push open the ocean blue cellar door.

The door was pulled out of her grasp to rise on its own.
The final light of the day flooded down with the cold. In
the opening, in silhouette, stood Zaitsev.

He held the door open and looked down at her.

Chekov called out, "Vasha? What are you doing here?
Come down and close the door. You're letting out the
heat."

Zaitsev stepped into the cellar and lowered the door.
He walked past Tania to the edge of the mattress. He
nodded at Shaikin, who stood beside Irina. He looked at
Chekov and jerked his thumb toward Tania at the steps.

"Interesting decision to bring Tanyushka along, Anatoly. Did she make it for you?"

Chekov lowered his head. Shaikin gave Zaitsev a
thumbs-up.

Zaitsev took the Luger off the bed and held it up to
Tania.

"Yours?"

Chekov spoke. "Mine."

Zaitsev handed the pistol to the little sniper. "Put it
away."

He looked back into the shadows at Tania. "Recruiting, Tania? Danilov will be jealous. That's his department."

Zaitsev turned to Chekov and Shaikin. "After today, tell them goodbye," he said evenly. "No more. Understand?"

Both men nodded.

Zaitsev bowed his head in mock gentility. "Ladies." Then he walked over to Tania and spoke to her. "You're leaving." He put his hand under her elbow.

Tania jerked her arm free. "What do you mean, I'm leaving?" She pointed at Chekov and Shaikin. "If they stay, I stay."

Shaikin raised his arms in exasperation and exhaled as if he'd been skewered.

Tania's tone was sharp. "Besides, what are you doing here?"

"You've been given an order, Private."

"By whom?"

"By your sergeant."

Tania laughed. "Are you still my sergeant in a whorehouse?"

Zaitsev thrust his arms up to open the door. "That's enough." He grabbed Tania's wrist and pulled her up the steps. She hit him in the back with her other fist.

"Tania," Chekov called through the jingling of their rifles and stomping boots, "don't be like that. It's just a little fun."

Shaikin's voice chased them. "I told you, Anatoly."

Outside, Zaitsev let her go and slammed the doors down with a bouncing clatter. She stomped off.

Zaitsev ran and grabbed her again. He brought his face close. "What were you doing down there?"

She tried to yank away. He put both hands on her wrist and jerked her arm down hard.

"Stop it. What were you doing in there?"

He can ask me this? she thought. He can visit whores and then ask me what I was doing there when he arrived?

"Shaikin and Chekov invited me. I went to see what it was about. And who invited you?" She reached down with her free hand and grabbed his crotch. "Him?"

She let Zaitsev go before he could force her to. "Leave me alone," she said.

Zaitsev released her arm. "Calm down. Listen to me."

She put her hands on her hips and spread her legs, as though she were readying for the ground to shift.

He took two steps back. He thinks I might swing at him, she thought. He could be right.

"I came to get you out of there," he said. His hands worked with his voice, illustrating his words. "After I left you in the trench, I turned to come back to you. To talk. I saw you leave with Shaikin and Chekov and head this way. By the time I figured where you were going and caught up with you, you were already inside."

Tania pointed back at the cellar doors in the snow.

"And why did I need to be hauled out of there so quickly by my sergeant? Why me and not Shaikin and Chekov?"

"Tania, that . . ." He pointed, too. "That is a man's place."

"And I don't belong in a man's place." Tania lowered her hand and her voice. "Is that it?"

Zaitsev took a breath to buy time for an answer. When none came, he shrugged.

Tania thought of chess. If a white king could shrug when he's in checkmate, he would look like Zaitsev right now.

"Is that it, Vasha?" She brought her hands to her breasts. "What do I have to do to be treated like an equal by you? Do I need to kill more? I will. Just tell me."

"Tanyushka," he said, "you're a woman."

"Ah," she said with angry sarcasm, "I see. So that's what's in the way. My woman's body. Yes, yes, Vasha, thank you for making it so clear for me what it is I need to do. I need to stop making love to you."

She snapped her fingers. "There. It's over. No more. Now I'm not a woman. I'm just another sniper."

"Tania . . ."

"No! We're both men now. It's OK. We can talk like men. You've obviously been here before, Sergeant. Why don't you go back inside now and join the party in the men's place? Hurry, though. They close after dark. But you must know that already."

With that, she ran into the debris.

TANIA SEARCHED FOR SOMETHING TO THROW when Zaitsev's steps approached the hanging blanket.

Beside her on the floor of the snipers' bunker stood a full vodka bottle. She'd tried to drink the stuff during her hour of sitting in the cool dirt of his corner, but she'd lost interest in getting drunk. It's just one more way to feel lousy, she thought. I have enough ways.

She picked up the bottle.

Zaitsev pushed aside the blanket. Tania cocked the bottle back to heave it but set it down. She would throw words instead.

"Go away and fuck someone else."

She folded her arms and legs tightly around herself like a beetle that had been touched.

Zaitsev walked to where she hunched against the bunker wall. He hung his machine gun, helmet, and canteen on a hook. He knelt in front of her. She drew in even tighter.

"Find some other whore, Sergeant."

He winced. Her pain was his; it flowed around them.

"I don't want to smell those women on you."

"Tania . . ."

"Go on, Vasha, go have your fun."

"Tania, I—"

"Shut up!" She reached for the bottle.

Zaitsev took the bottle and set it out of the way.

Tania tried to poke him in the eyes with her stare. She did not blink, feeling she'd crack if she did. She knew she had frozen stiff in the whores' cellar. Even before she looked up at his form outlined in the doorway, she'd recoiled from the awakening of her body and emotions when Irina and Olga had paired off with Shaikin and Chekov. Her anger at Zaitsev's sudden presence there and his patronizing attitude, following her to take her out of the "man's place," shoved her all the way down into the dark waters inside her, beneath the ice, where she sat now.

How dare he humiliate me in front of Shaikin and Chekov! Treat me like a dog that's gotten off a leash and must be chased down and retrieved! Tania, you're a woman, he said. Those two whores were women. Is that how he sees me?

She rose to her feet to gather her machine gun and the vodka.

Zaitsev's voice stopped her. "I'm sorry."

Tania laughed, facing him. "Don't apologize. We're both free. We can both make choices. Right now, I choose. I choose to get satisfaction for my woman's body somewhere else."

She saw Zaitsev's shoulders droop. His face tumbled, his hands fell. Good, she thought. Even as I freeze, he melts.

"Tania, don't . . ."

"I already have. We both have."

He stepped forward. Zaitsev the hunter, she thought. Let's see how he performs now, how he tracks and hunts. Let's see what he finds in this great frozen forest.

Zaitsev looked stricken. He sat at her feet.

Without looking up, he spoke. His voice held the

mournful sound of wind in empty buildings. Listening to Zaitsev, she grew sadder than him.

"What can I say?" he began. "It's hard for me, too. There's so much killing. My friends die. My family waits in Siberia. Every day, every awful day, there's no rest, no break. And now, this . . . this Thorvald is hunting me."

Tania knelt in front of him. She laid her rifle and the bottle in the dirt.

Zaitsev did not look up at her. He paused, acknowledging that she was near him. She looked at his crown, at the thick, short hairs crowding, reaching to her.

"After you left, I went hunting. I just roamed, I couldn't concentrate." He held out his hands as if showing her something small and tender. "I came looking for you. I had to find you and talk. To tell you you're important to me. You're how I survive. If I lost you, this would all go back to being a hell again."

Zaitsev brought his face up to her. His eyes shone. He blinked as if looking into the sun.

"Now I feel like you're someplace I can't follow."

He reached to her lap for her hands; she allowed him to take them. His grip was warm, firm.

"Tania, forgive me. I didn't know what you meant to me. I didn't know what made me follow you there and act like that. You were right. I . . ."

Tania pulled back her hands. She brought her knees again to her chest, wrapping them tightly with her arms. She lowered her head onto her drawn-up knees. With her eyes open, looking into the small, dark cave made from her face, arms, and knees, a tear skimmed down her cheek. She shook her chin to make it fly off and land on the dirt floor.

She felt him move closer. His voice came from near her forehead, buried in her arms.

"I do now," he whispered.

Then Tania's hair was in Zaitsev's hand, pulling up to

bring her face out of her cave. She knew the lamp was betraying her, that the path of the tear must be glistening.

He leaned over her. His lips grazed her cheek, dipping into the trail of the tear. He cupped it with his lower lip and followed it to her eye. His breath in the wetness on her face was lush.

She wrenched her eyes shut, squinting in a spasm as the ice inside her fissured and cracked open. Instantly she flew up through it; the water, no longer frozen but warmed now, fell from her, cascaded out of her closed eyes, down her cheeks, into his scooping lips. She flew out and above herself, her body left behind to convulse in his arms. She looked down and saw everything around her, the corpses and hatred, and shame, all of it, out in the open now, shimmering and cleansed in her raining tears.

Zaitsev held her. His arms were wings, freeing her from the ice, flying her high into the cloudburst, into the wind blowing through the ruins of the city beneath her, soaking in her rain.

TWENTY-ONE

BLOOD HAD SEEPED THROUGH THE THIN LINEN covering the body, blotting into a rosette above the head. Damn it, thought Zaitsev, with the number of blankets they're airlifting to us over the Volga, couldn't they spare just one thick one to lay over Morozov?

Konstantin Danyelovich Morozov had been one of Viktor's bears and a friend of Zaitsev's in the 284th, a fellow Siberian. Now he was a large corpse, shot through the cheek beneath the right eye, the back of his head split open. The bullet that killed him had bounced off his telescopic sight, smashing it.

Zaitsev stepped away as two men lifted Morozov's stretcher onto the back of a sled. They would pull it to the caves at the water's edge, the storage area for the dead, to await evacuation and burial once the river froze.

After the Volga turns solid, he thought, we'll see these bodies link into a stream of sleds, like black ants teeming away from a picnic, thousands without end. Bodies going, blankets and vodka returning. But still no ammunition. No reinforcements.

That's a sure signal that something is up. The Germans have hurled as many as ten divisions at us since August. We've countered with less than five divisions of reinforcements. My snipers haven't had a full complement of bullets to work with in the entire month of November. Even Atai Chebibulin has been frustrated in his efforts to find extra ammo.

The generals and *politrooks* keep telling us to hold out. Hold out for what? We've been given the job of drawing as many Nazis into the city as possible and then keeping them here. We could wipe them out of Stalingrad right now with enough men and ammo on our side. The Nazis are shivering, hopeless. The force has gone out of them. They're not soldiers any longer, just the limp, molted skins of former fighting men. But Stalin and his generals are holding back their thrust, hoarding our ammo, keeping us in check. It means they're building up to strike back. They must be. They haven't forgotten us.

Something is coming. And it's coming soon.

Thorvald knows it, too. He must. He's a colonel. He's not like me, a dirty little sergeant getting his information through the grapevine or out of sterilized articles written by the likes of Danilov. He's been flown in to kill me, just me. He goes home when he's done it. He'll want to do it soon.

Zaitsev looked across the frosty crust forming at the river's edge. He'd seen many frozen rivers in Siberia. He knew this ice wouldn't be thick enough for trucks and horse-drawn carts until mid-December.

And Morozov, also a Siberian; Zaitsev shook his head. Morozov would see no more rivers, nor sky nor life.

Zaitsev turned away. Another friend. Another hero carted off on a sled like baggage, one more memory to safeguard and avenge.

Morozov.

This has Thorvald's smell. Thorvald is talking to me. He's writing messages, drawing a map of where to meet him, scribbling in the blood of Baugderis, Kulikov, Morozov.

And Shaikin.

Ilya Shaikin had been shot through the neck while spotting for Morozov in sector fifteen on the southern rim of the city center. The sector ran along the front line below the Lazur in the afternoon shadow of Mamayev Kurgan. In this thin slice of downtown, Red soldiers were burrowed inside several formidable and well-placed buildings. These had become impregnable strongholds, with wave after wave of Germans crashing against them only to be repulsed by withering Russian counterfire. These fortresses were so steadfastly defended that they'd become landmarks on Red Army maps. In most instances they carried their former names, such as the House of Specialists, the state bank, and the beer hall. But in a few cases the previous stature of a building had been superseded by a new identity, arising out of the remarkable adventures of its Russian defenders. Such were the L-Shaped House and the Old Mill, whose names evoked murmurs of awe for the fighting prowess of their guardians. The most famous of all the strongholds was Pavlov's House. The badly damaged apartment building had been unofficially renamed for the indomitable Russian sergeant Jacob Pavlov, who with twenty men had occupied the ruin on Solechnaya Street on the front line since September 29. Pavlov continued to deny the Nazis access to the Volga, which was only two hundred meters behind him. He'd held so long in place that the commanders had taken to calling him "the Houseowner."

In the past three days, Zaitsev and Viktor had received reports of renewed German sniper activity south of Mamayev Kurgan, near the city center. Medical units had come under fire while evacuating the wounded in the alleys and streets in the area around Pavlov's House. Two officers and a private had been shot through their hearts. One nurse had been killed by a bullet under her chin, another wounded by a bullet through the neck.

It made sense to Zaitsev that Thorvald would avoid the factories: the sheer numbers of dead there would obscure his handiwork. It would hide his scent, the scat of slaughter, which he trusted would draw his quarry, the Hare, to him.

That dawn, Shaikin had volunteered with Morozov to scout the reports of German snipers in sector fifteen. "You can't be everywhere at once, Vasha," Shaikin had said at the end of the meeting in the snipers' bunker. "Just in case it's our Headmaster shooting up the place. I'll go have a talk with the wounded nurse. Then Morozov and I will take a look.

"Oh, by the way," Shaikin said, readying to leave, lifting the blanket in the doorway, "I'm sorry about yesterday afternoon. Chekov and Tania talked me into it. She should never have been in that cellar. You were a good fellow about it."

"Why should you be sorry, Ilyushka? Why would it matter to me if Tania was there?"

"Vasha," his friend said with a smile, "let me use Chekov's words, his exact words, when he told me. He said, 'Comrade Zaitsev is a very silent sniper, you know. But he's quite a loud loverboy.' "

Shaikin's last laugh was muted behind the dropping blanket.

Now Shaikin lies in a field hospital for evacuation. Tania had run to tell him about it in the afternoon. "Vasha! Morozov is dead, a bullet to the brain. Shaikin has been shot through the throat. Shaikin dragged Morozov's body out of their trench to where an artillery spotter saw them and sent help. Morozov's body is at the Lazur. Shaikin is in the hospital in sector thirteen in critical condition. They said he had his hand clamped over his neck, Vasha, to keep the blood in."

•   •   •

"ILYUSHKA."

Shaikin opened his eyes, the begging eyes of a maimed animal.

Shaikin gasped, "Vashinka." The name was almost lost in the gush of air from the wounded man's mouth, as though he had to fully empty his lungs to push the word through the gauntlet of pain in his throat.

Zaitsev looked down on his friend. Shaikin was sunken into a stretcher propped on bricks. His neck was wrapped in clean gauze. His hand was crusted red between the fingers from his own blood.

Shaikin clenched his eyes. Inhaling, his mouth remained open in a suffering circle, a small dark well. Zaitsev was stricken by the gurgling deep in his friend's throat.

"Don't talk, Ilya." He put his hand on Shaikin's bloody fist. "Nod your head. Was it Thorvald?"

Shaikin squeezed Zaitsev's fingers. His eyes opened. His head shuddered up and down. Yes.

"You talked to the wounded nurse? Was it him, too?"

Shaikin winced. It seemed not from pain but from a thought.

He squeezed Zaitsev's hand again and spoke.

"Nurse."

His burbling voice was more sorrowful for Zaitsev than the bandaged throat and faded face.

Shaikin's mouth twisted. "Dead," he said. He brought his hand up to his neck to point at the bullet entry point where blood was now seeping through the bandage. "Nurse, here."

Zaitsev recalled what Tania had told him that morning. Two officers and a private, shot through the heart. Then the nurses and Shaikin, pierced through the neck like gaffed fish. Morozov, killed by a bullet through his telescopic sight. Like Baugderis.

Thorvald's stench again. He's shooting everything in

sight, even medical officers and nurses. And he's doing it with a flourish, an unmistakable style, so I'll be sure to recognize his tracks.

Four days ago he displayed his abilities on the dummy Pyotr on the eastern slope of Mamayev Kurgan. The next morning, he shot Baugderis and Kulikov. Then the Headmaster moved south and waited. What was he doing? Why the three-day gap?

He was looking. He was searching for the perfect blind, a shooting cell into which he could disappear and kill anything Russian moving near him. And he found it. He can approach it invisibly and escape immediately. I know him. There, in his little fortress, he's curled up like a serpent, bringing down five medical personnel in the past two days and this morning the two snipers who confronted him, Morozov and Shaikin.

Yes. He's settled in. He wants this over with. He's making it clear; he wants to go home. So he's engraved an invitation in lead and copper and flesh and blood and sent it to me.

Come, the Headmaster has written. Come, Chief Master Sergeant Vasily Gregorievich Zaitsev, to the same spot where your friends met me today. Ask little, dying Shaikin. He'll gurgle out the address for you.

Come, Hare.

Thank you, Headmaster. I accept.

THE TEMPERATURE DROPPED MORE QUICKLY than the light. Zaitsev hunched his stiff shoulders. A cold ache ran down his neck to his lower back. For two hours, without break, he sat staring into his periscope.

The contours of the ruins and rubble dimmed through the eyepiece while the curtain of dusk lowered. He was in the identical spot that Shaikin had struggled to describe for him, where Shaikin had taken his bullet. Behind Zait-

sev was a black patch in the dirt like a hunter's blaze on
the trench floor, where Morozov had fallen. Zaitsev surveyed one more time the bank of apartment buildings
southwest along Solechnaya Street. He leveled his gaze
and looked to his right to take in the 250 meters of open
ground in Ninth of January Square, with its spilled fountains, broken benches, and uprooted shrubs and trees.
The park had become a perplexity of trenches, destroyed
vehicles, and craters. The square was bordered on his left
by three blocks of Solechnaya Street. At the left-hand corner of the park, across the street, was Pavlov's House.
Behind the square, running along its northwest boundary,
opposite where he sat, were shops and office buildings
interrupted by alleys and avenues. This, Zaitsev judged,
had been the heart of Stalingrad before the war.

Finally, he lowered the periscope with hands numb and
weary. He'd accomplished what he'd come to do: memo-
rize the details of the front line from this vantage point. If
anything changed over the next several days, any rock
moved or brick stacked, he would know.

He pulled off his white mittens to blow into his hands.
He cracked his knuckles and stretched his palms to ani-
mate his grip. From his pack, he pulled a pad and pencil
to draw hurried sketches in the dying light.

Zaitsev stretched his legs, which had tightened from
sitting for so long in the biting air. Beneath his feet was
the stained ground where Morozov's blood had pooled
and soaked down. Zaitsev slid a few meters to the side. It
was not proper to linger on this spot where one friend had
splashed his life into the earth and another had been mor-
tally wounded. It seemed somehow a sacrilege for him to
sit here, as if on graves. Spirits were here, where a man
had died. He thought how his old grandfather would have
lectured him for thinking this way; Grandmother Dunia,
shaking her birch stick, would have told him to respect

those spirits and listen to them, they are of the dead and
know things we do not.

He put away his pad and pencil. I remember the details
well enough, he considered. Besides, that isn't the type of
mistake I can expect from Thorvald. The Headmaster will
make a far bolder error than just moving a brick or lighting a cigarette. And when he does, the powers hovering
above this blood will help me find him, to set loose his
ghost to haunt wherever it is he lies last.

For the first time since he'd learned of the Nazi's presence in Stalingrad, Zaitsev felt his forest instincts open
up. The whispering voices of his father and grandfather
and of the ancestors who'd won their lives in the taiga had
been silent until he'd come to sit in this place, which he
knew Thorvald was watching. The voices had been waiting for clues, familiarities, keys to unlock his deeper
knowledge. Thorvald was a prey he'd not hunted before,
and the voices had kept their silence.

But now, with Thorvald finally within range, with the
evidence of Morozov's death and Shaikin's dying fresh in
the winter-hard dirt near him, Zaitsev's intuitions came
alive. Thorvald was a man, certainly, and the Hare had
hunted hundreds of them by now. But the Headmaster
possessed powers of no man he'd ever faced. This Nazi
could shoot marvelously. He could carve a face with bullets in a stuffed dummy in seconds, firing his single
weapon as if he were two men. His abilities with distance
must be uncanny. He'd killed both Morozov and
Baugderis, putting bullets through their telescopic sights
while Kulikov and Shaikin, two of the most experienced
hares, had watched from beside the victims, then were
themselves hit. He knows the battlefield. He's been traced
to Mamayev Kurgan, then to the Red October, and now
here to this park in the city center.

Thorvald is bold. He crawled into Kulikov's trench to

take his rifle. He's twisted, perhaps even rabid. He shoots anything, wasting bullets on dummies and nurses. He's cruel. He's smart. And like any other man of flesh and blood, he's surely scared to be in Stalingrad.

The Headmaster is focused, with only one task: to catch me. He's like a mad timber wolf that no longer eats or drinks but only kills. Everything the beast does is directed toward that lone goal. That's a weakness. It can betray him.

Zaitsev stood slowly to look over the square one last time for the evening. The light had decayed, and now the shadows seeped into the ground. It was time to leave. Zaitsev shouldered his sniper rifle, then bent to pick up the periscope. On the trench floor at his hand, somehow darker than the falling night, was the blood mark of Morozov.

He said to the blood, "I'll be back in the morning."

TWO HOURS LATER, ZAITSEV WALKED INTO THE snipers' bunker. Kulikov stood.

"Vasha."

"Nikolay!" Zaitsev hugged his friend. He kissed him on each cheek, then held him at arms' length. "You're back. How are you? How's the head?"

Kulikov tilted his brow to let Zaitsev examine the bandage wrapped above his ears.

Zaitsev poked his finger tenderly over where he knew the stitches were. "Well," the Hare said with a smile, "it's still attached. That's better than some."

Kulikov's grin faded. In the moment of jocularity, Zaitsev had forgotten Baugderis. He thought now of the smashed face and of Morozov and Shaikin. And others.

"I'm well," Kulikov said. "They shook me out of bed this afternoon. I heard what happened to Ilya and Morozov."

Zaitsev laid his rifle and pack in his corner.

"I've found him, Nikolay. Shaikin sent me right to him. I can feel him. The son of a bitch, I can feel him."

Kulikov looked into Zaitsev's eyes. The little sniper swallowed hard, but his face remained a mute mask. Many times Zaitsev had marveled at the silence of Nikolay Kulikov's face. It told nothing of the man's inner workings. His features, even his arms and legs, always manifested a stillness, like the moon. Zaitsev was sure this was why Kulikov was the most invisible on the move of all the snipers. He carried silence in his bones.

Zaitsev thought back four days to the trench where Kulikov and Baugderis had set up their tin-can gambit. Kulikov, unconscious, had awakened to his sins, visited on him by the bloody hole in Baugderis's head and the gash in his own. Kulikov has a score to settle. And Thorvald has his rifle.

"You want to come, Nikolay? We've both seen him work and we've both lived to tell. We can get him."

Kulikov blinked. "Tania won't mind?"

"What . . ." Zaitsev stopped. He shook his head and walked to the corner. Next it will be Danilov and a damned weekly column in *In Our Country's Defense*.

"No, Nikolay. Tania won't mind. Sit down."

Kulikov plopped to the floor. Zaitsev did not hear him move even while he watched Kulikov slide into the flickering shadow below the lamp's base. He chooses the darkest place, Zaitsev observed.

Zaitsev described the details of the location where Shaikin and Morozov had met Thorvald. He didn't know how the Headmaster had managed to shoot the two snipers. But at this stage, how it had happened was less important than where. He and Kulikov would wage their own, fresh battle against the Nazi supersniper.

"The sun rises at our backs and sets in front, slightly to

our right. So we'll have the advantage in the morning and early afternoon. We'll have to force a few shots out of him to get an idea of where he is. That shouldn't be too hard. The Headmaster seems all too eager to pull his trigger."

Kulikov said nothing. His slate-colored eyes were intent; he seemed to listen through them.

Zaitsev continued. "We can move. But I have a feeling he'll stay put. He's found a spot he's sure will be good enough to get me. So long as he thinks he's hidden, he'll stick to his cell."

Kulikov spoke. "How does he know he didn't shoot you when he shot Shaikin and Morozov?"

Zaitsev thought for a moment before answering.

"He doesn't. But I think he'll watch the place where he shot his last two snipers. If nobody else shows up to play with him tomorrow or the next day, he'll figure it was me he killed and the game is over. But if someone comes to face him, he'll guess that finally I'm in the trench across from him, that I got the word about his telescope shot on Morozov and the other nasty tricks he's played. After all, that's exactly what he intended. I think we've got one or two more days while he sits in his shooting cell waiting to see who drops by."

Kulikov rose. "I'll get some sleep. Oh-four-hundred here?"

"Yes, Nikolay."

Without a sound, Kulikov was gone. Zaitsev sat, looking into the wavering circle of shade beneath the lamp where the sniper had sat. Only seconds after his departure, it seemed Kulikov had already been gone an hour. How does he do that? Zaitsev wondered.

He turned off the lantern and lay on his bedroll, his pack under his head. He stared into the pitch of the bunker.

Tomorrow. Tomorrow begins the duel.

The cold air of the dirt floor crept up his cheek. He pulled his blanket higher. He listened to his own breathing and felt his pulse in his neck.

Thorvald. Colonel Thorvald. Just a name, just bloody holes in bodies, just guesses and conclusions so far. Tomorrow Thorvald becomes fact, becomes real for me, real as a bullet.

He wondered what a bullet felt like burning into his own flesh. He hadn't yet been wounded at Stalingrad, though he'd seen a thousand wounds. What was the pain like? And to be killed . . . did the death blackness come riding on the bullet instantly, before pain could grip you, everything silent and calm while you drift over into eternity? Or was it horrible to die with a bullet between the eyes? Was it a sudden bursting of every agony that lies coiled and waiting in the body, set loose, rampant for the few seconds before the senses quit? Zaitsev felt an itch between his eyebrows where a bullet might drill the next day. He rubbed his face to make it go away.

Thorvald. Zaitsev reviewed his lessons to the hares on how to deal with an enemy sniper. The process of finding the sniper begins with learning the enemy's front line of defense. View and catalog every physical detail possible. He'd done this hours ago. Next, study and understand how and where others were shot in the area. Zaitsev recalled his ten minutes that afternoon beside the agony of Shaikin and earlier with Morozov's body. The bullet to Morozov's head had been deflected off the rifle scope. The scope itself also revealed nothing. Where had Morozov's rifle been pointing when struck? Shaikin didn't know. He'd been looking through the binoculars at a moving helmet just above a trench along Solechnaya Street. He was calling Morozov into the shot on the helmet when Thorvald lashed out. Zaitsev reasoned that either there was some troop activity spreading near Pavlov's House or Thorvald had a helper carrying that helmet on a stick.

The mistake had been Shaikin's and Morozov's. They should not have been shooting. They'd gone to Ninth of January Square to locate Thorvald, not to engage him. When they bit on the bait, probably the helmet, the Headmaster flexed.

The next step is to fathom your enemy's strengths and weaknesses. Avoid his strengths; aggravate his flaws. If he's a skilled marksman, like Thorvald, test him with feints and false positions; give him easy targets to lull him into revealing his position without making yourself a target. Mock his skill by pretending to be a freshman sniper yourself; make small, controlled mistakes to swell his confidence in the contest. If he's impatient, if he's hot to shoot and go, like Thorvald, then drag him into a long and complicated battle. If he's stubborn, like the Headmaster, then distract his attention, irritate him through those distractions, wear down his concentration and his physical ability to see through his scope, to shoot accurately. If he's taken the initiative, like Thorvald, then take it back.

When it comes your turn to shoot, make it count. Remember the old folk wisdom: measure it seven times, cut it once.

The blanket in the doorway rose and fell. Careful boot steps crossed the blind floor to Zaitsev's corner.

He opened his lids, seeing nothing. He pulled his hand from beneath the blanket. Lying flat on the bedroll, he reached into the night. The cool air nipped at his wrist. A leg brushed against him.

He heard her curl up on the floor beside him. Her heels ground the dirt when she crossed her legs and settled.

She took his hand in both of hers and held it without squeezing, as if his fingers were fragile. After a minute in the dark, feeling her cup and fondle his hand, she spoke.

"Kulikov was a good choice. I'm glad he's back."

He breathed heavily once; it sounded to him, to his surprise, like a sigh. The bunker, so cold and inky moments before, seemed to feather around him now, to pulsate and fan out like a crow's wings, with Tania at his side. She gives the world, every moment of it, a dynamic, he thought. Things shift in her presence as though she makes them uncomfortable.

"Stay tonight," he said.

He hadn't intended to say this. But damn, he thought, she draws things out of me, pulls my ideas through my mouth and hands and fashions them into words and actions before I can stop them.

"No, Vashinka," she whispered. "You meet Thorvald tomorrow morning. You need to be pure. I'll wait."

She held his hand for another minute of swirling time and darkness. Zaitsev saw nothing, not even the night. His mind stood still, linked into Tania's while her fingers tumbled softly like a mouse playing in his palm. She surrounds me, he thought. Even sitting beside me, touching only my hand. She takes me.

He took his hand back and reached to her forehead to dig his fingers deep into her hair. It was thick, the strands like straw; he could not have pulled his fingers straight up and out of it. He slid his hand down her forehead and across her eyes and nose. He touched her face gently, like a blind man, enough only to ruffle water. His heart and his consciousness were in his hand, crowding into his fingertips like tourists to a window for a glimpse of her. At her neck, the flesh at her collar, he stopped. He dropped his hand beside him on the blanket.

I must be pure, she told me.

Tania stood. Her clothes rustled and broke the spell.

She walked to the blanket. "It's time for the Headmaster to learn a new lesson," she said into the dark. "How to die. One bullet, one lesson, from the Hare."

Tania lifted the blanket. A rim of moonlight silhouetted her legs and waist in the doorway. Her form slipped away.

"Kill him, Vasha," she said, and was gone. The blanket tumbled across the opening. A cold gust filled her space in the room and crawled on the floor next to Zaitsev where she had been.

TWENTY-TWO

IT WAS LATE AFTERNOON WHEN NIKKI AND
Thorvald arrived at Ninth of January Square. Thorvald's
interest soared immediately upon seeing the park.

The space was ideal for his mission, he said. He peeked
above the low stone wall and swept his hand back and
forth over the dusky panorama, 250 meters square, as if
feeling it for lumps or irregularities. The park allowed him
vision in a wide range. The sun would set at his back and
put him in shadow in the afternoon. There were plenty of
hiding places in this, the western half of the park: several
burned-out tanks, an abandoned redoubt, and lots of rubble. The other side of the park, the Red side of the line,
was smoother. Most of the fighting in this area had centered on the building to their right, called Pavlov's House.
The Reds were hanging tough in there, though the park
itself had remained an empty fighting ground, a no-man's-
land. "Perfect," Thorvald called it.

Nikki crouched behind the safety of the wall while
Thorvald rose with his excitement to scan the park's terrain through his field glasses. After a minute, almost
standing upright now, Thorvald said, "Ah, yes. There."

He hurried along the wall fifty meters to his left. Nikki
followed him. They stopped at a breach in the wall where

a tank had smashed through. Ten meters in front of them lay a wide sheet of corrugated metal atop a pile of bricks.

Thirty minutes later, Thorvald had commandeered a shovel from a soldier to their rear. When full night had fallen, Nikki was set to work digging a foxhole under the sheet.

He loaded the dirt from the excavation onto a canvas tarpaulin. The colonel dragged the tarp from the hole and dumped it behind the wall. Thorvald told Nikki to be careful while digging not to move or alter in any way the alignment of the bricks facing the Red side of the park.

Two hours later, Nikki looked out from the shooting cell he'd created. The hole was now deep enough for a man to rise to his knees, just skirting the top of his head against the metal roof. The sheet would keep the colonel totally in shadow all day. The hole, the bricks, and the sheet would hide not only his body but also the noise of his rifle. He could lie here in the neutral zone, out of sight and sound—even out of the Russian wind—aiming east between the bricks.

Nikki completed his labor, then crawled out of the hole. He sat in a tired heap beside the colonel.

Thorvald was chipper. "Well, let's see what we have here, Corporal." He skittered under the metal.

Nikki heard him laugh, hidden in the cell.

"Oh, this is very good." His voice under the metal was clanging and eerie, its source invisible.

THE NEXT MORNING, THORVALD CARRIED WITH him into the cell several blankets, two boxes of ammunition, a thermos, and two sandwiches. Nikki was left ten meters back, behind the wall, also with provisions, to wait for the colonel's instructions.

Thorvald sat silently in his nest until late afternoon. With the sun behind him, with Nikki watching through

binoculars, the colonel fired on several Red medical personnel, visible only for moments hustling in and out of
Pavlov's House with wounded. Nikki winced at every report from the rifle, though they were muffled and swollen
and not the sharp cracks he was used to. The shots were
like body blows, making his stomach quiver.

Nikki despised Thorvald's shooting at nurses and medical workers and the glee the colonel took in hitting them.
After each trigger pull, Thorvald counted up the score:
"One . . . two . . . aaaand three." Though Nikki days
before had wrestled his conscience to the ground, he
struggled now to hold it still while the colonel killed more
unsuspecting victims. He knew the answer to his own
question before he asked it: Was it right? Should nurses,
medics, and wounded soldiers be cut down and used for
bait for the Hare as if they were nothing more than car-
rots and cabbage set under a rabbit trap? Yes, of course.
Stalingrad is no longer about right and wrong or winning—only surviving. No, these were not military targets.
But what I'm trying to do has nothing to do with the
military. I want to go home. How many would I let die for
that? Nikki couldn't name a number. All of them.

The second morning began like the first, before sunup.
Thorvald crawled into the hole and again stayed quiet until the afternoon, when he fired twice with automatic
speed, paused, and fired a third time. All he said to Nikki
was, "Three more."

That night, Thorvald and Nikki walked to their separate quarters downtown without conversation. It seemed
the colonel had entered a realm of concentration; once
he'd laid his eye to his scope, he did not look away or
flinch until he'd hit his target. The duel with Zaitsev had
been joined; the target was selected but not yet beneath
the colonel's crosshairs.

The third dawn at Ninth of January Square, just as the

sun restored the park's colors, Nikki heard Thorvald's tinny voice.

"Corporal. We've got company."

Nikki unwrapped the blanket from his shoulders and grabbed his binoculars. He prepared to raise his eyes above the parapet. Then Thorvald hissed from inside his lair.

"Stay down. Snipers."

For the rest of the morning, Nikki sat hunched at the foot of the wall. He was on edge, wondering if the Hare himself was finally within the colonel's sights.

He waited for hours. Boredom jangled against his alertness; his nerves wore raw. At midday, with the sun at its highest and the shadows underfoot, Thorvald's voice slunk out of the hole.

"Go thirty meters to the left. Stop there and put your helmet on the shovel handle. Raise it over the wall just enough to make it look like your head. Walk with it to the left. Nikki, do you hear me?"

"Yes, sir."

"Do it. And if the helmet gets hit, drop it quickly."

Nikki snatched up the shovel. On his knees, he scurried to his left the thirty meters. He took off his helmet and raised it on the shovel handle just above the wall.

After moving no more than ten meters, the helmet snapped around with a clang, struck by a bullet. The shovel blade stung his hand. He dropped the shovel and heard the trailing echoes of a shot from across the park. He gathered in the tool and helmet and rushed back to his perch behind Thorvald.

"I didn't hear you shoot, Colonel," he called into the hole. "Did you?"

"Yes." The canned voice sounded tired.

"One-two, Colonel?"

"One-two."

Nikki waited, then asked, "Was it Zaitsev?"

Thorvald blew out a breath. Nikki imagined the colonel rolling over now to nap in the warmth of the blankets and the afternoon heat radiating from the metal sheet, like a bear that has eaten its fill.

"We'll find out tomorrow."

FIRST LIGHT WAS AN HOUR AWAY. NIKKI SAT BE- side Thorvald, their backs against the stone wall. The col- onel rested before his crawl down the shallow trench into his shooting cell.

Nikki's anticipation ran high on this fourth morning at Ninth of January Square. He agreed with Thorvald that the Russian snipers of the previous day had most likely been only some of Zaitsev's recruits. The Red master sniper himself was probably not among them. The ruse of carrying the helmet had been too basic, too poorly exe- cuted to be the work of the Headmaster. Had Zaitsev, the keen man of the forest, been the one watching, he wouldn't have taken the bait. Surely he would have recog- nized the feint as the work of an ordinary German marks- man and would not have gone on the attack the way those two Red snipers did. Zaitsev's goal was Thorvald, no one else. The Hare would not have given up his position for any lesser prey. But if the Ivan snipers across the park had been just a hunting party, perhaps scouting on Zaitsev's behalf, they would have been more likely to engage any target that presented itself, especially a German sniper heartless enough to fire on wounded and medical staff.

Today and tomorrow will tell. If Zaitsev is dead, there'll be no response. The Reds won't send any more pupils after Thorvald. He's shown them several times over that such an act is suicide. If there's more Red sniper activity across the park this morning or tomorrow, it'll be Zaitsev.

At last, it will be Zaitsev.

Thorvald had rested enough. He gathered up the pack

containing his thermos and the sandwiches made from his remaining cheeses and meats. He had enough to keep them in lunches for four more days. That, the colonel supposed, should be ample.

Thorvald took up the captured Moisin-Nagant. He grimaced, turning to crawl into the cell. Nikki wondered, Where does he get the patience to watch and wait all day? Look at him. He's flabby and delicate. Where does the will come from to be this supersniper, the most dangerous marksman in the Third Reich? If there were such a powerful force inside him, wouldn't it be on his outside as well, in his muscles, in his flesh?

But it is, it is, Nikki; he could hear the colonel's voice explaining it to him. It's in my eyes and in my hands, you've seen it. Sometimes in my voice. I put it in my bullets. The will is in the flash of powder, it flies inside the lead and copper jacket. I become the German supersniper when I grip my rifle.

"Stay on your toes today," the colonel said. Thorvald was up on his knees. "Don't move until I give you instructions. I think we might snare ourselves a rabbit before the day is out."

The colonel crawled on his belly behind the wall and under the metal sheet. He pushed his pack and rifle in front of him through the light snow that had fallen in the night.

Nikki sat bundled in a blanket. The dawn smelled crisp. The wet, heavy weather that had lain over Stalingrad like a damp sponge for the past week had sailed through the night before; this day was going to be clear, with little wind.

The last star of the waning eve winked low on the eastern horizon above the Volga. The star fought with the rose and purple hues of the climbing sun for its last glowing moments. Sound and sight will carry a long way today, Nikki mused. It'll be a good day for hunting.

• • •

NIKKI WOKE TO THE SUN FULL IN HIS FACE. HE
raised his chin to warm his neck. He pulled back his white
camouflage hood and took off his helmet. The sun was
not high enough to warm the top of his head, but the
absence of wind gave the chill a pleasant touch. He
thought back to the dry cold and powdery snows covering
his father's fields in Westphalia, how the cattle and sheep
stood still in the middle of the great white open spaces
after a snow, stupidly wondering where their earth had
gone. He thought about his sister, how on those coldest
days she made lunches of ham and cabbage for him and
his father when they came in kicking snow and dung off
their boots. They'd sit in the kitchen beneath the brown
photo of his mother, dead many years, as many years as
Nikki was old. She would have made you a good mother,
his father always said, and Nikki would smile at his sister
across the table, the sister who mothered him.

It was never so cold at home, never so deep in the
bones as the cold you felt in a foreign country, at war,
waiting to die, to kill, to survive, waiting.

He took off a mitten and reached for his two sandwiches. He unwrapped one of them and ate it. He should
have saved the food for when he grew hungrier later in
the day. But uncertainty made him eat it now, when he
wanted it.

Nikki sat in the cemetery silence of the wall, the rare
blue sky and the hard wreckage strewn all around. For a
while he did not think about Thorvald, curled up fat and
white on the ground like a grub. Nikki looked up to the
height of Mamayev Kurgan, at the railroad tracks running
behind the alleys, everything charred and broken, so clear
today. He imagined himself the only man alive in Stalingrad. What would he do if that were so? Build himself a
home from the pieces? Rise to his feet and walk

away . . . to where? No, he would sit right here in the sun. He'd eat his last sandwich. Maybe he'd go into the grub's nest and eat his sandwiches, too.

Nikki sat through the afternoon. He couldn't move away from his spot near the break in the wall, for Thorvald might at any moment need him. He stretched, rolled onto his stomach, and pulled the blanket over him. He wanted to hum or sing to himself but would not. He wondered, Does the colonel believe in God? Does he ask God for strength? Or is he like me, a believer only when he needs God, when he's in trouble? God, get me out of this. Please, God, I believe, I always believe, even when you don't hear from me. Get me home safely and I'll believe harder, I promise.

In the late afternoon the sun splashed long shadows across the park, lowering itself to shine over Thorvald's hidden shoulder in his hutch. Nikki ate his last sandwich after playing a game with himself to see how great a hunger he could accumulate. He'd passed the hours watching the hunger grow. The pang in his stomach helped keep him alert.

Thorvald's voice. "Nikki. Are you there?"

Nikki, so long bored, had to think of an answer.

"Nikki?"

"Yes, Colonel, I'm here."

"It's time to see if we have any company."

Nikki held his breath.

"Did you see anything, Colonel?"

"Perhaps. I'm not sure, but I might've just caught a flash in the same spot where the two snipers were yesterday."

"Is it the Hare?"

Thorvald's stunted, buzzing voice carried a grin. "Well, it's where I believe Zaitsev would be."

Yes, Nikki thought, it is. Zaitsev, the newspaper hero. He would come to the same spot where his friends had died. His sense of revenge would bend toward the dramatic. The Hare doesn't know Thorvald, but the colonel knows him. He's been watching that same spot all day, waiting for the sun to drop just so, to create just such a reflection.

"Put your helmet on the shovel handle again. Move fifty meters to the left, then hoist it and walk to the right."

Nikki scrambled for the shovel. Behind him, he heard Thorvald speak, or sing, to himself in his nook.

"Here, little rabbit. Here, bunny, bunny."

TWENTY-THREE

"THERE. THERE, VASHA! I SEE SOMETHING. A . . . a helmet. Look. Quick, damn it!"

Zaitsev had just finished his hour long shift poring over the park through his periscope. His eyes were exhausted. He'd slid on his mittens and been slumped back against the wall for no more than a minute when Kulikov spotted something.

He pulled off the gloves and scrambled fast for his periscope. Kulikov continued to curse.

"Where?" Zaitsev asked, slamming his chest against the wall. He raised the periscope above the bricks. "Where?"

"The wall at the far end of the park. Behind that tank. There. There!"

"Nikolay, calm down. I'll find it." This was as animated as he'd ever seen Kulikov. He's very intrigued by this Headmaster. Oh well, I've been living with Thorvald for a week now. Nikolay has just gotten started.

"He's moving right to left," Kulikov whispered.

No need to whisper, Zaitsev mused. Thorvald's close enough for a bullet, but we can still speak normally.

Zaitsev panned across the wall 250 meters away. The sun setting in front of him made it difficult to identify shapes, giving everything in his scope a ghostly aura.

Thorvald, of course, knows this. He's positioned himself so that the sun makes this his time of day, his advantage. Mine was this morning. Thorvald knows that, too; the morning passed with no sign of him.

"Found him?" whispered Kulikov.

Not yet. Not there. Past the tank. Along the wall, not there . . . what is that? Is it a stone? No, it . . . yes, it moved. A helmet, it must be. The range of the periscope was taxed at this distance, but right now Zaitsev trusted Kulikov's vision and instincts more than his own. Is it actually moving, he wondered, or is Kulikov's nervous chatter making me want to see it move? "I see it," he said before he was sure he really did. He watched closely the wavering gray lump at the edge of the wall. His tired eyes slowly began their automatic task of compensating for the glare and the hazy focus of the scope's optics at this distance. The lump did move. There. Certainly. It was a helmet.

"I see it," he repeated.

"He's your meat, Vasha. What do we do?"

Zaitsev watched the swaying helmet. It moved unnaturally, in jerks rising and falling, not at all like a man walking behind the far wall. It was a poor imitation, a helmet on a stick, bobbing as if the wearer had only one leg or were walking on his knees. The wall there was tall enough for a man not to have to walk on his knees to stay covered unless the man were holding up a stick with a helmet on it. No, this is not the Headmaster. The bastard is lying hidden elsewhere, within sight and range, waiting for me to fire as Shaikin and Morozov did. He's waiting for me to give away my position. This helmet carrier is an assistant, a clumsy assistant.

With a pang, Zaitsev lowered his eyes from the periscope. This lowly ruse, this freshman bit from the Headmaster, insulted him. This was not the opening move he'd anticipated. He didn't know what he'd expected, but it was not this.

"It's a trick. A very poor one." Zaitsev blinked to ease the tension around his eyes. "We'll do nothing."

Zaitsev and Kulikov watched the helmet rise and fall along the ridge of the brick wall. After several minutes, whoever was carrying it grew weary in the arms and lowered it.

The sun dropped until it lurched below the ruins on the western edge of the park. The light was too low for telescopic sights now. The only target this late in the day, the kind Viktor Medvedev and his bears excelled at would be a lit cigarette or a muzzle flash somewhere in the gathering darkness, not the kind of error the Headmaster would make. Or would he? After all, he'd walked a helmet on a stick in front of the Hare, a disappointment. The Nazi's far less than brilliant; he was not even craftsmanlike.

Thirty minutes later, after full night had descended, Zaitsev and Kulikov gathered their packs and rifles to leave.

"Where is he?" Kulikov muttered. "Damn him."

Amused, Zaitsev observed to himself how Nikolay, the quiet one, had grown absolutely talkative over Thorvald.

When they returned to the snipers' bunker, Medvedev and Tania were waiting. Zaitsev reported on the day's long inactivity, ending with the helmet ploy. For half an hour he listened to their opinions on what tactics he and Kulikov should employ. Then Kulikov raised himself off the floor in silence and left.

"Did we hurt his feelings?" Medvedev asked.

"No," Zaitsev said, "but he's taken this duel with Thorvald personally. My guess is he wants it too much to listen to advice. I don't know. It might still be Baugderis bothering him. He'll be all right. I think that's enough for tonight."

Medvedev rose from the floor. "Maybe I'll hunt your park tonight," he said. "Perhaps the Headmaster smokes."

Zaitsev laughed. "If he does, light one up for him."

Across from Zaitsev, Tania sat cross-legged, watching Viktor take his leave.

"How is Shaikin?" he asked her.

"I don't know. I don't want to know. I tell myself he's alive."

Tania rubbed her palms on her knees. Zaitsev sat with her in the hush, trying to calm the percolating things in his breast that wanted to reach out and pull her in.

She spoke. "Thorvald. Why is he behaving like a freshman?"

Zaitsev shook his head. "To make me think it's not him. To make me mad. I can come up with ten reasons why he does everything he does. And then I don't know anything."

Tania stretched her legs. The outlines of her calves and the stems of her pelvis showed through her white canvas pants.

"The Headmaster wants to know if it's you he's facing. He knows you, Vasha. We can assume he's read all the articles about you. He knows the Hare wouldn't shoot at a helmet on a stick. When you held your fire today, you told him you were there."

Tania rubbed her hands together. Then she stopped and looked into her palms as if looking into the bottom of a teacup for mystical clues.

She continued: "He's being unpredictable. You're the one who's acting in a pattern."

Zaitsev lay back on his bedroll, ignoring her comment. What does she know? he thought. A woman, still mostly a freshman herself. She's not out there with me staring into the haze and shadows, looking for her own personal assassin. Pattern. The only pattern I'll follow is this one: When

I shoot, somebody dies. One man, one bullet. Thorvald will be no exception.

But Tania's comment gnawed at him. Is she right? I'm hounded by detail and nuance in this battle with Thorvald. Could she be seeing it more clearly from a distance than I see it up close?

Shit. She's right. A pattern. Thorvald knows it. One man, one bullet. My stated, *printed* creed. No, not a creed. My damned brag is what it is. He knows it. He's read it I don't know how many times in those articles. I ought to wring Danilov's thick neck for putting all that information about me into *In Our Country's Defense*. He's put strings on me, made me into a puppet Thorvald can pick up and make dance. Thorvald knows how I hunt, all my patterns. When I didn't fire at the helmet this morning, he knew it was me, just like Tania says. And when Shaikin and Morozov did fire yesterday, Thorvald knew he wasn't facing me then. I should have stopped talking to Danilov, told the little troll there would be no more interviews. But I didn't, did I? I liked it; I rolled in it like a dog in high grass. And now my smell is so strong, Thorvald can track me with it. Hero? Fucking idiot! I'm facing a supersniper I know nothing about, and he's staring across no-man's-land at an enemy he's read a book on.

And he's using my tactics against me. Pretend to be a freshman. Lower your enemy's guard. Make him careless. Irritate him. Rattle his calm, wear down his endurance. The helmet on the stick. Not a stupid ruse at all. It made me angry. He knows it. Worse, he's lecturing me in my own tactics.

Zaitsev's mind raced to the dozens of times he'd played these same games with other Nazi snipers. Make them angry, turn the battle into a vendetta, make it personal. He recalled a month ago, one morning near the Barricades, when he'd shot one of two German snipers who'd burrowed behind a railroad mound. After his first bullet, which he was certain had split the nose of the first sniper, he'd raised a sign over his position with the number 10 scrawled on it with a charred stick. The number signified a perfect shot in a marksmanship competition. After a few quiet minutes to let the Nazi boil over the gall of this bizarre Russian sniper, Zaitsev simply put his helmet on the stick. He marched it along the top of the breastwork and, within moments, Chekov knocked down the second German sniper. The hot fool simply couldn't contain himself and fired on the helmet. The lesson: never let it become personal.

Tania's right. I'm locked into a pattern. Thorvald has me confused and angry. He's guiding me as if I were on a bridle. I've transformed this duel into a personal vendetta to repay him for killing my hares. He hunted them as the best way to get to me. It worked.

Before Zaitsev could respond to Tania, the bunker's blanket was pushed aside. The brass buttons of a wool greatcoat, the ones down the chest of Captain Danilov, entered the room.

To Zaitsev, Danilov looked wrong in the snipers' bunker, even though the commissar had been there many times before. Tonight, wrapped so tightly in his duel with the Headmaster, Zaitsev was stung by the fat man's presence. This is a place for fighters, he thought, men and women who are strong, deadly, vital, and hard. Here is this soft little man, shorter than a hare and wider than a barrel, standing in the middle of the room where others, better than him, have stood and would not stand again. Zaitsev sensed an ugly urge to sit on Danilov or rest the lantern on him as though he were a table.

"Comrades." Danilov greeted Zaitsev and Tania jovially. The lamp's sallow light darkened his amiable smile.

"Comrade commissar," Zaitsev acknowledged the *politrook*. He felt the interruption keenly; he wanted to continue dissecting the Headmaster with Tania for the next day's hunt.

Danilov did not sit. Good, thought Zaitsev. When he sits, he stays.

"Chief Master Sergeant," the commissar began, "what happened in the search for the German master sniper today?"

Zaitsev shook his head. "Nothing. But I'm sure I know where he is now. We have agreed, the Headmaster and I, that we should meet across a park downtown."

"Excellent," Danilov said. "I like the idea of the park. A wide-open space. Nothing between you but distance. Little to hide behind but your wits. A wonderful scene. I should like to see it."

Zaitsev's and Tania's eyes ran to each other. She heard it, too! Danilov wants to come with me.

"Tomorrow," the commissar added.

Zaitsev spoke immediately. "No, you can't go."

"Certainly I can." Only Danilov's lips moved.

Zaitsev made two fists. He shook them at the commissar.

"This is not what you think it is! This is a battle of concentration. The Headmaster and I are linked into something beyond what you can put into one of your articles. The Headmaster is not going to be patient with any mistakes. He's a killer."

"And so are you, Hare. You speak so well when you're excited, did you know? I'll be here two hours before dawn."

Danilov turned to leave.

Zaitsev shouted, "No!"

Tania tugged on his pants leg.

"Yes," she said.

Danilov turned to the snipers. "Private Chernova," he said, eyes twinkling like moonlit waters, "thank you for your support. The Hare can be a stubborn man, can't he?"

"Yes, comrade, he can be. But just before you came in, we were discussing the tactics of the Nazi sniper. He's a most complex enemy, and I'm sure Comrade Zaitsev understands that the more help he can get in catching him, the better."

Danilov hung in the doorway, his nose in the air. He seemed to sample the room for danger.

The commissar looked at her. Danilov wonders the same as I, Zaitsev thought. What's Tania's game?

Danilov turned on his heels. "In the morning, then." He was gone with a tired sweep of the blanket.

Zaitsev waited, looking at the blanket, at the only thing in the room Danilov had touched. He felt words and impulses knocking at his brain, angry questions to throw at Tania. He sat quietly, preferring first to lie still behind the cover of silence.

"Vasha, look at me."

He turned and blinked once, slowly.

"Yes?"

She smiled. "I may have just done a very smart thing, or it may be very dumb. Can I tell you why it was smart?"

"Yes."

"There's something undeniable about Danilov. We both have seen it. You even went back to get him last week because of it. Remember? When you came hunting with me on Mamayev Kurgan."

Zaitsev felt a moment building, like a swell of water. Tania was reaching out to him, and he wanted to reach back. He deeply wanted the inertia and warmth of Tania; his temper had to be dismissed into the cold and dark, out with Danilov.

Tania cocked her head. She rose to her knees and leaned her face so close that her blue eyes filled him, as if her eyes themselves were breathing onto his cheek. He blew at her like a bug to be brushed kindly away from his face. She blew back, softly, sexily, barely enough to shimmy a candle flame.

"Whenever he's around," she whispered, rubbing her nose against his, "things happen, don't they? You said so yourself. So take him to visit Thorvald. And see what happens."

AN HOUR AFTER DAWN, THE GERMANS SURGED again at Pavlov's House.

Zaitsev, Kulikov, and Danilov could not see the fighting, which was two hundred meters from where they sat behind the park wall. The attack came from the south side of the building, blocking their view. Still, the sounds of artillery and automatic weapons seared the air. The smoke of guns and dust from the wounds inflicted on the walls of Pavlov's House crept across the open ground. The thump of shells pounded in the ground beneath them, sounding down the street like someone beating dirt out of a carpet.

The attack exhausted itself by midmorning. Machine-gun fire issued again from the windows of the apartment building. Sergeant Jacob Pavlov, the Houseowner, was still at home.

Zaitsev and Kulikov kept their eyes sealed to their scopes. With the morning sun at their backs, they did not fear reflections off their sights. The Headmaster might catch a peek of us, Zaitsev thought, but he already suspects we're here. He won't be surprised. Also, in this battle haze, it's unlikely he'll see whatever we might show him well enough to shoot at it.

Danilov sat next to Kulikov. The commissar's shoulders were hunched over another of his notebooks. Only the small of his back rested against the wall. That morning, when the commissar had met Zaitsev and Kulikov outside the snipers' bunker in the dark cold, he had tucked under his arm the battered loudspeaker and the battery pack and microphone.

"We'll have a little chat with the Nazi colonel this morning," Danilov remarked in place of a greeting to the two snipers. Again, Zaitsev thought of the commissar as a barrel, rolling up to them, full nearly to bursting.

Danilov puffed up. "The Headmaster will talk back to me, and then you two can shut him up."

Zaitsev had used all his powers of persuasion to talk the commissar out of bringing the loudspeaker. Maybe tomorrow, he'd said. Let's lie low a while longer, get a better idea of whom we're dealing with. Behind the commissar's head, Kulikov had made childish, hilarious faces.

Zaitsev looked at the rear of Pavlov's House. Dormant for the past two days, it was smoking and threatened this morning. Tania was right. Danilov is an event in human form.

The commissar closed his pad with a clap of paper and rammed the book into his pack. He rolled onto his knees with a grunt to put his belly against the wall. He whispered to Zaitsev, "Have you found him yet?"

Zaitsev sighed. "I have absolutely no idea where the Headmaster is. I just know he's out there somewhere across the park. Before I can find him, he has to either make a mistake, which he will not do, or make the first move, which I must force him to do. The bad news is, when Thorvald moves, people get their heads blown off."

Danilov reached again for his notepad to record the Hare's statement.

Kulikov lowered his periscope and laid his arm lightly on Danilov's wrist.

"Commissar, please. Stop scribbling. It drives me crazy."

Zaitsev added, "He's right. It's distracting." He grabbed a spare periscope. "Would you like to help us scan the front?"

Danilov rocked to his toes, ready for action.

"Yes. Of course. Where should I look?"

"You patrol the wall on the other side while Nikolay and I watch the terrain."

Danilov snatched the periscope. Quickly, almost greedily, the commissar turned and brought the lens to his eye. Zaitsev watched him. The commissar is safe so long as the sun is at our backs and he stays low. The air is hazy. He won't see anything. Let him look. Zaitsev took off his own steel helmet and crawled behind Danilov.

"Sit still," he said. He took off Danilov's fur hat and put his helmet in its place. Danilov kept his gaze in the eyepiece, facing the park. The helmet sat higher on his head than it should. Damn, thought Zaitsev, the man has a head like a bucket.

Zaitsev patted the helmet on top to push it down. It didn't move.

"Stop that," Danilov whispered. He's all business now, Zaitsev thought. He plays the sniper fighter like a child.

"Good hunting, Commissar."

"Thank you. Go back to your post."

Zaitsev shook his head. Give him an hour with his eye at that periscope and he'll be out of wind. Maybe he'll go back and write an article about someone else and Nikolay and I can concentrate on taking care of the Headmaster.

Zaitsev slid back to his periscope. He raised it slowly above the wall and hurled his vision across the park. Nothing had moved in the three days he'd been watching. Not a stone, not a brick. Wherever the Headmaster was when he shot Morozov and Shaikin, he's still there. He's had no reason to move; we haven't given him one. He hasn't fired a shot since we got here.

Minutes passed, touching Zaitsev no more than the morning breeze. All of his senses had climbed into his eyes and hands to blend in the periscope. His voice, his sense of smell, his touch, his thoughts—all were magni-

fied and cast over the pitted landscape. He had no idea
what to search for other than some unknown clue he
trusted would be revealed to him, some sign of life in the
rubble and mist in front of him.

Don't worry, he mused, that's Stalingrad out there; it's
the perfect backdrop for a waiting, seeking sniper. It will
betray life inevitably.

Where is he? Where is the snake? So many crevices,
windows, shadows, craters, debris, the sun, the haze, the
wind, the cold, fuck! It's huge and dead all around me.
And out there, like the point of a needle sticking up out of
a rug, is that one invisible, deadly thing looking for me,
knowing me, waiting for me. Waiting for my head with a
bullet and a splattered ending, a sad story tonight beneath
the lantern in my bunker and a sled ride along the riverbank to the cool storage of the caves. Maybe Tania will
say goodbye to me beside the Volga this afternoon, then
tomorrow at dawn sit at this spot behind the wall to
avenge me. Will it snow and cover my blood mark before
she can swear revenge over it, before my ghost can hover
here and keep her safe?

Nothing in the rubble. Nothing in the buildings, the
shadows, the snowy patches, the trenches, the tanks, the
craters.

Nothing. Where?

A rustling movement beside him snagged his concentration, sucking it out of his eyes. He pulled his head from
the lens. His thoughts, flung so far outward across the
park, were slapped by the moment at hand, the rough,
cold feel of now. The abruptness of the change left him
dizzy.

He turned to Kulikov, kneeling next to him. Nikolay
stared intently into his own periscope, unmoving. Zaitsev
leaned back to see around Kulikov. There, Danilov was
slowly straightening his knees, sliding his belly up the
wall. He clutched the periscope tightly in his mitts, ram-

ming it against his face. The commissar's cheeks bulged beneath his hidden eyes, squeezing them outward like dough under the eyepiece.

"Commissar, get down," Zaitsev ordered. How long has he been standing up so straight? he wondered. Damn it, I should've kept an eye on him.

Danilov answered in a voice taut as a bowstring. "I see the bastard."

Before Zaitsev could speak, Danilov leaped fully to his feet. His helmeted head and the shoulders of his greatcoat were above the parapet.

"There he is!" Danilov took one hand off the periscope. "I'll point him out!"

"Get down!"

Kulikov dropped his scope and slid to his right. He grabbed the commissar's legs to yank him down behind the wall.

In that instant, Danilov was propelled backward from the wall as if by a shove. His hands flew from his sides, flinging the periscope into the dirt. His legs kicked up and struck Kulikov in the chin, he fell so hard. The helmet tumbled from his head.

Danilov's head was intact. An upper chest shot. Even while the commissar fell, Zaitsev found the hole ripped in his greatcoat below the right collarbone.

Danilov lay for several seconds. Zaitsev and Kulikov were stunned, jolted by the rashness of the commissar's action and the suddenness of the bullet. He'd been above the wall for no more than two seconds. In that thin slice of time, Thorvald hit him.

Danilov began to thrash, squirming like a grounded salmon fighting to flop itself back into the river. The mound of his stomach jerked and his back arced off the ground. He started to roll over, flailing his arms.

Zaitsev lunged to hold the commissar down. Kulikov

laid his weight over the commissar's legs, struggling to keep him still.

He's in shock from the wound, Zaitsev thought. We've got to hold him until he regains his senses or faints.

Danilov grunted, straining to rise off the ground.

"Lie still!" Kulikov shouted in Danilov's ear. "The pain will pass!"

Danilov heaved mightily against the two men on top of him.

"Get off me, damn it!" the commissar screamed. "Get off me!"

Zaitsev looked into Danilov's eyes. They were wide open and clear.

"Let me go! I'll kill the son of a bitch. I'll kill him myself! He shot me, the fucking bastard son of a bitch! Let me up! I'll kill him!"

Zaitsev and Kulikov released their grips. Danilov sat up, his face as red as Zaitsev had ever seen a face not covered in blood. The veins in the man's temples and neck strained against the skin. Danilov had spasmed in shock not from the wound but from fury. He was livid beyond expression. The tough little bastard.

Danilov looked at the hole in his right shoulder. Gray wool threads stuck up from the tear in the fabric as if air were escaping from the opening in his body. Zaitsev saw no blood, but he knew that beneath the coat and uniform, the commissar must be bleeding badly.

"Shit!" Danilov shook when he said the word. He brought his eyes up to Zaitsev kneeling beside him.

Zaitsev laid his hand on the commissar's good shoulder. "Are you all right?"

"Yes. I'll live." He paused. "I've never been shot before. It hurts."

"So I hear. We'll have to get you back now."

"I'd love to stay, but I think I'm bleeding."

Zaitsev smiled. Danilov blinked and parted his lips in an unsure, weakening smile.

Danilov made as if to lie back. Zaitsev put his hands under the commissar's neck and back to lower him. Danilov sighed.

"Thank you, Comrade Hare."

Zaitsev leaned his face close. "What did you see? Where were you looking?"

"I was looking at the wall, as you told me." Danilov's voice carried a quiver of displeasure, as if the question implied he could have been looking elsewhere, not properly following Zaitsev's instructions.

"Yes, of course." Zaitsev eased his tone. "What did you see? You said you saw him."

"Yes, I did." Danilov held up his left hand for Zaitsev to pull him to a sitting position. The *politrook* spit once in the dirt. It was in anger, though it seemed one good spit was all he could muster.

"I saw the bastard's helmet," he said. Spittle, veined with crimson, dangled from the commissar's chin, hanging unwiped and sad. "He was walking along the wall. That's what I saw."

Zaitsev was not surprised. Of course. The Headmaster, the Head Gamesman. Still the freshman bit, is it? Still trying to make me mad enough to jump. His game worked, but he bagged an unintended prey.

Zaitsev looked to Kulikov. "Nikolay, did you see anything? A muzzle flash, a reflection?"

Kulikov shook his head. "Nothing."

Nor had Zaitsev seen anything. Thorvald had made the first move, just as he'd warned Danilov. And Zaitsev had gotten nothing to show for it but a wounded bulldog commissar.

"Commissar, allow me, please. I must take a look at your wound."

Danilov's eyes opened a little wider.

"No. It's all right," he replied weakly. "I'd rather a doctor look at it."

Zaitsev stroked the commissar's shoulder gently.

"Comrade, the wound might tell me something about where Thorvald is hiding. There are ways."

Danilov squinted his eyes.

"It will hurt a little," Kulikov said from behind.

Danilov nodded drunkenly. "Yes. Of course. Proceed."

Grunting through gritted teeth, Danilov helped Kulikov to unbutton his greatcoat, pulling it gingerly off the right shoulder. The sea green jersey beneath the coat was muddy with blood. Zaitsev cut the tunic away from the wound. He carved a piece of cloth for a wipe and another for a bandage.

"Hold still. I need to clean it."

"As you see fit." Danilov leaned back against Kulikov.

A red trickle spilled from the wound's lower lip. Danilov's meaty shoulder was thick with black hair. Zaitsev toweled the blood from the area, making Danilov wince.

"Only for a moment," Zaitsev whispered.

The puncture was clean and round. A purple bruise had painted a uniform circle around the hole. This indicated a straight-on bullet path, according to the old lessons grandfather Andrei had taught him on the skins drying on the walls of the hunter's lodge. Look at the entry wound, Vasha, the old man had said, pointing with his walking stick. The bullet leaves a track against the skin, just like a paw in the snow. Thorvald is probably at ground level. What do you think, Grandfather? It's hard to tell at what angle Danilov's chest was turned to the park. But the commissar's injury has bought us one bit of information, at least.

"You were facing straight ahead, weren't you?" Zaitsev asked while Kulikov helped Danilov replace the tunic and coat over the right shoulder.

"Mmm-hmmm. Yes, I think so."

"I'm sorry this happened."

It's his own damned fault, but why add insult to injury? Now isn't the time to lecture him.

He rubbed the commissar's blood from his hands with the strip of cloth. I shouldn't have brought Danilov along. I should have refused, even after Tania's intervention. But Tania will have her way; she wanted Danilov here, and here he lies. This is what she intended, the result she foresaw. She coldly sent Danilov to this bullet, manipulated me into allowing it. Why? To help me find Thorvald or to rid us all of Danilov? In either event, the commissar will be leaving Stalingrad alive. He's lucky. The doctors at the field hospital will take out the bullet lodged in his shoulder, and then, when the river freezes, it's a sled ride across to Krasnaya Sloboda for you, Commissar. Ah, well. Whom the gods choose to spare, let them live in peace. Perhaps the commissar has spirits swarming about him, protecting him. If so, then spirits, listen to me: go with Danilov. Repay him for his injury in your service and protect him. He has pluck and toughness, even if he's dangerous and stupid. In the ways of the forest, like an animal, that makes him an innocent.

Kulikov helped Danilov to his feet, keeping his head low. Zaitsev watched them leave. The two walked in rhythm, attached to each other, skinny and fat like a boy with his hurt pony.

Zaitsev thought of the bullet in Danilov's shoulder and the blood he knew was warming the commissar's side and legs, perhaps pooling in his boots. How did this come to be? Batyuk gave me this assignment, to find and kill the Headmaster. Why? He's just one man. Why all this effort to wipe him out, why the bullets lodged in Shaikin, Morozov, Baugderis, Danilov, the nurses, the wounded? Why am I sitting here, dueling to the death with a single sniper instead of working in the factories to protect Russian troops, furthering the battle for the city?

There in Danilov's aching, wounded posture was his answer. Stalingrad is no longer just a battle for a spot on a map. It has become a war of ideas between Hitler and Stalin, between the generals of both armies ripping up this land, toppling these buildings. Stalingrad is Hitler's deepest stab into Russia. He won't allow himself to be stopped here. Likewise, Stalin is making his firmest stand here in the city named for him. Knowing its strategic importance to Hitler, Stalin has marked the city for death in order to preserve the *rodina*'s life. And the real result of these two leaders' ideas, hatched in the safety of their mighty castles, is dripping out of Danilov right now: blood. Bodies and destruction—these are far more real than ideas, yet so much less important to the leaders. And here, squared off like fighting cocks, Thorvald and I are no longer men but ideas. We've been made larger, given importance beyond our bodies. For the watching propagandists such as Danilov, for the opinion makers and the newspapers and the generals, for Hitler and Stalin, it's the Hare versus the Headmaster, the Russian legend against the German marvel. Whichever of us gets the bullet, he'll bleed not just blood but a headline and a story; one dictator's schemes will be furthered, the other's will be discredited. And one more body will be made cold and dead as the black ink of the newspapers and propaganda that will surely flow with the blood.

Oh, well, Colonel. Musings won't kill you for me. I'll need a bullet. So let's begin in earnest.

Zaïtsev took up his helmet and put it back on his head; the steel was cold from lying on the ground. He picked up Danilov's periscope. I saw nothing. Kulikov saw nothing. Danilov saw the walking helmet.

How could Thorvald shoot without Kulikov or me seeing a flash? The Headmaster is at ground level. But he must be deep in the shadows, hidden in darkness, nestled in it. He can't shoot without making a flash. Where would he be, to see us but not worry about his muzzle glare or have no fear of a reflection from his scope? He must be in an extremely well disguised spot, someplace I wouldn't think to look for him, someplace he's confident I wouldn't be looking when he squeezed the trigger and his barrel sparked.

Where is that kind of shooting cell out there? Where?

Zaitsev reached across the park with his senses and his intuition, creeping with them like a jungle cat among and under the foliage of facts and perceptions. This was how he'd always hunted, as a boy in the taiga, as a man at war.

He recalled the scene: Danilov was on his feet for two seconds, no more. Thorvald is close to shoot like that, to see so clearly through the mist with the morning light in his eyes. And the even ring around the entry wound? An open mouth whispering in his grandfather's voice.

Where?

First, he has an assistant. Thorvald told him to put the helmet on the stick again. The Headmaster must be close to the wall, behind it or in front of it, to give voice commands to the assistant. Probably within ten meters. How else could he have set the trap?

Where?

Zaitsev scanned the terrain through the periscope. He selected a range to his left and to his right, a logical perimeter within which the Headmaster must be to fire the shot that hit Danilov and leave a uniform hole and bruise ring in the commissar's flesh.

On the left edge of his shooting range were several ragged craters, a toppled fountain, and a burned-out German tank. The tank faced east, toward Zaitsev's position. He'd looked at this tank a hundred times during the past two days, but now the empty metal hulk bore a new significance. Was Thorvald inside? He could be. It was within range and close enough to the wall to work with an assistant. Thorvald could easily slide under the tank before dawn and enter through the emergency escape hatch. He could shoot out of the driver's view slit or the hole left where the turret's machine gun had been salvaged.

But this was not a position for an experienced sniper, especially a devious one. He'd have no quick escape route in case of an infantry or mortar attack on his position. His vision of the battlefield would be restricted, limiting his targets, and Thorvald had shown no inclination toward being selective with his victims.

Zaitsev swung his vision north to the right side of the range he'd selected. He concentrated on the wall. He imagined the Headmaster in a lair, calling to his assistant behind the wall. "Put the helmet on the stick and walk with it. Shake it up and down like you're making popcorn over a campfire. Do it so badly the Hare will feel my hand slapping him in the face!" The periscope brought Zaitsev to the lip of another crater. No, he's not in an open hole in the ground, he thought. Several humps of snow-covered rubble swelled on the park like white insect bites. He's not behind any of them, either. On the far right was an abandoned German bunker, a small pillbox made of sandbags, stacked concrete, and wood beams. Could Thorvald be in there? Certainly. Zaitsev leaned into the periscope as if he could send his eyes into the air like hawks, out to the fortification to inspect its features, then carry the details back to him. Zaitsev felt the crevices of the pillbox with his vision, knocking on it, calling out Thorvald's name: are you in there? How would Thorvald approach this shooting cell? How would he leave it? What were his firing angles? No, he's not in there. Like the burned-out tank at the other end of the range, Zaitsev could not believe the Headmaster would choose such an obvious firing cell, one a lesser sniper might select. He moved the periscope to the center of the park, inspecting the rubble near the foot of the wall. More piles of bricks, more craters, and some metal sheets littered the ground.

Zaitsev paused in his search to inquire of himself if he were growing tired. He'd been staring through the periscope for two hours now, since Kulikov left with Danilov. The sun had risen to its noon seat. He checked his hands, eyes, his folded legs, his concentration. Don't make these guesses and decisions if you aren't razor sharp, he chided himself. Do you need a rest? If so, then stop. Don't make a mistake. You must be alert, with your ears up, your nose in the wind. You're all right? You can continue? Good. Then tell me: is he in the tank, the bunker, in a crater, behind a pile of bricks, in a building, behind the wall? Are you sure, Vasily? Tell me if you're sure. Is it your instinct, or do you know for a fact? Tell me now.

No. He's somewhere else. Somewhere I'll find him. I am sure, because it is my instinct.

He is the Headmaster.

But I am a hunter. I am his hunter.

TWENTY-FOUR

HE NOTICED THE MOTION FIRST. A GRAY OB-
ject bobbed atop the wall like a baby bird above the ledge
of its nest. The thing twisted left and right, then shook up
and down like an angry fist. After watching for several
seconds, he recognized it as a field periscope, a favorite
tool of the hidden Red sniper.

"Nikki!"

He concentrated into the scope to slice the crosshairs
through the battle haze hanging on the park. A Russian
stronghold at the right corner of the park had come under
attack earlier that morning; the attack had faltered an
hour before, but smoke and dust lingered above the open
ground, catching and reflecting the light like a Berlin driz-
zle to obscure Thorvald's vision.

He turned from the scope. His left eye, closed for most
of the morning, was slow to open. The vision of his right
eye—his aiming side—was filmed with a translucent,
magnified image of the wall on the far side of the park. In
the darkness of his cell, the image hovered like a reclining
ghost.

He called again for Nikki; the sunlight dancing around
but not into his hole caused the apparition on the right

side of his vision to crinkle and disappear like burning paper. He blinked.

The corporal answered.

"Yes, sir, Colonel."

"Get the helmet and the stick."

Thorvald looked back through the scope. Who is this morning fool with his periscope swaying like a seasick child? He can't be a sniper. He's too eager, trying to take in the whole battlefield instead of moving precisely, imperceptibly, to avoid detection. No, this periscope is not in the hands of a sniper, at least not a veteran one. It must be a third party, perhaps an inexperienced officer or observer.

Nikki has confessed that he told the Reds I'm here to kill their Rabbit. This idiot might be someone who wants to record our little war. An intelligence officer, a correspondent for that stupid front newsletter of theirs, whatever. But certainly not a sniper.

I can put a bullet into that periscope. I could scare the piss out of the clumsy watcher, I could splatter glass all over him and all over Zaitsev, who I'm sure is sitting nearby. Why doesn't Zaitsev tell him to get down or go away and let a sniper do his work? This is no place for whoever that is. I could twitch a finger and demonstrate that for him. I wonder what the waving periscope would do if I told Nikki to hoist the helmet.

But I won't. Because this is too easy. Zaitsev must be baiting me. Yes, that's it. He's watching for me to shoot, hanging this target out like a salt lick. I see it now: there's a trap in that periscope's single eye. I won't come out of hiding, Rabbit. You must do better for me.

That periscope. Stupid. I could put the crosshairs there, right on the mirror and lens. Zaitsev won't see my muzzle flash. I'm far enough back in the darkness of this hole. He'd have to be looking right at me to spot it. There.

Right in the middle of the periscope, if the cretin would hold it still for a moment.

It would feel good to show Zaitsev firsthand whom he's up against.

Wait. Feel the rifle, blend it into the hands. The wood in both palms, skin of the rifle, my blood warming the wood. My cheek against the stock, laid there, resting, still as wood. The metal against my eye socket and the trigger under my finger, smooth, also skin but harder, wanting something from me. The scope pulls my eye in and throws it out bigger, to that periscope. The trigger wants something from me.

Suddenly, surprisingly, the periscope jumped high above the wall, exposing a helmet and the top half of a man's torso. The man raised a hand and pointed at Thorvald.

Thorvald fired.

What happened?

The man fell down.

Damn it! Thorvald thought. Damn it! What happened? I fired.

He dropped his rifle. His ears rang; the report was captured and showered back on him by the metal roof and the bricks. He skidded away from the opening between the bricks as if there were a dog snapping at him there. He dug his face into the dirt, expecting Zaitsev's round to come flying in the next instant. He brought his knees up to his chest, balled in the dirt, waiting for the burn of a bullet.

Seconds passed. Thorvald's muscles ached from the hard squeeze he'd locked his body into. His heartbeat soared in his temples. His breathing rattled in his open mouth. His eyelids were shut hard; behind them, his eyeballs jumped left and right. All over his body, his skin fizzed with fear.

Slowly, Thorvald relaxed his grip on himself. No bullet

had answered his. Not yet. He moved cautiously, straightening in the dirt, not knowing what motion might betray him. He felt pickled in dread. He hated the sensation of being watched, of thinking the Rabbit could see him through a scope, the nausea of wearing, if only for a second, the cross hairs.

He saw me. He must have. The damned Rabbit tricked me, he got me to jump at his bait. He must have seen me.

Thorvald shook his shoulders and legs as though shaking off a coating of ice. He was cold on the outside, hot deep within. The cold was strong on his brow. He wiped a hand across his forehead and pulled back damp fingertips.

He lay on his back for several minutes to ease his nerves and control his breathing. He looked up at the wavy underside of the metal sheet. Like a coffin lid, he thought. Almost a coffin.

Why did I do that? Why did I pull the trigger?

Calm slowly returned to his gut. He could think more clearly now, without panic. Damn Zaitsev for making me feel that. Damn him. I hate the fear, I hate it when it comes.

He'll be repaid. He will. Yesterday, this was just an assignment, one that interrupted my work at Gnössen. This was a job I did not want. But now he will surely die. Now this is personal. The Rabbit dies soon.

But the first order of business, Heinz, is to stay German, stay orderly, even with the fear. It is so, yes? Good. Now proceed, coolly, precisely.

I wonder, why did I shoot? In fact, it's not so important. I understand, I pulled the trigger because I was ready to pull it, keyed up. The target got itself shot. That's the way it works when it works, without thought.

All right. But what made the periscope stand up?

He replayed the moment he'd pulled the trigger. The crosshairs were on the moving periscope; then, without reason or warning, the man leaped up to expose his head and torso. Thorvald had felt the stock slam into his shoulder. He didn't remember whether he'd adjusted his aim upward to follow the head. A chest shot is probably what he sent. Just as well. It was a hit, no question.

The target rose. He pointed.

This way. At me.

He must have seen me. He pointed this way.

At me. I fired. He went down.

Who else could he have pointed at? Who else?

Who else is there? Nikki?

Nikki.

Thorvald turned toward the rear of the cell. He heard the immediacy in his own voice.

"Nikki!"

The corporal did not answer.

He shouted again. He can't hear me in this damned hole, he thought. He waited.

The corporal called from behind the wall.

"Did you shoot, Colonel? I thought I heard you. Did you get him?"

"Where were you?"

"Fifty meters to the right with the helmet on the stick."

Thorvald stiffened. "You put the helmet up?"

"Yes, sir. You told me to."

Thorvald would have slapped the boy had he been facing him.

"Corporal, I told you to get it ready. Not to put it up. You almost got me killed!"

A shiver ran up Thorvald's back at the words. He recalled himself curled up like something moist found under a rock. It degraded him; it cut into his sense of command here in Stalingrad.

"Corporal, sit right where you are and stay there! You will do nothing, nothing until I tell you! Understand?"

Nikki sounded confused, contrite. "Yes, sir. I thought—"

"Quiet!" Thorvald let it come out of him, the stain of shame the fear had left behind when it withdrew. It felt good to make it leave. He tipped his head down as if to pour more out of his mouth onto Nikki.

"Don't think! *I* will think. You sit and wait until I speak. Nothing more. Now sit!" He knew he was speaking to the corporal as though the boy were a disobedient mutt. He added, for meanness, "And stay!"

He squirmed to the front of his hole, his face flushed with vexation. He looked out between the bricks. The man with the periscope had seen Nikki's helmet. That was what happened, was the reason he'd jumped.

Who was the jumping man? He wasn't a sniper; no sniper would have risen above the wall. What was he doing in my battle with Zaitsev?

And what did Zaitsev have to do with what happened? Did the Rabbit control the situation? Was the jumping man a planned bait, or did it just happen? Did Zaitsev, knowing I had used the helmet on the stick each of the past two days, get some fool to come along on his hunt for me? Did he tell him, "If you see a helmet above that wall over there, stand up and point it out to me"? Could the Red legend do something like that? Is he cold enough to use live bait on me? Or am I even facing Zaitsev? Perhaps the jumping man was part of another advance patrol of lesser snipers, more student bunnies on the lookout for signs of me. Or someone else, some unlucky soldier unaware of the magnified eyes watching the park, someone who wandered into the midst of our battlefield, some sympathetic journalist from America or London, rambling along the front looking for news.

What happened?

Thorvald admitted that he did not know.

This troubled him. He'd relied on outsmarting the Rabbit. Up to now, events had unfolded under his control; even Nikki's betrayal of him to the Russians hadn't proven to be more than a waste of a few days. But this latest incident had taken place on its own: Nikki's raising of the helmet without his knowledge, the jumping man across the park, his instinctive shot. Thorvald was not comfortable with instinct. He considered himself a man guided by intellect. Whereas instinct was part reflex and part gut feeling, intellect came not from the stomach but from the mind. The result of instinct was luck, but intellect begat control. And the Germanic mind was the finest in the world at control.

The morning sun ascended and the shadows decreased. It was not yet afternoon, and though the sun was in front of him, his hole remained filled with shadow like brackish water in a bowl. He looked at his watch, bringing it close in the dim light. 10:45. He asked himself again: Did Zaitsev see my flash? If he did, he would have returned fire, wouldn't he? One man, one bullet. He would have ended it if he could have. Can I conclude that he didn't see me? Was I right, that this shooting cell under the metal sheet and surrounded by these bricks, this innocent-looking pile of debris, is a perfect sniper haven? Am I safe here? Perhaps. I might indeed be safe here.

For now, I'm stuck. I can't crawl out until after nightfall. What will Zaitsev do next? Will he make a move? Will he try me again with another bait? Or will he grow impatient and careless? Will I get my shot today at the Rabbit's ears?

Thorvald picked the Moisin-Nagant out of the dirt. He cradled it again in his hands. He wrapped the sling around his left wrist, brought the wooden stock gently against his right shoulder, and lowered his eye to the cool metal of the scope. He shrugged once, hefting the rifle into place to fit in his grasp, against his cheek, in his arms. His finger crept to the trigger.

Well, Rabbit, he thought, you have an audience for the rest of the day. What would you like to show me? I'll put a bullet in it for you. I see you, but I don't think you can see me.

For the next three hours, Thorvald lay still, watching the wall where the jumping man had appeared. After the shock and anger of the morning, his stamina seemed to treble. He could now gaze through the scope for an hour at a time, needing only a few minutes of rest before he lowered his head back to the task. I can do anything, he thought. The Rabbit knows it.

Gazing down the scope past the fine black lines of the reticle, Thorvald indulged in an intuition. He sensed he could smell the Rabbit's fear flowing across the park. It was an acrid, rotten smell, like urine.

The sun shone straight overhead now. This was the time of day when neither Thorvald nor Zaitsev was in danger of reflection. The buildings around the perimeter and the debris sprawled in the park stood on their shadows. Thorvald's hole was at its darkest during this time; he felt invisible and bold.

Thorvald envisioned killing Zaitsev. He imagined the Rabbit in his sights, his finger hauling back the trigger. He saw Zaitsev take a bullet in the head but not fall. Zaitsev just stood where he'd been struck. Other Russians came and poured concrete over him and made a statue, right on the spot. At the bottom of the statue it read, *Killed in action by Heinz von K. Thorvald, colonel, SS, 11/17/42*. Thorvald saw himself telling the story in the Berlin Opera House to the fashionable ladies and men, recounting his grueling duel on the Russian steppe, in the hell of the ruined city at the spearpoint of the German invasion. I will tell them of the cat-and-mouse game between the two supersnipers and how extraordinary my enemy was. German intelligence will later find a copy of the Red newsletter that sadly reports the famous Rabbit's death. The article exhorts all Russian soldiers to avenge their hero's murder at the hands of Heinz von K. Thor-

vald, colonel SS. Someone will coin for me a nickname
that will stick, a flattering, one- or two-word sobriquet. All
the real heroes have them, like the Rabbit. I will be the
Teacher, the Sniper Master, something of the sort.

And Nikki. Yes, Nikki. What to do about the young
corporal? Will Nikki be an asset to me back in Berlin? He,
too, will know the true story of my duel with the Russian
supersniper. Will he tell his version accurately, how my
cunning trapped the Rabbit and blew off his head? What
if he lies and tells his mates in the barracks how it was
really his knowledge of the battle and the city that nabbed
Zaitsev? "I pointed Thorvald at the Russian," he might
say. "All he did was pull the trigger." If I'm the only one
who tells the story back in Berlin, then I will control it.
No worries there. Yes, I promised to take Nikki back with
me. But what's the value of a promise to an admitted
traitor, a liar, and an uncooperative dunce who almost got
me killed this morning? We'll have to see. We'll talk, Nikki
and I, when Zaitsev is dead.

While Thorvald's mind paraded images of his own ce-
lebrity, his tireless body and eyes stayed acute for any
motion on the far wall. When the movement came, it
didn't seem sudden to him, even after his long wait. There
it is, he thought. Zaitsev's move. Or Zaitsev's mistake. It
doesn't matter which.

A white shape appeared above the wall. It was too
small for Thorvald to tell exactly what it was. From the
way it moved, it was part of a man, a hand inside a mitten
perhaps, the side of a shoulder or even a white-hooded
head. The target stood out well against the mottled scenery. Thorvald swung the crosshairs no more than a millimeter to the left. A voice said to him, Wait—wait until
you're sure what you're firing at.

He answered the voice: To hell with waiting and to hell
with Zaitsev. He doesn't see me. I can do whatever I
choose. I'm invisible. Besides, I'm angry. I feel like shoot-

ing right now. It's what I do best. So let the Rabbit see some more of what I can do.

Zaitsev is the sniper who waits. I shoot.

The white target had been up for no more than three seconds when his aim was centered, perfect. The crosshairs were calm.

TWENTY-FIVE

"DANILOV WILL NOT DIE."

Zaitsev jerked around, amazed again at Kulikov's ability to move undetected. He hadn't heard the little sniper's return. Kulikov's hands were smudged with the commissar's dried blood.

Danilov had been conscious when they reached a field hospital at the limestone cliffs above the Volga. Kulikov stayed only long enough to have a nurse inspect the commissar's wound. She prodded it with a cloth and a metal tong, drawing Danilov's ire. He seemed to have a reserve of nastiness left. Kulikov wished him luck and hurried back to the park and Zaitsev. He'd been gone less than three hours.

Upon retaking his place beside Zaitsev, Kulikov asked a question he'd mulled over while making his way along the river and through the ruins.

"If killing you, Vasha, is Thorvald's only assignment, why would he waste a bullet on a target any experienced sniper would know was not another sniper? Why'd he risk his position just to hit a fat man with a periscope who couldn't keep his head down?"

Kulikov had concocted one answer in his head, but he wanted to see what Zaitsev thought before speaking.

Zaitsev replied quickly. "Because the Headmaster doesn't think we can find him."

"And," Kulikov said, smiling, "he'll probably stay where he is until we drag him out by his feet."

Zaitsev put a finger to his head. "I've been doing some thinking while you were gone, too, Nikolay. Take a look at this."

He showed Kulikov a meter-long plank. He pulled off his white mitten and stuck it atop the board.

"We'll raise this over the wall and see if it draws a shot. If he hits the glove, we'll have a hole in the wood we can read a lot better than that mess he made of Danilov's shoulder."

Kulikov nodded. "He likes to show off."

"Right. Maybe we can get him to show us where he is."

Zaitsev took the measure of the daylight. The sun was high; there'd be no risk to Thorvald of emitting a reflection. He just might take the bait.

"Ready?" Zaitsev positioned the board in his lap. "Let's wave hello to the Headmaster."

He lifted the plank. The glove cleared the wall. Zaitsev moved it once to the right. Hello, Colonel.

He counted under his breath. "One . . . two . . ."

The end of the plank shook as if hit with a bat. A bullet ripped through the white palm of the mitten. The vibration stung Zaitsev's hands.

He snatched the board down, pressing an index finger against the wall to mark where the bottom of the board had been. With a bit of soap, he marked a line on the wall.

Cotton stuffing and splinters mingled in the hole in the center of the glove's palm. The bullet had gone straight through to leave a jagged aperture in the wood roughly as big around as a finger.

Zaitsev slid the mitten off the board and put it back on his hand. The two holes, in the palm and in the glove's back, let in hard dots of cold against his skin. He made a fist in the glove and shook it at Nikolay Kulikov, kneeling next to him.

"Yes," Zaitsev said. "Yes, Nikolay." Then he motioned at the sun. "Let's wait an hour or so and let him cool down. Then we'll watch until dark."

Kulikov pulled back his white hood. He removed his helmet and rubbed his hand through his short-cropped hair.

"Vasha," Nikolay asked, "did you hear a rifle shot after the bullet hit the board? Or even when Danilov got hit?"

Zaitsev furrowed his brow. "No."

He thought back to the moment seconds earlier when the glove was struck, and to when Danilov had been knocked down that morning. He tried to part the veil of excitement that is always present when bullets fly; it clouded his memory like the clogged skies overhead. He couldn't recall hearing even the echo of a rifle on either occasion.

He looked at Kulikov and smiled.

"Another odd little piece for the puzzle, Nikolushka."

Kulikov pulled from his pocket a bottle of vodka, mostly finished. He handed it to Zaitsev.

"The Hare," he said.

"Nikolay," Zaitsev answered.

He reached for the bottle with his perforated mitten. He looked at the hole, at the spot on the back of his hand. He froze with an intuition; he could feel the bullet pass through his mitt, the shot burrowing and burning through his hand. In his imagination, he sent the gloved hand, punched through like a railroad ticket, away from his arm and over the wall to follow the bullet's course backward, the hand pulling itself along as if down a rope, back to the barrel of the rifle that fired it.

There you are, Colonel Thorvald. Hello.

Zaitsev snapped back to his body, his right hand hovering in the air. Kulikov stared at him, waiting for him to grasp the bottle. Zaitsev reeled in his focus and took the vodka.

The Hare raised the bottle to the far side of the park and toasted again.

"The Headmaster."

NIGHT WAS TWO HOURS OLD. FAR TO THE NORTH, the sky shivered with artillery flashes. Around the park, it was quiet and black. Zaitsev listened to the rumble of explosions. He thought of the city as a sleeping giant; he was at the feet, the other end was snoring.

Surely Thorvald has crawled away by now. The Headmaster has not shown himself to be a night hunter. Zaitsev reached for the plank. He nodded to Kulikov.

"I think we can do it now."

Kulikov struck a match and held the flame near the mark scratched across the wall. Zaitsev raised the plank slowly to re-create the exact position he'd held it that afternoon.

"All right, Nikolay."

Kulikov skidded back from Zaitsev. He hoisted a flare gun and fired.

The pistol blazed with a thumping recoil. Three hundred meters overhead, the flare ignited as its small parachute opened to cast a golden glimmer over the park.

Kulikov set the smoking pistol down and moved quickly to Zaitsev. He raised his face to the board, held by Zaitsev. He looked through the hole as if through a telescope. Kulikov kept his eye to the board for several seconds. Then, while the light from the flare rained down in ocher sheets, he knelt next to Zaitsev. He put his hands on the board to push it against the wall and keep it level with the soap mark.

"Your turn, Vasha."

Zaitsev released the board to Kulikov. He stood, closed his left eye, and looked through the hole.

The opening framed a section of the center of the park, a level bit of ground fifty meters wide running in front of the wall. Thorvald must be somewhere in this field, he thought.

The shadows from the falling flare were stark, shifting black; the park bore the hue of straw. Zaitsev knew every detail that fell within the bounds described by the hole. Piles of debris and two craters, that was all. The burned-out tank, the bunker, and the larger pieces of the battle all fell outside the circle. This was as Zaitsev expected. He commanded himself to find Thorvald's nest. It's concealed in this level area in front of the wall. It's all so flat—what could Thorvald hide behind? Look. Remember. Think. Feel. Where would you be, Vasily? What would you use for a blind? Fly to that side of the park, then look back over here. Think like Thorvald. What are you behind?

Stop.

There was never any sound from the Headmaster's rifle! The reports from his shots did not sail across the park. They did not bounce off the buildings around us. Kulikov heard nothing. I heard nothing.

Behind? No.

Thorvald was not *behind* anything! He was in something!

Or under. Under!

That sheet of metal. Where is it? There. It lay over a pile of bricks, almost flat on the ground. Innocent, simple, nothing notable about it in a landscape of debris. Zaitsev had seen it so many times he'd grown accustomed to ignoring it. But it was there, in this rounded range of possibility through the hole in the board. The park was finally dimming in the flare's failing glow. Yes, the Headmaster's shooting cell could be beneath the metal, behind those few bricks. Dig a trench under it. Crawl up before dawn.

Be out of the wind. Talk to your assistant ten meters behind you. The assistant stays hidden behind the wall to carry that damned helmet. You're in shadow all day under a metal roof; all you have to do is lie in the dark and fire away, with no worry about reflections off your scope. Surrounded on all four sides, no rifle report will escape such a hole to float the 250 meters across the park. To spot your muzzle flash, an enemy would have to be staring straight down your barrel when you pulled the trigger, exactly the wrong place to be.

Perfect. So perfect that the Headmaster will violate the sniper's first rule of survival: shoot and move. Pull the trigger, then pull out. He's stayed in this cell, first shooting up the medical staff, then Shaikin and Morozov; today he shot Danilov. So many bullets from one spot. He's confident. Yes. Until we drag him out by his feet.

Zaitsev backed away from the plank. He stood straight, looking over the wall to watch the flare crash into the park. The flare fizzled, a tiny volcano for a few seconds, then extinguished. The park was black again.

Kulikov slipped to his side.

Zasitsev said, "He's under that sheet of metal. He's dug a hole under it."

Kulikov did not speak. This was his way of agreeing.

"He'll come back to it tomorrow." It felt good to Zaitsev to stand tall here at the wall. It felt defiant.

Kulikov said, "I'll sneak across the park and take a look. Let's see if his nest is really under the metal sheet. What do you think?"

"No, Nikolay. It's not worth the risk. I think he's gone home for the night, but who can tell? He may have left a guard just in case we try it. Let's leave it till morning. He'll be in there. Trust it."

Though he'd told Kulikov not to crawl out to look under the metal, Zaitsev's imagination slithered over the flat park and under the sheet of metal. There indeed lay Thorvald, peering out through the bricks. Hello, Headmaster. Excuse me. Zaitsev gazed through the Headmaster's scope, back to this side of the park. There, wearing the black cross of the scope, was the head of the Hare. There I am. A nice clean shot, Headmaster. Take it. Congratulations.

Just 250 meters. A bullet covers such a distance in a heartbeat, stopping that heart.

"He won't move," Zaitsev said, turning away from the park. "So we'll have to."

Zaitsev and Kulikov collected their packs, rifles, and periscopes. On his feet, Zaitsev felt the weight and straps of his gear. He sensed a rush of freedom, like a boy again, packed and ready to head out on a hunting trip. He looked into the dirt at the base of the wall. Under the night, he could not see Morozov's blood, but he wished it a farewell. He thanked the spirits of this spot for their help, for their insights. Thorvald had shackled him here for three days. Now he was breaking away.

He walked, Kulikov behind him. The night was quiet save for the grinding of their boots in the dirt and pebbles. He heard his own footsteps, then Kulikov's light steps moving out of sync with his. He tried to lay plans for the next day's confrontation with the Headmaster, but Kulikov's presence close at his rear spooked his concentration, like a bevy of quail flushed from the brush.

He stopped. "Nikolay, please. Wait here for a little while. I want to go ahead alone and do some thinking."

Kulikov sat on his pack.

Zaitsev turned, grateful for the man's loyalty. He stepped along the wall slowly, listening to the rhythm of his lone tread in the frozen dirt. He looked over the wall into the open park. He saw only pale shapes; the night sky bled bits of light. The light from the stars had been his favorite light in the taiga. He once believed that stars were little rents in the sky where the grand brightness of the universe beyond the sun and moon shone through to the earth. His mother had told him the stars were God's ten million eyes watching. God. What role, he wondered, has God played in Stalingrad?

The soft stomping of shelling came from the factories, their distant flashes no help to him here by the park. He rested beside the wall thirty meters from where Kulikov sat. He eased himself down, crossing his legs, and pulled off his mittens. He rolled back his white hood to remove his helmet, then unfastened the top two buttons of his coat. The wind was light, a curtain of cold. He let the chill brush over him. The calm gave the night a distilled purity, a clarity the world does not have when the wind is high. Let the night in, he thought. He breathed deeply to fill his lungs with the cold; let the night speak. The stars, the earth, the cold, even the city, let it in. Join it.

He closed his eyes and exhaled.

"Bai ya nai," he said. God of the taiga. It was a Yakut offering to bring the hunter luck.

He chased his thoughts outward. Thorvald. I know where he is. I've read him. Zaitsev let his thoughts pick up speed. Thorvald. He knows me. So what do I do about it? I must be something else, not me. Not the Hare. Not what he expects.

The cold scratched at his cheeks and neck. It awakened the parts of his body where he carried the instincts and senses he trusted most, from long before—his gut, his shoulders, the back of his neck, and wrists.

Thorvald is expecting the Hare. So I must be something he does not expect. He knows I can be the night, the earth, the ruins.

I am Russian. The city is Russian. He knows all this.

A moan of artillery from the north tolled in the ground. He opened his eyes.

The city is German, too.

German.

I will be German.

He knows all my tactics, all the ones I've taught, the ones described in detail by Danilov. This time I'll use one that hasn't appeared in *In Our Country's Defense*.

I'll use a tactic the Germans themselves taught me.

Zaitsev put on his helmet and pulled up his hood. With numbed fingers, he buttoned his coat and slid into his mittens. He looked into the canopy that twinkled with stars and artillery.

"Thank you," he said to the spirits of the night and the battle.

He walked quickly to where Kulikov waited. "Nikolay, I have an errand for you. It requires your talent for silent movement."

Kulikov answered with a keen look, like a hound eager to track.

"Go," Zaitsev said, thrilled to be in action after so long a time waiting, "to the eastern slope of Mamayev Kurgan. Bring me back a mortar shell."

TWENTY-SIX

THORVALD DRUMMED HIS FINGERS IN THE DIRT. Six dawns in a row, he thought, six days lying in this awful hole. And what do I have to show for my dozens of hours staring across this little park? Nothing but a rabbit who won't come out of his hutch.

Face me, Rabbit. We'll have a contest. Competition targets, clay disks, name it. Whoever is the better shot wins. The loser shoots himself in the head, and we'll be done with it. But let's do it, Rabbit. Enough of this cold crawling down the backs of our necks and dribbling down our ribs all day. Enough of sandwiches and cheeses. It's time for a dark beer and a steak served on bone china and starched linen instead of stale food from a paper bag on a filthy floor.

Look at what you've done now, Rabbit. You've moved thirty meters to the left from where you've sat the last three days. You've carved out a notch in the top of the wall. You must have worked late last night. But just an hour after dawn I saw your ruse. A nice effort, little bunny. It almost fooled me. I believed for a short while that this was your game for today, a test for me. You wanted to know, was I keeping notes on the terrain? Did I have it memorized? Would I spot a small alteration in the contours on your side of the park? Yes, of course, Rabbit. Elementary. Among the first lessons I teach at Gnössen. You forget, I train your kind. Then I remembered, I haven't seen your kind before. You go beyond the lessons; that is your renown. It's why I was called from Berlin to kill you. So I began to look farther than your little notch. Could it be a fake? Something to draw my attention away from another ploy? I had the morning on my hands, why not spend it speculating, yes? And I searched. I burned up my eyes like cheap batteries, scanning every centimeter of your wall. Then five minutes ago, there it was: not quite a flash but a glimmer of light, brighter than the wall. A yellow taint, brass or gold like an old wedding band. Twenty meters to the right of the notch, you've dug a clever little yellow tunnel at the base of the wall. Is that a mortar shell you've slid into the hole? How wily of you, Rabbit. You didn't think I'd see that, did you? Two positions: one obvious, to anchor my attention, another one hidden to kill me. Excellent. You would have passed my class at Gnössen, Rabbit. But with only a second-level grade. Were I your teacher, I would have made you shake a handful of rocks inside your tube to dull its sheen. We all make mistakes, Rabbit; don't feel bad. It was just a tiny falter I couldn't expect a Siberian sergeant to avoid. One can't think of everything, can one?

What's the time? Damn, I've been watching for five hours. It's late morning. The sun is shoving high past your shoulder; it's your advantage, and you haven't made your move yet. You're waiting for a mistake on my part. It won't happen, Rabbit. I've caught you. Just make a move and I'll trigger my trap. Will you take action, or is your strategy to kill me with boredom? How could this be? You're reputed to be a superman. Are you really not a master sniper at all but simply some plucky hayseed from the Urals? Perhaps you're too scared to act. Or worse, perhaps you're a hoax. You don't even exist. Oh, no, that can't be! Zaitsev, a myth? A ruse of the Russian military press, a propaganda trick to whip up morale among the miserable? No, impossible. In fact, *too* possible. Think, Heinz, what evidence have you seen of a Zaitsev? None. The Reds have seen plenty of me. I've made shots that will leave them talking about me for months. But I haven't seen the first round from the Rabbit. One man, one bullet? Could it be a lie, just some tinsel to cover the fact that he never shoots because he doesn't exist? Oh, shit. Shit, is this a joke?

That does it. The next Russian I shoot, I tell Nikki and the generals that I hit the Rabbit and I'm getting on a plane to Berlin. It'll take days before the Red newspapers come out and claim that I missed him. By then, I'll be gone and the generals won't bring me back.

Nikki. I'll take him with me. A gentleman's word is his bond. He'll be able to tell them in Berlin how many times I've crawled into this evil dark nest. I'll keep Nikki close to me, keep my power over him; he won't lie about me. If I say I got the Rabbit between the eyes, he'll be as eager to believe it as me. I'll make Nikki a sergeant because their uniforms look better and I don't want to be around a corporal at the opera. I'll make him my driver, yes, better than a sniper, he doesn't seem to like guns. I'll keep him away from my students at Gnössen. No need for them to hear more than one version of my time in Stalingrad. I'm a teacher, after all. They need to look up to me.

And what if Nikki is right? What if the Russians are indeed readying a colossal counterattack somewhere? What if, while I'm lying in this hole on the edge of this giant scab that used to be a park, I'm not even facing Zaitsev but just some more junior snipers? Perhaps the real Zaitsev is ten kilometers away, preparing to take part in a bigger, more vital mission. Why would they take him out of action and assign him to find just me? Who am I to be so important to command the sole attention of the great Rabbit? It was easy to send me after him; I wasn't

doing anything important, just cooling my heels in Gnössen, in the mornings teaching boys how to shoot other
boys, then knocking down traps in my free afternoons.
Pull! Mark! Ah, Heinz, there is the very real possibility
that Zaitsev is a hoax, a fake, just like that notch carved in
the wall. But it really doesn't matter now whether that's
Zaitsev across the park or any other Ivan. Because some
Red bastard, the next one I see, is going to die. Maybe I'll
bag two this morning, one in the notch and another in the
tunnel. Yes.

And look there, in the notch. Presto. Just when my
patience was wearing thin. There's a helmet. Is there a
head beneath it, or is it just a helmet on a stick? It moves
the way a man moves, smoothly. I think there is a head
beneath that helmet, a head that's alive. For the moment,
anyway, it's alive. I'm going to put a bullet through it. I'll
turn that head into a skeleton key to unlock this casket
I've been lying in. It's my wish granted.

And what of the cunning little tunnel low and to the
right? Is there another head waiting for me there? Move
the reticle down, to the right, let the crosshairs crawl over
the stones. There it is. The tunnel. Shiny, brass. Still
glowing. Look close. No, no one home. But I know someone is there, waiting just out of sight. Now, Heinz, go
back to the helmet in the notch. How long has this one
been there? Does it matter? He's there now and I am
here. I am also there, with him, my eyes touching his
helmet like his own skin. Stay there another few seconds,
clever little Russian. I am stiffening in my coils, girding to
strike. I'll shoot the one in the notch first, the high target.
Pull! Then I'll haul back the bolt and swing low for the
mortar shell. Mark! I'll send off two shots, just so.
Whether the Rabbit is in front of one or the other won't
matter. Any head in either place is going to pop like a
dropped melon. Look to the head in the notch first. He's
bold, this one, with the sun at his back, moving his helmet

in and out of my sight, sliding in and out of my crosshairs.
He can't see me. No reflection comes from my hole; I'm
wearing darkness like the new black uniform I'll wear in
Berlin. What's he looking at? He seems to be . . . there,
that's the barrel of a rifle resting at the bottom of the
notch. He's looking to my left. He thinks I'm over there. A
shot! He just fired at that bunker. Idiot. He thinks I'm a
fool to be in there. Do they think there's no Thorvald?
Like there's no Rabbit? Listen to the sound of his rifle
shot, aimed at an empty bunker, a waste. All of this is a
waste. Well, die Russian, in the bottom of the notch.
Move in one more time and stay there, let me put the
brand of these thin lines across your helmet like a cross
over your grave. But first, Heinz, quick! Take one practice
swing from the notch down to the tunnel. Just like the
trap range. Start high. Pull! Now the bolt! Back, forward,
speed and balance. Now swing low, to the right, there!
Perfect. Mark!

Wait. What is this? Yes, yes, yes. There *is* someone
home in that tunnel now. A circle of glass sitting on top of
a black dot. That's a scope and a rifle looking this way,
into my darkness. So. They've finally figured out my hiding place. And they're getting ready. That shot at the
bunker was clearly another fake to confuse me. Well, my
friend in the tunnel, hold yourself there. Don't move from
behind your scope. I will clear up all confusion in another
few moments.

That scope in the tunnel is watching, waiting for me to
fire first. That is the Rabbit looking through the mortar
shell, I'm sure of it. Pleased to meet you at last, Russian
supersniper. Just in time to say goodbye. Poetic, really,
and heroic in a way; it depends on how the story is told
later.

Perhaps you're hoping to spot my muzzle flash when I
shoot out the head in the notch, Rabbit. Perhaps. That's
likely to be your plan. But will you see *me* here in my

darkness? No. You'll have to make a blind shot, a perfect shot, guided only by a pop of blue light, lit and gone in a fraction of an instant. I don't believe you have that brand of skill. You are more the stalking hunter, the visceral, faithful, stupid man of nature than you are a trained and practiced marksman.

This, then, is the finale of our duet, Rabbit. I'll tell you what: I'll make it into a race. I'll even take a handicap. Here are the rules: If by miraculous luck you're looking in the exact place when I kill your companion with my first shot, I'll show myself to you with my muzzle flash. You'll then have about three seconds to find my head in the darkness before I swing low to find yours in the light. The fastest hands, the clearest eye, and the best shot wins. Wins all.

Ready, Zaitsev? I, Heinz von Krupp Thorvald, the German supersniper, will now display for you what is truly meant by "one man, one bullet" twice over. Pull! The high notch. Mark! The low tunnel.

It's a contest you cannot win, Rabbit.

Now, little helmets in my sights. It's time for Nikki and me to board our flight home. Wings and coffee.

First, the high target. The helmet in the notch.

Let the pulse ease.

The crosshairs. Still. Black. Sharp.

There's a beauty to this.

The target waits. It beckons the bullet, dead center.

Die now, first helmet. The high target.

Pull!

Loud. I pulled the trigger.

The bullet was true.

He's up. There he is.

A man. His arms are spread. He's fallen.

Why did he jump up like that? Strange. He should have gone straight down, crumpled. I know it was a hit.

Heinz! Forget him! The second target. The tunnel.

Find it. Move!

Yank back the bolt. Smooth. Fast. Ram it home.

Swing, swing down, right and low.

Now find the Hare. Find his gleaming tunnel.

Where is he? Find him! Fast!

Too much movement. Damn it!

Where is he?

How much time has elapsed? Too much!

Seconds. Only seconds, Heinz.

Stay calm. He can't see you. Find him.

Stop! There's the mortar shell.

There's his scope, with his soft eye behind it.

The low target. Ease the pulse.

The crosshairs. The beauty.

Mark.

I am finished.

TWENTY-SEVEN

ZAITSEV LAY ON THE GROUND, STOMACH DOWN, his feet spread behind him for balance.

He slid only the first centimeter of the Moisin-Nagant's barrel into the brass casing he'd worked into the bottom of the wall the night before. This was today's trick, a German ploy from the slopes of Mamayev Kurgan. Zaitsev hoped that after dueling for four days, Thorvald would not be vigilant enough to spot this small opening. It had taken him hours of chipping away at the stones to make the shaft for the mortar shell. Kulikov had lent him inspiration, working silently beside him through the cold night. Kulikov's task was to cut a V-shaped notch into the wall with his trenching tool, twenty meters to Zaitsev's left. Neither man exchanged a word until both jobs were completed.

It was a simple idea. Draw the Headmaster's fire with a feint. The gash in the wall was calculated to be so obvious it would be spotted by the Headmaster as soon as the morning light was full enough over the park. This would lock in Thorvald's attention to keep him from blundering onto the mortar shell at the base of the wall to his right. In that small tunnel, pointed directly into his lair, lay the true sting of this day's tactic, the Hare's rifle.

Zaitsev's hope was that if he was staring straight into the darkness beneath the metal when the Headmaster fired at Kulikov, he might spot the muzzle flash. If so, he would risk a blind shot at the flash point. If he missed, he would scare Thorvald out of his position and the duel would surely start over in a different location in the city. As unpleasant a result as that would be, it couldn't be helped. One man, one bullet? It sounded good. But Thorvald was not just a man. He was a killer ghost. It was best to seize on the first, and probably only, opportunity when it presented itself, even if the shot was less than certain. The hunt for the Headmaster had taken several days and lives; it might also take several bullets.

The sun was high now and favored Zaitsev's position, perhaps only for another hour. It's time to move, he thought. The Headmaster will expect something from us while the light is out of the east. Zaitsev laid his cheek on the cool wooden stock. He crept his eye up to the scope, creating as little motion as possible. He swung the crosshairs to the metal sheet, which lay on a pile of bricks. He raised his cheek a millimeter, lowering the center of the cross to the black depth between the bricks, into the dark den of the Headmaster.

"Now," he called to Kulikov.

Zaitsev knew what his partner was doing. A minute before, Kulikov had laid a brick on top of his head and donned his helmet over it, tightening the strap under his chin. The brick lifted the helmet ten centimeters above his crown. Both men hoped this would be enough margin of safety for Kulikov's scalp. They agreed that a helmet jiggling on a stick would not flush out the Headmaster. The helmet had to move naturally; it had to be on a man's head. Kulikov consented to the plan without comment. A brave comrade, Zaitsev thought, and a man confident in his ability to move with precision.

With his helmet raised so, the scheme called for Kulikov to lean in and out of the notch to catch the Head-master's attention with the movement. Then . . .

Kulikov fired the shot, the next step in the plan. The bullet was aimed at the empty bunker to their right, a random round to tweak Thorvald's attention and a message that the Red snipers did not know where his hiding place was. The rifle crack flew past Zaitsev; he tied his thoughts to the sound as if they were a note to a pigeon's leg, to have them flap across the park into Thorvald's hole, where he would read *We don't know where you are, Colonel. You are safe. Come out.*

The crosshairs were like two swords in Zaitsev's hands; he was ready to wield them. He snuggled tighter to the scope. His finger caressed the trigger. Come out, Head-master. You snake. Make a move.

Seconds passed. The crosshairs bounced once. His pulse throbbed in his hands. Ease off, he thought. Don't go to him; let him come to you. Let him earn the bullet.

It's not working. The Headmaster isn't home this morning. He's already gone. Could he have left without finishing our duel? No, never; he hasn't bagged his Hare yet. Or has he? Danilov. Did he think he hit me when he hit Danilov?

No, not the Headmaster. He knows I'm here. Don't be impatient. He's there. He's under the metal sheet, down in the blackness I've erected this cross over. We're knotted together, the two of us. He can't leave. Our eyes and hands are tangled above this park right now and cannot be untied except through death. He's in there. I feel him there.

Zaitsev recalled Baugderis's pink, exploded face and the black blood hardened over the head of Morozov. The Headmaster had shot both snipers through their scopes. Through the scopes, he thought, marking the beginnings of alarm; is he staring at me right now? Are his crosshairs boring into this mortar shell, stretching across my scope?

Has he spotted me, has the sun betrayed me after all my careful steps? These passing seconds—is he using them to wait for his own pulse to settle, to squeeze his trigger with my soft right eye for his mark? Thorvald can do it. I've seen the results. Baugderis, Morozov. I know he can shoot as fast as two men. Danilov. Kulikov. Shaikin. The dummy Pyotr. Was I wrong? Does Thorvald know this mortar shell trick? Did the Headmaster teach this to his boy killers at his Berlin school?

Staring across the crosshairs, Zaitsev winced. Nothing, he thought, nothing but flat blackness. He clenched his teeth.

All right, Thorvald. Come on, damn it! Come on! Let's be done with it! If you see me, show me! Come on!

A faint blue flash winked almost faster than Zaitsev's eye could grasp it. But there it was, deep in the Headmaster's hole.

To Zaitsev's right, Kulikov's feet scuffled in the dirt. The little sniper's rifle clattered on the ground.

Kulikov cried out, "Aaayugh!" He stood, his arms flared out, then fell hard away from the wall. His back thumped the ground; his breath gasped on impact.

Nikolay! The Headmaster shot him! He missed the brick and hit Nikolay!

Zaitsev's hands tried to release the rifle. His cheek pulled a millimeter off the scope. Nikolay! I've got to tend to him. He's down! The bastard shot him!

No! a voice commanded him. No! Stay in place!

He became rigid around his rifle. Nikolay's spirit can't be helped now. The Headmaster. Focus, Vasily.

The flash. It was him.

A second passed. Fear crept up his spine like a wolf, low and powerful. Is another bullet on its way, this one for me, from the Headmaster? Another second ticked on his forehead. I've got to shoot. But I can't. I don't see him, only my eye's memory of the muzzle flash. What if I miss? The Headmaster will answer.

A third second. He held his breath; his heart and lungs seemed to be outside him, big as barns, filled with frozen air and coursing blood. His eye winced once.

The fear leaped onto his shoulders. It clawed and barked around his head and eyes. The fear bit into his neck, and another second passed.

Here, Vasha, take the spear, a voice from the taiga cried in his memory. The fear has power. Kill it and take its power! Take the spear! Do it! You are one of us, Vasha, a hunter!

Yes, a hunter.

In that moment, he stabbed as hard as he could.

There was nothing beneath his crosshairs but black. A blind shot, into the evil eclipse of Thorvald's hole. The fourth second. The last one.

Zaitsev cast a curse into the bullet. The Headmaster thinks his time in the darkness is done. He is wrong.

His darkness is just beginning.

Now.

The rifle snapped into his shoulder, the report cracked in his ears. Beneath the crosshairs, the hole remained clamped shut.

"Did you get him?" Kulikov's voice!

Zaitsev dropped the rifle and spun away from the mortar shell. Kulikov was on his rump, propped on his elbows. The front of his helmet was punched in. His face and the tops of his ears were coated in brick dust.

Kulikov grinned. Zaitsev was dazed. The fear withdrew into the shadows of the forest inside him. Kulikov stepped out from those shadows. All happened at once.

He exhaled. The wind was in his lungs again. He grabbed up a small stone and bounced it hard off his friend's chest.

"You son of a bitch! You're not dead!"

Kulikov played at taking his own pulse. He shook his head.

Zaitsev threw another pebble to make his friend cover his face with his arms.

"Why didn't you tell me you were going to jump up like that?" Zaitsev asked. "It scared the shit out of me!"

Nikolay tilted his head. More rust-colored dust trickled onto his shoulder. He took off the helmet and dumped broken bits of brick into his lap.

"I thought," said Kulikov, "it might buy you another second or two if I made a show of it. Maybe the Headmaster would stop and admire his handiwork. I don't know, it seemed like the thing to do at the moment."

"At the moment," Zaitsev grumbled, pretending to be vexed. But Nikolay might have been right. The Headmaster had not gotten off his second shot in three, even four seconds.

"Well," Kulikov asked, "did you get him?"

"I don't know." Zaitsev shrugged.

Kulikov swept dust from his shoulders.

The Hare laughed. His happiness surfaced at seeing Nikolay unscathed.

"Here." Kulikov tossed Zaitsev a flattened gray slug he'd sifted out of the shards of brick in his lap. "This was sent for you. I think it came out of my rifle."

Zaitsev fingered the lump of lead. He felt the Headmaster's hands on it, just as he'd sensed his presence in the hole beneath the metal. He looked into the sky and tried to understand what had happened, whom he had just faced. The Headmaster. A phenomenal, fearsome man with a rifle. Thorvald has a strong spirit. So do I. That's what we hunted in each other, how he called me and how I heard him in this massive boneyard of Stalingrad. Thorvald's spirit is like tar; if you touch it, your hands will be smeared with it. The bullet in Zaitsev's palm, which might have ended up in his head, felt black as pitch, almost sticky with the death it might have been. He tossed it away.

He looked at the puncture in the front of Kulikov's helmet, an ebony dot directly in the middle of the forehead. Thorvald's shot had been perfect.

Zaitsev reached into his pack for a loaf of black bread.

"We'll wait until tonight, Nikolay," he said, bringing the dark crust to his lips. "Maybe we'll get our chance to drag the Headmaster out by his feet."

"And if he's not in there?" Nikolay asked, reaching for the bread.

"Then," the Hare said, sitting back, "I don't know."

TWENTY-EIGHT

THE PUNCH OF GUNFIRE KNOCKED AWAY NIKKI'S drowsiness.

No! They're shooting at me. Coming fully awake, he tensed to roll over and run. Blood bounded in his temples. He realized suddenly he'd heard only an echo off the high ruined walls.

The shot had not issued from the colonel's hole only ten meters away. The bang wasn't muffled; there was instead a crispness to it, like a field of banners snapping. The shot came from the other side of the park.

Zaitsev. He has fired.

Nikki pressed his chest against the wall. If Zaitsev has at last pulled his trigger, it can only mean the colonel has flushed him out with some trick or other. Thorvald will be answering in another moment. Here it comes. And away we go, home.

Seconds passed, ten perhaps. The quiet kicked at Nikki's stomach. Shoot, Colonel. Kill him. What are you waiting for? Nikki wanted to cry out around the broken back of the wall. Shoot! Get him!

Nikki laid his palms against the stones. He dug his nails into the mortar as if climbing the wall from his knees. Shoot, Colonel. Please.

The answering shot burped out of Thorvald's den. The report broke Nikki's grip on the wall. He released his fingers from the stones and sank back to his knees. He brought his hands to his face and bent his head, almost prayerful. "Yes," he whispered.

Four seconds later, an echo bounced again off the ruins from the opposite side of the park, from the Red snipers.

Nikki's head jerked out of his hands.

How could it be? Two shots from across the park? But the Hare is dead. The colonel drew him out, made him fire first, then punished him, killed him. Who's shooting now? Thorvald missed? No. Thorvald hit somebody when he fired, that's certain. He never misses. It must be the Hare's assistant, yes, that's who it is, firing back wildly in a vengeful rage, the Hare dead beside him, the Hare's brains splattered on his cheek.

Nikki wanted to holler into Thorvald's cell: You got him, Colonel! Are we going home tomorrow? How many sandwiches are left, eh? Let's eat them all!

Nikki turned his back to the wall. He hugged his knees for warmth and gazed up at the mute, mangled buildings across the boulevard. The sun shone brightly on their empty faces. Sad, he thought, these giant husks, remnants of life that can't fall down, dead and still standing. I wish I knew what they know, how to be dead and stay on my feet. It might make dying easier to take. Are you alive enough, buildings, to tell me what you heard, what you saw? Did Thorvald get the Hare? I'm small and behind this wall, I don't know what's happened.

The black windows of the buildings kept a watch like buzzards in a line; they would not wink at Nikki to give him a clue who had survived, the Hare or the Headmaster.

Nikki lowered himself into the well of sleep. There's nothing I can do, he thought. I can't call to the colonel.

He dislikes interruptions. He won't speak to me all day, it's just his way. He's probably napping in there; the action's over for the day, maybe longer.

The November sun weighed on the chilly air. Sit still, he thought. Huddle behind this wall and block the breeze. The stones will warm during the day. Nikki took off his gloves and unwrapped a sandwich.

Time, he thought. Time has a heaviness you can feel when there's nothing you can do but wait, when it sits across your shoulders like a yoke.

NIKKI'S MIND RACED FOR AN HOUR. THE SUN dipped below the horizon. The quiet around him went undisturbed.

Thorvald's hole is the most silent, the blackest part of the world, Nikki thought. What is he doing in there? Is he asleep? Should I wake him? Maybe the colonel has set up another trick to nab the Hare, something in the night. Yes, something to surprise Zaitsev. Thorvald has deciphered some Russian tactic that's going to take place tonight, and he's lying in ambush. That's why we're still here. But the colonel has never worked after the sun goes down; we always leave the park the minute it gets dark. The temperature drops, and I know how he hates the cold. He grumbles like an old woman about it. What is he doing in there?

Nikki kicked his boots on the ground to sting his heels. He rolled to his knees and bounced in a crouch. His hips ached from the cold ground.

The afternoon had been sunny, almost comfortable at Nikki's post facing into the light. Now the heat slipped away from the wall's stones and the earth beneath him, sucked out into the night. The next morning was going to be foggy. Over his father's pastures, fog often followed a starry, cool night. Am I going home? he wondered. How far am I from home? Two thousand kilometers. Come get me in Russia tomorrow morning, fog; land around me, and I'll walk away from Stalingrad under you. I'll walk all the way home at dawn. The fog will cover me, no one will see me. I know where the creek lies on the edge of our property, even in the fog. If you follow the creek, it widens and flows east to the River Elbe. The river flows through low, easy hills that roll like green over young bones. I'll jump all the way over the creek this time. I'm older now. I fell in up to my knees the day before I left for the army. I could jump it easily now, even carrying a pack on my back. The dog will try, too, but he never makes it, misses by a meter. He'll splash in, then swim over and shake. He'll run ahead, scaring up the cows, announcing my homecoming. I'll walk right up out of the haze. The dog's barking will hide my footsteps, so my father won't hear me coming until I'm on the front stoop. He'll send for my sister at the hospital, and while we wait for her we'll eat breakfast together, and we'll talk, not about the war, but about the cows and the dog.

A rumble like a small peal of thunder tapped at Nikki's senses. Not thunder. It was metal, a sheet of metal being jiggled and moved.

Thorvald is pushing aside his metal roof. What's going on?

Nikki crept to the edge of the wall and leaned his head around the stones enough to see the colonel's cell. Two wraiths under the moonlight, men in white camouflage, gripped the sheet above Thorvald's cell and slid it aside. One carried a rifle with a scope. He pointed it down into the hole.

Nikki held his breath. With the metal gone, the moonlight showed only the scuffed bottoms of the colonel's boots. They were stacked; he lay on his side. The soldier with the rifle stepped over the bricks into the hole and kicked. Thorvald's boots rolled over, the black tips pointed

now to the night sky. The second soldier reached down
and tugged to withdraw a handful of papers. He brought
them close to his face beneath his hood and the speckled
moon. He released a few of the pages and kept the rest,
nodding to the other. This man took Thorvald's rifle, the
Russian Moisin-Nagant. With the papers and rifle in their
hands, the two figures bent low and jogged back into the
park, donning the darkness over their white outfits.

Nikki watched the two soldiers fade. Even if he'd
brought his rifle with him, he would not have shot at
them. He could have killed at least one. Perhaps it would
have been the Hare. No matter. It was over.

He walked around the wall to look down into the hole.
Thorvald lay on his back in the Russian dirt, his right arm
raised as if volunteering for something, hailing a cab or
waving farewell from a distance. The hollow in the
ground, exposed now from above, the broken rocks and
bricks lining the wall, the sandwich sack and thermos, a
scattering of white papers, all made Thorvald appear to be
a relic dug up at an excavation, a well-preserved corpse
lying in the middle of his personal effects. The colonel's
white parka was unzipped; his coat within had been rifled.
The left arm lay at his side. The upper half of his right
arm, where his shattered head had come to rest after the
blast of the bullet, was blotched. A large discolored patch
of earth lay beneath the elbow. The white moon looking
down with Nikki worked a vulgar alchemy, drawing the
color out of the dried blood, turning red to black.

Nikki stood; he was high above Thorvald now, the
first time he'd felt this. He sensed no danger standing
up in the park. The Hare was gone. The colonel was
gone. All the guessing, the gamesmanship, the paranoia,
the intent watching, all the twists and bends of the
sniper duel—all was ended. The park had reverted to a
part of Stalingrad; it was no longer a strange place filled

with sweeping, deadly crosshairs but something tired, dismal, and familiar.

He looked at the moon, remote and white, the same moon glowing over his home far away. He wanted to leap away from this corpse in its uncovered crypt. He'd catch the rim of the moon, pull himself in, and crawl through the pearly tunnel in the sky over Russia and Poland and into Germany until he was above the meadows of West-phalia. He'd jump down and ride the snowflakes into the pastures like the gnomes of fairy tales.

Thorvald had been Nikki's only hope of going home. For the week since he'd met Thorvald at the Gumrak air-field, Nikki had dreamed of his father, his sister, and their farm. Nightly his father walked to him and held him with the warm touch of a wish. He looked now at the real city, its dark and evil walls, broken streets, every bit of it a citadel for death, and he realized that this was the home Thorvald had bequeathed him.

Nikki's heart fell into the hole with Thorvald. His dream of home was nothing more now than the moon, a small white token hung against the great blackness over Stalingrad. He turned, resisting his urge to reach down and take the colonel's sandwich sack.

He walked into the night, along the route he and the colonel had taken each of the past three evenings to Lieu-tenant Ostarhild's office. His steps were solitary without Thorvald on some side of him. He searched for his por-tion of grief over the colonel's death, for the officer who'd shown him some trust and kindness. There was nothing, only disappointment. Nikki recognized again the growing ease with which he accepted death; it had crossed his path so often, a groove was worn in him. But the colonel had been special, if only for a week. He'd been a spyglass to let Nikki see far beyond Stalingrad, with stories of Ger-man high life, elite ways, and sandwiches made from still-fresh Berliner cheeses, the opera in evening gowns and dress blacks, the trap-shooting crowd and their oiled shotguns. Nikki wanted to know if he could still feel the passing of a man who'd touched his life before dying. If only he could reach death inside him and lay his hands on it, he could fight it with emotion, drive it away with tears, pound its spell out of his breast with his fists. But the death of Colonel Thorvald did not lift him up out of his soul, just as the white-clad body lying in the park would not rise from its hole.

Nikki felt only the nearness of death. It was like a neighbor you watch day and night, to whom you have never said hello. He was unable to cross the distance, the little alley, to death, to sit with it and embrace it. He was cursed with being a watchman at death's house. He saw the beginning of the end of everything. The war, the soldiers, the nations, all will die, he thought. Everything will die but time. This left him empty, exhausted. Time and me. We will not die. Time and I will go on and on, watching lonely death reap his fields, come and go.

I see now that I have been assigned to time's regiment. Just as well. I have no other duty at hand.

He walked to his basement in the bakery. He did not duck behind cover or stop to listen to the yapping of small arms fire the way he and the colonel had done on their return trips. All the way, until his head lay on his pack, Nikki carried the sensation of being atop a horse that knew its way home. He believed he could have closed his eyes and walked straight from Thorvald's body to his bedroll.

NIKKI WOKE AND GLANCED AT HIS WATCH. PAST eleven o'clock, almost afternoon. He walked across the street to Lieutenant Ostarhild's office. It was empty. The desk was a mess, covered with maps and transcripts of prisoner interrogations. Nikki sat in the lieutenant's chair.

The vantage point gave him a sense of the friendly young officer; he was harried, obsessive, a worrier. The world viewed from behind this desk was closing in.

Nikki pushed through the stacks of papers. Below the first layer of sheets was a calendar opened to the day's date, November 19, 1942. Ostarhild, or someone, had been at this desk early that morning and had left in a hurry, in a flurry of paper.

Hunger snagged at Nikki like a nail catching his clothes. He pondered pulling out the lieutenant's desk drawers to find a snack but thought better of it when footsteps fell in the hall.

He rose quickly. Before he could reach the door, a captain entered. Nikki came to attention but did not salute.

"Sir," he said.

The officer, an older man with a bald pate and glasses, waved in a combination of salute and dismissal. He moved with haste to Ostarhild's chair. He busied himself in the papers.

Without looking up, the captain said, "Yes, Corporal?"

"Sir, do you know where Lieutenant Ostarhild is?"

The captain found one report he was looking for.

"Are you one of his spotters?"

"Yes, sir. Corporal Mond, sir."

The captain set down the page and looked up. His face was as wrinkled and white as balled-up paper. The chair and the desk did this to him, made him fret, just as they did to Ostarhild.

"Your officer is out on the steppe right now, Corporal. Go about your duties."

Nikki did not move. He had no assignment now that the colonel was dead. He wanted to report the end of Thorvald to someone, to conclude the business.

"Sir, I have no duties at the moment. I have just been—"

"Corporal," the captain broke in, "I cannot speak with you right now. But since you're one of Ostarhild's boys, I'll tell you this so you won't hear it secondhand and get it wrong. Maybe you can help keep the panic down."

Nikki shifted his stance. The Russians. Here it comes. The end, the finish of everything.

"At oh-seven-thirty this morning, heavy Red forces counterattacked from Serafimovich in the northwest. Several thousand artillery pieces opened up on the Rumanian Third Army. At oh-eight-fifty, waves of Red tanks and infantry attacked out of the fog. The Rumanians broke ranks and are in retreat. Ostarhild is out there trying to assess the damage."

The captain seemed to be out of information. Nikki waited.

"It appears," the captain said with finality, "the Reds are trying to encircle us."

"Yes, sir."

"Now you know what I know, Corporal. Dismissed."

Nikki looked at the captain for several seconds. The officer returned his gaze, admitting his helplessness.

Nikki shrugged. "Dismissed to where, sir?"

"You know best, Corporal, I'm sure." The captain looked again into the papers.

Nikki reached the door. Behind him the captain spoke in a voice wrung dry as salt.

"Try to stay alive, son," he said. "That's the best I can tell you."

TWENTY-NINE

TANIA SAT IN ZAITSEV'S CORNER, WAITING FOR the party to begin.

A dozen snipers milled about the bunker. Atai Chebibulin delivered a ringing crate of vodka bottles and a stack of chocolate bars, then departed humbly into the night, asking Tania to congratulate the Hare on his victory.

Viktor said again, "He'll be back from his meeting with Chuikov any minute. All of you, keep your hands off the vodka."

Tania took her sniper journal from her backpack. The booklet's bent black cover showed its usage. It had been inscribed forty-eight times.

She stopped at a page bearing Zaitsev's signature. She ran her thumb over the ink of his name, feeling his hands on the page. Nowhere else in his body, she thought, is Vasha's strength so clear, so expressed, as in his hands. Sometimes in his eyes, yes, but they are closed when we make love. Always in his hands. He says he's powerful like a bear cub, which before it's one year old can break a man's arm. He's an artless lover, Vasha is. We probably both are, grappling on the floor under so many coats. But he's a strong lover and sincere, and I give him all I have.

He loves me, though he doesn't say it. I trust him with my life. Would I die for him? I don't know. Would I die alongside him? Yes.

Zaitsev's victory. If Danilov were here, it would've been described in grander terms, Communism over fascism, Russian will over German arrogance, good triumphs against evil. Is it so great, so momentous, that Vasha killed the Headmaster? One stick, one rifle erased from Stalingrad? Does that warrant cheers and toasts? Yes. Thorvald was the Nazis' best, their generals' handpicked hope, and he was crushed. Yes, we can drink to the death of hope for all the Nazis.

Tania heard footsteps outside the bunker. She put her journal away and stood. Vasha entered. He endured the cheers and thumps on his shoulder blades with his eyes locked on Tania's.

She folded her legs and sat again in his corner to tell him to accept the praise: Take the center, Vasha. We'll have our moments later, you and I, in private.

A bottle was thrust into his hand. He held it up to show it off as if holding Thorvald's head and tipped it into a big swallow. He gulped deeply, and the snipers applauded. He swept the bottle from his mouth and leaped up at Viktor to grab him around the neck in a headlock. He buried his nose in the Bear's scalp and inhaled, then gasped out the burn and pep of the vodka.

The others snatched bottles from Chebibulin's box and raised them. Tania laughed and clapped her hands at the toasts.

When the last tribute had been offered, Nikolay Kulikov stepped to the middle of the bunker.

"This," he said, pivoting slowly in the dirt, his palms facing the gathering, "this is the story of the Hare versus the Headmaster. Vasha, if I tell any lies, you shoot me."

"How would I know if I'd hit you?" Zaitsev laughed. "You'd fake it."

This private joke between the two revealed the end of Kulikov's account. He scowled at Zaitsev.

Kulikov told the story: how the Headmaster had been sent by the German high command to kill the Hare. How several comrades—brave Morozov, crazy Baugderis, handsome Shaikin—painted a map in their blood of the spot where the Headmaster waited, across Ninth of January Square. Then, of all unlikely heroes, the pug Danilov had been the key, getting himself shot but giving Vasha the inspiration for the plank of wood and the white glove. The flare at night, scanning the empty tank and bunker and craters and then, finally, the metal sheet across the park where they guessed the viper kept his nest. The subterfuge the next morning with the hollow mortar shell, Kulikov's decoy shot at the bunker, then the Headmaster's answering round striking the brick beneath Nikolay's helmet. How he got the sudden impulse to stand and throw out his wings like a bagged mallard.

"Like this." Kulikov beat his arms in the air for the rapt snipers. "Aaaaargh. He got me!"

With his hands in the air, freezing this moment of his tale in time, Kulikov whispered, "The Headmaster was confused. He hesitated." Nikolay pointed at Zaitsev behind him. Zaitsev laughed. Quiet Kulikov was a wonderful storyteller.

"Vasha zeroed in on the blue flash of the Headmaster's muzzle deep in the dark hole." He let his voice climb. "Firmly, calmly, as only a true hunter could do, the Hare let a few seconds pass, to allow the Nazi's head to settle. The Headmaster was setting up his second shot. He'd got me, and now he was bringing back his bolt for the bullet that would come for Vasha. But Vasha waited with courage until the last possible moment, when he repaid the Headmaster's first and only mistake, the one he made under the Hare's crosshairs. Vasha fired his lone bullet of the duel into the blackness and blasted the Headmaster's unseen head into his sniper journal. Which I signed as witness, of course."

The snipers clapped. Nikolay wasn't finished. At the end of the story was the German's white body and the blackened, blasted face lying in the hole under the metal sheet.

"We pulled the metal sheet back like we were opening a tin of caviar. And I took back my rifle"—he knocked his chest with his fist—"completing my victory."

The snipers waited. Kulikov lifted his bottle. "To Vasha. The best of us all."

The others, even Viktor, repeated the toast and drank.

Zaitsev rose. He thanked Nikolay and the snipers for their help and their own victories against the enemy. Then he made his report to them as their leader.

"Let me tell you what General Chuikov told me tonight. Right now, there are seven hundred and fifty thousand Germans surrounded on the steppe. Yesterday and this morning, a million Russian soldiers, thirteen thousand artillery pieces, and nine hundred tanks staged a counterattack to isolate the German army from its supply lines. The enemy is trapped in an area fifty kilometers long by thirty-five kilometers wide. The Germans are calling it *der Kessel,* the 'cauldron.'

"Stalingrad is the eastern boundary of the cauldron. And though the Nazis have got ninety-five percent of downtown, it's our job to keep them here until they can be finished off or Stalin can force a surrender."

Viktor stood. "Sounds like we still have a job to do, boys." The Bear glanced at Tania and smiled. He did not correct himself to add "and girls." Tania stuck out her tongue. Viktor made a show of pocketing his vodka bottle to take the celebration out into the night with him and to lead the others to do the same.

The snipers rose and filed out, except Tania. She made

no attempt to hide the fact that she was staying behind while the others shook the Hare's hand one more time.

Zaitsev sat next to her.

"While Nikolay was talking," he said, "I wondered just how good Thorvald really was. He must have been phenomenal."

Tania snorted, impatient with this sort of humility, that Vasha would actually pause to admire a German. Vasha marveled that he had somehow beaten the Headmaster. And why not. He was right: Thorvald never missed. The butcher's bill the Headmaster had rung up during his one week in Stalingrad was frightful. But Vasily Zaitsev was the most dangerous man in the Russian army, perhaps the most lethal with a rifle in the world. Was Thorvald better? They would never know, Tania thought. The Headmaster was dead, and that was the measure of his skills on this day.

Zaitsev took her hand. His fingers were warm from all the congratulations. Tania preferred his hands cool at the beginning, fresh to her touch, so she could warm them herself.

"Thank you for the party," he said. "It was a surprise."

"I have more."

He squeezed her hands. "I'm sure. But now I have a surprise for you. Chuikov thinks the Germans are going to try a breakout soon. Tonight, four hares are going to kill Paulus."

Tania's eyebrows went up. "Cut off the head of the Sixth Army and the body will lie still."

"Exactly. Chuikov asked me to lead the mission."

Not a mission, Tania thought. An assassination.

"And which three hares are going with you, Vasha? I hope this is my surprise."

"You'll be my second in command."

Zaitsev told her he'd also selected two new hares from the latest sniper class. Tania knew them both. One, a

Lithuanian Jew, Jakobsin, tall and slender, had dark skin that seemed to sizzle with electricity when he spoke. He's a talker, Tania thought, but she'd seen him quiet and mean. He's strong and can shoot. His eyes, narrow and black, see as straight as crows fly. And a woman, Yelena Mogileva; she'd lived only a hundred kilometers east of Stalingrad on the empty steppe of Kazakhstan. Tania knew little about Mogileva. The woman had said few words during her sniper training. She was skinny, but her hands were big like a man's, with pronounced tendons and blue veins. Her cropped hair, once jet, was graying. Tania couldn't guess the Kazakh woman's age, couldn't tell much about her at all except that she'd definitely handled a rifle before she was handed one in Stalingrad; she was a good shot and could sit unwavering for hours behind her scope. Mogileva had her own reasons for joining the snipers; whatever they were, Tania hoped they were good enough. Why is she coming? Why do we need two women along on this mission? Vasha's teaching her, I suppose, the same way he taught the rest of us. I'm pleased Vasha selected me. He's flattering me, telling me he doesn't consider me a woman in battle. He wants me near him in danger; he trusts me when the time comes for killing.

Intelligence had pinpointed the German Sixth Army's command bunker in the downtown sector. Paulus was reported to be holed up in the Gorki Theater at the south end of Red Square.

Zaitsev checked his watch. "After midnight, we'll each carry two satchel charges. We'll work our way down the riverbank, then slip past the House of Specialists to the rim of the park. Chuikov said that Paulus's offices and bedroom are on the western side of the building. We'll plant the charges at the base of the wall."

Tania knew the rest. She'd done it all before. They'd

424   D a v i d   L .   R o b b i n s

light the eight charges, then scurry under cover of the detonation to the icy edge of the Volga.

"That much dynamite," Tania laughed, making Zaitsev grin, "ought to bring down the house tonight at the Gorki Theater."

SHE WATCHED HIS HANDS SHUFFLING THROUGH the canvas backpacks. He checked each for charges, counted the dynamite sticks, and inspected the wires and connections. He was meticulous; his respect for the implements of death was plain.

Her fascination with the Hare's body moved her, like it had many times. In her mind she saw him naked through his white camouflage uniform. Beneath the faint lantern, his arms and chest were hairless, lean, and blanched as linen. For a short man, his muscles were long; the smooth cords beneath his skin flexed when he set the parcels near the door of the bunker.

"All set." He looked at his watch. "It's almost midnight. Where are they?"

She leaned against the cool dirt wall. Jakobsin and Mogileva would come under the blanket in a few minutes. Those moments until their arrival belonged to her and Vasha.

He moved to the opposite wall. He pressed his back against it, as she had. They looked at each other across the bunker, almost mirror images.

"Do you think," she asked into his eyes, "this will continue?" She reached her hand out and waved it back and forth. "You and me?"

Zaitsev's jaw worked. He said nothing.

"We're soldiers. We're also lovers. The hand does not fit the glove."

"Are you saying it's over?"

"I can't say. I know I'm only truly alive when I'm with

you. I know I'm desperate. For love, for revenge, for this to be over, for this to continue. I'm pulled, Vasha, pulled apart, and I can't make the pieces fit back together."

Tania lowered her face. The lamplight fell from her cheeks to hide her eyes behind the veil of her hair.

"What I'm telling you, Vashinka, is that I'm scared. I'm lost every second. It was easier before, when all there was inside me was hate. Now the battle is inside me, too, between love and hate, and I'm being torn up just like the city. I don't know which I want to win; I fight them both. It's not over. I . . . I just had to tell you I don't know what it is we've started."

Zaitsev walked to her and stopped an arm's length away. She wanted him to touch her; she wanted him to make the decision for her now, to take one side or the other in the battle and win it.

"It would be beautiful, Tanyushka, to love you forever. To marry and live and work beside you. To teach our children how to shoot like their mother, the partisan."

She heard him chuckle at her old nickname. She smiled beneath her shadow.

"I don't know either, Tania. We bathe in each other's life every night, and in the morning we go out and swim up to our necks in death. It's strange and twisted and spinning, and I can't catch it to take a good look at it. All I can do is let time and the fates figure it out, because they're the only ones who know what's going on with the world and with you and me."

Tania raised her head. It would be beautiful, he'd said.

"And what," she asked, "is it you want?"

Zaitsev seemed to answer the question inside his head first. Approving of the words with a nod, he spoke.

"To love you forever. To never let you go."

Tania's breath snatched in her breast.

Zaitsev reached for her hand. He pulled her forward,

away from the wall. There is the strength, she thought, in the hand.

So. He loves me. Then he should know me. I will open up to him, this one man.

Smiling close to his lips, she asked, "Do you remember, Vasha, when I said I had more surprises for you?"

His grin curled lasciviously. "Tania, we don't have time. Not right now."

"We have time for this one. I should have told you sooner. I was afraid you would send me away, or that Danilov would take me out of the hares. But now I have to tell you. Because of what you just said."

Zaitsev crinkled his brow. "All right. Tell me."

Tania pulled back from his grin to gauge all of his face. "I'm an American."

She noted no movement of his eyes or his arms around her waist. He stayed impassive, his body stock still; the hunter, she thought, waiting, always waiting.

"No," he said, "you're not."

In English she answered, "Yes, I am, you cute little Siberian. You have no idea what I'm saying, do you?"

"Tania, you're speaking English."

She returned to Russian. "We do that in America."

"You're not American."

"I am. My parents are Russian. They live in New York now."

Zaitsev began to swell with this; Tania sensed him on the move, the hunter rising from cover to engage.

"What are you doing here?"

"Fighting."

"Are you a spy?"

Tania slapped his chest with an open palm. The knives, pistol, bullets on him all rattled.

"No!"

"Then how did you—"

Tania bridged his lips with a raised finger.

"When there's time, Vasha. But you understand why I couldn't say anything before, and why you have to keep this our secret. If the *politrooks* find out, they'll make me a hero, just like you, but only in newspapers. They won't let me fight. Please say it's all right. Please."

Zaitsev shook his head. At first Tania thought that he might reject her or the idea that she could be foreign, not Russian. But he made the head shake comic, an overblown gesture, rattling his brains hard, with a smile.

"Yes, Amerikanushka," he said, feigning dizziness with crossed eyeballs. "Yes, it's all right."

He straightened out his eyes and pulled her to him more tightly. "When the war is over, can we go to live in Florida?"

Tania laughed heartily at this.

The sounds of boot steps slipped past the blanket in the doorway. Zaitsev let her go and stepped back. He shrugged. See, he seemed to say, I have to let you go so soon.

No, you don't, Tania thought. She rose to her toes and thrust her face quickly at him. Just before he could avoid her, just when the blanket lifted, she kissed him with a quiet smack of her lips.

There, she thought. The moment needed to come full circle; it had to be closed with a kiss, even a small one.

She stood quietly, her hands behind her at parade rest while he addressed the two new hares. The tall dark man and the thin woman had come only one step into the bunker. Their faces showed their awe at being included on this foray with the Hare himself.

Zaitsev did not look at her until all four of the snipers had loaded up their rifles and explosive packs. While the two new hares were filing out the bunker door, he mouthed the question "New York?" to her behind their backs. She grimaced at him and mouthed back, "Stop it." Like this, with serious miens now in place, Zaitsev and

Tania walked up beside Jakobsin and Mogileva to go out
into the Stalingrad night to assassinate General Paulus.

The four burdened snipers picked their way down the
Volga cliffs to the ice. They moved crisply along the high
limestone wall. The night was thinned by a wedge of
moon shining behind the clouds like a peeking child.
Tania imagined the landmarks they passed beneath,
checking them off on a memorized city map. The beer
factory. The state bank. The House of Specialists, which
marked the southern extreme of the Sixty-second Army's
beachhead along the Volga. Ahead one kilometer was the
main ferry landing, in German hands now. Tania remembered floating past it clinging to a timber with Fedya and
Yuri in the burning river. This night, she returned as a
sniper on a secret mission with the famous Hare, who
loved her, who never wanted to let her go. Who wanted to
live with her in warm, sunny Florida, America.

To her left, gossamer light shimmered on the icy Volga.
The river was black and cold. But above and to her right
the city cast down a heat like a match held near her
cheek. The sticks are still up there, she thought. The city
felt as if it were burning, the flames leaping out of its
entrails just as they had the first night she'd seen Stalingrad from the opposite bank.

The battle continues here and across Russia, she
thought. So long as the sticks live on our soil, there's still
a job of killing to do.

Forget Florida, America.

The hate had ambushed her again. It's so strong in me,
so solid, she thought, surprised how quickly it reared to
the surface. The part of me that does not hate is so thin,
less than my skin. I can almost stand back and look at the
hate. I can describe it, touch it, like a statue inside me.
The statue grows; it's filling me up. The hate has become
me. Oh, Vasha, I want . . . I want. But the hate is all of
me. Every step we take on this ice, every crunch of my

boots, I hear the guns, see the bodies jerk and fall, pile upon pile. Will they never stop falling?

The Kazakh woman stumbled ahead of her. The noise laid the whip to Tania's temper. "Get up," she mumbled; all the jocularity and tenderness she'd shared with Zaitsev in the sniper's bunker only an hour before had dissolved.

But the sound of her own voice broke the spell of hatred like the snap of a hypnotist's finger. The quick spur of anger at Mogileva returned Tania to the night chill, the rifle and dynamite packs slung across her shoulders, the mission and the line of snipers walking in front of her.

The abrupt release swirled in her stomach. Just walk, Tania thought. Don't think. Just follow the tall man in front of you. Vasha's at the head of the line. Vasha will take care of it all. He'll point you at the Germans and let you kill them. Tonight, tomorrow, and again, just follow Vasha. Stay close to him. All of life that is not war and hatred will wait. Just stay close to Vasha.

The thought of closeness touched Tania. Stay close to him, she repeated. Stay with Vasha.

Deep inside, in the center of the hardness that was her pain, a thrill hovered like a hummingbird in her breast. You are alive, Tania, it said. You move, you live, you love. Just stay alive.

In that suspended second, Tania knew the beating warmth of a heart that had not turned hard, a heart that did not belong to the statue of hatred but was hers, soft and quickened and hers.

Ten meters ahead, Mogileva tripped and fell forward. Out of the woman's boots, like from a rocket, exploded a blast of orange light. Sand and ice ripped out of the ground, riding the detonation. Tania froze, wondering even while shrapnel from the mine clawed into her stomach if she had found love too late.

She fell onto her back, her arms spread wide as if in greeting. She could not move; a weight pressed on her chest and abdomen, crushing her to the ground. Her mouth was engulfed in thirst, but she could not swallow. A blue spot like a welder's torch hovered in her eyes. She felt nothing. Then came the strong coursing of her pulse and something slipping out of her stomach, a rising heat, as if someone had left a door open there into the cold night.

Slowly the weight was lifted and laid beside her. She lolled her head to look at Jakobsin. The length of his white front was blackened and torn. Smoke ghosted from his tattered face and chest.

Hands dug beneath Tania's shoulders. Her head was lifted into a lap; a jumble of arms and legs gathered her in. She struggled to halt her rolling eyes. The rising in her stomach called her to come down there, to leave through the open door. No, she thought. In a little while. Let me stay a bit longer.

She heard the voice of Vasily Zaitsev. She could not break out of herself to hear what he was saying. His hands were under her head, but the hands were not strong enough somehow to keep her eyes still. Where is he, she wondered? He is all around me.

A shaft of agony leaped from her stomach and rose to her throat. She opened her mouth to cough it out. Warm ink burbled on her breath and ran down her cheeks.

Tania could not move, though her senses reeled in a tempest of confusion. She closed her eyes to shut it out. Too much, she decided. Too much going on. Are these Vasha's hands? Where is he?

The ground disappeared beneath her. She was turned to her side; her head and her right arm dangled, pointing at the earth. Let me lie back down, she thought. It was warm and quiet, and I felt pain only once.

Tania became aware of a pressure against her stomach. Something was tight against her there; the warmth escaping out of her had stopped. Now there was only pain, the stabbing of a thousand blades deeply into her, past her spine, out into the night like the glow from a flame. She was burning. The torment kicked at her in a rhythm, pounding like the stomping of boots.

The pain cleared her faculties. She was alive, yet— Oh, it hurts! What happened? Panic circled her senses like a jackal. I'm wounded, in the stomach, an explosion. Pain and blood. Jakobsin dead. Mogileva. A land mine. The blast. What's happening? Where is Vasha? Arms are under me, Vasha's arms, legs running. Oh, the steps hurt! Go slower. No, run! Run with me, don't let go!

The salt taste of blood filled Tania's mouth. In her midsection, the ache threatened to envelop her. She opened her eyes.

Zaitsev holds me to him. He presses against me, closing my wound with his chest. Run, Vasha! He's my bandage; his life holds mine inside me while we run.

Stay close to him, Tania. Stay alive.

Oh, run, Vasha, run!

Tania swished her tongue to clear her mouth. A dribble spilled over her lips.

In English she murmured, "Run."

Zaitsev's gait slowed. He spoke. His breathing was fast and heavy but his words were clear.

"Stay with me, Tanyushka. We'll make it to the hospital."

Tania could form no answer. She'd spent her strength. So many things to say, and all she could utter was "run" in the wrong language.

She began the slide down into her body, into the joggling pain, to splash in it, then to slip beneath it into unconsciousness.

THIRTY

SHE MOANED ONCE, TERRIBLY, WHEN HE STUM-
bled. He righted himself quickly from his knees, never
letting go the pressure, keeping his bloody chest pressed
into Tania's open gut.

Zaitsev ran again. The sand hissed under his skimming
boots, the sound mingling with his pounding breath. His
mind swerved between panic and focus: Tania's limp
weight in his arms terrified him, and her blood was running into his boots.

He tried to make himself blank, to drive forward like a
machine beyond thought or fatigue. Images hurled themselves at him, all of Tania—sleeping, naked, laughing,
aiming her rifle, racing beside him in the flashes of explosions. He pushed through them, popping the memories
like bubbles until the night was empty of all but the body
in his arms and the running.

He came to a barbed-wire checkpoint, dodging a shattered horse cart on the dark beach. Pulling aside a rickety
gate to let him through, the guards said nothing. He
regained his pace, and a voice shouted after him, "Go!"

The medical station was fifty meters ahead in the base
of the limestone cliff. It was where Shaikin had lain
clutching his neck. Shaikin had died in that cave.

Zaitsev pushed through the blanket in the doorway to the medical station. He stood panting in a short hall; the walls and ceiling were built from timbers buttressed by metal beams. A bare light bulb swung from a hanging wire. Three soldiers lay on stretchers in a line on the floor. A nurse in green fatigues bent over the soldier farthest from Zaitsev.

Now that he'd reached the field hospital, Tania felt heavy in his arms. His panic spurted at the thought of releasing her. She was going to be given over to this nurse who hadn't even turned around to see him holding her. He swallowed and spoke.

"We need help."

The nurse lifted her head. Like a winded horse, Zaitsev chuffed hard through his nose. He knew his face must show his terror.

The nurse moved to him, her hands reaching to support Tania's head. "Lay her down here," she said.

The nurse pulled Tania's head to guide Zaitsev to an open space on the floor. He wrapped Tania tighter in his arms.

The nurse saw the madness. "Sergeant."

He did not move.

She spoke sternly. "Sergeant. Lay her down. I must look at her wound."

"Where's the doctor?"

The nurse checked beneath Tania's eyelids while she talked.

"He's in surgery. I'm the triage nurse. He'll be with her as soon as he can. Put her down."

Triage. This woman decides who goes before the doctor. If I lay Tania down, she'll die on the floor. She'll die waiting in line behind these stretchers.

The nurse stepped back. She seemed to be calculating Tania's chances from what she could see while Zaitsev

held her, looking at the amount of Tania's blood on him.
She pointed at the floor.

"Lay her down or she'll die in your arms."

The words stung him. He knew death, and he knew
this nurse was wrong.

"No."

Behind Zaitsev, a snap sounded. Another snap, like
plastic, then a voice.

"What's going on here?"

The nurse kept one hand beneath Tania's head and
motioned with the other.

"He won't put her down. I have to look at her. She's
bad."

The doctor threw two splotched surgical gloves into a
bin. The man was old, the oldest Zaitsev had seen in Stalingrad. He was tall and thick-waisted, with his head
shaved bald. His blue eyes were rimmed in exhaustion.
The doctor's white apron was fresh, barely soiled with
blood. His stoop disappeared when he held out his arms
to Zaitsev.

"Give her to me. We'll see what we can do."

Zaitsev balked, though he felt a surge of faith in the old
man. His arms ached in their lock around Tania.

The doctor shook his head, solemn as a great oak.

"She won't die in my arms either, son. Give her to me."

The doctor touched Tania. Zaitsev lowered his arms to
let her body roll back from his breast. The nurse stayed at
Tania's head; Tania's arms flopped when the doctor took
her.

Zaitsev looked at the dripping rip in Tania's coat. It was
big enough to put his fist into.

"Doctor." He intended to plead somehow, but the old
man and nurse had already assumed all of Tania's weight
and turned from him. They laid her on the floor.

The doctor's hands flew at Tania, pecking at her like
two white chicks. The nurse returned to the line of

stretchers. She knelt at all three; when she was done, she called to the doctor, "Stable." To the man on the last stretcher, the nurse leaned close and mumbled.

The doctor unbuttoned Tania's coat and tunic. With scissors he sliced through her undershirts, pulling aside the burgundy pieces like a velvet curtain. His hands and apron began to streak with red.

The wound jumped at Zaitsev. A pit the shape and size of an open mouth was torn in the left side of her abdomen, below the rib cage. Poking out of the hole was a pink, veined glob; the pressure inside her body had caused part of her small intestine to boil through the opening. Pulses of blood escaped around the edges, dribbling down her side to pool on the floor.

The nurse returned to the doctor's side. Zaitsev moved behind her. Tania's face was waxen; her eye sockets and cheeks were shadowed as though rubbed with charcoal. Her face stunned Zaitsev; it looked hollow, like a skull.

The nurse slapped a gauze sheet in the doctor's outstretched hand. He clapped it over the wound and pushed down. He spoke urgently. "Lift her again."

Zaitsev stepped between the doctor and nurse and dug his hands under Tania. He tried to be careful.

The doctor squawked at him. "Come on, boy!"

They carried Tania into a large room off the hall. Two tables held the center, both ringed by glaring electric lights hoisted on poles. The low grumble of a gasoline-powered generator came from somewhere in the walls. One table was empty and covered with a fresh white sheet. On the other table a soldier lay unconscious; beside him, a second nurse wrapped gauze around the stump below his right knee. His detached leg was bundled in cloth on the floor, still in its boot.

Zaitsev laid Tania on the table. The doctor took his hands from the bandage above her wound to put on clean plastic gloves; the nurse pushed down on the gauze in his stead. With her free hand she searched under Tania's chin for a pulse. Zaitsev backed away from the table and bumped into an elevated tray of surgical instruments. They rattled, but none spilled. The nurse and doctor ignored him, busying themselves with preparatory movements and intense chatter. The doctor asked rapid-fire questions, and the nurse responded in one- or two-word bursts.

The doctor moved to the middle of the table to swab Tania's naked torso clean. The nurse removed the bandage from the wound and threw it in a bucket beneath the table. With another swab, she painted an orange coating around the opening where the balloonlike intestine was sticking out.

"Ether?" the nurse asked.

The doctor wagged his head no.

Without an order, the second nurse shut off the lights at her table. She left the amputee soldier and came to stand beside Tania opposite the doctor and the triage nurse. The doctor examined the gleaming tools at his elbow while both nurses donned surgical gloves.

Zaitsev drifted to a corner behind the old man. He expected to be asked to leave the surgery room; he was ready to refuse. The doctor and nurses leaned over Tania and did not even look at each other while they worked.

The doctor held out his hand. A nurse selected a scalpel from the tray and put it in his palm. He drew the knife down Tania's abdomen, crossing the center of the wound. With another stroke, he sliced the corners of the hole to widen it.

The nurses on either side of the table slipped their fingers beneath the flaps of flesh the doctor had laid open and eased them back. Zaitsev felt himself swelling with the urge to push the three of them away from Tania and take her in his arms again. His dread pulled him a step forward.

Wet loops of Tania's small intestine filled the gaping hole. The doctor pushed it about with his fingers and bent his head.

"A few small lacerations," he mumbled to his nurses. "We can come back for these." The women did not move.

The old man tugged the mass aside and probed under it. He held out his hand again. Another scalpel filled it. The nurse beside the doctor sponged blood from the living crater.

Zaitsev watched the doctor and the women work with swift certainty inside Tania. Zaitsev himself was no stranger to the insides of living things. He'd skinned a thousand animals in the taiga, buried his hands in their viscera, yanked them out, and thrown them to his dogs. So long as he kept his eyes on the surgery, on the hands of the doctor, on the exposed organs, his anxiety stayed in check. It was when he looked at Tania's blond hair draped on the table, her hands quiet as wood beside her, that his own gut quivered.

Months before, the moment he'd begun killing in Stalingrad, Zaitsev had reconciled himself to dying. It was the commerce of battle; he risked his own life in order to take others. But he'd not anticipated dying in pieces. Tania seemed the biggest part of him; if she died on this table, that part died, too. He'd be left alive without her, gutted, then stranded in an icy landscape to survive somehow without her passion and heat.

And just before this terrible thing happened, such news. An American. What kind of a woman was this, to come so far, to fight so hard and give so much for Russia, from America? What kind of woman? Zaitsev quietly shook his head.

The doctor dug the scalpel deep into Tania. The triage nurse laid a clamp in his gloved palm, now glistening like a ruby. The doctor wriggled his wrists as if tying a quick knot. One of the nurses lifted a pail from the floor. The doctor pulled up and held Tania's red spleen in both hands like a gob of mud. He dropped the organ into the bucket.

Zaitsev shuddered. He balled his hands into and out of fists. His fingers were still tacky with Tania's blood.

The nurse opposite the doctor leaned to look down into Tania. She nodded at the doctor. Again he held one hand out for a clamp, then flicked the scalpel. With a twist he took from Tania her left kidney. This, too, he dropped into the bucket.

A fountain of blood shot from the cavity. The doctor stepped back in surprise, then dove with both hands into the hole. Blood sprayed uncontrolled for several seconds until the doctor quelled it. In the silence after the shock, the doctor and nurses looked at each other through red, dripping masks.

"Clamp it! Clamp!" the doctor commanded.

The triage nurse stabbed her hands down beside the doctor's. In a moment, they were done. The doctor turned from the table to wipe his face with a linen. Zaitsev saw Tania's blood clinging in the wrinkles around his mouth and eyes.

The doctor, vibrant and sure moments before, had become old again. Speaking to Zaitsev, he seemed tired and sad.

"A piece of shrapnel tore up her spleen and kidney. She could live without them. The best thing to do was remove them."

He wiped at his eyes with the napkin. Zaitsev said, "Yes."

The doctor glanced back at Tania. Zaitsev looked with him, visualizing again the red liquid pillar that had leaped from her middle.

"The shrapnel was imbedded in her left kidney. The tip of it was protruding from the rear of the kidney. It had perforated the aorta. I didn't see it. When I took the kidney out, the aorta ruptured."

Zaitsev said only, "Yes."

"Sergeant, I've done what I can."

Behind the doctor, the two nurses released their grips on the flaps of Tania's abdomen. They stepped away from the table in unison, waiting beside the unconscious body in a silent and final tableau.

Zaitsev would not let it be final.

"You're not letting her die."

The doctor sighed. "It has nothing to do with me."

The old man turned away but stopped and looked back at the sound of the hammer clicking on Zaitsev's pistol.

The gun was leveled at the doctor's heart. Behind him, the nurses took another synchronized step backward.

"You told me she wouldn't die, Doctor. You can save her."

The doctor pursed his lips to compose his answer. No fear showed in his eyes from the danger aimed at him. He lifted his head to speak as if addressing a student.

"Sergeant, this patient you brought me has lost a spleen, a kidney, and a lot of blood. I don't have any stores of blood to replace what she's lost. All we can do this close to the front line is stabilize the wounded until they can be moved across the river. The tear in her aorta can be repaired. It will take me twenty minutes to do so. But with the blood she's lost already, the kidney she has left has probably been irreparably damaged. If it hasn't, it will be before I can return blood flow to it. She will go into renal failure and die."

Zaitsev did not lower the weapon. Tania was alive on the table and the doctor must return to her side.

"She will die, Sergeant. And in the twenty minutes I spend stitching her back together, it's also possible that one of the wounded men waiting in the hall may also die. Can you live with that?"

Zaitsev looked at Tania on the table. Her heart continued to beat; it was in a trench, in dire trouble, fighting to live. Those soldiers lying on stretchers in the hall were in their own trenches. He was not here for them.

"I have no choice," he said, raising the gun to the doctor's head. He spoke to Tania, to tell her he was coming. "I love her too much to have a choice."

The doctor glanced back at his nurses. They stood motionless, white as painted angels. The old man removed a glove and rubbed his hand over his bald head as if to warm it like an egg, to hatch what he should do next. He looked at Zaitsev's pistol.

"If you're going to wave that gun near my patient, Sergeant, please sterilize it."

He peeled off the other glove and threw the pair into a corner. When he returned his eyes to Zaitsev, the gun was holstered.

The doctor spun on his heels to the table. He was animated again, grabbing fresh gloves and snapping into them. With his hands raised, he announced to his nurses, who'd jerked into action when he did, "He loves her, ladies."

The nurses pulled back the carved sheets. Again they exposed Tania's insides, working without words. Blood-soaked sponges and gauze littered the floor beneath the table. The nurses daubed sweat from the doctor's face with bandages. Zaitsev's back ached; he was afraid to move, afraid he might alter some fragile dynamic in the room. Once, Tania groaned. Zaitsev gritted his teeth, longing to crawl into her unconsciousness, to stand beside her and battle their way out together or die shoulder to shoulder.

At last, the doctor clutched a needle threaded with gut. He dipped into the hole and pulled out and snipped. He sewed like this for a long time, seeming to repair a dozen fissures inside Tania. When he was done, he stood back from the table and took off his plastic gloves. The triage nurse began stitching Tania's skin, closing her wound.

The doctor came close. Zaitsev tried to read the man's blue eyes, hidden beneath tufted white brows. The doctor looked into Zaitsev's face, then glanced away. His hands rose and fell, as if weighing something.

Zaitsev looked at the surgeon's hands, the fingers long and wrinkled, like twigs. Have these old hands saved Tania? He wanted the doctor to report quickly on Tania's condition, but he could see the man was picking his words carefully. Why? Zaitsev wondered. How bad is the news?

He prodded. "Doctor?"

The old man dropped his hands—their work seemed done for now—and dug them into his coat pockets.

"I put everything back in order," he said. "She's in shock. I can't say how long it will last. One or two days, I suspect."

"When she wakes up?"

Zaitsev watched the man inhale.

"If the remaining kidney survived the surgery, we'll know. She'll have to urinate. If the next forty-eight hours passes and she doesn't make water, conscious or not, she's dying and it cannot be stopped."

The nurse completed the last black stitches on Tania. Two straight lines intersected on her belly, leaving on her the dark mark of the crosshairs.

The old man laid his hand on Zaitsev's collar. He patted once; the touch was light.

"Remember, Sergeant," he said. "whatever happens to your friend, she has no choice, either."

The doctor walked away; his stoop reappeared across his shoulders. Two white-clad orderlies entered the surgery room and lifted the stretcher of the soldier whose leg had been cut off. The soldier's head tossed; he was awakening. The orderlies walked past the soldier's amputated leg and carried him out.

The nurses clicked off the lights around Tania. One followed the orderlies and the doctor out of the room. The other, the triage nurse, returned to the front hall.

Zaitsev walked behind the triage nurse into the hall. She kneeled beside the soldier lying on the nearest stretcher. The man's chest was circled in gauze. The nurse lifted his eyelids. She peered into the eyes for only a moment; she'd become skilled at recognizing death. Without looking at Zaitsev, she stood and moved to the next stretcher. This soldier greeted her with an outstretched hand.

Zaitsev put his palm on the corpse's cool forehead. The man had been older than he, a peasant, judging from the rough skin and thick fingers. Zaitsev reached beneath his own coat to the pocket of his tunic. He removed the medallion given to him by Chuikov, the Order of Lenin, and pinned it on the silent breast.

IN THE SMALL RECOVERY WARD, ORDERLIES IN white smocks slipped in quietly almost every hour to lift the wounded from the room's four beds onto stretchers, to carry them out for evacuation. Zaitsev heard a few of the soldiers whimper when they were moved. Others, the ones resting after surgery, he watched wake groggily to discover parts of their bodies lopped off or bandaged and searing. Tania was left alone. He sat beside her—he had not released her hand since she was laid in the bed.

The doctor visited Tania's bedside the morning after she left his surgery table. He pulled back her blanket. He reached his hand up between her naked legs to feel the bedsheets there, her pubis and her thighs. They were dry. He looked beneath her eyelids and took her pulse and temperature.

The doctor looked down at Zaitsev.

"Has she moved at all? Spoken?"

"No."

"Have you eaten?"

"No."

The old man patted Zaitsev's shoulder. Again, the touch was light, almost fragile.

"You won't be any help to her if you pass out from hunger, Sergeant. I'll send you some bread and cheese. Please eat."

Zaitsev accepted the food from an orderly, though he ate with only his free hand. Tania lay motionless beside him. Her shallow breathing and her hand, which several times trembled, were the only clues to her clinging life.

He searched for ways to send messages to her. He laid his head down and spoke softly in her ear to tell her stories: of hunts they'd shared, the first time he'd laid eyes on her in the Lazur and how beautiful she'd looked, the ice house they'd blown up, the first time they'd made love. That he wished she'd been beside him when he'd dueled Thorvald, that it probably would have been the partisan and not the Hare who killed the Headmaster.

With his finger he drew pictures on her palm of deer and wolves; he sketched bull's-eyes and faces and the rising sun of Florida, America. He squeezed her hand in rhythms. He held her hand to his cheek and his lips. He wiped away his tears with her thumb.

Every few hours, Zaitsev felt under the blanket for moisture, the way the doctor had done. Each time, when he found her dry, he felt parched himself. It's such a simple thing, Tanyushka, he thought. Just make water and save your life.

The first time he held up the blanket, he touched her bandages. He remembered the pink and red turmoil he'd seen beneath them, the bits of her sliced away and tossed into a bucket. He lowered the blanket and wept.

Tania's coma crossed into a second night. Zaitsev rested his head on the bed. Once, an orderly jiggled his arm to wake him, then lifted a half-full urinal left beside Zaitsev's chair. The orderly smiled hopefully, but Zaitsev shook his head. The urine was his, not Tania's.

Zaitsev was dozing when her hand twitched. Without lifting his head, he pressed back. When her fingers imitated the squeeze, he raised his face to see her looking at him.

"Hello, Vashinka."

He had no words ready.

"Tania, I . . ." He stared in wonder. Pink had chased some of the pallor from her face. "How long have you been awake?"

"Not long."

He held her hand in both of his. "I stayed here, Tania. I never left."

She tried to bring her other hand around to cover his, but something stopped her. The effort made her wince, but she said through it, "I know."

Tania opened one of his palms. She dragged her finger around it in two circles and dotted the center for a bull's-eye.

Zaitsev brought his lips over hers. Her lips were dry.

She whispered into his cheek. "I'm in a lot of pain, Vasha. Am I dying?"

Zaitsev buried his eyes in her hair. He nuzzled her. If she's dying, the doctor said, it cannot be stopped.

"I don't know, Tania." He wasn't sure what to tell her. "You lost a lot of blood. They took out one of your kidneys."

Tania looked at the ceiling. She nodded as if she knew what he would say next. He remembered she was a doctor's granddaughter.

"We've been waiting for the other kidney to start working."

Two orderlies entered the ward bearing a wounded captain to the bed farthest from Tania. His neck and shoulder were wrapped in fresh white gauze. The man was conscious.

"Careful," he said to the orderlies lowering his stretcher. The officer propped himself up on his good arm to help the orderlies shift him from the stretcher to the bed.

"Damn," the man said through gritted teeth. He sucked air.

"Vasha . . ." Tania licked her lips. "I'm thirsty."

Zaitsev stood to get an orderly's attention. His hand left hers. She grabbed for him, grunting in pain.

"Vasha. Don't . . ."

He looked into her wracked face. He wrapped his fingers around hers and felt her rising strength.

"Tania?"

She smoothed the ache in her eyes. "Don't . . . let go."

Zaitsev smiled and sat. Time and the fates, he thought. I want to stay. To never let her go. How long will the fates let me stay? Do they care what I want?

"Orderly. Some water here."

One of the orderlies beside the wounded captain left to fetch the water. The other one folded the officer's stretcher.

The captain lurched to his good shoulder to lie so that he could look at Zaitsev and Tania. His big head was shaved slick, and light reflected off his pate. The man had a large jaw like a horse.

"Damned unlucky," he said. "She going to be all right?"

"Yes, sir," Zaitsev answered.

"Me, too. Bullet went clean through." The captain looked around the ward. "Glad just to keep my arm in this place." The man grimaced and lay on his back. He kept talking. "Took twenty thousand prisoners yesterday. Germans were damned surprised when we jumped up behind them."

The orderly came with a cup of water. Zaitsev held Tania's head up to drink. Water dribbled down her chin when she swallowed. He dried her gently with his sleeve.

Tania laid her head on the pillow. Her eyes were closed.

"We're winning," the captain said, then fell silent.

THREE

THE CAULDRON

THIRTY-ONE

"EVERY SEVEN SECONDS A GERMAN SOLDIER DIES in Stalingrad. One . . . two . . . three . . . four . . . five . . . six . . . seven. Every seven seconds a German soldier dies in Stalingrad. One . . . two . . . three . . ."

The man beside Nikki got to his feet. He walked to the radio, which sat on a workbench. He tuned in the other military station.

None of the dozen soldiers on the factory floor moved. They sat, each man huddled into himself. The station came in.

". . . five . . . six . . . seven. Every seven seconds . . ."

The soldier shouted, "God in heaven! What happened to Lale Anderson's show?"

Another soldier lifted his eyes. "The Reds jam the broadcasts. It comes and goes. She'll be back on in a little while. Just sit down."

"God in heaven," the standing one mumbled again. He walked out the door into the neighboring shop room.

Nikki looked about him. Only that morning, Christmas Eve of 1942, he'd linked up with this motley squad in the depths of the Barricades factory. With these men, Nikki had spent the day improvising Christmas decorations. A small tree was fashioned out of metal rods wrapped together with wire. Cotton balls from medical kits served as bulbs. Stars cut out of colored paper hung from the iron boughs, and cups of oil and water with a wick of twisted threads served for candles beneath the tree.

The soldier who'd walked out in disgust at the jamming broadcast had arrived two hours ago. He, like Nikki, was one of the thousands of German nomads set loose over the city by the demise of their units. This soldier—Nikki did not know his name—had retreated from the outer reaches of the Cauldron on the steppe. In his platoon of engineers, he'd been the last man alive. He wandered east to the city center. When he could stand no more cold, the whipping weather drove him indoors. He walked through the Barricades, unsure of what he was searching for; feeling only a growing hunger and weariness. The men of this squad, as they had with Nikki, invited the engineer to join them for a Christmas Eve meal. Earlier that morning, they'd killed and cooked their two Doberman mascots. The rest of their original company, which had numbered over fifty a month earlier, when they were first assigned to the Barricades, were no longer alive to vote against the feast. The engineer settled into the ring of new comrades and accepted a smoke. He related without emotion the fate of his squad. They'd all died when their vehicle was hit by tank fire in one of the hundreds of skirmishes with the Reds on the rim of the *Kessel*. He'd been lucky; he was riding on the truck's running board and was blown free of the explosion. He ended his tale with a shrug, repeating a word softly, with a somber laugh. "Lucky."

Since Thorvald's death five weeks before, Nikki had also become a battlefield wanderer. Lieutenant Ostarhild was presumed dead on the steppe, but Nikki's assignment to the intelligence unit had not been countermanded, so he felt free to continue his expeditions around the city.

He became a collector of forlorn tales. The men, from the ruins downtown and Mamayev Kurgan to the factories, all believed they'd been forsaken. Their hope that Hitler would rescue the Sixth Army before they were annihilated was being starved and bled out of them an hour at a time.

Despite the Russians' commanding position on the steppe and the weakened state of the German troops there, the Reds never quit their harassing attacks in the city proper. Nikki understood the Russian tactic: if they can keep us on the defensive here in the city, we can't switch to the offensive. We can't break out of the *Kessel*. This is their aim, to eradicate the Sixth Army.

In the face of this constant onslaught, Nikki had witnessed courage and feats of determination that redefined what he knew of the human spirit. German soldiers— exhausted, demoralized, and without enough food, ammunition, or even hope—had continued to fight with discipline across Stalingrad. The Reds gave them no rest, not even leaving their holiday radio broadcasts untouched.

But if Nikki was to give his intelligence report tonight, he would not tell of the fortitude and order of many of the German troops. He would describe scenes of horror. He'd seen black-eyed men, cannibals, circle like vultures waiting for the wounded to die, to snatch them away while still warm. These ghouls were hunted and shot on sight; special patrols had been organized to ferret them out. Even so, roving bands of human-flesh eaters, fatter and rosier of cheek than their starving comrades, haunted the corridors and rooms of the factories and houses. Their number was growing along with their boldness and desperation.

In his account of these last days in Stalingrad, Nikki would also tell of incredible, numbing stupidity. He'd watched He-111s, those few that could find breaks in the weather to fly over the *Kessel,* drop their supplies not on Sixth Army positions but on top of Russians who'd learned to mimic German signal flares. In other places inside the ring, Nikki saw famished German soldiers run to be the first under a parachute when it lowered its cargo to the ground. The men fought each other to tear at the collapsed chute, ripping the silk away to get at the pine crates, shoving like rude piglets. These men opened shipments not of the ham and milk powder, bullets and warm clothing that would keep them alive but tons of marjoram and pepper—this for troops who were killing rats and dogs and grilling them. Another time, the Luftwaffe made the men a gift of a thousand right boots. Nikki's favorite story in all of Stalingrad this past awful month was the airborne delivery into the Cauldron of a million carefully wrapped Swedish contraceptives.

Mostly, Nikki would report upon doom. Each day over a thousand soldiers in the surrounded pocket died. Many succumbed to wounds suffered against the advancing Reds on the steppe. Others had taken their bullets fighting in the city. But by far, the vast number of corpses Nikki saw piled and protected from the cannibals by their sullen mates had been ravaged by frostbite, typhus, dysentery, or starvation. There was no fuel in the *Kessel* to run generators for heat or tanks for defense or trucks for transport out of the ring. As a Christmas gift to his remaining quarter million men, Paulus allowed the slaughter of the Sixth Army's last four hundred horses. These were animals that were themselves withering away from too much duty and not enough food. The men, the weather, the fighting, and even the rare laughter were all spoiled and dying in Stalingrad. Everything inside the Cauldron, like a poisoned river, had been seasoned with doom.

Nikki remembered the holiday feast he'd shared with the men around the radio only an hour before. For the first time in weeks, his stomach was full. He did not let himself think about what lay in his gut. The meat had been red and warm, lapping over his plate in a large portion and well flavored with marjoram. He rose stiffly, the way he always did after the big Christmas Eve meals at home. He walked into the adjoining shop room.

The chamber had a heavy oaken floor designed to hold machinery weighing several tons. Overhead the weary remains of lifts and pneumatics hung in tatters. Chains cascaded from the walls and rusted rafters, giving the room the jangling feel of a dungeon. The machines had been unbolted from the floor and moved months ago by retreating workers. All that remained was a metal lathe in the corner. The engineer who'd walked in from the steppe stood by it with his hand on the gearbox.

Nikki approached quietly and looked at the lathe. The nameplate riveted to the motor housing carried the inscription of the machine's maker: *Oscar Ottmund, Boblingen, Deutschland.*

The soldier stroked the nameplate. "Back home, I was a machinist," he said.

Nikki nodded. "I was a dairy farmer."

"I've never been to Boblingen. Is it nice?"

"I don't know. I never got very far from Westphalia. Cows don't take holidays."

The soldier stroked the lathe casing. "I could make this work, you know. Back home. I could make this sing."

Nikki patted him on the shoulder. He was close to Nikki's age, though the war had made them all older.

"Not me," Nikki laughed. "If it doesn't moo or fire a bullet, I'm lost."

The soldier laughed. The war had made them brothers, too.

Nikki searched his pockets for something to give the soldier. It was Christmas Eve. He found nothing.

"What's it like out on the steppe?" he asked.

The soldier dropped his hand from the lathe.

"Russians. They've got it. Ten thousand artillery pieces,

a thousand tanks, a million men, all of them running back and forth. You don't know where they're going to hit next. They come out of the fog, out of the snow, the sky, the ground. The steppe's full of ravines and crevices. We roll past them and they jump up behind us. You can't see distances because of the snow. And every night, they keep up the noise."

The soldier pinched his nose to ape the tinny sound of loudspeakers. " 'German soldiers,' " he squeaked, " 'lay down your weapons. Your war is over. Come over to warm food and shelter.' "

The soldier grinned. He let go of his nose for a breath, then pinched it again and continued.

" 'Manstein has retreated. Hitler has deserted you. Winter has found you. Every seven seconds a German soldier dies in Stalingrad. One . . . two . . . three . . .' "

He dropped his hand from his nose. "Over and over."

Nikki understood. Months back, when he'd first encountered Russian propaganda, it had seemed silly, easily ignored. But inside the Cauldron, any offer of relief, even from a Red loudspeaker, had to be considered. Surrender or death. Everyone in the Sixth Army knew one or the other was their likely fate. The repetition of the messages broadcast on the battlefield or here on the radio joined with the lice, hunger, danger, and raw fear to strip the men's nerves another layer.

"Tell me," Nikki asked, "about Manstein."

For every soldier in the Cauldron, the name Manstein symbolized hope. Field Marshal Erich von Manstein was going to smash through the Red ring and free them from the *Kessel*.

It was common knowledge that the Sixth Army was too weak and short on supplies to force a breach in the enemy forces. The breakthrough would have to come from outside. The rescue mission had fallen to the brilliant Manstein, hero of the July siege at Sevastopol. For the month since the circle had closed around them, rumors flew among the men. "Hitler hasn't forgotten us," they agreed, gripping each other by the shoulders, holding on to one another as if to keep themselves from floating off the planet. "Hitler's sent Manstein to come and get us out."

On December 12, twelve days earlier, those hopes became a reality when Manstein struck. The field marshal led thirteen divisions out of Kotelnikovo, striking furiously at the Russians in a narrow salient out of the southwest. After ten days of hard charging, hacking at the Reds in repeated lightning attacks like an ax against a tree, one of the panzer divisions, the Fourth under General Hermann "Papa" Hoth, pushed to within forty kilometers of the Sixth Army's perimeter.

"I watched them coming," the soldier said. "Every night, we'd look south. We could see the flashes getting brighter, you know; we could hear the fighting when the wind was right. We'd jump up and shout, 'Give it to them, Papa! Come and get us!' We knew they were coming. We knew it."

The engineer turned full toward Nikki, to be certain to impart all of his story with the pain behind it. His eyes narrowed, projecting the images into Nikki's eyes.

"Last night the lights started fading. We just stood there in the dark, with our hands out, you know, like children. And then the lights were gone. Manstein had turned around. We got quick orders to pull back. The Russians were coming our way. That's when our truck got hit."

He patted the lathe. "So here I am. That about settles it, I think."

Nikki studied the engineer's hand on the machine. He could sense the connection there, an old, true one. This man had loved his machines. They'd put his feet on the ground, walked him into manhood with their screeching and sparking. The same was done for me in the fields by Father's cows. I was raised among them, understanding their ways, nature's habits. Now it was all near an end.

The engineer's gentle strokes on the lathe were like a man touching his own tombstone. Without looking up, the soldier said, "I think I'd like to be alone, Corporal."

Nikki nodded. He wanted to pat the man on the shoulder. He reached out but did not touch him. He walked away.

The sound of a single rifle shot beat Nikki to the doorway. He did not want to turn back to look but he could not overcome his sense of his own fate, an urge to watch and remember what was happening here in the last days of the Sixth Army in the Cauldron. Others, he knew, would ask someday about the sorrow of these men. Nikki would tell them.

He would tell them about the quiet machinist lying beside the lathe from Boblingen in an empty shop room, facedown in a spreading scarlet bloom of despair. And the gaunt men in the next room with bellies full of dog. These were men who did not get up from their places on the floor to see what had happened to the quiet fellow who'd shared their Christmas Eve meal or even inquire about him when Nikki sat back down in their circle.

Nikki spent that night in the Barricades factory. He did not go again into the shop where the engineer lay dead. Let the room be his shrine, Nikki thought. Let him lie there in peace near his lathe. It's a better place than any I could drag him to.

The conversation around the lantern was hushed and strained, as if coming from under a great weight. The men talked of their homes, their civilian jobs, their women and children. One spoke to the group in a voice almost too hushed to hear and described himself as though he were already dead. He wondered how his family would fare with him gone forever. His wife and three boys would go to live with his mother, who'd make sure the boys learned some manners and read some books. His wife was a good woman, a hard worker, but coarse, a country girl. This sent each man into a reverie of his own over the fates of his kin after his death in Stalingrad.

In the hallway, the two guards waited for their hour-long shifts to end. Nikki said he did not have his rifle with him but would take a turn on guard. One of the men thanked him and handed over his Mauser.

Nikki walked to the hall carrying the weapon. He'd not held a gun in more than a month, not since he'd carried Thorvald's. The heft in his hand, heavy with purpose, brought images bursting out of his fingers and arm. Gripping the rifle, he felt he'd grasped again a link in an endless, evil chain, a succession of guns, swords, knives, arrows, spears, clubs—weapons extending backward and forward into time. He saw bodies scattered everywhere, ten billion bodies lying across time, across an eternal barbed-wire fence. He held the rifle away from him. Look at this thing. Metal and wood, that's all it is. But it's also a door, an opening that the devil and death and all that hates man and life can march through. Amazing what this thing can do, amazing what we'll do with it in our hands. Nikki leaned the rifle against the wall. He turned his back and walked to a window overlooking a factory courtyard.

He stood at the window, absorbing the precious calm of this Christmas Eve. After a while, a barrage bathed the concrete walls and floor of the courtyard in shimmering red. A pop of green added its tint to the shadows in the courtyard. The two colors swirled, mingled, and were joined by amber and white flickers from overhead. In the night sky, hundreds of colored flares raced their sparkling tails into the sky to explode at their highest points.

Nikki ran to the stairs. He climbed two stories for a better view and sprinted to a window to look over the courtyard wall.

In a giant semicircle, spreading from the Orlovka River far in the northeast to Tsaritsa Gorge on the Volga downtown, German soldiers lobbed flares into the sky to salute the holy season. The display was awesome and beautiful, as if the giant rim of a volcano were erupting while the center remained dark. The ring of colored fire in the sky marked the outskirts of the German troops in the *Kessel*.

Everything around Nikki danced; his hands, cheeks, and white tunic jittered in the flashes of color. After minutes, the lights and crackles faded and slowly, reluctantly, stopped.

Then the silence over the city was deeper, as though when the merriment was done it had crashed and left a crater. Nikki turned from the window. Through the broken glass came the sound of men's voices drifting on the wind.

"O Tannenbaum, O Tannenbaum, wie grün sind deine Blät ter . . ."

The song grew, spreading around the Cauldron the way moments ago the fireworks had. Nikki sang, too.

Inside the ring we are perishing, he thought, his voice rising with the unseen others. But up there where we send this song, beyond the clouds, touched only by the tinsel of starlight and moonlight, it is a silent, clean, good Christmas.

NIKKI WOKE WITH A START IN HIS CORNER. His joints groaned; overnight, his limberness had been sapped by the icy floor. He rose to his knees, and the chill greeted him. It was colder by far than the day before.

He limped to a window where the men went to relieve themselves. Working the buttons on his pants, he looked east toward the Volga. Snow whipped over the landscape like salt pouring from a box. During the night a blizzard had settled over the city. The temperature outside must be deadly. Merry Christmas, Nikki thought, to the Sixth Army.

When he was done, he walked through the room past the waking squad members. Their grumbles showed the misery of rising to another day of Stalingrad. Nikki climbed the stairs again for a look west out the window, over the courtyard toward the steppe.

His vision was stopped by a curtain of driving snow. The wind wailed wrathfully outside. Above the moaning gusts he heard the unmistakable pounding of artillery. Cannons and *katyusha* rockets were raining down with the snow into the Cauldron onto German heads this Christmas morning.

Nikki and the men busied themselves ripping up floorboards to build a fire. By late afternoon, the blizzard had slackened. Scraps of metal were arranged on the floor to make a brazier; wood was laid in it and lit with newspapers. The fire's wash warmed Nikki's hands and face while his back stung with the cold.

From the small radio, the scratchy voice of Joseph Goebbels filled the room. Hitler's minister of propaganda narrated the military's Christmas show, claiming it was being broadcast from around the empire of German-held countries. The minister assured the public that all was well and strong with the Nazi armies fighting for their future.

Goebbels's high voice screeched from the radio like a maddened eagle. His confidence is shot thin, Nikki thought. He's using too much force, pounding down his words like artillery, like he's trying to kill something with his voice. He's trying to kill fear, kill doubt. Everything everywhere is fine, he says. Everything is good for Germany. We're winning, the world cowers from us. Don't worry for your sons. They're wrapped warmly in Germany's destiny.

The minister of propaganda chanted out a list of cities

conquered by the Wehrmacht, taking his audience on a grand excursion of the Third Reich's front lines. In each locale, the soldiers gave a brave rendition of a holiday carol to send a reassuring Christmas wish home to their loved ones.

"And now, from Narvik," Goebbels crooned. The men around the radio joined in while soldiers stationed north of the Arctic Circle on the Norwegian coast led them in "Good King Wenceslas." Even singing, Nikki suspected the carolers were not really in Norway but in a professional studio in Berlin. The singing was too good, too sharp, to be a chorus of fighting men.

"And in Tunisia," Goebbels shouted when the song was done. Another expert male chorus rendered "Stille Nacht, Heilige Nacht." The men around the radio swayed, their faces flickering in the firelight. They touched shoulders while they sang. The glow reflected off the rims of their eyes and on moist trails down their cheeks. A tear welled in Nikki's eye. He wished for the teardrop to grow. He sang while it swept down his chin. He rejoiced in the tear's chilly damp. It was good to feel so full, to cry and sway with these men, lost as he was. The watering of his vision as he blinked gave a prism to the sparkling flames in front of him.

". . . *stille Nacht, heilige Nacht, alles schläft, einsam wacht . . .*"

Nikki sang and cried. He sensed at last the break he knew was coming, like the snap of a frayed cord. He was no longer, in his heart, a soldier of the German army.

He was finally unbound as he sang, evicted from his duty by the lies and manipulations pouring from the radio as well as by the senselessness he'd witnessed and taken part in over the past four months. Goebbels is doing his duty, telling the German people all is calm, when the whole black truth is we're dying here in Stalingrad, in

Europe, Africa, everywhere. And soldiers and civilians around the world, they're dying with us, doing their duty.

Nikki let his tears flow. Enough. I've done my duty in Stalingrad. I've left behind me a warrior's trail of bodies. It's what was asked of me. Now it's done.

Duty. We Germans cling to it like it was a shawl to keep us warm. We'll do anything in its name. How cold will we be when the shawl is ripped away, when the liars are silent at last and the duty we had to their lies dies with them? What will the believers do then? They'll claim they didn't know, their leaders were false to them! Better to kill duty at the first sign of a lie from your leaders; smash duty right then. Throw it off you like a snake that's dropped on you from a tree!

With duty gone from around your shoulders, you see all the lies clearly because duty makes you blind. Look down at duty, with a broken back now, hissing weakly up at me from the floor. I see everything revealed. Hitler. Stalin. Churchill. Mussolini. Roosevelt. Hirohito. Like the men singing on the radio, a chorus of liars. They must be liars because this war they've told us to wage *cannot* be the truth for mankind. It must be an insane lie!

I have no duty to Germany any longer. My allegiance is only to me now, to my life, given to me by God alone. My love is only for my family. Because Hitler has abandoned me and lied to me, my contract with him is broken. I won't kill his enemies, and I will not meet my fate under his orders. I am free.

". . . *schlafe in himmlischer Ruh, schlafe in himmlischer Ruh.*"

The melody waltzed to a close. The men stopped swaying. Many wiped eyes on their sleeves.

"And now," Goebbels's voice bellowed with pride, "from Fortress Stalingrad."

The men stared at each other, incredulous.

"From here?" one said.

"I don't believe it!"

"There's no one from the radio here! When did they get here? Today in the blizzard?"

"This is shit! Goebbels is lying!"

"Did you hear that? Fortress Stalingrad? Damn it!"

"Was the whole show a lie? What do you think?"

Nikki rose from the circle of shocked soldiers. Now they know, too, he thought. Good. Men should know truths while they die.

Nikki leaned down before he walked away from the fire. He touched the soldier nearest him on the shoulder.

"Thank you," he said. "Merry Christmas."

The man looked up with wet eyes. His brow was crinkled and imploring. His mouth hung open. His features spoke to Nikki: You are on your feet. You are going somewhere. Take me with you.

Nikki took his hand from the soldier's shoulder. "I'm going home," he said. Should the soldier rise and come along, Nikki would be glad of the company.

The man gazed up at Nikki. His face, turned from the fire, was halved by shadow. He shook his head, his grief a weighty crown.

Nikki walked to the door. Behind him, the broadcast of the Christmas carol from "Fortress Stalingrad" cracked off like an icicle.

NIKKI FOUND HIS BEDROLL IN THE DARK. Exhausted and cold, he laid his head on his pack. The tips of his fingers and toes ached with a white sort of pain as if crusted in ice. He wiggled them while he curled on the floor. Sleep overtook him quickly and carried him to morning on dreams of walking through a swirling mist.

Just after dawn, a motorcycle roared by his window to the battered department store across the street where Ostarhild had kept his desk, where the haggard captain now sat. Nikki stood to see the goggled, snow-caked rider run up the steps. More news, he thought. More intelligence. More truths about what's happening here and out on the steppe. Good. Tell them all, messenger. Get on your motorcycle and spread the word.

Nikki had nothing to eat. He could have found a field kitchen to give him his day's ration of two ounces of bread, one ounce of meat paste, and a third of an ounce each of butter and coffee. But he didn't want to wait in line today. He would stay hungry to help keep him alert.

He looked at his rifle, left leaning against the bread shelves for a month. He took in the basement walls, his backpack, his bedroll, and the lantern without fuel. These were all the protection afforded him by the German army. They were not enough.

With his knife he cut his canvas pack into strips and swaddled his boots. He sliced the bedroll into three long pieces, wrapping one strip about his torso beneath his coat. One went around his shoulders. The last, cut again, was divided into pieces to cover his neck, ears, nose, and hands.

He walked up the steps to the street. Snow twirled in corkscrews on the wind. The sky was locked tight in clouds. His wrappings stole the edge from the cold.

He tucked his arms and walked west ten blocks to the No. 1 Train Station. He chose a train track, wrenched and tangled but still a steel ribbon running true to the south. He followed it.

Nikki moved through the city. Bundled men hurried past him. No one stopped to ask where he was going. Each soldier was deeply involved with himself. Cutting through the whipping chill, they flapped their arms and leaned at the waist, ducking their heads to make themselves smaller targets for the biting cold. These men are just staying alive, Nikki thought. Everyone does it his own way. Life, no matter how many people are around you, is a private chore.

For four hours Nikki followed the rail. Often it disappeared beneath the snow. He kept to it by dragging his boots deeper to find the big wooden ties. Sometimes the rail curled up out of the snow like a crooked metal finger beckoning him onward.

He walked past many landmarks, famous for the fury of the fighting around them in September and October. He recognized Tsaritsa Gorge, Railroad Station No. 2, and the bloody grain elevator. The grain silos, hard by the Volga, had been held for ten days by fifty Red defenders against three divisions. Now the elevator was blackened by fire and silenced by the heaps of dead needed to win this pinpoint on a map for Germany.

South of the grain elevator, Nikki left the city center and entered the residential outskirts. The wooden workers' houses and shacks here had all been trampled by tanks and artillery. Nothing was left standing, not even trees. Snow covered the landscape to form smooth white hillocks interrupted only by a board or a pipe sticking out of random drifts. The neighborhoods were gone, the residents evacuated or killed. In their place were the invaders, stumbling around, huddling in foxholes against the wind or peering over the tops of trenches.

By early afternoon, Nikki had walked six kilometers past the grain silos. The growing concentration of men kicking aimlessly through the powder and tanks with snowy faces told him he was nearing the southern frontier of the Sixth Army's hedgehog formation. Some of the men strung barbed wire. Others knifed through the weather on their way to a tent or a trench, or just to keep moving, Nikki could not tell.

Doom, he thought. It thickens with the snow, it darkens with the hours. It grows on these men's faces like beards.

He approached a group gathered around an oil drum holding a wood fire.

"Is there a lot of action here?" he asked.

A soldier looked straight into the fire.

"What do you mean by 'action'? Fighting?"

"Yes."

"Sure, there's plenty of action. We fight the cold, the lice, the shits, hunger, each other."

The man looked south across the open, glistening land where Russians were massed behind the veil of wind-driven snow.

"And yeah, we fight them when they want. Where you from?"

Nikki nodded his head behind him, to the north.

"Downtown," he said.

"Oh, fuck. You've seen it. What are you doing here?"

"Walking."

The soldier's smile lifted the blond stubble on his cheeks. "Yeah."

Nikki took off his mittens to hold his hands close to the jumping flames in the barrel.

"Have the Reds taken many prisoners?"

"You mean," the soldier said, "do the Reds take prisoners?"

Nikki nodded.

"Yeah. Sometimes. Sometimes not. Depends on how mad they are that day. Usually they're pretty mad. You can hear them going crazy, screaming and shooting at prisoners, guys who've dropped their guns and put their hands in the air. The Rumanians west of here are getting hammered. It's nasty. I saw it, and I ran back here and I'm staying here. I'd rather starve, thank you. Fucking Russians. It isn't right."

"They've got a reason to be mad," Nikki said.

The man spat into the fire. It hissed quickly and was gone.

Nikki reached under his parka to his inside pocket for the envelope containing his orders. The papers were stamped *Intelligence*. Nikki remained assigned to Lieutenant Ostarhild's unit of gatherers and listeners. He was cleared to go anywhere on the battlefield unescorted. He put his mittens on and clutched the envelope. He wanted the papers ready now.

Nikki turned from the fire to look south to the Russian lines. The cold slapped his cheeks. He pulled the canvas muffler over his mouth and nose. He spoke to the man beside him through the wrapping. The cloth caught his breath and warmed his lips.

"I'm a dairy farmer," he called through the freezing wind and the crackling of the fire. "From Westphalia."

Nikki walked into the whirling white.

EPILOGUE

ON THE AFTERNOON OF JANUARY 8, 1943, THE
Russian forces manning the Cauldron around Stalingrad
paused in their liquidation of the encircled Sixth Army to
await the results of a surrender offer tendered by the Russian command to the commander of the German forces,
General Friedrich von Paulus. The terms of surrender
were generous, accompanied by a promise from Stalin to
annihilate the Sixth Army if it continued to resist. The
next day, the offer was refused and the battle resumed.

The decision to reject the Russian proposal was made
not on the scene by Paulus but by Adolf Hitler from his
Wolf's Lair castle in East Prussia. Anyone who had seen
firsthand the suffering of the Sixth Army could not have
asked them to fight another day.

Hitler determined that Paulus and his emaciated,
shivering troops would remain in "Fortress Stalingrad."
They would be a tragic but strategic sacrifice, one neces-
sary to tie down Russian forces and allow the remnants of
Army Group Don under Manstein and Sixth Army Group
B near Rostov, commanded by Field Marshal Fedor von
Bock, to retreat north. Hitler correctly feared the resur-
gent strength of the Red Army, and he needed Manstein
in place to bar the coming Red advance.

At 0805 the morning of January 10, the Russians renewed their attack on the Cauldron in a massive action, triggered by an hour of artillery bombardment blanketing the German positions. At precisely 0900, a thousand Russian tanks and waves of fresh infantry leaped into the fray. The ring drew tighter by the hour. The Reds knifed into the Nazi forces, reclaiming in a single day hundreds of square kilometers that it had taken the invaders months to conquer. German infantry and motorized divisions fought bravely but without stamina. Their resistance shattered quickly.

Throughout January, German soldiers surrendered in groups of thousands. Appearing more like ragged scarecrows than men, they stumbled out of the mists and swirling snows, hands behind their heads, weapons dropped at their feet. Scraps of cloth bound their heads and boots. Starvation bulged in their darting eyes.

Despite the pitiful condition of the surrendering enemy troops, many of the Reds could not relinquish their burning hatred for the Nazis. Their anger had been stoked white hot by the invasion of their homeland, news of the Nazis' cruelty in the occupied territories, the terrible, ongoing siege of Leningrad, and the rhetoric of loathing spread incessantly by the Communist agitators. Each Russian bore the pain of the *rodina* in the same hands he carried his machine gun.

Entire companies of Germans, Rumanians, Hungarians, and Italians were mowed down without remorse while they advanced under white flags. The murdering Russian units went unpunished, receiving the tacit and vengeful sanction of their generals and of Stalin to exterminate the enemy. By the third week of January, the Sixth Army, which two months earlier had numbered over three hundred thousand, had been massacred—starved, frozen, and hacked—to less than ninety thousand men.

On January 30, Hitler wired General Paulus that he

had been promoted to the rank of field marshal, knowing that no German field marshal had ever surrendered his forces in battle. Hitler hoped that his beleaguered commander would take the hint and commit suicide, salvaging what Hitler deemed to be one final, heroic act. Paulus did not shoot himself; instead, before dawn, he surrendered to a young Russian lieutenant, Fyodor Yelchenko, who sat in a tank outside Sixth Army headquarters in the decimated Univermag department store, pointing his turret directly into Paulus's window.

All organized German resistance in Stalingrad ended on February 2. Massive columns of prisoners streamed north out of the city. The captives shuffled across the Volga through blinding snow, then east to holding camps. Those who could not keep up with the march received a bullet in the skull from NKVD guards and were left beside the road.

The lines of prisoners passed through small villages untouched by the war. Though the Red Army had stopped the Wehrmacht at Stalingrad, the citizens east of the Volga displayed their hatred for the Germans as if they themselves had been in the grim battles. Old men and women broke into the prisoners' limping ranks to slap at them or steal from them lighters, fountain pens, packs, hoarded bits of food, even writing paper. In several instances, Russian soldiers guarding the towns vented their wrath by firing indiscriminately into the trudging columns.

Bivouacs for the prisoners were set up along the way, rarely more than hastily-thrown-up tents, drafty barns, or windowless factory rooms. Straw was strewn on the ground for bedding. Each morning, fewer prisoners rose to continue the march east. Many of the men died in the night from starvation and cold. Typhus also struck them down, contracted from the lice riding in their crevices.

Finally, the survivors were loaded onto trucks and driven to labor camps across Siberia.

At the outset of the German invasion, Stalin had relocated many Soviet industries east of the Ural mountains. These factories needed rail links to the western half of the nation. The Axis prisoners were given inhuman burdens of labor, bending their backs over picks, shovels, and sledgehammers twelve hours a day in bitter Siberian weather. They went into tunnels to set dynamite charges. They split boulders and loaded the rocks onto truck beds or built retaining walls into the carved-away sides of mountains. Often at night, they were lectured by Communists about the evils of their governments and fascism. Many of the captives appeared to turn against their countries to cheer for world socialism. The louder they bellowed, the less cruel was their treatment. Doctors, nurses, food, clothes, even mail and some news appeared as the years moved past, making it plain that the Russians wanted some prisoners left alive to use for chips on the postwar world's political gaming tables.

Not until 1948 did Russia release its first Stalingrad prisoners. The political pressures of the Cold War served to slow the repatriations to a trickle. Nonetheless, by 1954, only two thousand Germans remained in Siberian prison camps. These were men whom Premier Nikita Khrushchev identified not as prisoners of war but "war criminals," men who had been tried and sentenced by Soviet tribunals for atrocities against the Russian people. After painstaking negotiations, these men, too, were finally amnestied and released.

Of the million and a quarter invading soldiers who rode across the Russian steppe to the gates of Stalingrad in August of 1942, fewer than thirty thousand ever returned to their homelands.

ACKNOWLEDGMENTS

The author would like to thank Mr. John F. Young of Ithaca, New York, for his invaluable company and assistance while researching this book in Russia; Dr. Jim Redington of Bath County, Virginia, my longstanding best friend, for his invaluable guidance in all matters medical in this volume, for decades of adventures and calm counsel, and for allowing me over the years to walk alongside his loving family; my agent, Marcy Posner, of the William Morris Agency, without whom this writer and this book would remain just wishful thinking; and Ms. Katie Hall of Bantam, who as an editor is a wish granted.

BIBLIOGRAPHY

The author wishes to recognize and recommend the following historical works on Russia and the Battle of Stalingrad:

Beevor, Antony, *Stalingrad: The Fateful Siege, 1942–1943*. Viking, 1998.

Chuikov, Vasili I., *The Battle for Stalingrad*. Trans. H. Silver. Holt, Rinehart and Winston, 1964.

Clark, Alan, *Barbarossa: The Russian-German Conflict, 1941–45*. William Morrow, 1965.

Craig, William, *Enemy at the Gates: The Battle for Stalingrad*. Reader's Digest Press, 1973.

Glantz, David M., and Jonathan M. House, *When Titans Clashed: How the Red Army Stopped Hitler*. University Press of Kansas, 1995.

Jukes, Geoffrey, *Stalingrad: The Turning Point*. Ballantine Books, 1968.

Keegan, John, *The Second World War*. Penguin Books, 1989.

Schroter, Heinz, *Stalingrad*. Trans. C. Fitzgibbon. E. P. Dutton, 1958.

Seth, R., *Stalingrad: Point of Return*. Coward-McCann, 1959.

Shipler, David K., *Russia: Broken Idols, Solemn Dreams*. Times Books, 1983.

Tantum, William, *Sniper Rifles of Two Wars*. Historical Arms Series no. 8. Museum Restoration Service, 1967.

Two Hundred Days of Fire: Accounts by Participants and Witnesses of the Battle of Stalingrad. Progress Publishers, 1970.

Werth, Alexander, *Russia at War, 1941–1945*. E. P. Dutton, 1964.

———. *The Year of Stalingrad*. H. Hamilton, 1946.

Zaitsev, Vasily, *Za Volgoi zemli dlia nas ne bylo* (For us, there was no land beyond the Volga). Moscow, 1971.

Fedya's poem, "The Washing River," is the work of Ms. Karen Johnston of Seattle and used by permission.

ABOUT THE AUTHOR

DAVID L. ROBBINS lives in his hometown of Richmond, Virginia, where he works full time on novels and part time on the blues guitar and jazz harmonica.

Turn the page for a preview of
David L. Robbins's newest historical thriller

The End of War
A Novel of the Race for Berlin

Above his head, in the cold, dark, wind-creaked rafters of the tobacco barn, Charley Bandy sees withered souls.

Clustered five stalks to a stick, stepped several rows deep, they are hung upside down as though in punishment. The ten thousand leaves fill this lower reach of heaven. The air reeks of tar, thick, like the times Bandy has smelled blood.

Brown and drying, crowded and alike, these are not the souls of soldiers, Bandy thinks. No. The spirits of the battle-torn shine and are upright in a much higher neighborhood. There's room among war heroes where they are, what they earned for eternity with their courage and their deaths is space, distinction. Bandy is having a melancholy moment, he knows; he's being drawn back. He shakes his noggin to rattle the pull away. But the tobacco leaves drip their sticky scent and the odor is so much like gun smoke and gauze and the morning mists of Europe.

He lowers his gaze to the dirt floor of the barn. Several empty tobacco baskets lie about, waiting for another moist day to put the tobacco in case, that condition where the humidity is high to make the leaves supple enough to be handled. But this has been a dry winter, and the burley tobacco leaves, though sufficiently air-cured now dangling on their sticks overhead, can't be touched without breaking like ancient parchment. This Christmas came and went with little gift money. The family is edgy, waiting for the weather to cooperate and put the tobacco in case long enough to bundle it into hands, arrange the hands into the big woven baskets, then truck it all to the auction hall down in Marshall. The family needs to make some money, get school clothes, fix some machinery, buy next season's seed. Only a third of the leaves have been stripped and separated. The lowest leaves, called "lugs," and the paltry tips at the top all get tossed on a pile outside the barn to be used as ground cover and fertilizer. The broad middle leaves, the "smokers," get sold for bulk tobacco. The best leaves make it as far as cigar wrappers. A good, heavy harvest of smokers pays some bills.

Inside the house Bandy's mom and dad, wife, sister and brother-in-law, dozen or so uncles and aunts and cousins and their kin, wait for 1945 to arrive in another ten minutes. Every one of them lives nearby, a dog wouldn't get tired jogging between all their houses, either in Big Laurel, Little Laurel, Shelton Laurel, or on a rural road associated with no town. They are tobacco farmers up here in the Appalachian hollers. The clefts between the high slopes are narrow, and arable land comes only in slim patches, always beside the roads. Nothing makes a buck better on so little land as tobacco. The Bandys, the Ketchums, the Wallins are woven together by marriages and births like the tobacco baskets, broad and firm and white, hundred-year-old clans of soil and nicotine, pocket knives, and Saturday nights at the Masonic dance hall.

The clamor of his family's revelry—generational, those kids still awake squeal, the adults clink glasses and toast what they're going to do next year, the old folks cackle, the oldest ones cough—skim like sounds over a lake, tinkling and clear to Charles Bandy through the crisp, frostless mountain night. The mountain doesn't know it's New Year's Eve. The war doesn't know it's New Year's Eve.

Bandy opens his palms to the kerosene lantern he brought to the barn. He washes his hands in the little heat above the vent and thinks of the GIs freezing right now in foxholes and slit trenches in France, Belgium, Holland, Luxembourg, and Germany. Pall Mall and Lucky Strikes are dangling from beard-shrouded soldiers' lips right now. Surely some Tennessee tobacco is glowing over there.

The barn door slides open. Leaves in the rafters rustle their wrinkles; the barn takes on the feel of a cave coated in restless bats. This eerie sense disappears in just a moment, because it is her and no room she enters is a cave. She shuts the door. She has another lantern with her.

"Charley."

"Hey."

"What're you doing out here? Everyone's inside. It's almost time."

Bandy hears the piney woods in his wife's voice. Her accent is sugary, with rounded corners, not the serrated Appalachian tongue, not the mountain laurel. She comes from the flatlands, from Hendersonville, North Carolina. Her people farm tobacco down there, too. Flue cured, where they keep a fire stoked in the barns day and night. They've got big plots of land, not the sloped slivers Bandy's tribe makes pay. The two met at Vanderbilt when he was a senior and she was a freshman. He graduated in journalism, then she got her teaching degree. They married and stayed in Memphis four more years. She taught third grade, he took photos for any rag that would buy them. Then eleven years ago he carried her up here to the mountains and everyone, kids, parents, family, farmers, fell over themselves for her. She could be mayor if there was a mayor; they have a postmaster and a sheriff, that's the extent of the government in these hills.

"You all right?" she asks.

"I'm fine, Vic."

"Well, come inside. Everyone's missing you. Your mama asked me to come get you."

"I'll be along directly."

"Charley, I'm not going to celebrate the New Year with you out here in the barn. I have spent enough time without you already." He thinks Victoria is referring to their wartime, years gouged out of the last decade, years of fear for her, and that she wants to make him sorry for it right now, again. But she steps up close and says something different, sweetly.

"You have been working way too hard since you got back. Your daddy's roof. Alvin's fence. Jane and Edgar's tractor. What about our house?"

She sets the lantern on the dirt floor. She slips her arms around his waist. "What about me?"

Bandy takes in her brown hair nestled under his nose. She's only five feet five, he's a good six-footer. She's got that teacher scent, squeaky clean, a role model for the kids, for sixteen years of marriage now. She's still cute, the cheerleader she used to be in college keeps dancing and doing splits in her eyes and smiles. Except for the difference in height, they look very much alike. Both have mousy hair, both are lean-faced with brown eyes. Perhaps that's why they took to each other with such speed when they met sixteen years ago, they recognized they were cut from the same tobacco-stained cloth. Bandy breathes her in. For a moment he can't smell the leaves in their firmament, or the war in its new year.

"Victoria?"

"Yes, doll?"

"I love you."

His wife squeezes him. She is happy right now, and that

makes this the moment to tell her, because he must yank the happiness away from her. It's the only fair way to do it.

"I'm going back."

She does not release him, or even flinch. Her head rests on his chest, her ear gentle against his heart. This saddens him; she knew it was coming. He hadn't even fooled her, hadn't once in the two weeks he'd been home given her a single moment to believe he might stay.

"Haven't they gotten enough out of you?"

The "they" is *Life* magazine, Bandy's employer for the past eight years, since the magazine's inception in 1936. He is a staff photographer. His name is known nationwide for his byline, Charles Bandy, LIFE SPECIAL CORRESPONDENT, for the remarkable black-and-white images he has captured of war and warriors, of both friend and foe. His exposed negatives go via military courier from the battlefield to London censors, then by wire to New York, then onto the glossy pages of *Life*. Just days after the pictures are taken, the hopeful and weary eyes of the home front stare into the magazine as though into a crystal ball, for it is there that they witness their sons and fathers and enemies far across the ocean, they peer through haze and exploding earth and risk. America wonders and weeps through Bandy's camera.

Bandy makes no reply to his wife's charge. She has not lessened her grip about his waist. Nor has she taken her ear from his chest, as though to make certain that he indeed has a heart, to be leaving her again.

She speaks into the wool of his sweater. There is no sadness in her voice. She is not appealing to him, not beseeching, but prosecuting a point. She thinks he is wrong to go back and will try to prove it.

"Nineteen thirty-six, the Spanish Civil War. Nineteen thirty-seven, the Sino-Japanese War. Nineteen forty, the Battle of Britain. Nineteen forty-one, Manila, Tobruk. Nineteen forty-two, Libya and Egypt. Guadalcanal."

Victoria now lifts her head from his breast. She sniffles. She has lost the struggle to stay calm in the list of his assignments and the misery of his absences. She grabs at his brown eyes with hers, which are unblinking and damp. The yellow lantern light creates small suns in the wet trails down her cheeks.

"Nineteen forty-three, Sicily, Messina, Salerno, Naples. Nineteen forty-four, D-Day, for God's sake, you were in the first wave. Normandy. Holland. Belgium."

Bandy weakly smiles down at her. "You've been following my career."

She is not amused and answers in a quiet voice. "I've been praying for your life, Charley."

Inside the house, only a hundred feet away, someone calls out, "All right, y'all! One minute! One minute!" Someone else squawks a noisemaker and a child shouts, "Not yet!"

At this Victoria releases her arms from around him and steps back.

"I want children. Your children. I'm not getting any younger. You get killed, what am I going to do? You think about that?"

"Always."

"And? It doesn't seem to make you want to stay home."

But this time he had come home from the war really wanting to stay. Two weeks ago the Germans were beaten. France had been liberated. Italy switched sides. The Russians were gathering along the Vistula River in eastern Poland for their final thrust to Berlin. *Wehrmacht* soldiers were surrendering by the tens of thousands to Eisenhower's and Montgomery's troops. The war was expected to end by Christmas, January at the latest. Odds were that Hitler would sue for peace once the end was in sight. So Bandy had figured that was it. He had notified the magazine, said his goodbyes to those men and officers around him—the soldiers always changed. The instinct of the war photographer to sense where the action will happen next is his greatest asset, more vital then any facility with a camera, because a bad shot of action is better than a great shot of nothing—and had boarded a plane west. He traveled for three days to get home. Then the morning he arrived, December 16, even while he set down his duffle and held his wife, the Germans launched a massive winter counter offensive, with two hundred fifty thousand men, thousands of tanks and artillery pieces. The assault was staged opposed to all logic. It was a last roll of the dice against the American and British forces in Belgium and Luxembourg, launched through the thick Ardennes forests, the biggest battle yet on the Western Front. Hitler attempted to drive a wedge into the Allied forces, recapture the port of Antwerp and reclaim the initiative. In the first few days he succeeded, stabbing west to a point just shy of the Meuse River on the French border, forging a pocket that became the name of the battle, the Bulge. Eisenhower responded to the German attack by mobilizing six hundred thousand men. The American airborne commander of the surrounded town of Bastogne, when asked to surrender, replied to the Germans, "Nuts. The Battle of the Bulge will be won in the next few weeks, Hitler will turn back." But the war has been prolonged by who knows how long. Now it looks like it won't end until somebody—either the Reds or the Western Allies—assaults and takes Berlin. Hitler has screwed Bandy's plans.

Bandy says to his wife, motionless in his arms, "I'll be back."

Victoria takes this like a slap. She even starts to bring up her hands to fend off the words. She bites her lip and turns away.

"In a box, Charley?"

Inside the house, Bandy's dad calls out, "All right! Here comes 1945, the best damn year of 'em all! Right?"

Answering shouts agree, the best damn year of 'em all.

The family counts down from ten, nine, eight, seven . . . Noisemakers start to blow seconds early.

Bandy stands four feet from his wife. One of her tears dots the dirt floor, and they stand apart, separated by an ocean.

January 1, 1945, midnight
Kuntsevo Dacha
Moscow suburbs

All the bells are ringing.

Even this far outside Moscow, twenty kilometers, the Marshal can hear them. He leans his nose close to a chilly windowpane. He has pushed aside the thick blackout curtain to gaze into a moonless, overcast dark. The glow of Moscow is missing from the horizon, shrouded for safety's sake. All the other structures nearby in his compound are likewise extinguished. The night has total victory outside, save for the lanterns of his security guards strolling the crunchy ground around the dacha. The distant din of the bells is incongruous, joy and hope playing against such blackness. This is the Russian way, he thinks. Beauty meshed in tragedy, never one without the other for us.

Along the same wall where the Marshal stands, one of his generals thrusts aside the curtain of another window. This general turns to the others in the giant banquet room—Politburo members, military men and their wives, all pomaded and powdered, brass and lace. The general calls out to them, "Hear the bells!"

The Marshal does not swivel around but keeps his back to their cheers for the new year, the kisses of men given first to their comrades on both cheeks, then to the women on lips, the bear hugs and handshakes. He turns only to the general near him looking out into the same inky Russia.

He says, "Close the curtain, Comrade General."

The general hesitates only for a moment, in surprise. He lets go the curtain and it falls into place.

"Yes, Comrade Stalin," he says, inclining his forehead. "My apologies, Comrade."

The general makes his escape back to the arms of his fellows and women. Stalin continues to stare through the glass at nothing.

He looks west, towards Poland. There he has his two generals, Zhukov and Koniev, his two studded fists, poised on the Vistula with a million men and ten thousand artillery pieces and twenty thousand tanks. Before the month is out, he will brandish those fists and pound the Germans first out of Poland, then into pulp in their own homeland. He will not unfurl those fists, will not wipe the blood off them, until he wipes them on Hitler's shirt in Berlin.

That's the lair of the beast. That's the trophy the world wants. Whoever captures Berlin wins the war.

The English and the Americans long for the prestige of it. They've turned back a nasty winter offensive from Hitler. Their noses have been bloodied one more time. Plus, Hitler has stepped up rocket bombings of London. All this will make them push back even harder, move even faster into Germany. Now they will believe even more that Berlin can be theirs.

But Berlin belongs to Russia. By might. By sacrifice.

He trusts none of his generals. The taking of Berlin is too vital to delegate control to anyone but himself. Stalin has taken control of the coordination of all three fronts involved in the assault on the German capital, First and Second Byelorussian and First Ukrainian.

Nor does he trust that English bulldog Churchill or the cripple Roosevelt. No matter Churchill's lengthy toasts or Roosevelt's slavering courtship. They will do anything to take Berlin from Stalin.

That is why anything is warranted to take it first.

He holds back the curtain for a minute, breaking his

own hard rule, staying apart from the revelers behind him. When he hears the party fade at his back, he lets the curtain relax, and turns. His boot heels clack, he comes to attention at the window. With the report, all eyes are on him. Even the chattiest of them shuts up. Stalin stands like a rock, a chipped boulder, really. He knows how squat and ugly he is, with a face pockmarked by childhood smallpox, short forehead, squinty hazel eyes, only five feet four inches tall. Do any of these leaders and ladies rapt now before him know that the second and third toes on his left foot have grown together? He's a grotesque little gnome, chiseled from a poor quarry. No, he thinks, they don't anymore see Iosif Vissarionovich Dzhugashvili, the little Georgian bandit. They see only Stalin.

Rightly so, he thinks. Rightly so.

The Marshal casts his eyes over the pack, forty or so of them invited here to his dacha to celebrate the new year. They stand ramrod straight out of fear or respect, he's not concerned which. Who are these suit fillers and dress curvers? All of them, even the women, are his creations. What power they wield they possess only in his name. The shoulder boards, the stiff shirts, boots and handbags, flesh and bone would end up crackling on a bonfire with a wave of his hand, and within hours some forty others would stand here gaping. Who are these newcomers to the new year of the Red victory? What have they done to stand here before Stalin and not be swept away? Nothing. There's not one left who knows Stalin as less than a god, who has any claim at all to pity should his god turn on him. Not one of them with the bells ringing far away, full glass in hand, woman in tow, eyes stuck on Stalin, would hesitate to put a knife in Stalin's back if he could get away with it. They want power. These are the ones Stalin is wary of. The ones who do not desire power, Stalin despises.

But the power is Stalin's alone, his right. None of these celebrants was there half a century ago to study with the boy Iosif, the seminary student of ten years. Who among them ran and hid with Koba, the revolutionary? Or shivered in exile with the hard young Stalin who never once left Russia, while others waited in Paris for the revolt to begin in St. Petersburg? Or as a political prisoner who made five escapes? Which of them sat at the right hand of Lenin himself, or battled the Whites at Tsaritsyn so fiercely that the city was named after him, Stalingrad? What man alive has branded his own name on the revolution more than Stalin?

These frippish fools know only Stalin, "man of steel." They knew Lenin, but did they know the young firebreather Vladimir Ulyanov, who took his nom de guerre from the river Lena in Siberia, where he was exiled? And you can bet they remember that bastard Trotsky, but do they recall him when he was that bastard Leon Bronshtein, the wire-haired Jew who adopted the name of one of his jailers? Today Trotsky lives abroad, fearing for his life. And that loudmouth Lev Rozenfeld, who would have us call him Kamenev, "man of stone." Where is he now? Under a granite marker where Stalin put him ten years later, after arrest and a very public trial and an admission of guilt. Stalin killed a few other birds with the stone Kamenev, flung him to fell Bukharin, Zinoviev, Rykov, Tomsky, and the rest who would deny Russia the leadership of Stalin.

Those men knew both Lenin and Stalin in the early days. They too were coauthors of the Bolshevik uprising. They held power of their own making. But they spoke of things regarding Stalin that history has proven to be lies. They dared consider that they and not Stalin might be the true interpreters of Lenin, that they were the brightest lamps for Russia's path. History has proven them wrong. Look around now. They are gone, all of them, with their families and everything they touched. Steel proved stronger than the river, the stone, the prison keeper. History is Stalin's courtyard, while their names are dust on the bricks. How many? Dozens, hundreds, thousands, Stalin does not keep tabs like some Arbat merchant of the goods that have gone through his hands, no one calls Stalin to account.

He notes the Moscow bells have stopped.

He does not know how long he has stood like this, rigid, staring over the crowd's head, hating ghosts in the air. A minute, perhaps a second. When did the bells stop? It seems to him that even time does his bidding. He relaxes his eyes, widening the sockets. He takes a breath and runs two fingers over his moustache.

The young ambassador to the United States, Andrei Gromyko, lifts his glass.

"Comrade Marshal," he says. "It would be an honor to have you make the first toast to the new year."

Stalin thinks he will do so and that he will watch a bit more closely this upstart politico who lifts his glass first.

Stalin steps forward from the window. "Bring me a glass."

When his hand is full, he raises the drink in toast. Stalin is a teetotaler. But for the beginning of this year of victory, he will drink vodka. His hand in the air is still below the chins of many in the room. The rest of the glasses go up, and just for a flash Stalin fights his claustrophobia; his eyes are so far below all the crystal hoisted and packed above his head, he senses he is beneath a shining and crowding weight, like the surface of a sunlit lake.

He takes a step backward. This relieves him; he speaks.

"In a matter of days, the mighty Red forces gathered on the Vistula River will strike the first blow towards the heart of the German beast. In 1945 we will put an end to this senseless and horrible war to defeat fascism. In the years we have fought the Hitlerites, we have lost over twenty-five million soldiers and civilians. That is more than ten Russians for every meter of land between Moscow and Berlin."

Stalin watches the faces grow somber. A few of the

glasses waver in the air. He lets the moment hang; some boots shuffle. He has invited the millions of war ghosts into the room where everyone can see them. These legions of Russian dead join the spirits which only he sees, overwhelming them into anonymity. Now Stalin feels comfortable.

"There is not a single Soviet citizen who has gone untouched by this war. Every man and woman in the ranks, every factory worker, every farmer, has a score to settle. Our soldiers will fight from what they have suffered. They will fight from what they have witnessed and from what they have lost. Atrocities scar every village and city the Germans have touched. Have no fear that we are about to win. Have no fear of Hitler. I give you my word we will wipe our asses in Berlin soon in the new year."

Men in the crowd smile at Stalin's coarseness. The women titter behind gloved hands. "To the victorious Red Army! *Na zdrovya!*"

Glasses are turned bottoms to the ceiling, all of them. Stalin watches elbows and swallows and satisfied gasps. When they are done, his own glass still full, he makes a private toast.

I will take Berlin. The cost is of no concern. Whatever it is, we've already paid most of it.

He drinks. The gathering applauds.

"Budenny!" Stalin yawps. "Did you bring your damned accordion?"

A spry old marshal of the Red Army puts up his hands. "Yes, Comrade Stalin, of course. You know I can't come to a party without it. I always get sent home to bring it back."

"Then play us a polka. Let's dance to some German music!"

The military man hurries to a corner and returns, strapping on his weathered accordion. He stamps his boot four times to set the tempo, and launches into a rousing Prussian tune. Couples set down their glasses and partner up.

In moments the room is swirling, stamping with gaiety. Budenny, the former cavalry officer, is quite the catalyst. Stalin sidles out of the way.

The accordion renders waltzes, folks songs, ballads. Stalin fetches his English Dunhill pipe from his place at the head table. From a pouch he pours another bowlful of shredded Herzegovina Flor cigarettes and lights up. He paces the room through clouds of blue smoke, enjoying the dancers, savoring his pipe and his separateness. He has reduced his need for human relationships to almost nothing. He has seen two wives die. First, beloved Kato in their youth, from disease. Then the traitorous Nadezhda, who committed suicide in 1932 after arguing with him over politics. Yakov, son of his first marriage, an artillery commander who surrendered to the Germans—a coward, only cowards surrender. Vasili, a sniveler. Daughter Svetlana, acid-tongued like her mother, estranged. Stalin, the *vozhd*, the supremo, cannot afford the normal human luxuries of emotion or values. He must have steel cords where others have nerves. How can he dote on one, or two, or twenty, when he must envision and guard the future for hundreds of millions? He cannot want for himself when an entire nation is told every day, "Stalin is thinking of us."

He wonders, what could be lonelier?

Stalin watches his guests grow drunker with the dancing. Marshal Budenny has made himself quite popular tonight.

"Semyon," he calls to the musical marshal. "Rest your hands for a moment. I want to see your feet in action."

Budenny halts his playing. Sweat breaks on his brow from an hour of the accordion's buttons and keys. The dancers freeze like figurines.

Stalin walks to the gramophone. No one else in the room moves. He picks out a disk and slides it beneath the needle. The dancers lower their arms, no longer porcelain dolls but uneasy humans. Out of the gramophone bell emerges a scratchy ditty, a balalaika plucks a fast-paced folk melody along with a clarinet, drums, and a wailing violin.

Stalin approaches Budenny. He puts his arms out to relieve the old man of the accordion.

"Dance for me, Semyon. The Gopak. I have seen you do it, you're magnificent."

"Comrade," the marshal raises his palms in defense, "not in many years."

Stalin sets the accordion on the ground.

"And many years from now, you will say that you did it tonight. Dance, Semyon. To victory."

Stalin steps back. He claps his hands to the music. The crowd joins him now and they form a rousing circle around Semyon Budenny, a seventy-three-year-old marshal of the Red Army. The gray warrior squats on his haunches, crosses his arms and kicks out his heels in the classic Cossack dance.

Budenny dances with fervor. He begins rickety but soon limbers and is impressive for his age. The others shout "Urrah!" and clap in time to the music. Stalin studies Budenny's face. The dancing marshal keeps a pleasant smile. Stalin knows that Budenny is in great pain.